Laura,
Thanks for th
support.
M

War Torn:

A King's Assassin Novel

M.M. Brownlow

Eloquent Books

Eloquent Books
An imprint of Strategic Book Group
P.O. Box 333
Durham CT 06422
www.StrategicBookGroup.com

ISBN: 978-1-60911-882-2

Dedications

I would like to dedicate this book, first and foremost, to my family. They have been nothing but supportive. I would especially like to thank my husband, for being my sounding board and for providing such wonderful ideas. It takes a lot to put up with constant book talk.

I would like to dedicate this book to my friends and colleagues. Having an unending supply of people willing to read my drafts over and over again makes this whole process a lot easier.

Finally, I would like to thank my small but growing group of devoted readers. Knowing that there are people who are eagerly awaiting this book makes it much easier to maintain focus.

Prologue

The world was just beginning to lighten with the coming dawn. Shapes slowly became distinguishable in the gloom, colorless in that odd pre-dawn way, leaving behind only shades of gray. Dew covered the grass, and late summer flowers were just starting to open slowly, sending faint whiffs of fragrance into the air.

There were birds starting to rustle their wings and wake in their nests, but it was too early for the farmers to be about yet, so there was no movement visible in the main area of the small village. The same wasn't true in the surrounding countryside, where human shapes were flitting around the edges of the settlement, moving between and around the buildings.

Suddenly, color bloomed in the dimness, fire igniting along the edges of the thatched roofs of a number of the village homes. More pinpoints of light appeared along the edge of the village as archers lit their oil-drenched arrows to fire into the buildings. With each passing minute, more houses were adding their light to the growing glow, and the fire spread rapidly along the dried thatch.

The smell of smoke and the crackling of the fire quickly woke the village dogs, which in turn woke their masters with their howls and barks. Men, women and children began to pour from their burning homes, trying to escape the growing conflagration, but instead of safety, they found armed men waiting for them. The soldiers slaughtered the villagers wherever they caught them, with no mercy shown to anyone, regardless of age or gender.

When the slaughter was over, the armed men gathered as many horses, sheep and cattle as they could, finished burning the buildings, and set the nearly ripe crops on fire. When they left, there was nothing but complete desolation left behind them.

Petyr felt sick, looking at the wholesale destruction of the small village. There were corpses strewn here and there, and some had partially burned during the obliteration of the buildings. A few dogs wandered mournfully along the roads, looking for their masters, and some chickens were going about their normal business, unconcerned by the death around them. Aside from the members of the Bacovian army, there wasn't another living person in the area.

"How is it that they always seem to know where we aren't?" Petyr asked himself, shaking his head and dislodging some ash from his unruly brown hair. He'd been struggling with this question for a few weeks now. The Bacovian army was a large one, but they couldn't cover the entire border, and the Madelians always seemed to strike at those tiny gaps in their defenses. This was the third such village that Petyr had seen recently.

"Commander?"

A voice interrupted Petyr's thoughts, and he turned towards the man who addressed him. The man's red and black uniform, streaked here and there with soot, was testimony to the work he had just completed.

"This village is just like the others, sir," the soldier continued when he knew that he had Petyr's attention. "There is nothing useful left. They took what herd animals they could and burned the fields. We could likely track them, if you wanted to. They made no effort at all to hide their tracks."

Petyr shook his head again, knowing that the culprits would have made directly for the border, just as the other groups had in the past. Even though the embers were still smoldering here, he knew that his much larger group would never catch up, and his orders directly forbade him from splitting his command for any reason. His only consolation was that they seemed to be getting closer, reaching the villages sooner, but it still wasn't soon enough.

The war with Madelia, now about two months old, was not going well for Bacovia, or at least that was how it seemed here on the front lines. Petyr felt that their tactics needed to be adjusted, and soon, but the higher ups weren't listening to the likes of him.

As Petyr organized his men into teams to gather and bury the bodies, he realized just how useless the exercise was. The villagers didn't care if he buried them or not – he was doing this strictly for his men, because they expected it. But Petyr had a different idea. He was tired of the deaths of so many innocents, tired of the enemy constantly going unpunished. Petyr knew that it would be against his orders, but he had to do something. It was about time that someone did.

"Anders," Petyr called, signaling one of his men to come over. "I have another job for you."

"Of course, sir," the solider replied. Anders didn't question his orders, regardless of what they may be, but Petyr knew that Anders was itching for a fight as much as he was.

"I'd like you to gather together a squad of men," the commander explained. "They need to be men who share your… opinions about how things are being handled. I want you to take the squad across the border and deal with the Madelians who did this."

"Yes sir!" Anders acknowledged. "I will be across the border within the hour." He threw Petyr a quick salute and hurried away to gather his men. Petyr smiled grimly at his lieutenant's back as he watched him go. At least some of them were going to be able to exact a bit of revenge for the attack that had destroyed this village.

Chapter 1

Eryk desperately ducked the sword that was coming very quickly towards his head, and backpedaled as best he could, trying to get out of the swordsman's range. His opponent was too quick to let him get away with that however, and Eryk quickly found himself dodging another strike, this time aimed at his midsection.

"Aislynn! Do you think you could possibly hurry up and get over here?"

Eryk whipped his head around to look for his bodyguard, flipping his shoulder-length black hair into his eyes briefly.

"Stop distracting me!" Aislynn called back from somewhere over to the left of the young king. She faced off against two opponents of her own, and was unable to rescue Eryk from his attacker at this particular point in time. She stepped up her attacks in order to get to him as soon as possible.

Aislynn had had only a few instants of warning before this attack began, and she was just lucky that she had been practicing with a quarterstaff this morning. It was also fortunate that she was able to use this particular weapon to fight off two attackers at once, holding the long piece of wood in the middle and using each end separately to deflect the incoming blows.

Determined to get to the king's side, Aislynn aimed a quick attack at one of her assailants, directing a blow towards the man's head, followed quickly by one at his knees. As he danced back out of the way, she whirled and managed to take two steps towards Eryk before her other attacker blocked her movement in the king's direction.

Snarling, Aislynn sprang at the man, raining blows around his midsection, which he was unable to block effectively with his more cumbersome sword. One of her attacks got through his defenses and he doubled over, breathless, dropping his weapon to the ground. She took another step towards Eryk before her remaining attacker rushed forward, forcing her to stop again; the attacker tackled her from behind, preventing her from reaching her goal.

Eryk saw Aislynn fall, and he immediately took an instinctive step towards her.

"Stop!" Aislynn cried out. She had seen Eryk move and had instantly stopped that ridiculous notion. "Pay attention to Branden, and ignore me!"

Aislynn knew that Eryk still had a lot of trouble with the idea that she was *his* bodyguard and not the other way around, which is why they often practiced as a pair now. She and Byron, the captain of the royal guard, were determined to train Eryk to the idea of fleeing a fight as quickly as possible, and Aislynn was quite ready to beat the idea into him if necessary.

She turned her attention back to Mateo, who was trying to get his feet under him in order to attack her where she lay prone on the ground. She rolled onto her back and lashed out with her quarterstaff, forcing her guard to roll quickly away and out of the range of her weapon. Mateo, like his twin brother Marcus, was also fighting with a sword this morning, and so he had nothing with which to attack the princess at range, which was definitely working in her favor. Given a brief reprieve from attacks on her, she turned her attention briefly back to Eryk.

Branden, who had the honor of trying to disarm or disable the king this morning, wasn't going easy on him. Eryk, having forced his attention back to his own fight, brought his sword up just in time to parry a flurry of attacks. The friends had often sparred together over the years, and Branden was proving that he remained the better swordsman of the two.

Eryk could see Aislynn looking in his direction, appraising the situation, and he didn't want Branden to notice her scrutiny, so he took a quick step to the side, forcing Branden to move with him. Now Branden had his back to Aislynn, which proved to be his undoing a few short moments later when Branden suddenly found himself falling forward, tripped by Aislynn's quarterstaff.

With Branden temporarily out of the way, Eryk moved again towards Aislynn, to help her regain her feet. This time Byron stopped him.

"Where are you supposed to be going?" the captain called, freezing Eryk in his tracks for the second time this morning. Eryk sighed and stepped back before reluctantly turning away from Aislynn and sprinting across the courtyard to where Byron was waiting, holding a bow and a quiver of special blunted arrows.

Eryk took his weapon and turned back to the ongoing battle, trying to determine the best way to help Aislynn. Poor Marcus was still out of the fight, having taken quite the blow to the stomach from Aislynn's staff, but Mateo and Branden were both advancing on the bodyguard, who had regained her feet and was crouched, ready to defend herself from their attacks.

Eryk took careful aim, not wanting to hit Aislynn, and let an arrow fly. Just as Mateo aimed a strike at Aislynn's thigh, he felt a thump into his side as Eryk's arrow hit home. Knowing that a real arrow on that trajectory would have punctured his lung, he stepped back out of the fight with a smile and a nod to his "killer". That left Branden to face Aislynn alone, and it didn't take her long to disarm him, sending his sword flying out of his hand with a practiced twist of her staff.

As Aislynn and Mateo helped Marcus to his feet, Byron turned to face Eryk, an angry scowl on his face. He was actually very pleased with the progress that Eryk was making, but the king continued to overlook certain important concepts.

"What do you think you're doing out there?" he demanded angrily. "Twice you stepped out of line. Twice!"

Eryk looked down at the smaller man sheepishly. "I know, I know, but it's just so hard. I can see her there, in trouble, and I just *need* to go and help her."

"Remember what happened last time you went to help her?" Byron asked ruthlessly. He knew that Eryk still blamed himself for the injuries Aislynn had received a couple of months ago.

Shortly after Aislynn's arrival in Bacovia, newly appointed as Eryk's bodyguard, she had been attacked in her chambers by one of the very assassins who were trying to kill the king, and who had successfully managed to kill Eryk's father. The assassin had been unwittingly helped by Branden, Eryk's best friend, who had been under the influence of a powerful drug at the time. When Eryk had arrived to help, he was unarmed since he hadn't been thinking clearly at the time, and Aislynn had to sacrifice herself in order to save her charge. She was very lucky to have survived the wounds she had received, and the scars she had as a result of that attack were extensive.

Eryk shuddered with the memory, now looking more guilty than sheepish.

"She can take care of herself," Byron added, a little more gently. "I know that you still have trouble wrapping your mind around the idea of a princess taking care of herself, but she's an assassin first and royalty second. You should know that by now."

Aislynn and the others joined them as Byron finished lecturing Eryk. Marcus was still looking a bit unsteady, but he was walking under his own power. The twins, Aislynn's official bodyguards, walked on either side of their princess, all three of them about the same height at a few inches short of six feet tall. The men had light brown hair, kept short to help control the curls, and it looked very pale against the dark blue and silver uniforms that Marcus and Mateo still insisted that they wear. The rampant bear of Evendell, Aislynn's home kingdom, was evident on the breast of both jackets.

"It's okay," Marcus was saying as they came up. "I know the risks going up against you, and it's not the first time you've landed a good hit."

"I know," Aislynn replied, "but I should be disciplined enough to not actually hurt you if I connect."

Aislynn blushed, suddenly realizing that she hadn't pulled the force of her blow because Marcus had gotten between her and Eryk. That protective feeling that had started when she had first arrived here had developed into something more over the past months. She supposed that having a physical *need* to keep your protégé safe wasn't a bad thing in her line of work, but the intensity of the feeling sometimes scared her a little. This had only been practice, after all, and she had known that Eryk was in no real danger.

"Nicely done, gentlemen," Byron complemented the newcomers with a smile and a nod of his head. "You nearly had him that time, Branden."

"You wouldn't be saying that if Cheta had been playing today," Branden said with a laugh. He turned his gaze to the wolf, Aislynn's companion, who was sitting peacefully at Byron's side. It was unusual for Cheta not to be part of Eryk's defense, a decision made jointly between Eryk, Aislynn and Cheta herself. Though she looked like a wolf, Cheta was something far more, a magical creature known as an *eesprid* that was bound to Aislynn as her ally and a reminder of her home. The wolf had her own opinions about any number of things, including whether or not she would participate in any given sparring session.

With the continuation of the war with Madelia, Byron had thought it prudent to open up the early morning practice sessions he shared with Aislynn, and sometimes Eryk, and recruit some help. Having the three extra gentlemen there to attack and distract had added another level of difficulty to Eryk's training, and was serving to reinforce the idea that Eryk was to flee the battle as quickly as possible. Aislynn had agreed that the increased difficulty would be good for Eryk, and she knew that she could certainly use the additional practice, especially against multiple opponents. Sparring only with Byron, though she enjoyed the time she spent with him immensely, wasn't enough to mimic all of the real situations that could arise, though the two of them still practiced alone from time to time. The exercise was also good for Cheta, who didn't get as much exercise as she used to now that Aislynn spent most of her time in the castle. Her joint role as Eryk's bodyguard and his chief advisor kept her very busy.

Checking the position of the sun, Aislynn realized that the sparring session this morning had taken longer than normal, and they were running a little late. It wasn't a big problem, since everyone present would be having breakfast together, but it would mean a rushed meal before the council meeting scheduled for later this morning.

"Sorry to break this up gentlemen," she said, interrupting Byron's ongoing critique of everyone's performances, "but we all have to leave and get cleaned up. Half of us have a council meeting soon, so we should really grab something to eat." She grabbed Eryk by the hand, ready to drag him off into the castle if needed, and she waved Marcus and Mateo away to go and get themselves cleaned up. Aislynn knew that Eryk's guards were waiting for him just outside of the barracks, so she'd be fine for a little while without her own guards.

Life had gotten very complicated after the assassination attempts against Eryk earlier in the summer, and a balance between her role and the need for visible bodyguards had needed to be established. To add to the difficulties, Marcus and Mateo had never forgiven themselves for not being on duty the day Branden had attacked her, and she had had one or both of them by her side nearly every moment since then. That was just another example of the changes that had occurred during the past months.

Her struggle to find a balance between the men in her life was something that occupied her thoughts a lot too. Before she had come to Bacovia, she'd been nothing more than an assassin, very good at her job, but far too busy with it to even consider romantic relationships. She'd attended and trained at the Academy for nineteen of her twenty-three years, and her job was literally all she had known. Here, she had met not one, but two men who looked at her as more than just a highly trained killer. On one hand, she had Eryk, who was convinced that Aislynn would be perfect as his queen, and on the other side of the equation was Byron. The captain wasn't willing to jeopardize his friendship with Eryk, despite the fact that he loved Aislynn, and so he had backed away. Byron felt that Aislynn was destined to be Eryk's, but nobody had really asked Aislynn's opinion. Her life was far too complicated.

Aislynn and Eryk dashed across the courtyard and up the stairs into the castle proper, followed closely by two of Eryk's guards, dressed in the standard red and gray uniforms of Bacovia's royal guard. The servants were used to the two of them running around here and there, and the pair didn't cause a fuss as they took the stairs up to the second storey two at a time. They parted ways at the landing with a quick chaste kiss, and they each went to their own suites to change, Eryk's guards keeping pace with their king.

Marja was waiting for Aislynn, and she pounced on her as soon as the princess walked through the door.

"Where have you been?" she demanded, her blue eyes glinting with anger. "You are nearly an hour late!" Marja, always one for propriety, had never been able to understand Aislynn's seemingly less than serious attitude about everything. Marja, the daughter of a noble family in Evendell, had come to Bacovia with Aislynn to help the princess fit in at court. The two women had been friends their entire lives, but they had very different views about what was important and what wasn't.

Aislynn didn't even bother to answer Marja's question, knowing that it was rhetorical anyway. Marja knew exactly where she'd been and what she'd been doing, which is why there was hot water for washing awaiting her in her room. She stripped out of her dirty clothing and washed quickly, and then turned to the bed and the dress waiting for her there.

With an eye to the late summer weather, Marja had selected a dress that was a lightweight creation of cotton and lace. The pale green color brought out green highlights in Aislynn's brown eyes, and the dress skimmed her curves in a way she knew Eryk would find appealing. Leave it to Marja to select clothing for her with Eryk in mind, Aislynn thought to herself with a chuckle as she undid her braid and shook out her long, straight brown hair.

When she was finished with the last of the buttons, Aislynn slipped a pair of daggers into their hidden sheaths and whirled out of the room to find Marja and Cheta waiting for her. Marja gave her outfit a quick glance, and satisfied that Aislynn now looked like a proper princess, the three of them left the room and headed down to the dining hall.

The gentlemen were already waiting when Aislynn and Marja entered, and Byron watched, as he always did, as Aislynn glided into the room. He loved to watch her move, and he still felt relief knowing that her injuries had not permanently disabled her. The way he watched her was strictly innocent, or at least as innocent as he could make it, more the way one would watch a dancer with appreciation. Byron and Aislynn were honest with each other about their feelings, but aside from a single kiss, they had never acted on those feelings and Byron was determined that they never would.

With the ladies present, everyone took their places at the table, and Eryk signaled the servants to bring in the meal. The king sat at the head of the table, and Aislynn sat across from him. Byron occupied the spot to Eryk's right, while Branden sat to Eryk's left, beside Marja. That was another recent development.

After Branden's incredibly poor judgment with the Madelians and his attack on Aislynn, Eryk removed him from the role of chief advisor, appointing Aislynn in his place. After Aislynn had recovered enough from her injuries to take on her new duties, Branden and Marja had both often found themselves alone and at loose ends. They had naturally gravitated towards each other, and a relationship began. Aislynn had to admit that the two blonds made a very cute couple, and they were now engaged to be married. The pair was planning to say their vows at the Harvestide Festival, just over a month away.

As the meal progressed, the conversation turned, as it always did, to the war.

"So what's the latest news?" Branden asked, trying to keep the eagerness from his voice. Since he no longer had a position on the council, he often felt that he was out of touch with the most up-to-date information. He found that asking for that information was nearly as difficult as not knowing what was going on. He hated being on the outskirts of the court and council.

"Things are not going well, according to the latest reports," Eryk replied. "We are not losing a lot of men in battle, but we are losing a lot of villagers, livestock and crops. The Madelians have adopted a strike-and-run technique that our army just cannot keep up with."

Aislynn could feel Eryk's distress coming to her through the magical link she shared with him, despite the fact that he kept his face smooth and his voice even. Eryk had become a master of hiding his emotions since his coronation, but he couldn't hide them from her, regardless of how hard he tried. The mutual protection spell that bound Evendell and Bacovia together had a number of interesting side effects, including the ability Aislynn now had to sense Eryk's location and mood.

"Lord Geoffrey is becoming impossible to work with," Eryk continued. "He's very set in his ways, convinced that the way he has directed wars in the past is the only way, but this war is not like the others. The enemy will not stand and fight, and Geoffrey just isn't able to adapt."

"What are you planning to do?" Byron asked, though he already suspected that he knew the answer.

"I have someone coming to speak to the council. He has been very successful adapting his company to a wide range of situations, and I'm confident that he'll be able to adapt his strategies to match the Madelian tactics too." Eryk left it at that, not willing to say for certain that Lord Geoffrey would be replaced as the commander of Bacovia's army until after he had met with the newcomer.

"And how is everything else going?" Marja wanted to know. "I know that war can be disruptive."

"So far, so good," Aislynn answered her. "Because Bacovia has such a large standing army, we have been able to keep conscriptions to an absolute minimum, so the majority of the citizens have been relatively unaffected so far. Those who live near the border are the ones who have been most affected, of course, and we are doing what we can to send the refugees east to safety. We will be able to get the harvest in, the way things are going, and it looks like it will be a good one, despite the crops we have lost so far. Everyone will be fed through the winter, at least."

"But if this continues through the winter," Eryk continued, "the spring planting could be in jeopardy, especially if Madelia starts making gains across the border. We can't afford to lose a lot of the arable land that is currently being used as a battlefield. It is definitely in our best interest to end this war as soon as possible."

"And how are you going to do that?" Branden asked. "If it was as easy as just 'ending it', then you would have done it already."

Eryk didn't have a ready answer for that question. This issue had been plaguing him for weeks. He had a few ideas rolling around in his head, but nothing concrete enough to be worth mentioning, at least not yet.

As the meal ended, Byron excused himself first to stop by his office quickly to get some paperwork before the council meeting. Marja and Branden followed soon after, heading off to spend some time together while everyone else was otherwise occupied.

Eryk rose and moved over to where Aislynn was waiting.

"Well, your Highness," he said as he offered her his arm, "shall we saunter over to the council meeting?"

Aislynn rolled her eyes, but put her hand on Eryk's proffered arm. "If we must," she replied with a melodramatic sigh.

As the couple moved off down the hall, followed closely by the obvious protection of Cheta and Eryk's guards, many of the servants they passed paused in their duties and bowed to them respectfully. They had definitely become a pair in the eyes of the castle staff, one rarely seen without the other, and everyone was generally pleased with the match. Aislynn was no longer the unknown foreign princess she had been when she had first arrived. Now everyone knew her as someone who treated everyone fairly, and someone who didn't make many demands, both characteristics that set her apart from most of the nobility they usually served.

"My compliments to Lady Marja," Eryk commented as they walked. "Her taste, as always, is impeccable."

Aislynn looked up at him, trying to determine from the look in his blue eyes if he was being serious, and she decided that he was. All she could feel from him right now were the standard feelings of love and carefully suppressed desire that she had come to associate as normal for Eryk when he was thinking about her, which seemed to happen a lot.

"I will let her know that you approve of her choice of attire," Aislynn replied with a small smirk. "I do wonder sometimes if she picks out my clothing with my comfort in mind, or your pleasure."

Eryk laughed, grateful to have an insider helping him to woo and win Aislynn's hand. Despite the fact that he had not mentioned the prospect of marriage even once since midsummer, he had not given up the idea. It was only a matter of time. Eryk knew that Aislynn was very skittish about the idea of marriage, though he didn't quite understand why, so he had been very careful not to push her. He didn't want to scare her away, so he was giving her time to get used to the idea.

"Well, let's get this over with," he said as they reached the council chamber. He pushed the door open, and they walked in together to face the assembled representatives of the kingdom of Bacovia.

Chapter 2

The eight members of the council were assembled and waiting for the arrival of their liege. As Eryk entered, the hum of conversation quieted, and those few council members who were standing quickly took their seats. They had been on their best behavior ever since Eryk had abruptly replaced two of their colleagues in the middle of a council session a little over a month ago.

The two men, responsible for overseeing the finances of the kingdom and the merchants, had disagreed with something Eryk had said, and instead of offering him their opinions in a civilized manner, they had had the audacity to yell and argue with him in front of everyone. Eryk had calmly summoned one of the guards from outside the room, had the councilors escorted out of the chambers, and there were two new members in their places when the next session convened a few days later. The rest of the council had subsequently learned that the two gentlemen in question had been lining their own pockets with crown money. They had reacted the way they had because Eryk's suggestion would have ruined their little side business.

Aislynn looked around at the assembled councilors as she walked to her own chair, positioned to Eryk's left, smiling slightly at Byron when he met her eye. Most of the other councilors turned their faces away, refusing to meet her gaze. They actually ignored her as much as possible, knowing that she was at least partially responsible for Eryk's new confidence and his full understanding of exactly how the council was supposed to work. They couldn't get away with the bullying tactics that they had used when he'd first assumed the throne. Aislynn's upbringing, despite the oddities of her assassin training, had still had its fair share of political teachings, and she had taught Eryk some of the lessons his father hadn't had the time to teach him and Eryk hadn't had the inclination to learn. Aislynn didn't mind the council ignoring her though, since she had free rein to watch them while they pointedly *didn't* watch her. She had managed to pick up a lot of interesting information for Eryk just from watching their body language during these meetings.

"So what is on the agenda today, ladies and gentlemen?" Eryk asked as he took his seat and called the meeting to order.

"Well, Sire," answered Lord Geoffrey, "we need to discuss the progress of the campaign." Lord Geoffrey was in his element these days. Before the war, he had been *old*, but now he had a sparkle in his eye and a spring in his step. War was what he knew, and the peacetimes had worn on him.

"And the impact of the war on the coffers needs to be addressed also." This came from Lady Mataline, one of the newly appointed councilors and the one in charge of the money in the realm. She was a middle-aged woman and she had never married, which left her free to perform her duties for the king and council.

She had come to Eryk's attention after her father had died, when she had appeared at one of his earliest sessions of court. While her father was living, she had helped him to manage his growing business, and it was with her aide that he became as prosperous as he had. When he died, Mataline's uncle had wanted to inherit the assets and the business, complaining that a woman would not be able to manage things effectively. A brief conversation with her had proven to Eryk's satisfaction that Mataline was more than capable, so he had ruled in her favor, and when the financial position became available on the council, she was the first person he had thought of to fill the role.

Aislynn liked Mataline a lot, but they were very careful not to associate during council meetings, which could compromise Mataline's position with her colleagues. Instead, it was common for Mataline to find Aislynn in Eryk's study, or in her garden, where they would visit and chat for a little while. Aislynn found that it was nice to have someone besides Marja to escape with, if only for a short time.

"Well, let's start with the finances then," Eryk said, nodding to Mataline to give her report. Fortunately, it wasn't as bleak as it could have been. The biggest drain on the kingdom coffers was supplying the army, not paying them. The large standing army was a benefit in this case, since they paid soldiers the same amount now as they always had. However, wars consumed, and keeping the army stocked with food, tents, blankets, weapons, and all of the other things they needed while on campaign, did cost money.

"So what can we do to increase the amount of money we have available?"Eryk asked, turning to look at three of the men ranged along the left side of the table. These gentlemen were responsible for the merchants, the artisans and the diplomatic relations between Bacovia and the surrounding kingdoms.

"Well I know that the harvest looks to be good, despite the losses of crops and fields to the north," said Lord Harmon. "I know that we are going to need to keep more of the surplus than usual this year, but I can see if there is someone who will pay us well for what we can afford to part with."

Lord Harmon was a very small gentleman, wizened and stooped with age. His eyes were his one truly defining feature, bright with intelligence and humor. Everyone he worked with liked him, and he was a master of negotiation with Bacovia's foreign allies. Aside from Byron, he was the only councilor who would meet Aislynn's gaze, and she could remember a number of humorous stories that her father had told her about some of the negotiations Harmon had worked out with King Jackob and Evendell.

"And we can see if we can find some way to increase production and shipping of goods," suggested Lord Aeron, gesturing to Lord Philip seated beside him, who nodded in agreement. These two gentlemen oversaw the merchants and artisans, respectfully, and they each had a lot of pull with their fellows.

Satisfied with the proposed plan of action, Eryk moved on to the next order of business.

"Next, then, we need to address the losses caused by this war with Madelia," Eryk stated, looking pointedly at Lord Geoffrey. The commanders in the field controlled the battle, but Lord Geoffrey determined the overall plans. He was the one who made the decrees that affected how the troops deployed.

"Reports from the front indicate that our losses have been minimal to date," Geoffrey responded, confused by the look he was getting from Eryk. As far as he knew, everything was working fine.

"That's because we haven't done any fighting!" Lord Harmon pointed out bluntly. Geoffrey looked offended, and opened his mouth to defend himself, but Eryk interrupted him.

"Reports indicate that Madelia isn't massing her forces anywhere for us to attack directly. Instead, they are attacking isolated villages, killing everyone they can find, stealing what they can, and destroying the rest. The losses Bacovia has sustained to date are, in fact, far above what I would consider acceptable. Right now, we have lost about seven citizens for each solider that has been killed in battle."

"But casualties of war are to be expected," Geoffrey responded. "What do you expect us to do?"

"We have to find some way of protecting our citizens, and ideally, some way to strike at a larger portion of Madelia's army at once. In addition, it would be a very good thing if we can end this before winter. I'm opening the floor to suggestions."

The room was quiet for a few moments while the councilors mulled over the problem silently. In all of the recent wars that Bacovia had fought, the enemies had come and struck at the kingdom head-on. Bacovia's superior numbers had been an asset every time, turning the enemy away from the borders without too much difficulty. The strike-and-run tactics that Madelia was using were much harder for them to counter.

"Well if you want to end this quickly, we can always cut the head off of the snake, so to speak," suggested Harmon with a look at Aislynn. She knew that he was referring to the assassins her kingdom was known for, and not her directly, but the implication was eerie. The fact that she was, herself, one of those assassins was something that was largely unknown in this court. “If we kill Queen Vivien, the war will be over while Madelia tries to sort out succession. We could fortify the border while they do that, and if the new ruler wants to try and attack us, then they are more than welcome to try.”

The councilors greeted Harmon’s suggestion with a few nods of approval, but most did not look convinced that his idea would succeed.

“Maybe we could try and get a large concentration of their soldiers in one place and try to wipe them out in one blow,” Father Jonas suggested, looking for another possible quick solution. Nobody really wanted a long, drawn out war.

“What would possess them to come in numbers to attack at a specific point?” asked Aeron. “If they were willing to do that, don’t you think they would have done it already?”

“They’re likely afraid of our numbers,” suggested Geoffrey proudly. “We would need to bait them if that plan is to have any chance at all of being successful.” Geoffrey turned to look at Eryk, and Byron followed his gaze, shaking his head.

“We will not be using his Majesty as bait for the Madelian army,” Byron stated firmly. “We wouldn’t be able to keep him safe enough to let him onto the battle field, and if they can’t see him, I can’t imagine that they would come and walk into your little trap.”

“What else would possibly get them to mass in one place for us?” Mataline asked. Nobody had an answer for her, and the room remained silent.

“Are there any other suggestions?” the king asked, looking around the table at his councilors.

“Well, there was one other suggestion that has been brought forth,” Harmon spoke up again. He seemed reluctant to share this information for some reason, and Eryk had to gesture for him to continue.

“I received a missive just this morning,” the man continued slowly, “from Madelia. It seems that Queen Vivien is interested in forming a treaty between our kingdoms, something that would be sure to end the war.”

“We’ve already tried the treaty route,” Byron commented. “Their emissaries brought assassins into the court; assassins who killed Tarren, who tried to kill Eryk on numerous occasions and who attacked the princess."

"Yes… well… this is a different treaty agreement," Harmon said, looking more uncomfortable by the minute.

"Just spit it out, man!" Geoffrey commanded. "You're wasting our time."

"Vivien proposed an alliance by marriage," Harmon finally blurted out. "She comments that since neither throne has a direct heir, and since the land disputes have been causing problems for decades, joining the two kingdoms would be the ideal solution."

Eryk was shaking his head before the man had even finished speaking, and didn't give the council any time at all to discuss Madelia's proposal.

"I'll think about it, but if we assume that this war is going to continue on for a while longer, what can we do to protect our villagers?" Eryk asked, trying to move the conversation along.

"Well the Madelians seem to be attacking isolated villages, keeping a step or two ahead of the army detachments we have making rounds up there," Geoffrey said. "If we plan to give up on a massive battle to end this war, then I suppose we could split the army up into little detachments and have a garrison stationed in or near each village."

"Is that really practical?" asked Lord Philip. "Wouldn't it make more sense to train the villagers to form a militia and try to fortify and defend the towns in some fashion? Surely there's enough wood up there to build walls around the villages."

"Do we have the resources to supply that many militia groups?" Byron asked, looking to Mataline for an answer.

"I'd have to look into it, but my immediate response is probably. We don't have a lot of extra money, but I do know that we already have a decent stockpile of basic weapons on hand. Is that not true, Lord Aeron?"

Aeron nodded his head in agreement. "We do currently have a number of spears and short swords that were destined for the front lines. We could divert a certain number of those to the frontier villages for militia use. And a number of the villagers would have their own weapons, of course."

"Lord Geoffrey," Eryk said, turning to the army commander. "Could you appoint men to train the militia forces? I think that it would be a good idea to send small squads of soldiers to the villages, to help speed along the training. Perhaps divide the villages into groups and assign a squad to a group of villages?"

"Yes, I do think that could work. I'll think of some good men, with training experience, and get the squads organized as soon as possible. Could you divide up the goods to be transported to the villages Lord Aeron?"

Aeron nodded his agreement and made a note for himself. "It will be done within the next few days," he promised.

"Well this plan of action at least helps to protect our citizens, and I'll take everyone's suggestions for ending this war into consideration," Eryk said. "Is there any other order of business to be discussed today?"

"Well, your Majesty, there is just one more thing" replied Father Jonas, turning his gaze upon Aislynn. "It is especially important with the proposal from Madelia on the table."

Byron sat up a little straighter in his chair. He knew where this was going, and it wasn't going to be pretty. He'd brought this subject up to Aislynn about a month ago, and the result was such that he had promised himself NEVER to bring it up again.

"With the hazards of the war, your Majesty, you do really need to reconsider taking a bride. I know that you're not directly involved in the fighting yourself, but one never does know what will happen when a kingdom is at war, especially since our current enemy has already tried to have you killed on numerous occasions." Jonas paused briefly to take a breath, and then continued right away, determined to have his say.

"We don't really understand the delay here. You have obviously made your choice. She is always with you and we know that she performs all the duties of a queen anyway. The realm needs a *legitimate* heir, your Majesty."

"How dare you!" Aislynn asked in a very quiet voice. She was up and out of her seat, anger apparent in every line of her body at the implication of what Jonas had just said, and who would blame her? The accusation that she was sleeping with Eryk would be enough to ruin any nobly born woman's reputation, let alone a woman who was royalty.

Because he was watching her reaction, Byron saw Aislynn's right hand twitch, and knew that she was struggling with the idea of launching one of her hidden daggers at the man. Byron had known that this discussion wasn't going to be pretty, and now he wondered if there would be a new councilor at the next meeting to replace the one that Aislynn was about to kill. Nevertheless, he made no move to stop her.

A quick glance around the table showed Eryk that while Jonas may be expressing the overall opinion of the group that he just marry Aislynn and get it over with, the rest of the councilors would never have phrased things quite the way he had. Eryk could feel Aislynn at his side, nearly vibrating with the rage she was keeping in close check, and he was honestly as surprised as Byron was that Jonas wasn't already dead where he stood. The princess had a very volatile temper, though she rarely lost control of it in public. Her years of disciplined training saw to that.

"I do not appreciate the slur against her Highness's honor," Eryk began quietly. "You have absolutely no right to make accusations like that, especially if you cannot prove them. Neither of us has acted inappropriately, and it's none of your business with whom I choose to spend my time. I will get married when I am ready to be married. I would advise you to leave this chamber now."

Throughout this whole lecture, Eryk sat motionless in his chair at the head of the table. He spoke quietly and calmly, and somehow the effect was considerably more frightening than if he had been yelling and screaming. Father Jonas, realizing that he had erred badly, rose quickly from his seat and excused himself, nearly running from the room.

"Well then, if there is nothing further..." Eryk really didn't wait to see if anyone had any other business they wanted to present. Everyone desperately wanted to be somewhere else, but none more so than Aislynn. As soon as Eryk stood, ending the meeting, she was striding down the length of the room and out of the still open door, Cheta jogging along behind her. Eryk desperately hoped that she wasn't going to hunt Jonas down.

He turned his despairing glance back to the remaining council members. The men kept their faces carefully neutral, but Mataline met his gaze with a sympathetic look of her own. Eryk knew that she would have gone after Aislynn if she could, but he also knew of the lengths the two women were going to in order to keep their friendship a secret from the rest of the council.

Eryk dismissed the council properly, and then slowly made his way to his study, trailed by one of his guards. He knew that Aislynn had likely gone to one of two places, depending on just how angry she was, and he decided to check the closest location first.

Reaching his study, Eryk knew that his guess had been a good one. The other half of his pair of guards was standing outside the door, indicating that the princess was inside. Moving through the study, he approached the door to the garden apprehensively. Sometimes it was better to let Aislynn work out her anger herself, he had learned, but it was hard to decide when to leave her alone and when she needed a sounding board. He stepped cautiously out into the garden, warily checking for flying objects, and looked around. Aislynn was on her knees beside a small garden plot, ripping weeds angrily out of the ground with a total disregard for the dirt flying through the air and the grass staining her dress.

"Why can't they just leave us alone?" she demanded as he approached. He had gotten used to her knowing when he was nearby, and it no longer startled him when she started speaking without him needing to announce his presence.

"Because they can't," he replied as he knelt down beside her. He took a deep breath, steadying himself before broaching the dangerous topic. "The kingdom needs a direct heir to the throne, and I want it to be my child and not my cousin Davin. I've grown over these past months, I'm accepting my responsibilities, and I realize what everyone expects of me. And I'm willing to be patient and wait until you are ready, even if they aren't. I love you."

He paused for a moment and then continued. "Unfortunately, the council is going to keep bringing this up, so you're going to have to get used to that and try to keep a rein on your temper."

Aislynn looked up at him with a scowl. "You know as well as I do that I'm not angry about the fact that they want you to marry. How could that man even *think*…?" She trailed off.

"Well we do spend a lot of time together, starting very early in the morning and often ending late into the night, depending on what needs to be done. It is a somewhat logical conclusion that we are also spending some intimate time together in the bedroom." Eryk smiled a little, and Aislynn could feel that he wasn't displeased with the idea. She stopped pulling weeds out of the garden and turned to face him.

"You still should have chosen someone else while you had the chance," she said with a sad smile. "It would have made all of this a lot easier on you."

"And easier on you. But I don't want anybody else, and I know that you feel the same way about me, even if you won't let yourself act on those feelings." Aislynn blushed and looked away, as much of an admission as Eryk was going to get.

"Just promise me that you'll think about it again, okay?" He leaned forward, kissed her softly on the forehead, then rose and went back into his study, leaving Aislynn alone with her thoughts.

Aislynn watched Eryk leave the garden, and glanced over to where her wolf lay sprawled in the sunshine. With a sigh, she turned back to her garden and resumed yanking the weeds out of the soft ground. She found that gardening was a good way to vent her anger, and an acceptable way.

Once again, she replayed the events of the council meeting. Her immediate reaction to the proposal from Madelia had been anger, but she didn't really want to examine *why* it had been anger. Ever since Eryk had made his feelings towards her known, she had been encouraging him to find someone more suitable than she to be his queen. Now there was a perfect candidate, so why was she so against the idea? Was she truly falling in love with Eryk or was she just possessive of the man she was bound to protect with her very life?

Chapter 3

Eryk walked back into his study, closing the door behind him. He would just leave Aislynn to gather herself together, and he knew that she would rejoin him when she was ready. If he needed her before she was ready to come back inside, well she wasn't too far away.

As he turned away from the door and began to walk over to his desk, he froze. There was something not quite right about the room, but he couldn't put his finger on it. He slowly drew the sword he now wore everywhere he went, and backed slowly up to a wall. Eryk knew that ideally, being backed into a corner wasn't the best place to start a fight, but he didn't know what was making his hair stand on end, so it was better to be safe than sorry and have his back protected.

The attacker came from his left, flying at him out of the deep shadows beside the floor-to-ceiling windows. Eryk brought his sword up quickly to block the descending overhand chop, and the weapons met with a loud clang. Instead of pressing the attack, however, Eryk's attacker stepped back, bringing his sword down as he moved.

"Very nice, your Majesty," Byron complimented. "Your training is coming along very well. How did you know I was there?"

"I just felt that there was something wrong with the room," Eryk explained.

"Good." Byron was very happy with this evidence of Eryk's progress. He had come a long way from the person who had presented himself early one morning a couple of months ago practically begging to be taught. Who would have thought that the king's guilt and his determination never to endanger Aislynn again would have had such great results?

"So how is she?" Byron asked, nodding towards the garden and relaxing into a less formal tone. He was only a year or so older than the king, having recently celebrated his twenty-sixth birthday, and the two of them had known each other for years.

"She's okay, but frustrated. She wants the council to leave us alone, but I told her why that wouldn't happen. And I asked her to think about my proposal again."

"That was dangerous, especially coming right on the heels of Jonas' accusation. What possessed you to do that? I had never thought you were a stupid man." The captain said this with a smirk.

Eryk laughed. "I asked her because I love her, and it would make things so much easier if she would finally agree to marry me. I admit that part of me wants to use the power I now have to change the kingdom's policy on arranged marriage and make it possible to arrange the wedding behind her back. Do you think I could get Jackob's consent?"

Byron laughed, shaking his head. "You are a glutton for punishment, aren't you?"

"She's worth it," Eryk proclaimed, with a smile. "What else brings you here, other than to spring a surprise attack on me, that is?"

"Well it seems that you have a visitor from the east, your Majesty," Byron said, all business again. "He says that his name is…"

"Lord Warren," Eryk interrupted. "Excellent! He's here earlier than I thought he would be. Please show him in immediately."

The man Byron escorted into the king's presence a few moments later was tall and well built, wearing a red and black uniform very similar to that worn by the Bacovian soldiers. The quality and cut of the fabric was far above standard issue, however, showing the man's rank and status. He had curly red hair that he wore cut short, likely in order to fit more comfortably under the helmet he carried under his left arm. A sword rested in a worn scabbard at his left hip, ready to draw at a moment's notice, and from the look of him, he knew how to use it. He came to stand in front of Eryk's desk, and bowed at the waist.

"Greetings, your Majesty. I hope that I have arrived quickly enough for your needs. Your summons sounded quite urgent."

"You are here more rapidly than I thought you would be. How did you manage that?" As he spoke, Eryk moved around to the front of the desk and took Warren's hand in a firm grasp. "Welcome back! Come… sit and we'll talk for a few minutes."

Seeing that Eryk had everything well in hand, Byron excused himself and quietly left the room. It was obvious that Eryk knew the man, and Byron wasn't too concerned about the king's safety with both Aislynn and the pair of guards nearby.

"So how have you been?" Eryk asked as he settled himself into a comfortable chair.

"Well, all things considered," Warren answered, taking a seat on the couch. "So you're the king now. I'm sorry that I missed the coronation ceremony."

"That's fine. I know that you have been very busy getting your command established. I've heard really good things about it."

Warren beamed with obvious pride. "It's been a lot of work, but the men have stepped up to the challenge. I brought some of them with me, like you asked."

"Perfect. We've been having a lot of trouble with the ongoing conflict against Madelia, and I think that your experiences with your men would be a tremendous help."

"Tell me what's been happening," Warren insisted, leaning forward a little bit towards Eryk.

Just as Eryk was about to explain the situation at the border, Warren sat up abruptly, turning at the sound of footsteps. Eryk looked up, and saw Aislynn entering the room. She looked a little disheveled, with her hair a bit tangled from the breeze outside and some dirt marks on her green dress, but the way the sunlight brought out the highlights in her hair and illuminated her face made Eryk's heart skip a beat. Cheta moved up to sit beside her mistress, and Aislynn smiled at the look on Eryk face, to say nothing of the feelings pulsing between them.

"I thought I heard voices," she explained, looking at Warren, who rose and bowed to her.

"Aislynn, this is Lord Warren, an old friend of mine. I asked him to join us here because he has some expertise that may help us turn the tide of battle against Madelia."

"Pleased to meet you," Aislynn said with a smile. She had to look up at him to meet his eyes, which was unusual for her. She realized that Warren was even taller than Eryk, and the king topped six feet.

"Well, if you're just getting caught up and you don't need me, I'll see you both later." With a whistle to Cheta, Aislynn turned and left the room, leaving the gentlemen to their discussion.

As Aislynn left the study, one of the guards on duty outside the door fell into place behind her. She had gotten used to having someone following her around, and the castle guards now took turns rotating that duty with Marcus and Mateo so that she had someone nearby at times when her twin guards couldn't be. It also made Eryk feel better knowing that she had some help in case she needed it, and what made Eryk feel better made her life easier.

Once she had finished having her little tantrum in the garden, Aislynn had realized that her dress was a mess, as was her hair, and she needed to change. Marja was still out somewhere with Branden, so she was left to her own devices, which basically meant that looking like a proper princess was a lost cause. She slipped out of the green dress, and struck with sudden inspiration, Aislynn found a riding dress to wear.

Eryk would likely be in the study the rest of the day with Warren she realized, so she decided to take advantage of the lovely weather and go for a ride. With autumn fast approaching, it wouldn't be long before the weather would prevent her from heading out into the countryside. Winter came early here at the edge of the mountains.

Aislynn nearly skipped back out of her room, gathered her guard with a look and headed down to the stables, Cheta racing along ahead.

"I hope you're up for a ride," she called over her shoulder to the guard. She didn't recognize this one, but there were so many men in the royal guard, and they rotated so often, that she really wasn't surprised. She toyed with the idea of swinging by the barracks to get one of her own guards, but decided against it. She was a part of Bacovia now, for better or for worse, so she may as well get used to having Bacovian guards. She saddled her horse while the guard got one of his own, and they were riding out of the city gates within a half hour.

Aislynn loved the feeling of freedom she got when riding through the fields and forests around the capital city. Cheta loved to run too, and the two of them didn't get away often enough as far as the wolf was concerned. With a laugh, she spurred the horse into a gallop, drawing ahead of Cheta and the guard who trailed along behind.

Aislynn soon found herself at the field where she and Eryk had spent some quiet afternoons before the war started to occupy all of their time. She dismounted and walked out into the sunlight, leaving the horse to graze at the edge of the trees. As Eryk had suspected, his duties had curtailed a lot of his freedom, but he had taken her advice often enough that they had visited this field on more than one occasion since he had assumed the throne. This was one of their favorite places, and Aislynn decided that it was as good a place as any to think about his proposal. Again.

Eryk had decided, unequivocally, that he wanted Aislynn as his queen. She knew that, as he had made his position very clear, spurning any of the other women who had been in consideration. The question was whether she wanted to *be* Eryk's queen. On one level, she knew that she did, and she was reasonably certain that she would be happy in the position. However, on another level, the level where her duty was a part of every fiber of her being, she just wasn't sure that she could take that step. It had nothing to do with love, and it had nothing to do with compatibility. It had everything to do with duty, and Aislynn still couldn't reconcile her duty as a bodyguard to keep Eryk safe, and her potential duty as a queen to have children. How could she justify the inability to do her job as a bodyguard in order to provide Eryk with his heir?

Aislynn knew that her father had said that it could work if she wanted to make it work. It had worked before, apparently, so logically it could work again, but did she want it to? And of course, she couldn't forget about Byron. The captain *said* that he didn't want to interfere with Eryk's claim to her, but Aislynn suspected that if she decided to pursue Byron that he would change his mind about that. What would make her happy? She spent the afternoon wandering back and forth across the field, thinking about the problem from as many different angles as possible.

She examined her reaction this morning, when Marcus had gotten between her and Eryk. Had it been protectiveness or possessiveness? If it was possessiveness, would she be able to stand the sight of Eryk with another woman if she made it clear that she would never marry him and he would have to get his heir elsewhere? Would he even choose another with Davin waiting in the wings to be king one day? If only she hadn't gotten so close! If only her emotions weren't so tangled up in this…

The sun was starting to set and Aislynn was walking more in shadow than in sunlight when she realized that she had better get back to the castle if she was going to be in time for dinner. Eryk, she knew, had been with his friend all afternoon. From this distance, she couldn't tell if they had stayed in the study, but she did know that they had stayed in the city. It wouldn't be long before he realized that she wasn't there, and she didn't want him to worry. Did *that* mean that she was ready to marry him?

As Aislynn rode back to the city, all she knew was that she was lucky to be here in Bacovia. In any other kingdom, she'd be wedded and bedded by now, regardless of her opinion on the matter. She was lucky to have the choice and she knew that she was lucky that Eryk was a patient man. She wondered how long that patience would last as she rode through the castle gates with a sigh.

Leaving her horse in the hands of a groom, Aislynn ran up the stairs and kept right on running until she reached her room. The water in the basin in her room was still warm, but Marja had come and gone, so it was up to her to get herself ready for dinner. She quickly washed up and pulled the pins out of her hair as she moved across the room to the wardrobe. She tossed the pins carelessly onto her dresser and grabbed the first dress she put her hands on, stepping into it with hardly a skipped beat.

This dress was one that her seamstress Anna had made earlier in the summer season, and it sported the off the shoulder sleeves and tight bodice that were the style right now, but with a loose and flowing skirt as per Aislynn's preference. Her position as the king's chief advisor set her a little apart from the court as a whole and she was free to do what she would with her clothing, within reason. She quickly laced the dress up the side, ran a comb through her hair, and hurried out of the room.

The dining hall was full by the time she arrived, but fortunately, nobody was eating yet. Unlike breakfast, which usually only involved the five of them, close friends all, dinner was for the entire court. The courtiers seated themselves based on rank, with the highest-ranking nobility sitting closest to the head table on the other side of the room. Given her position on the council, and her rank, there was nowhere for her to sit *but* the head table.

Since she was last into the room today, she would have to make the uncomfortable journey across the hall alone. Aislynn felt like everyone was watching her as she walked, a situation that still made her skin crawl, and it was with great relief that she arrived at her destination. The men all rose from their seats, Byron pulled her chair out for her, and they all sat once again.

"Now that we're all here," Eryk said with a smile, "let's eat." He signaled to the servants, and the platters of food started to circulate among the diners.

"So are you all caught up now?" Aislynn asked Warren with a smile. He was sitting to Eryk's right, on the other side of Byron.

He nodded. "It has been a long time, and it's nice to see Eryk again. It's also wonderful to see he outgrew that awkward, gangly stage he was going through last time I was here."

Eryk laughed at that. "You weren't much to look at either," he pointed out. "I remember that every time you went out into the sun, you came back in with your skin the same color as your hair." The rest of the dinner continued that way, with lighthearted banter bouncing back and forth between those seated at the head table.

When dinner was over, Eryk rose from his seat and moved down the table to Aislynn's chair. He pulled her chair out for her, and offered her his hand. As she took it and rose, he bent close and asked the question she'd been waiting for.

"What were you doing this afternoon?" he whispered softly into her ear.

"I was thinking," she replied truthfully.

"And?"

"I'm still thinking."

With a sigh, Eryk released her hand and moved out into the dining hall. After dinner, it was his custom to visit among the courtiers and council members. He felt that his father had been too distanced from his court, and one of the first things he had done after assuming the crown was to change that by instituting dinners for the whole court. Aislynn found the enforced social parade annoying and exhausting, so she usually escaped into a nearby garden once she made sure that either Marcus or Mateo was on duty at the king's back. Everyone in the court knew where she went, so if anyone wanted to talk to her, the members of the court could easily find her there. Therefore, tonight, true to her custom, she left the room and took refuge in the fresh air outside.

She wasn't there long, walking among the night-blooming jasmine and moonflowers, before she heard footsteps behind her, crunching on the gravel of the pathway. Turning, she was surprised to find Warren walking towards her.

"Seeing as it is a lovely evening, I was hoping that I could join you, your Majesty," he said as he closed the distance between them.

"Your Majesty?" Aislynn repeated, confused.

"Is that not the proper term of address?" Warren asked, with a smile on his face. "I'm sorry that I missed your wedding."

Understanding dawned and Aislynn laughed. "Highness is the appropriate term for me, my Lord. I'm not Eryk's queen."

Now it was Warren's turn to look confused. "I just assumed, watching him when you walked into the room and the way he…" He trailed off, not sure how to continue.

Aislynn just smiled and turned away to continue walking along the pathway. Warren took a few quick steps to catch up to her and then slowed his pace to match hers.

"I don't understand," Warren admitted after a few minutes. "Hasn't he asked? It seems pretty obvious that he wants to, so if he hasn't gotten up the courage yet, I'm sure it's just a matter of time."

Aislynn didn't look at him, and trusted the night to hide her blushes. "It's not that he hasn't asked," she replied.

"Ahhhh. Well then, since you apparently have better taste in men, would you honor me with a stroll around the gardens?" Warren asked, laughter apparent in his voice.

Aislynn stopped and turned to look up at him, not entirely sure what to make of his invitation. This man was supposed to be Eryk's friend, a friend who had just admitted that it was obvious that Eryk cared for her. Was he making advances towards her, or was he just joking around? Deciding that he didn't seem like the type to go after the woman his friend was interested in, she accepted the invitation, resting her hand lightly on Warren's arm.

As they walked, they spoke about inconsequential things. She let Warren choose the topics of conversation, and it quickly became obvious that he didn't expect anything more from her than a pretty face and a few shallow responses. Aislynn rarely did what others expected, and now she began to direct the conversation a little until there was an opening for her to exploit.

"So Eryk said that you might have some ideas that could help us win this war. What sort of things have you implemented in the east?" she asked pointedly.

Surprised by the serious nature of the question, Warren paused and looked down at her to see if she was expecting a serious response or something that just brushed the surface of the issue. He met her bright, direct gaze, and decided that she definitely wanted a real answer.

"Well, it's really a multi-step process," he began. "We need to start by determining the pattern of the attacks on your forces. I know that they may seem random, but there will be a pattern somewhere. People are not truly capable of being entirely random, I've found.

"Once we find that pattern, we can begin to anticipate their attacks and prepare our defenses accordingly. The hope is to catch one or more of their little groups unaware and whittle down their numbers."

"What about the villages they have been attacking? Is it possible to find a pattern in those? I know that the plan is to begin training militia in the border villages, but weapon training of any sort takes time, and it would be better for everyone on our side of the border if we could anticipate the next village to be attacked and take measures to protect it."

"That's true, and looking at the villages will definitely be part of looking at all of the attacks in general. Nobody really has any idea how big Madelia's army is, so we don't know if it is one or more groups that are attacking villages. It would make a big difference if it was just one group that moves around a lot."

"True, but I doubt we can be that lucky. I'm guessing that there are at least two groups that are attacking the border villages," Aislynn suggested.

By this time, the pair had walked the periphery of the entire garden. They were back at the doors leading into the dining hall. Eryk was just finishing up with the last group courtiers, and he made his way outside as soon as his conversation was complete.

"Are you two enjoying yourselves?" he asked as he joined them.

"Definitely," Warren replied with enthusiasm. Aislynn just nodded.

"Mataline is looking for you," Eryk told Aislynn, inclining his head in the direction of the swiftly emptying dining hall. "I told her that I would send you along when I found you, so you may want to hurry."

With a nod of her head to Warren, Aislynn reclaimed her hand and proceeded through the open doors and into the dining hall to find Mataline. Warren just stood outside and watched her walk away.

"She's quite something, isn't she?" Eryk asked with a smile.

"She certainly is. She had some interesting thoughts on the progression of the war with Madelia. I know that I haven't been here long enough to know what's already been discussed, but she is certainly well informed."

"She should be," Eryk laughed. "She is my chief advisor, after all."

"Is she now?" Warren mused. "Well isn't that interesting."

Chapter 4

Eryk and Branden circled slowly, each trying to find a weakness in the other's defenses. Byron had declared this morning that Eryk would try to spar properly with Branden instead of using his usual duck-and-run tactics. Branden was a far better swordsman, so he had promised at the beginning of their combat to be a little lenient, using only the most basic attacks. Eryk, however, had become very adept at protecting himself, so Branden was having a hard time getting in a hit.

Branden decided to press the attack, surging forward while bringing his sword across for a cut aimed at Eryk's shoulder. Eryk jumped back while bringing his sword up to block. Their swords met with the ring of metal on metal, and then Eryk struck back at Branden with an overhand chop of his own. Branden danced back, easily outdistancing Eryk's reach, and then stepped forward quickly, sword leading. Eryk brought his sword down and across his body, blocking the attack, but he continued with the twisting movement he had started, pushing his sword up and stepping forward, forcing Branden back on his heels. Branden turned with Eryk to avoid losing his balance, and he managed to step away, freeing his sword and gaining some breathing room. They both dropped into defensive crouches again, getting ready for the next flurry of blows.

Branden advanced once more, ready to attack, but he noticed that Eryk's attention wasn't on him any longer, so Branden straightened and glanced over his shoulder to see what Eryk was looking at. On the other side of the courtyard, Aislynn and Byron had faced off, each holding a short sword and dagger. Branden turned to stand beside Eryk, and together they watched the two professionals begin their practice.

"You're sure about this, right?" Byron asked as he circled, a slightly concerned look on his face.

"Positive. Nothing I've done these past few weeks has so much as pulled at the scars. Marcus and Mateo are good, but they're not as good as you are, and I've been itching for a real workout."

Aislynn knew that Byron just needed the extra reassurance that she was ready for this level of exertion. This would be their first sparring match since Aislynn was so badly injured, but the healing magic that Eryk's royal physician possessed was impressive, and she'd healed well. She knew that Byron's concern stemmed from more than professional courtesy, and she appreciated it, but the two had agreed not to talk about it and so he said nothing else. His concession to using her favorite weapons instead of his own long sword was enough of an indication.

To show that she'd meant what she said, Aislynn lunged forward, sword leading the way. She didn't honestly expect to come anywhere near the mark and Byron didn't disappoint, leaping sideways and easily evading her. He didn't let her get her feet under her either, lunging right back towards her, sword cutting diagonally through the air. Aislynn blocked his strike with her sword and plunged her dagger forward towards his neck, but Byron brought his own dagger up to block. They stood there for a moment, blades locked together, until Aislynn sprang backwards with a laugh. She had missed this!

Byron took the lead this time, sending his sword out towards Aislynn's thigh while stabbing his dagger towards her opposite elbow, both attacks meant to disable. Aislynn blocked the sword first, bringing her weapon across her body and down, and then stepped closer to Byron, putting her weight behind her sword and forcing Byron to twist away from her. This left his right side exposed, and Aislynn immediately took advantage, driving her dagger forward towards his unprotected side.

Desperate to escape what would certainly be considered a lethal blow, taking him out of the practice and giving her the win, Byron kicked out, hooking his right leg around Aislynn's ankle and tripping her to the ground. In order to catch herself, she had to drop her sword, and it clattered to the stones, bouncing out of easy reach. Having Aislynn at a disadvantage, Byron moved to attack, but she twisted away from him and rolled towards her sword. Once she felt it under her hand, she grasped the grip and twisted over and up onto her feet. She stayed low, in a defensive crouch, waiting to see what Byron would do next.

They both moved at the same time, Aislynn springing forward just as Byron advanced towards her. The flurry of blows that followed was nearly too fast for Eryk and Branden to follow, and the sound of metal on metal filled the courtyard. The attacks and parries went on and on until suddenly, a sword was flying through the air. The watching men didn't know who had been disarmed until they saw Byron rushing towards the fallen sword, Aislynn close on his heels.

Byron barely slowed as he sprinted past his sword, just bending over to grab the hilt as he ran by. He knew that if he stopped to pick it up properly, Aislynn would be on him, and he'd be finished. Byron flipped his sword over to grasp it properly, and then turned to face his pursuer.

Byron could tell that Aislynn was starting to tire as she attacked him again. Her sword swings were slowing, and he knew that it would just be a matter of time. Soon, her parries would slow to the point where he could score the final hit. He just needed to keep her at bay a little longer.

Aislynn also knew that her time was running out if she wanted to win this match. She needed to end things as soon as possible, which meant she was going to have to surprise Byron with something. She could tell by the way he was standing that he was prepared to defend himself, so she opted for something very unconventional. Springing towards him, she crossed her weapons and drove them towards his chest. He brought his own weapons up to block, and as soon as her sword touched his, Aislynn pulled her arms apart, sending Byron's sword crashing into his dagger. Startled, he lost his grip briefly, but it was long enough for Aislynn to bring her sword and dagger to bear, one pointed at his heart and the other pointed at his head. With a rueful shake of his head, Byron conceded defeat.

"That was nicely done," he complimented, "if a little unorthodox.

It's nice to see that you are indeed feeling like your old self again." Aislynn just smiled and bent down to retrieve the dropped weapons.

"I'll definitely need to spar again tomorrow," she commented as she stood up with a barely suppressed groan. "If I'm this sore now, I'll be barely able to move tomorrow."

"I guess that means that tomorrow I'll win and bring the tally back to a more even keel."

Across the courtyard, Branden turned to Eryk with a look of astonishment on his face. He had never seen Aislynn truly fight before now. Until now, he'd only seen what went on in the practices since her injuries, so the princess had been holding herself back and going slowly to make sure she didn't affect her recovery.

"To think that I actually thought that I could beat her," he said quietly, with a rueful shake of his head.

"Well you were pretty drunk at the time, and drugged, so you certainly weren't thinking straight," Eryk reminded him with a smile and an elbow to the ribs.

"No kidding," Branden agreed.

Byron noticed the two of them standing there and started across the courtyard with a scowl on his face. As Aislynn excused herself to ease her sore muscles, Byron got the two young men back to work on their sparring. It seemed that their impromptu break was definitely over.

When Warren arrived at the dining hall for breakfast later that morning, he found it empty save for Branden. Seeing him, Branden called out a greeting.

"Everyone else should be along shortly," he said. "Knowing the ladies, at least, they're making sure they look their best before starting the day."

Warren smiled and walked across the room, seating himself at the table across from Branden.

"It's been a long time," Warren commented. "What have you been up to? I hear that you're due to be married soon."

Branden smiled and nodded. "Yes, to the Lady Marja. We're supposed to be wed at Harvestide."

"She's Princess Aislynn's friend, isn't she?"

Branden nodded. "When Aislynn and Eryk started spending so much time together, Marja and I found that our free time passed more quickly with company. Once we got to know one another, we decided to get married."

"About that whole 'spending time together' thing… How did Aislynn end up as Eryk's advisor? Wasn't that supposed to be your job?"

Branden blushed and looked away briefly. He had made a complete and utter fool of himself, getting involved with those Madelians. He still considered himself very lucky to be permitted at court, and even luckier to be the king's friend. His sister, Alexius, hadn't been so fortunate. She'd been banished from court for her role as an accomplice in the attack that had injured Aislynn so badly. Of course, his only role now was as the king's sparring partner, but it was better than nothing, right?

Looking back at Warren, Branden smiled a small, ironic smile. "Aislynn is… uniquely qualified to be Eryk's advisor," he said, choosing not to explain anything further.

"So she's got the king's ear, does she? Perhaps a little bedtime persuasion?"

"I'd not repeat that thought, if I were you," Branden said with a bit of a chuckle. "I have it on good authority *that's* not happening, and I understand that Aislynn nearly killed a man the other day for making the same comment." Warren laughed, thinking that Branden was kidding about that last part.

"So that's why she hasn't married him yet. She can get him to do what she wants and doesn't even need to sleep with him to get her way." Warren smiled at the thought. "She needs someone to take a firm stand with her, that's all."

Branden turned to look Warren directly in the eye. "Warren, I know that you've been gone a long time, and you likely don't consider me a friend any longer, but please listen closely anyway. The relationship between Eryk and Aislynn is complicated, and you don't have a hope in hell of getting anywhere with her, so don't even think about it."

Just then, Byron and Eryk arrived, and they came over to join Warren and Branden at the table. Eryk greeted Warren with a big smile and asked if he had slept well. They all spoke of inconsequential things until Cheta's appearance heralded the arrival of Aislynn and Marja. Eryk and Branden rose and went to join their ladies, as was their custom, leaving Byron and Warren alone at the table. As the four made their way back, Byron noticed the look of speculation on Warren's face and the gleam in his eye as he watched Aislynn glide across the room, her hand on Eryk's arm. This can't be a precursor to anything good, Byron thought to himself as he recognized the thoughts behind the looks, but the rest of their group joined them before he could say anything to Warren.

After the meal, Byron excused himself to be about his duties, and everyone else prepared to head out to the field where Warren's men had bivouacked. Aislynn and Eryk especially wanted to meet Warren's soldiers and find out exactly how they could make a difference in the war.

"Are we going to walk or ride?" Marja asked, a little concerned by the idea of having to walk the entire way out of the city.

"It would be faster to ride, my Lady," replied Warren. "I doubt any of us want to make the dusty trek by foot if we don't need to."

Marja smiled, happy to have the man echo her own thoughts, but then a thought crossed her mind. "But we're not dressed for riding," Marja explained, indicating herself and Aislynn. Always a proper lady, Marja wasn't about to ride on horseback if she wasn't appropriately dressed and prepared for the excursion.

Eryk laughed. "Well we can get a carriage for you, if you'd like. Branden can even keep you company, since I'm pretty sure that Aislynn won't be joining you."

Marja turned to look at Aislynn with an expression of near horror on her face, but Aislynn just shrugged. She knew that Marja really wasn't surprised that Aislynn would choose to ride, regardless of her dress. They'd had many a conversation about the princess's "inappropriate" behaviors.

"I'll ride sidesaddle, just for you," she promised her friend instead.

The issue of transportation settled, the five of them made their way to the stables. The grooms were a little puzzled by Aislynn's unusual request for a sidesaddle, but they did as she asked, and Marja and Branden settled comfortably into Aislynn's little used carriage. The princess knew that the two of them would appreciate the time alone as much as she would appreciate the fresh air.

Eryk gave Aislynn a lift into her saddle, and mounted his own big stallion while she settled herself into the odd contraption. She had never liked sitting sideways on a horse, but it was the least she could do to keep up appearances and make Marja happy. Besides, she thought to herself, Warren didn't know about her position as Eryk's bodyguard, so she figured she might as well *try* to act like a proper royal lady.

Aislynn was surprised to find that the ride through the city was quite pleasant. Warren rode close beside her, sharing stories and anecdotes about Eryk from their time spent together as boys in Tarren's court. The one that amused Aislynn the most was the story that Warren shared about Eryk's early weapon training.

"It was truly the funniest thing," Warren confided as he leaned over to pretend to whisper in Aislynn's ear. "We were all about ten or eleven, I guess, and it was our very first sword lesson. Until now, we'd only learned about knife fighting and done some archery. Eryk, of course, was always very good at archery, and was hopeless with the knives. Nevertheless, that was nothing compared to how horrible he was when he picked up that sword for the first time.

"Branden took to the sword like it was the natural extension of his arm. He was swinging it around easily and our instructor quickly got him set up with one of the older boys. It was obvious that Branden was going to be good with the weapon. I wasn't too bad myself," Warren added with false modesty. He continued with a barely suppressed chuckle.

"Eryk… well Eryk was a special case. As soon as he wrapped his hand around the grip and tried to pick the weapon up, we all knew that there was going to be trouble. Eryk was always a tall boy, but he didn't seem to have the upper body strength to match his height. The sword was simply too heavy for him to lift properly, and our instructor knew it. The man stepped forward to help Eryk just as the prince took the sword in a two-handed grip, brought it up and swung it around with all his strength. It was a good thing our instructor was quick on his feet or our dear Eryk would have sliced the man open! You should have seen the look on both of their faces."

Aislynn burst out laughing, easily able to picture the confused and embarrassed expression Eryk would have had on his face. She'd put that look there herself, once or twice. Warren joined her, his deep laugh rolling out through the city, leaving Eryk to ride alone and embarrassed. It had been a long time since Aislynn had laughed so hard, and Eryk had to wonder why he was always the butt of the jokes and stories that amused her the most.

Warren kept up a constant flow of conversation, and Eryk found that he was unable to get a word in edgewise. Soon, the way that Warren was monopolizing Aislynn's time began to make Eryk feel uncomfortable, and he felt jealousy begin to grow in the pit of his stomach. Aislynn, feeling Eryk's growing discomfort and jealousy through the link that bound them, quickly found a reason to excuse herself and reined her horse in to fall back to join him. She'd been finding Warren's attention a little stifling anyway and was just as happy to escape, but it was only a few moments before they reached Warren's encampment.

The soldiers had laid out their camp in a neat, organized fashion, with tents pitched in long rows across the middle of the plateau, surrounded by picket lines of horses. They could see men moving among the animals, grooming and feeding, as well as men practicing drills on horseback in an open space to the south of the camp. Aislynn turned to Warren, a look of confusion on her face.

"You've created a cavalry unit?" she asked. "What's so interesting about that?"

"These aren't just any cavalry," Warren was happy to explain. "They're light cavalry. Skirmishers. They are essentially incredibly mobile archers, able to dash in and out of combat, move from one area of the field to another quickly, lead the opening attacks and cover any retreats."

"That sounds impressive," Aislynn commented, "but I'd prefer to see it in action before I believe that this is our salvation. How many men did you bring with you?"

"There are one hundred here, your Highness, but we have nearly one thousand in the whole command back home." Warren looked over his men with pride. "They are highly disciplined, and the beasts have been trained for combat too, so they are weapons in their own right."

"How many men do you need in a group in order to be effective?" Eryk wanted to know. "Ideally, I think that we'd like to split your men up into smaller groups, in order to be able to cover more ground."

"Well the number of men and beasts needed really depends on what you want them to do. If you're looking for a group to run down those Madelians who are attacking your border villages, then groups of six to ten are likely big enough. If you want to use them for flanking advantage in large scale combat, then the more of them you have together, the more effective they will be."

As Branden and Marja joined them, the three on horseback dismounted and the group set off to the south of the camp to watch the men practice their drills. There was no better way to determine how best to use the light cavalry than to see the men and animals in action.

"Where's Cheta going?" Branden asked, watching the wolf head off away from the camp. His question drew Eryk's attention to the fleeing wolf too.

"She's taking advantage of being so close to the forest to go and hunt," Aislynn replied. "She should only be gone for a short time."

Aislynn didn't seem at all concerned by the apparent desertion of her *eesprid*, so they decided not to worry about it either. Eryk knew that Cheta had appeared shortly after Aislynn was born and had been the princess's friend and companion ever since. Since they had been together for their entire lives, Aislynn was obviously a good judge of whether or not to worry.

Eryk knew that there were differences among the assassins trained in the Academy that Aislynn's kingdom was well known for, sort of a difference in specialty. From what she had revealed to him, both types of assassin were taught to kill, but the *eesprid* were one of two signs that the kingdom of Evendell used to determine which children were meant to be trained as bodyguards instead of simple assassins. The wolf that was her companion was an indicator of the princess's specialized education, along with the strange eagle birthmark on her left wrist. Shaking his head at the strangeness of his assassin-trained bodyguard and some of her upbringing, the king drew his attention back to Warren and his men.

They spent the rest of the day watching the soldiers practice and gathering information to use to form a plan of attack at the next day's council meeting. Eryk was hoping that the novelty of the mobile archery units would encourage Bacovia's fighters and help to catch and decimate the enemy troops. By the time they were ready to head back to the castle for dinner, Cheta had rejoined them, and they made their way back up the mountain plateau full of renewed hope for a quick end to the ongoing conflict.

The evening air was cool as Aislynn walked in the garden, heralding the fast approaching autumn. She liked the crisp, clear air because it reminded her of her home in Evendell, where the leaves would already be turning. Nobody wanted to be fighting a war throughout the winter, and Aislynn hoped that the ideas they had developed today would help to make sure that a prolonged conflict didn't happen.

She was some distance away from the castle, at the far end of the garden, when she heard footsteps behind her. She knew that she should be safe here, even with Cheta off prowling the garden for mice, but she reached for her dagger anyway, waiting for the shape dimly visible in the night to define itself. She relaxed when she recognized Warren's broad shoulders and tall frame.

"Your men do you justice," Aislynn commented as he came closer. "They are everything you claimed that they were in your letter to Eryk. I know that Eryk is grateful to you for bringing them here, and he appreciates your help for tomorrow's council meeting, when we explain our new plans to the councilors. I'm sure our men will be happy to have your skirmishers fighting with them."

Warren didn't say anything as he continued to come towards her, but she could see the smile on his face once he got close enough. He stopped in front of her, so close that she could feel the heat of his body in the chilly air.

"You are a very interesting woman," he said, still smiling. "I find that I'm intrigued by someone of your status holding the position that you do here. You are so…independent, relying only on yourself." Not knowing what to make of the observation, Aislynn reminded silent, waiting for him to continue. He made her a little uncertain of herself, which wasn't something she was used to.

"You are very beautiful," he said, reaching up to caress her cheek, startling her with his brashness. His touch left tingles on her skin, and when his hand reached her chin, he slipped it behind her head, tangling his fingers in her unbound hair.

Suddenly, he stepped even closer, pulling her towards him at the same time. Leaning down, he kissed her passionately, his free arm reaching around her waist and pulling her against him. She could feel his heart pounding in his chest as he held her against him, and she could feel the hunger in his kiss. Involuntarily, she felt her body reacting to his barely controlled passion, starting to melt against him, but she forced herself to stiffen in his grasp.

He tried to draw her farther into the seclusion of the garden, and she pushed her hands up between them. She broke his grasp with difficulty and backed away from him slowly.

"I don't know what you think you're doing –" she started to say, but Warren interrupted her.

"You can't tell me that you didn't feel that," he said, stepping towards her. She took another step away from him.

"You felt the connection between us as much as I did," he stated. "You've been here for months, Eryk has asked you to marry him and still you are unwed, uncommitted. Ask yourself why that is and think about what just happened, and I think you'll come to realize –"

"I will realize nothing!" Aislynn spat, her heart pounding with fury. "I would advise you, Lord Warren, that you never lay hands on me again."

Aislynn whirled away from him and strode back to the castle, furious with him and with herself. She had to admit that she *had* felt something when Warren kissed her, but she stamped on that feeling, forcing it down and leaving only the fury behind. Cheta joined her as she walked the length of the garden, and she carefully avoided any of the remaining courtiers by cutting down the side of the garden and into the adjacent courtyard. Despite the well-guarded gates between the two, she was easily recognized and the men made no move to stop her.

Aislynn went immediately to her room, shutting the bedroom door carefully behind her. She was alone, Marja not having returned from dinner yet, so she undressed quickly and slipped into her nightdress before throwing herself onto the bed. Wrapping her arms around Cheta's warm body, she buried her face into the wolf's fur and began to sob.

The princess was still crying when Marja came through the main door of the suite a little while later. Concerned, Marja made her way silently across the suite and leaned against Aislynn's door. When she heard nothing but sobs coming from the other side, she knocked quietly.

"Your Highness?" she called quietly. "Is everything okay?" She knew that it wasn't, but she also didn't want to intrude on Aislynn's privacy if her friend didn't want her there. When she heard nothing, she turned the doorknob quietly and called again. "Aislynn?"

As Marja pushed the door open and looked inside, she saw a distraught Aislynn curled up around Cheta. The other woman raised her head to meet Marja's gaze briefly, and then pushed herself away from the wolf, refusing to let Marja see her as weak. She rubbed her hand across her red eyes and tear-stained cheeks and then met Marja's eyes again.

"Can I help you?" Aislynn asked, not quite able to keep her tone of voice entirely civil. She really didn't appreciate having her friend see her like this, weeping in her room. It just seemed so… pathetic.

"I was going to ask you the same thing," the blond replied with a tiny smile. "Do you want to talk about it?"

Aislynn thought about the invitation for just a moment before realizing that she really *did* want to talk about it. The impulse was unlike her, and Aislynn grimaced as she nodded her head. Marja came over and sat down on the bed beside Aislynn, but carefully didn't reach out to her friend. She knew enough about the princess to know that Aislynn agreeing to talk was unusual enough, so she didn't want to push it.

"Is it about Eryk?" Marja asked, picking the most logical person to be causing Aislynn so much grief, and she was surprised when Aislynn shook her head.

"No, not Eryk. At least, not directly," Aislynn clarified. Then she poured out the story of what had passed between her and Warren in the garden, even admitting to the feelings of passion that had stirred deep inside of her.

"Why haven't I said yes to Eryk?" Aislynn questioned, looking to her friend for answers. "What's wrong with me?"

"Well, considering the fact that you apparently now have three men vying for your attention, I don't think that there's anything wrong with you," Marja replied with a smile.

Aislynn blushed. "One of them is officially *not* vying for my attention, if you remember," she corrected.

"And that's likely part of the problem," Marja commented. "I'm sure it'll be fine. Everything will work itself out."

"Are you sure?"

"As sure as I can be. Eventually, you'll pick one of them, the rest will move on with their lives and things will be more peaceful around here."

Marja sounded so positive and convincing that Aislynn couldn't help but smile. Everything would be fine, she thought to herself, liking the sound of the statement. Everything would be fine.

Chapter 5

Aislynn woke with a start, her heart racing. As she lay on her bed in the darkness, hearing nothing but her own ragged breathing, she realized that it was just a dream that had awakened her. A dream that left her knees weak and her body trembling with uncontrolled emotions. She had been dreaming of Warren and last night's encounter in the garden, and the fury she had felt last night rose again. A rising wave of desire followed that fury, something that she squashed quickly and thoroughly.

Aislynn replayed the events in her head again as she lay there. Why hadn't she resisted or broken away sooner? Why hadn't she slapped him or something? The answer, unfortunately, was painfully obvious; she hadn't done any of those things because she had liked kissing Warren.

She rose quickly and dressed, suddenly desperate to begin her sparring practice with Byron. She was hoping to distract herself with exercise, work off some excess energy until she could sort out what she was feeling, and deal with it properly. Eryk had never kissed her like that… Aislynn stopped when that idea crossed her mind. Why hadn't he ever kissed her with the passion that Warren had shown her? And why did it bother her so much that he hadn't?

Aislynn shook her head to help clear away the unwanted thoughts, and walked quietly through the suite so as not to wake Marja. She could tell by the lack of light coming in through the window of the reception room that she was awake earlier than normal, but she moved out of her room and into the halls of the castle anyway. She was, as expected, quite stiff this morning, so she figured that she could use the extra time to stretch thoroughly before beginning her morning practice session. Marcus fell into place behind her without a word, and Cheta raced ahead, knowing exactly where they were going.

When Byron entered the barracks courtyard some time later, he was surprised to see Aislynn there already, and without Eryk. The two usually arrived together. He nodded a greeting to Marcus, who returned the greeting before leaving to switch shifts with his twin. Marcus knew that the captain of the guard was enough of a protector for his princess.

Byron watched Aislynn moving around the courtyard with practiced movements, working with a quarterstaff just like on their very first day. The easy way she moved led him to believe that she had been there for quite some time, exercise having loosened her stiffened muscles, and he wondered what was going on. This was certainly atypical behavior for her.

He walked out from under the archway, making his presence known, and Aislynn came to rest a short distance away from him. One glance at the haunted look in her eyes confirmed for him that something wasn't right, though she was trying hard to hide it.

"You're here early this morning," he commented, deciding to keep things light. He was still learning where the line was for them, somewhere between friend and more than that. He'd made his choice, backing down from a relationship in favor of Eryk, and Byron was determined to honor that decision, but it did mean redefining the rules between him and Aislynn.

"I couldn't sleep," she replied truthfully. "I figured that I might as well get some extra practice in. I was pretty stiff this morning, and this way I may actually have a chance of holding my own against you." Her tone was light, but her smile was very wrong. Even the way she held herself was off, lacking her usual confidence.

"Would you like to get started now, or should we wait for Eryk?" Byron asked, and Aislynn's slight flinch at the sound of Eryk's name gave him an idea of what was going on. There was only one way to find out, he thought to himself, taking a deep breath before plunging into the conversation. Was this crossing that line he was trying to establish?

"Did Warren hurt you?" he asked, very quietly, deciding to go ahead anyway. He really wasn't sure he wanted to know the answer to that question.

"No, he…" Aislynn trailed off, and she looked at him suspiciously. "How did you know something happened with Warren?"

"One, I know you better than anyone else here, except maybe Eryk. I know your body language and your various tones of voice, and I can tell that something isn't right," Byron explained. "Two, I saw the way he was looking at you yesterday, and I figured that he'd try something. I have to admit that he moved a lot faster than I thought he would, likely because he'll be leaving soon."

Aislynn's face brightened, thrilled by the idea. "That's right! He'll be gone soon and I won't have to think about him anymore." She wouldn't have to think about the way he had made her feel because he'd be gone and things could be normal again.

"Have you been thinking about him?" Byron asked pointedly.

Aislynn looked down at the ground, suddenly ashamed, and nodded. Why was she feeling ashamed? There wasn't anything wrong with her thinking about Warren. Neither of them were married or engaged. She should be flattered, shouldn't she?

"And?" he pressed.

"And nothing," Aislynn stated firmly, lifting her eyes and meeting Byron's gaze again. "I told him never to touch me again, and I meant it."

"You told him? First you don't hunt Jonas down, and now you *told* Warren… you must be losing your edge." Byron smiled, showing her that he was joking. In all honesty, if she killed someone every time she lost her temper, the castle would be full of corpses strewn here and there.

Byron walked over to the rack of weapons and chose a quarterstaff of his own. Turning back to face Aislynn, he signaled the start of their match. As they faced off, Byron admitted to himself that he was relieved that Aislynn wanted nothing to do with Warren. She would crush Eryk if she married another man, and Byron had to admit to himself that *he* couldn't stand the thought of it either. It was bad enough that he had to step aside for the king, and Byron did not intend to step aside for anyone *but* Eryk. There was a limit to what he could endure.

Aislynn slipped into the dining hall later than everyone else did, again. She had sent word with Marja that she was running late, and had asked that the meal start without her.

When she arrived, she found Eryk and Byron deep in discussion about the castle's defenses. They were discussing how to strengthen them in case of siege, and Branden was adding his own insights to the conversation. Marja and Warren were carrying on a conversation of their own, but Warren rose immediately when he saw her, a big smile of greeting on his face. He pulled Aislynn's chair out from the table for her, and as she sat, he leaned over quickly.

"Have you been thinking about me?" he breathed softly into her ear, just before sitting down again and picking up the conversation with Marja where he'd left off. He did quickly glance her way, and seeing Aislynn's blush, Warren smiled at the confirmation of his suspicions.

Despite the fact that he didn't even look at her for the rest of the meal, Aislynn found the time torturous and very uncomfortable. Everyone noticed her abnormal behavior, with Byron throwing her anxious glances, and Marja asking if she was feeling unwell. The feeling of loving concern coming from Eryk just made things that much worse. Aislynn knew that the days until Warren left would all be long and painful, but she was determined not to spend that time hiding in her room like a skittish child. She just decided to ignore the man as much as possible.

The end of the meal was a welcome event, and Aislynn realized that she was looking forward to a council meeting for the very first time. At least there, *he* would be on the other side of the room and she would be able to ignore him, she hoped. She would also have Eryk's steady presence right beside her, which she figured could only help to keep her grounded. When Eryk asked her to go to his study to get the updated maps for the council meeting, she jumped at the opportunity to leave the dining hall and compose herself before facing everyone.

Aislynn walked quickly to the study and easily located the maps that Eryk wanted. They had been working on them together a few days ago, drawing in updates as they came in from the border. She sighed quietly, remembering the number of villages they had marked as destroyed. The loss of life was astounding, and there was no end in sight. She did hope that Warren's men would give them the advantage Bacovia needed.

On her way to the council chambers, Cheta's low growl startled her, making her pause just as she approached a junction in the hall. Sure enough, as soon as she rounded the corner, there was Warren, obviously waiting for her.

"Did you sleep well?" he asked with a grin. Aislynn just glared at him and moved to go around him and continue down the hall.

Not wanting her to get away from him that easily, Warren reached out and grabbed Aislynn's arm as she moved to brush past him and continue down the hall. He whirled her around and pressed her back against the wall, kissing her forcefully. Without even thinking, Aislynn brought her knee up, catching Warren hard in the groin. As he backed away in pain, starting to double over, she helped him to the ground with a swift shove.

"I told you never to touch me again," she growled. "Consider that your final warning. If you dare to lay hands on me, just one more time, I will kill you."

As Aislynn stalked down the corridor, Warren started to smile to himself as he regained his feet, the pain slowly starting to fade. He loved her fire and her passion, and everything she said and did made him want her even more. She was royalty though, so he'd have to approach this more carefully than he was used to. Warren knew one thing for certain; Eryk wasn't man enough for her. He dusted himself off and set off slowly for the council chamber.

The council got right to work as soon as everyone assembled. Eryk laid out the maps and together they discussed the latest updates and the overall lack of progress that Bacovia's forces had been making since the beginning of the war. Warren outlined some ideas for how to best position and use his cavalry unit, and the council began to wrinkle out the final details of the new plan.

The final decision was to divide Warren's men into five groups of twenty men and horses. Lord Geoffrey would assign each of these five groups a section of the border to patrol, and their orders were to assist the foot troops already assigned to those areas. In addition, they were to pursue the groups of Madelian fighters that were continually striking across the border and retreating, engaging them and destroying them if possible.

The council would continue to work on a plan to try to draw Madelia into a large-scale battle, for which Bacovia's army was better suited. The debate continued as to whether this battle would occur on Bacovian soil or Madelian. There were pros and cons with either choice, so the council decided to leave the final decision until the next meeting. By the end of the day, everyone was optimistic that their new plan had a chance of finally evening the odds, or perhaps even tipping them in Bacovia's favor.

The councilors went on ahead while Eryk and Aislynn went to draft some missives to send with the cavalry, outlining the new plans and the duties of the cavalry and foot units. Eryk maintained that it was very important for everyone to know what was going on.

The couple entered the study, Eryk closing the door behind them as Aislynn laid the newly marked maps on his desk. As she reached over to get a pen and paper, Eryk came up behind her and turned her around to face him.

"Are you okay?" he asked, a concerned look on his face. "You've been acting oddly all day." He brushed a loose strand of hair back from her forehead as he spoke.

"I'm fine," Aislynn replied, smiling. "I just didn't sleep well last night, so I'm pretty tired." She loved the feeling of his hands touching her skin, she realized. Suddenly, she really wanted Eryk to kiss her, fiercely and passionately, and she leaned into him just a little bit, hoping to encourage him.

"Well in that case, why don't we leave these until the morning and go get some dinner? That way, maybe you can get to bed a bit early and catch up on some of that missed sleep." Aislynn nodded her agreement, disappointment shooting through her as Eryk stepped away and offered her his arm. She linked her arm with his, and together they made their way to the dining hall and dinner.

Aislynn just picked at her food, and the time passed quickly while she mulled over everything that had happened during the past day. She wondered how she could possibly sleep when she had no idea who would be playing that all-important key role in her dreams tonight. Aislynn also didn't speak to anybody for the entire meal, and she missed the glances the others threw her way as she stared at her plate and the unappealing food on it. When dinner was over, she thankfully fled to the seclusion of the garden, keeping Cheta by her side to warn her of unwelcome visitors.

She had come to realize, thanks to Father Jonas' comments and Warren's unwanted attentions, that she would have to continue to deal with knowing looks and advances from men for as long as she remained unwed and unattached, and she didn't want that.

Regardless of what she tried, she couldn't help but compare Eryk and Warren to each other. Warren was a professional solider, and his work required him to be strong, balanced and athletic, which made him a good complement for her. Eryk, despite his huge improvements, was still clumsy by comparison, but she was bound to him regardless.

They treated her differently too, with Warren essentially taking what he wanted from her, while Eryk asked her permission. She knew that she definitely preferred Eryk's method, finding Warren's aggression grating. Nevertheless, Warren's passion was thrilling and she admitted to herself that she was tempted to see where that passion could lead, while Eryk was so… restrained. Aislynn didn't know if he even had that level of passion in him, which would be a shame. Maybe she'd have to try to draw it to the surface… That could be interesting.

Still, even if she actively tried, she could not imagine herself with Warren. Eryk, on the other hand, was a different story. She liked to spend time with Eryk, and he truly seemed to enjoy her company too. He even liked to spend time with her if he wasn't forced to by the duties they shared. Finally, she knew that Eryk truly loved her, and had loved her for some time, and she loved him too. It was time that she admitted that to herself, and she smiled as she did it.

Of course, this would all be so much more complicated if Byron hadn't withdrawn his bid for her affections. She cared for Byron too, and having to try to decide between him and Eryk would have been difficult. Fortunately, she didn't need to worry about that, and with Byron removed from the equation, her heart made her choice so very clear to her.

"Well Cheta, I guess I've finally made up my mind. Maybe I'll be lucky and be one of those women who can't have children," she muttered to her wolf, who looked up at her with something that almost looked like a pleased grin. Aislynn felt oddly satisfied and happy with her decision, and she knew that Eryk should be along shortly, so she would tell him then. The whole "providing the heir to the throne" thing was just something she'd have to deal with, but Aislynn decided not to worry about *that* until she had to.

Suddenly, Aislynn felt a rush of anger along her link to Eryk, and she felt him getting closer. A courtier must have made him angry, and he was coming to find her to let off some steam. This usually happened once every couple of days since the war had started, and she figured that she'd let him vent his frustrations and then let him know the good news. She could see him now, coming closer in the night.

"I heard about you and Warren," Eryk stated without preamble as soon as he could see her in the darkness of the garden.

"Excuse me? You heard *what* about me and Warren?" This was certainly not how she had expected the conversation to go.

"I heard about how the two of you were out here in the garden last night, and how you were practically throwing yourself at him. Then, of course, there was this morning before the council meeting, in the hall. Now I understand why you've been 'thinking' for so long! You've been waiting for someone else, stringing me along and letting me think that I had a chance. I didn't know that you could be so cold. So cruel. How could you do this to me? I love you, and I've told you that I love you, and you're betraying me with Warren after he's only been here for a couple of days!"

Aislynn had gotten over her initial shock, and now she was getting angry. Eryk just kept talking, making these horrible accusations and not letting her get a word in edgewise. Finally, she stood and stepped right up to him, seeking to put a stop to the flow of ugly words, but Eryk just stepped away.

"Would you shut up for a minute?" she demanded. "How dare you come up to me like this, screaming accusations for the entire world to hear!"

"Do you deny them? Did you kiss him?" Eryk asked, and Aislynn could feel how much he was hurting behind the anger.

"He kissed me, totally unprovoked and uninvited. Yes, I'll admit that I responded to it, but so would you," Aislynn replied, more quietly. To prove her point, she reached up and grabbed Eryk, pulling his lips down to hers and kissing him ferociously. Feeling him relax, responding to her kiss, she broke away and stepped back.

"See?" she demanded. "It's a natural reaction."

"Only with you," Eryk pointed out quickly, furiously. "If it had been anyone else who kissed me, I would have pulled away, stopped, and not become lost in the moment."

Aislynn kept right on talking, not stopping to address Eryk's remark. "I have been nothing but loyal to you. Hell, I nearly gave my life for you! Twice! And this is how you repay me? By thinking the worst of me when you hear one little story?"

"One? Don't you mean two? Or are you denying what happened between you and him in the hallway? A servant saw the two of you together, so don't bother denying it!"

"To think that I have been beating myself up all day feeling guilty about what happened last night!" Aislynn screamed at the king. "I felt that I should have pushed him away more quickly, like I DID this afternoon, thank you very much! Apparently, I shouldn't have bothered thinking about you and your feelings at all."

Eryk stood there for a moment, not quite sure what to say. Aislynn took advantage of his silence to finish her own comments.

"I have apparently misjudged you," she said, quietly enough that Eryk needed to listen very closely to hear her. "I'd always thought that if we ever had a problem between us, we'd be able to talk about it, deal with it. Instead, as soon as there is a little hiccup in the way you see the world, you're screaming at me and accusing me of betraying you. It was just a kiss!"

"Well maybe for you it was just a kiss. You seem to have men hanging off your every word and following you around like lost puppies, hoping you'll deign to notice them. Must be nice to be kissed!"

"What are you talking about? Like you don't have the women in the court throwing themselves at you, hoping that you'll pick them. You're still unwed, so there's still a chance you'll pick one of them. Why not try them out first and see if they suit you?"

"I would never –" Eryk began, but Aislynn cut him off.

"No? You mean to tell me that there hasn't been anyone warming your bed these past months?" She looked at him incredulously.

"No, there hasn't," the king stated quietly, anger forcing the words out through clenched teeth. "Since I met you, there hasn't been anyone or anything. No bed warming, no kissing, not even any evening strolls through the gardens. Not since you."

Aislynn stared at Eryk for a moment, disbelief written across her face for him to see. Then she whirled away and stalked off back towards the lights of the dining room.

"I guess it's a good thing I agreed to meet with Vivien to discuss a possible marriage alliance, isn't it?" he called after her. "Maybe I'll get what I want from her, since it's pretty apparent that it'll be a miracle if I ever get it from you!"

For the second time into two nights, Aislynn was leaving the garden and heading for her room with her emotions tangled into a confused ball inside of her. As she continued to stride away from the king, refusing to acknowledge his parting attack, she realized that she had just come very close to making a horrible mistake. She was actually happy that Eryk had started the conversation.

As she walked away, Warren chuckled to himself. His hiding place in the deep shadows of the trees had provided him with a clear view of the explosive argument between the king and princess. Things had gone better than he had hoped, and now all that was left was to see if their relationship was as strong as Branden claimed that it was. And if it wasn't, he'd be here to pick up the pieces, claiming his prize.

By the time Aislynn reached her room, she could feel that Eryk's anger was fading from a boiling fury to a simmering rage, the kind that set in and lasted for a very long time. She suspected that it was going to be very uncomfortable around Eryk for the next while, but she wasn't about to back down. A single kiss, and one that was unasked for, didn't warrant this kind of treatment.

Sighing, she settled into bed wondering why, if she didn't deserve this treatment, was she feeling just a little guilty. She hadn't done anything wrong, after all. As Aislynn tried to puzzle that through, her previous sleepless night caught up to her with a vengeance and she slipped quickly into a deep and dreamless sleep.

Chapter 6

The sword slashed in from the left, aimed towards Aislynn's knees. She jumped over the low strike and brought her own sword slicing down to the right, forcing Byron to twist awkwardly in order to bring his weapon up to block. Wishing she had her dagger, the princess kicked out and connected with the back of the captain's knee, sending him stumbling forward a few steps while he regained his balance.

Byron spun back towards his opponent, surprised that she hadn't pursued him and taken advantage of his few moments of weakness. That's what she would normally have done. Instead, Aislynn just stood there in the courtyard looking at him with a scowl on her face.

"I can't believe he's dragging us all to the border," Aislynn stated, and not for the first time. "Of all the ridiculous, stupid things to do…"

"Have you told *him* how you feel about it?" Byron asked sarcastically. He was fully aware of the fact that the princess and the king were not currently on speaking terms and hadn't been since their rather explosive argument in the gardens two days ago. "Anything concerning his safety is your responsibility, after all, so you'd be well within your rights to mention it."

"I have," she snarled, bringing the sword in her hand whirling towards him. "He laughed at me and accused me of trying to manipulate him."

"There isn't a lot we can do about it," Byron commented as he brought his own sword around low in front of him, cutting towards her legs. "He and Vivien agreed to meet at the border for their discussions, so that neither side would have the advantage of territory. If he doesn't want to listen to your concerns, we're all going to have to go along with the plan."

"And that's another stupid thing," Aislynn growled, bringing her sword up defensively and stepping away from Byron. "Why would he possibly want to negotiate with that woman? She's already tried to have him killed once."

"We don't know that for certain. Just because her emissaries were harboring the assassins, that doesn't mean that she had anything to do with it. Durham was the one paying for them, not the Madelian crown."

Byron took two quick steps towards the assassin, slashing with his sword. She blocked easily, twisting her sword in her hand, and the two launched into a quick series of attacks and parries, effectively stopping their conversation.

Aislynn darted forward, sword leading, and made a jabbing attack towards Byron's midsection, forcing him to dance to the side and out of the way. As he moved, he dropped his right arm and brought his weapon crashing into hers before sweeping it out and away from his body. He stepped in right behind, coming close beside her as Aislynn twisted away from him, forced to move if she wanted to keep her weapon in her hand. Byron was suddenly behind the assassin, but she jumped away from him as her sword slid free of his, and she spun to face him.

Aislynn attacked again, this time using an overhead chop. The move would have left her body exposed to an attack from him if she hadn't been too far away. Instead, she was able to take a few running steps towards him as she attacked, her momentum adding a lot of extra power to the down stroke of her blade. Byron knew that Aislynn was stronger than she looked and didn't want to numb his arm by blocking her attack, so he sidestepped quickly instead, forcing Aislynn to pull her attack up short to avoid slamming her sword into the cobblestones of the courtyard. The abrupt halt of her forward motion left her briefly unbalanced, and Byron darted in to take advantage of her weakness.

Lifting his sword into the air, the captain brought the weapon whistling down towards the princess's head, turning to face her as he dropped his arm. Aislynn assessed the situation quickly, weighing her options, and dropped down to the ground below his line of attack instead of engaging him or trying to move out of the way. The first would likely have caused some damage, considering the force behind Byron's attack, and the second would have left her even more off balance than she had been.

As soon the attack whistled past above, Aislynn pulled her feet back under her and jumped back up, bringing her sword up in a vertical attack aimed at the junction of Byron's sword arm and shoulder. The attack would have cut his arm off if it had connected, but he brought his sword back across quickly, intercepting her attack.

"Besides, isn't this what you wanted?" Byron pointed out as the two stepped apart once more. "You've maintained that marriage isn't for you, so Eryk marrying someone else is getting exactly what you asked for, right?"

Aislynn looked down at the cobblestones, silently contemplating that idea. It was true that she'd told Eryk to marry someone other than her, on numerous occasions. This seemed like an excellent example of the old "be careful what you wish for" proverb.

Byron, for his part, thought that the idea was a fabulous one. The war would end, Eryk would be safely married, and he'd be free to pursue *his* heart's desire. But not until everything about the marriage was formalized between Eryk and Vivien. He couldn't make his claim clear until Eryk was officially committed elsewhere. Byron wondered for a moment about his use of the word claim, but then decided that the word was correct after all. If Eryk was going to be stupid enough to push Aislynn aside, then Byron fully intended to be the one to have her, even if he had to beat that upstart cavalry commander half to death to do it.

The two came together again, Aislynn's sword darting straight in and heading towards Byron's stomach. She was determined to work out some of her frustration by trying to take a strip out of her friend's hide, and Byron didn't mind being her partner at all, despite the inherent risks. He brought his sword twirling up and to the right, forcing Aislynn's blade away from his body and making her turn in the same direction, leaving her side exposed.

Byron stepped in closer, trapping her arm between their bodies. Since they were fighting only with swords this morning, he knew that he didn't need to worry about Aislynn stabbing him with her dagger, so he didn't mind being this close. The captain shifted his weight, preparing to hook his leg around her ankles and send her tumbling to the ground, but Aislynn just shifted the sword to her left hand and brought it curving around towards his unprotected back.

The captain, seeing the sword coming towards him from the corner of his eye, made a move to step back, but Aislynn used her now empty right hand to grab onto his shirt and hold him in place. Byron had the option of trying to twist his sword arm around to block her blade, but they were too close together and he didn't want to risk cutting Aislynn accidentally. He felt the point of her sword nudge his back, right above his kidney, forcing him to concede defeat.

With a chuckle, Aislynn excused herself to go and change before breakfast, and Byron walked back into the barracks to go and tidy up himself. As he went through his morning routine, he thought about the rather tense situation between the king and his chief advisor. Aislynn's anger had cooled by the time she awoke the morning after their fight, but Eryk's anger was still simmering, leaving Aislynn feeling hurt by what she perceived as unjust accusations on the part of the king. It was very obvious to the captain that they cared deeply for each other; Aislynn wouldn't feel so hurt by Eryk's current behavior towards her otherwise, and Eryk wouldn't insist on finding more ways to hurt her if he didn't love her too. It seemed to Byron that those who loved each other the most were the most able to cause each other pain. With a sigh, he set off to find Eryk before everyone gathered to break their fast.

"I am a stupid, stupid man," Byron muttered to himself as he walked down the castle corridor towards the king's study. "I am quite possibly about to sabotage my best chance at ending up with the woman I want. Why would I do that to myself?"

But of course, he knew why. Byron considered himself Eryk's friend, and as such, he didn't want him to make what could possibly be the biggest mistake of his life. Byron knew, beyond a shadow of a doubt, that marrying Vivien would not make Eryk happy, and he truly wanted the king to be happy. Byron also cared deeply for Aislynn and considered her his friend, perhaps even his closest friend, and while he wished there could be more than friendship between them, he wanted her to be happy too. Eryk marrying Vivien was most definitely *not* going to make her happy. But maybe *I* could make her happy, whispered another voice in his head, a voice that Byron squashed quickly.

"You're such a martyr," he told himself as approached the door. The guards on duty outside showed that Eryk was there, likely taking care of some unfinished paperwork before the morning meal.

"Being a martyr is not a good thing," Byron scolded himself under his breath, but he reached out and knocked on the door anyway.

Eryk was sitting at his desk when Byron entered the study. The early morning sun hadn't yet cleared the walls of the garden outside, leaving the room in shadow. In the light of the lantern perched on his desk, Eryk's bright blue eyes appeared dark, his black hair shone dully, and the shadows cast upon his face gave him an ominous appearance.

"What is it?" the king asked, looking a little concerned with Byron's presence.

Taking a deep breath, Byron plunged into the argument he had prepared, knowing that confronting the issue directly would get him nowhere. "I think you're making a big mistake," he said.

Eryk's expression darkened, his anger flaring to life again. "With Aislynn? I don't see how that's any of your business," the king stated firmly.

"No, by neglecting your training," Byron replied with a shake of his head, relying on his carefully planned speech. The way Eryk had immediately latched onto Aislynn as the source of Byron's concern didn't bode well, but the captain continued anyway. "If you don't practice regularly, you'll lose the skills you've worked so hard to obtain."

"I'm busy," Eryk said, gesturing to the piles of paperwork scattered across his desk. "I don't have time to spar in the mornings anymore."

Byron took another deep breath. "So you not showing up doesn't have anything to do with Aislynn's presence in the courtyard at dawn?" he dared to ask.

"Look," Eryk stated, glaring at the captain. "I said I was too busy, and that's what I meant. If I wanted to spar, I would do it whether she was there or not, okay?" The tone of his rebuttal sounded defensive even to Eryk himself, and the king sighed.

"I appreciate your concern, Byron," he said, a bit more calmly. "It's good to know that *someone* is concerned about me."

Byron, despite his intentions to keep this conversation as non-confrontational as possible, just couldn't let that comment pass. "She does care," he said quietly. "A lot."

As he knew it would, Eryk's anger flared to life again, burning just as brightly as it had before. "And how would you know that?" the king demanded. "Oh, yes. I forgot about how much time the two of you spend together."

"It's not like that, and you know it," Byron said, trying to keep his voice even. "You've known about our practices for months, and you've been there, seen us."

"You mean the practices I had to find out about by accident?" Eryk sneered.

"I explained that! You weren't the king when they started, and you didn't know about her role here in Bacovia at the time. With everything that happened after your father's death, innocent practices were far from everyone's mind when we were passing along information." Byron was starting to lose his temper now, something that didn't happen very often.

"Sure, Byron. Whatever you say," the king commented sarcastically. "So you say that she cares about me, huh? Well *I* certainly don't see it."

"Maybe you should look harder," Byron muttered.

"What was that? Did you say something, Captain?"

"Yeah. I said maybe you should pay a bit more attention to what's going on around you."

"Really? I know what's going on around me. We are at war! My people are dying, my villages are burning to the ground, and my army is ineffective. The woman who I thought would be my queen has proven to be nothing more than a common slut, and now I have a chance to do my duty and end this conflict before more people lose their homes, their families or their lives. Did I miss anything?"

The venom in Eryk's voice rocked Byron as he paraded out the list of tragedies going on the kingdom, and the way he had referred to Aislynn… The captain shook his head, and glared at the king. "Well I wish you all the happiness in the world. May you enjoy the peace this foolishness brings, at least until your queen stabs you in the back and takes both kingdoms for herself."

"Well I have experience with being stabbed in the back, so I think I'll survive," Eryk growled.

"Gods," Byron muttered. "I'd hate to see what you'd do if something really serious happened. All of this over a kiss…"

"Well if you care so much about it, why don't you take her for yourself?" Eryk ranted, standing up and coming around the desk. "You can be one more man on the string she seems to be building." Byron flushed at the king's words, though Eryk couldn't tell if it was in anger or embarrassment.

Byron looked up at Eryk as the taller man stood in front of him and glared. He ran a hand through his short blond hair and met Eryk's gaze. "Because she wants you," he stated simply. Then he turned on his heel and fled the study, leaving the king to think about what he had said. Or not. At this point in time, Byron was past caring if Eryk wanted to continue to act like a fool. Admitting that last bit of information to Eryk had been painful enough, and Byron wasn't about to put himself through this sort of pain again.

Shortly after breakfast, the retinue that Eryk was taking with him to the border began to gather in the castle courtyard in preparation for their journey. The trip would take two days, barring any unforeseen problems, and the wagons carrying the tents, food and other supplies had left shortly after dawn. The wagon drivers knew where the stopping point was for the day, and they expected to arrive early enough to set up tonight's camp before Eryk and his party got there.

"Who are you leaving in charge?" Aislynn asked Byron as she swung up into her saddle. In deference to the wide range of people traveling with them, she was wearing a modest riding dress instead of her usual pants and blouse. Her long brown hair was tied back from her face, and he could see the grip of her short sword sticking out from under her saddle's girth, within easy reach.

"I'm leaving Jon in charge," Byron answered. "Owen is coming with us, to rotate with Marcus and Mateo, so it seemed like a good chance to give him some leadership experience." Jonathan was Byron's junior lieutenant, and someone who Aislynn knew very well.

"That'll be good for him," she agreed.

In addition to Eryk, Aislynn and Byron, Lord Harmon, who as head of diplomatic relations would mediate the process, accompanied them. Marcus and Mateo would be Eryk's night guards, since Aislynn's presence near him at night would raise too many questions, just like here at the castle, and Owen would be Eryk's official daytime bodyguard. Aislynn herself would be armed, of course, and Byron would always be nearby. A squad of the royal guard also accompanied the whole group. They were riding into a war zone, after all.

As soon as everyone assembled, Eryk gave the signal for them to leave. A few of the guardsmen went first, followed by the members of the court. The rest of the guardsmen followed for now, but Aislynn knew that some of them would move out to each side to flank the party once they left the confines of the city. On the plateau below the capital, Eryk paused briefly to confer with Warren, and when they started riding once more, four of Warren's light cavalry joined the flanking guards, taking an even more outlying position.

"He's as protected as he can be," Byron commented to Aislynn once they were truly underway.

"He'd be safer in the city," she replied.

"True, but he wants to do this, and who are we to argue with him? He is the king, after all."

"No kidding," Aislynn commented sarcastically. With a sigh, she settled into her saddle, at least happy to be outside in the fresh, crisp air of early autumn. She signaled to Cheta, and the wolf bounded off into the woods that ran parallel to the road. Aislynn knew the wolf would scout around the group, an extra layer of safety, and she could return quickly if she was needed. Cheta also knew to send up a howl if there was any danger that was too close for her to risk returning to Aislynn's side with a warning, and Aislynn relaxed as much as she could.

"I wish this was all over with," the assassin commented, fingering the handle of the throwing dagger at her waist.

"So do I," Byron agreed. Personally, he couldn't believe that Eryk was still going through with this, but he had to admit to himself that a part of him was happy. Watching Aislynn look at Eryk though… Those looks were enough to make him squash that happy part of himself. He felt guilty taking pleasure in something that made her so very miserable.

Chapter 7

After two full days of travel, Eryk and his entourage arrived at the agreed upon area of the border between Bacovia and Madelia. Once again, Eryk's wagons had left early and arrived at their destination before the king, and the setting up of the camp was well underway when the royal party arrived. Eryk's tent was already up, and so were the tents intended for Aislynn, Harmon and Byron, and the four of them headed off to their respective quarters to wash off the dirt from their travels before dinner. Aislynn sent Cheta with Eryk and Owen.

When she emerged from her tent a short while later, Aislynn paused and looked across the field towards the other encampment. The Madelians were just as busy over on their side of the meeting area as Eryk's people were. The two flags bearing Madelia's winged serpent erected outside of the central tent and flapping in the breeze showed the reason why. The queen had arrived. With a sigh, Aislynn turned away from the scene and went to Eryk's tent, nodding a greeting to Owen as she entered.

"There is as much grandstanding in these sorts of negotiations as in any other type," Harmon was explaining as she entered. Byron gave her a slight nod of greeting and she turned to listen to the diplomatic advisor as Cheta rejoined her.

"In fact," the man continued, "a show of power is likely even more important here than anywhere else. That's one of the reasons the rules have been so clearly laid out." Harmon moved over to where a small field table was set up, and gestured to the map laid out on it.

"The two camps are both clearly marked, as you can see, and the meeting area is directly between the two. Each monarch is allowed one advisor and one guard; the rest of the entourages must remain outside of the lines that will be clearly marked on the ground surrounding the area."

"Are you sure you want to have me there?" Aislynn asked Eryk bluntly. "Lord Harmon would likely be a better choice."

Eryk shook his head. "I definitely want you there. I don't trust Vivien at all, and I know that you're good with reading body language. You may notice a subtle clue that I might miss or be too distracted to see, something that an assassin, a woman would catch but a king… a man wouldn't."

"Owen will accompany you as your guard," Byron said, joining the conversation for the first time. "He's excellent with thrown weapons, so I feel that he'd be your best defense if something were to happen. I'll coordinate with the commanders of the cavalry and foot soldiers, and find out how to make the best use of all of our resources. A show of power shouldn't be an issue."

"I don't want the cavalry to give anything away," Eryk commanded. "Make sure you keep them well back from the border. Just having horses isn't a big deal, but their modified saddles and tack give them their greater advantage, and I don't want the secret leaked if we can avoid it. They can practice their archery just like any other archer – on the ground."

"Certainly, your Majesty. I'll pass the word."

"You are expected at the negotiation table tomorrow morning at about two hours after sunrise," Harmon commented, checking a sheaf of notes that he held in his hand. "I need to go and meet with Vivien's representative now, and we will take care of setting up the meeting area together. If you have no further need of me?"

Eryk shook his head and dismissed the councilor, Harmon taking his leave with a short bow. The king turned to look at Byron for a moment, and then asked him to leave as well. The captain repeated Harmon's bow and left without a word or a backwards glance.

When he and Aislynn were alone, Eryk turned to face her. "I don't want to fight with you."

"Well that's good," the princess commented, "because I was tired of it days ago." There was a hint of sharpness to her speech, but Aislynn managed to keep a rein on her temper. Mostly.

"The sooner we get this over with, the sooner we can all go home," he continued, ignoring her comment. "I need your council during these negotiations, even if I can't stand to look at you right now."

"Fine," Aislynn said, nodding her head sharply. "We'll agree to disagree and move on." He may not like her, but she could feel that he certainly loved her still. Why was he going through with this sham? Oh yeah… because she'd gotten so caught up in the fight with him that she hadn't been able to tell Eryk that her head was ready to listen to what her heart had been trying to tell her. Well, it was too late now, and to tell him would be selfish.

Aislynn left the king's tent feeling exhausted, even though she'd done nothing but sit on the back of her horse all day. He'd been the one doing all of the walking, after all. Still, she retired to her tent early, turning over her guarding duties to Marcus and Mateo for the night.

Tomorrow was going to be the first of many long days.

A whisper of cloth on cloth woke her from a deep, dreamless sleep. Without opening her eyes, Aislynn kept her breathing even and slow, and inched her hand under her pillow to the hilt of the knife hidden there. She happened to be sleeping on her side, face to the side of the tent and her back exposed, a position that made her profoundly uncomfortable. Then the complete lack of sound in her tent registered, including the fact that Cheta was still laying silently at her feet. As she rolled over with a groan, her long brown hair fell across her face.

"Byron, you really shouldn't be here," she said, brushing her hair away from her eyes. "People are going to talk if you get caught, and I don't feel like dealing with that sort of scandal right now, thank you very much." A low chuckle from over by the door was her only answer.

"Seriously, go away."

"Nobody saw me, and I'm not going to get caught. You're not

planning to let him go through with this, are you?" Byron asked as he pulled the camp chair over and sat down beside the bed. Aislynn hadn't known that his night vision was good enough to see so clearly in the darkness of her tent.

"Of course I am," was her reply. "Is it dawn already?"

"Just before dawn, actually, so time for you to get up," Byron answered with another brief chuckle. "Do you *want* him to marry her?"

"Why do you keep changing the subject back to that?" With another groan, Aislynn sat up, letting her blanket fall down around her waist. She reached her hands up above her head, stretching the sore muscles in her shoulders, stiff from sleeping on the uncomfortable cot.

"Because he's making a mistake, you *know* that he's making a mistake, and it's your responsibility as Eryk's chief advisor to make that clear to him." The tone of Byron's voice was far from joking now. "He loves you, and doing this is just so *wrong*." He very carefully didn't add the fact that he knew that Aislynn loved Eryk back.

Aislynn sighed and turned her head and body to face Byron where he sat. "He won't listen to me, Byron," she explained. "And we're already here. In less than two hours, we're finally going to be sitting down at that table to begin the negotiations to end this war. It seems more than a little late to call the whole thing off. Besides, love has very little to do with marriage when you're a king."

"It matters here," Byron insisted, though the small voice in the back of his head was urging him to be quiet. He was going to ruin everything, the voice informed him. "We don't have arranged marriages in Bacovia because long ago the king decided that being in love with your queen led to being a better king. So yes, love does matter."

"This isn't an arranged marriage," Aislynn reminded him. "They are both consenting adults, coming into this with the full knowledge of what it all means. Hell, we're about to negotiate all of the terms and conditions of the thing! There are no surprises here, for either of them."

"You're right," Byron exclaimed, throwing his hands up into the air. "It doesn't sound arranged at all! So exactly how many cows is Eryk getting?" With a sigh, he stood up to leave.

"So be it," he stated. "You're obviously not going to listen to reason here." Then he turned and slipped back out of the tent. He'd tried his best, he told himself, running a hand absently through his short hair. He'd spoken to both of them, and there wasn't anything else to be done here. It looked like he'd be able to get what he wanted after all.

After Byron left, Aislynn got out of bed and dressed quickly. The air was chilly, definitely edging into autumn, and she felt the cold all the more keenly because of the warm bed she'd just left behind. The dress she'd chosen for today was a deep burgundy, with a high neck and long sleeves. It was very modest, and very traditional, and the intention was for Aislynn to appear as much like a princess and advisor as possible.

After dressing and settling a belt around her hips, Aislynn slipped a long bladed dirk into her hidden scabbard and ran a brush through her hair. The final touch was a thin golden circlet around her brow to mark her rank. She never wore the thing and it felt strange and constricting, but appearances were very important today. Lord Harmon had made that very clear.

Aislynn nodded greetings to Marcus and Mateo as she approached Eryk's tent, dismissing them from their guard duties, and the men bowed to her before they left. Cheta nudged her way past the flap, and Aislynn followed closely behind without announcing herself. She knew that Eryk was awake, and had been for some time, so she didn't see the need for it. So she was surprised to catch the king still in the process of dressing.

"I'm sorry," she apologized quickly, taking a step backwards towards the door. Eryk glanced up at her as he finished the last tie on his pants, then he reached down to pick up his shirt from the table.

"What?" Eryk asked, surprised by her reaction. She'd seen him without a shirt before, when they'd known each other for only a few days, and Aislynn certainly hadn't reacted like this back then.

"It's just… I don't know. It seems inappropriate for me to see you half-naked when we're about to go and negotiate your marriage," she explained, fumbling for the words she wanted. "You're… taken, I guess."

Eryk's eyes flashed briefly, sending a wave of grief and anger flooding down the link to her. "Yeah," he agreed. "I guess I am."

As Eryk finished dressing, Aislynn realized that he was wearing the same outfit he'd worn to his courting ball. The beige silk shirt made his black hair seem darker and his blue eyes seem brighter, and as he settled his little used crown on to his head, Eryk looked every bit the king he'd become. Soon after, Byron, Harmon and Owen joined them, and not long after that, they were all walking across the field towards the table erected between the two camps.

Harmon and his Madelian counterpart had worked into the night to get the meeting site arranged to everyone's standards, and the effect was amazing. Inside of the perimeter created by what looked like hundreds of flowers, was the table they had selected. It was a perfect square, and large enough for Eryk and Aislynn to sit beside each other along one of the sides, with two matching chairs on the opposite side for Vivien and her advisor. There was a canopy over the table to keep off both sun and rain, since the weather could be unpredictable at this time of year, and the banners of Bacovia and Madelia adorned the poles that supported the canopy. A shining white cloth covered the table itself and a more substantial breakfast for the delegates awaited. To one side, near the flower border, there were baskets of food and drink that had been prepared and were ready for later in the day.

Eryk settled himself into a chair at the table and gestured to Aislynn to join him. She did, unrolling a map of Bacovia and Madelia before she sat, and Owen took up his position at the king's shoulder while Cheta settled at their feet under the table. Only a few minutes after the Bacovian group settled into their places, a stir in the Madelian camp announced the imminent arrival of Eryk's future queen.

Vivien, Aislynn was startled to notice, was a very beautiful woman, and Eryk thought so too, given the feelings of awe and lust suddenly coming her way through her link. The queen was wearing a dark blue gown that caught the early morning sunlight ever so slightly as she walked. The dress hugged her body like a glove before flaring around the knee to allow Vivien to move properly, and there was nothing modest about the plunging neckline. Vivien's black hair shone in the sun, and the diamonds she had wound in her hair caught the light with every tiny movement she made. A matching diamond strand wound around her long, slender neck before dangling down between her breasts and brushing the top of her gown's neckline. Aislynn knew that Vivien was in her mid-thirties, which made her quite a bit older than Eryk, but the queen certainly didn't look older than her late-twenties. As she and Eryk rose to greet the woman properly, Aislynn also saw that Vivien was tall, nearly as tall as Aislynn herself.

"Your Majesty," Eryk greeted his counterpart, taking her hand and raising it to his lips. He kissed the back of her knuckles gently, just the lightest feather of a touch. "It is a pleasure to meet you."

"And you, your Majesty," Vivien purred in return, her dark eyes glinting. "Let me introduce my advisor, Lord Callum," she continued, indicating the man standing next to her. He had a warrior's lean, fit build, with wavy brown hair and hazel eyes that glinted in the sunlight. He was dressed in fine, well-made clothing, and Aislynn would guess that he was likely nobility in Madelia, but not from a highly ranked family. He nodded a greeting, but said nothing.

"And this is my advisor," Eryk said, indicating Aislynn. "Her Highness, Princess Aislynn of Evendell."

"Well, well, well," the queen commented as she sat down. "So the rumors are true after all. Bacovia finally has a woman in a position of true power." She looked at Eryk appreciatively while he resumed his seat. "That bodes well for our...discussions."

Aislynn, following the example of the lord across from her, said nothing and let Eryk and Vivien monopolize the conversation. The pleasantries had to be taken care of before any business could be discussed, and Aislynn was busy thinking of other things anyway. Despite her years of training and years of working as an assassin, Aislynn felt threatened and belittled by the woman sitting across from her. Vivien was a woman who knew how to take control of a situation and get what she wanted. She was confident and beautiful, and Aislynn hated her the moment she laid eyes on her.

"So the first order of business," Callum commented once the small talk drew to a close, "is determining how the kingdom is going to look once the marriage occurs."

Drawn back to the task at hand, Aislynn pushed the map across towards the other side of the table. "This is the current border," she said, indicating the appropriate line on the map. "We need to make sure the depiction of Madelia is correct so that the borders of Bacovia can be redrawn properly."

"What makes you think that it is the Bacovian borders that need to be redrawn?" Vivien asked, glancing down at the map that lay in front of her.

"That is the custom when two kingdoms are merged through marriage," Eryk reminded her. "It is the husband's kingdom that is expanded."

"We'll just have to see about that," Vivien purred, laying her hand on Eryk's arm gently. "That *is* what these negotiations are about, after all."

"That was an incredibly long day," Vivien sighed, leaning back against the table in the middle of her large tent. She kicked off her shoes and dug her toes into the thick carpets that covered the ground. She did like her comforts, even when away from home.

"It was just the first of many," Callum replied, sitting down in one of the nearby chairs. "We barely scratched the surface today."

"True, but it was a good start. I think we should be able to wrap this up in a couple of days." Lifting her arms, Vivien unwound the diamonds from her hair, throwing them carelessly on to the table. "In fact, I'd be willing to bank on it."

"Do you mean that?" Callum rubbed his eyes and then lifted his gaze to meet that of his queen.

"Certainly. I wouldn't joke about something as serious as that. We have no time to waste, so send the message tonight."

"Yes, your Majesty, right away." Callum rose to his feet to carry out Vivien's order. He gathered supplies from the small chest she kept for that purpose, and then quickly penned the missive that she dictated. He presented the paper to her, and the queen signed it and sealed it with the winged serpent symbol of Madelia.

Callum bowed low, as Vivien required of her subjects, and then left the tent quickly. The queen could be vicious when thwarted, so it was always best to do as she commanded rapidly and properly. He dashed to his own tent, wondering again at his master's foresight as he dug through his belongings until he came upon the rolled parchment waiting for him. Callum's master had known that he'd need to send this order to the squad of soldiers to the west.

He held the parchment Vivien had given him and released a small surge of power. Flames leapt from the palm of his hand, consuming the paper in a blink of an eye. He leaned over the brazier in his tent and blew gently, getting rid of the ash, and therefore the last of the evidence. Then taking the paper provided by his master, Callum slipped back out of the tent.

A short while later, as the sun started to sink below the horizon, a messenger cantered out of the rear of the Madelian encampment. Turning his mount's head into the setting sun, the soldier rode off to do his duty.

Chapter 8

Petyr led his command down the main street of another razed village. Like the others, every usable building had burned to the ground and all of the villagers were slaughtered. Petyr sent some of his men to hunt around the town for any survivors, not that he honestly expected them to find any, and set the others to digging yet another large communal burial pit. He was getting seriously tired of this.

He had barely finished surveying the damage when one of his lieutenants came running up. "Commander!" Anders called urgently, hailing Petyr before he'd even come to a halt.

"What is it?" Petyr demanded.

"This isn't like the other villages, Sir. Always before, the Madelians gathered the livestock and headed back towards the border, but not this time," the man explained. Petyr waited for him to continue.

"This time, it looks like they took any of the horses they could find, but killed the rest of the animals. They also took all of the wagons, Sir, and I think that they slaughtered the animals and used the wagons to carry the meat away."

"So? I don't understand the urgency here. Why does it matter if they kill the animals or herd them across the border? They're lost to us anyway." Despite the fact that he'd sent Anders and a squad of men across the border last time, the soldiers had returned empty-handed and defeated. The trail to the border may have been clear as day, but the

Madelians had faded into the countryside once they were on their own side of the imaginary line dividing the kingdoms.

"This time they're not heading back to Madelia. The tracks, a mixture of boots, hooves and wagon wheels, are heading *away* from the border and farther into Bacovia."

"Lieutenant, round up the men immediately and have them get ready to march. We need to follow that group immediately, and we need to catch them before they can do any more damage. No matter what, we can't let them reach the capital."

Realization dawned on the lieutenant's face. While it seemed like they had been out here forever, hunting down raiding groups of soldiers along the border, they were less then two days travel away from the capital city, and the king.

"Can we leave yet?" Aislynn was exhausted. After two days of negotiating, and two sleepless nights, she was feeling lightheaded and sick.

"Not quite yet," Byron replied ruefully. As she stumbled, he put his hand surreptitiously on her elbow to steady her. "You are going to be totally useless today, you know that right?"

"Yeah, I know," she acknowledged. "I don't think I've slept since that first night. My reflexes are shot, and so is my balance, apparently."

"You should have said something when you had a chance," he commented quietly, pitching his voice for her ears alone.

Aislynn stopped and turned to glare at him. "That is enough from you, do you understand me?" She meant the question to be threatening, but a huge yawn ruined the effect. Byron chuckled quietly, and she slapped him on the arm.

"Well the two of *you* certainly look like you're getting along nicely," Eryk commented wearily from behind the pair. He sounded as tired as Aislynn felt, and she looked back over her shoulder at him. There was a bit of bite to his voice, but it seemed like the negotiations had taken their toll on him too, and he didn't have the energy to fight with her. Aislynn could feel how tired he was, physically and emotionally, and over that was a feeling of relief. "Nice to see you're moving on," he said.

"Like you're not?" Aislynn snapped back at him, but again, she was simply too tired to fight with the king. They'd been over this before anyway, so what was the point?

"Let's get this finished and get home," Eryk said as he pushed past Aislynn and Byron. They followed along behind him and took their places at the table, Byron stepping in for Owen as Eryk's guard. This was the last meeting with Vivien, and everyone could hardly wait for it to be over.

Vivien arrived, looking resplendent in her red satin gown. She and Callum didn't appear the least bit tired, and Aislynn forced herself to push down yet another pang of jealousy. After only forty-eight hours, she had taken so many hits to her ego, Aislynn wasn't sure she'd ever recover. Part of her knew that she didn't need to compare herself to Vivien, but a larger part of her couldn't help herself.

"Let's just go over the terms as agreed, shall we?" Callum asked, laying out the documents that had been prepared.

Aislynn struggled to focus on the papers, and tried to ignore the feelings she was suddenly picking up from Eryk. The only good thing about being so exhausted was that his emotions had faded so nicely into the background over the past couple of days. For Aislynn to be feeling anything from him now, after yet another sleepless night, meant that the feelings were very strong indeed. And they were feelings of despair.

"The borders of Bacovia will be expanded to encompass what is currently the kingdom of Madelia," Callum continued. "Following the customs of Bacovia, the first male child produced of the union will inherit the throne of Bacovia."

Aislynn picked up the recount in order to explain the next part of the agreement. "The new kingdom of Bacovia will be divided into four principalities of roughly the same size. One of these principalities will be what is currently the kingdom of Madelia, and it will retain that name. Her majesty will continue to rule the principality of Madelia, and any of the principalities can be ruled by a subsequent child of the union, regardless of gender."

Back and forth, the two advisors outlined each of the terms that Eryk and Vivien had agreed upon over the course of the past two days. They had worked out living arrangements, details for the wedding, the procedure for recalling the two warring armies, pretty much anything either side could think of. When they finished, each monarchy signed the two copies of the document, which had been previously prepared under the watchful eyes of the advisors. The final step was to affix each of the royal seals, the eagle of Bacovia and the winged serpent of Madelia, completing the agreement.

While Eryk and Aislynn were busy at the negotiation table, Eryk's staff had been packing up his camp. There was a wedding to plan, an army to recall, and a populace to notify. All of these things took time, and the sooner they got started the better - especially with the recalling of the army. Therefore, not long after the seals were stamped on to the treaties, the king parted ways from his betrothed, and the Bacovians made tracks for the capital.

"You look miserable," Byron said softly as he reined his horse up beside Aislynn's gray. "Is there anything I can do to help?" Eryk's pending marriage was official – Aislynn carried the documents in her saddlebags – so Byron felt comfortable offering to be a shoulder to lean on.

"Thanks," she said, smiling sadly. "I'm fine though, honest. I'm just feeling…" Aislynn trailed off, unsure if she should continue or not. She had never told anyone about the link she had with Eryk, and she wasn't sure that she should start now.

"Feeling what?" he prompted her. "You can tell me."

She sighed, then glanced around to see if anyone was close enough to overhear what she was about to say. Eryk was riding ahead of them, flanked by Marcus and Mateo, and all three of them were far enough away. Owen was riding behind them, but when he noticed Aislynn looking around, he reined in his horse and fell back a little ways.

"You know what my job is, my real job," Aislynn began, meeting Byron's blue eyes. "Well, there are a few… side effects. I guess that's the best way to describe it. I have a link to him, one that goes only one way, and through it, I can sense him. His location… and his emotions."

Byron looked startled by her revelation, but remained silent. After a few moments, she continued. "What I'm feeling isn't entirely me. I'm feeling an overflow from him, worse than usual because he's so close to me right now. I guess I'm too tired to block it out." Silently, Aislynn added to herself that it was likely so bad because her own emotions were echoing his, something that had always led to a rather strong reaction in the past. She *was* miserable, though she'd only admit that to herself.

"Wow," the captain breathed after a few moments to process the information. "You mean to tell me that you can feel what he's feeling?"

Aislynn nodded, her long brown hair swaying with the movement. Some of her hair slipped over her shoulder and hid her face from view.

"And you let him sign those papers?" Byron couldn't believe what he was hearing. "You can feel what he feels for you, and you're letting him marry *her*?"

"I told you to drop it, Byron," Aislynn said quietly, menacingly. She pushed her hair back over her shoulder and looked at the man riding beside her. "*He* is the one who started that argument. I was just about to accept his proposal when he came storming up to me in the garden–"

"You were *what*?" Byron latched on to what he'd heard and swung around in the saddle. He reached out and grabbed the reins from her startled grasp, pulling her horse and his over to the side of the road. Bringing both beasts to a stop, he turned to face her again.

"How could you do that!" he exploded, shocking himself with his anger, and startling Aislynn. "How could you betray him like that?"

"Not you too! I didn't betray him. How many times do I have to explain that I didn't ask Warren to do what he did? I didn't want to be kissed, and short of killing him, what was I supposed to do?"

"That's not what I'm talking about. You love him! You must. You, the woman who never wanted to marry anybody, were about to become the king's betrothed and you let him sign that agreement. THAT is the betrayal I'm talking about."

Aislynn sat there in the saddle for just a fraction of a second before lashing out. She slapped Byron hard across the face, forcing his head to twist violently to the side.

"How dare you!" she spat, hands clenched at her sides. "I am not the one who is to blame here. He had already agreed to meet with her to discuss the terms of the marriage when he started that fight, so he had no intention of actually marrying me."

Byron's need to defend his king and friend warred with his need to comfort Aislynn, but his loyalty to Eryk won out. "Maybe if you hadn't taken so long to make up your mind, this would have been avoided," he commented bitterly. He was ready for the slap this time, and caught her by the wrist as her hand flew towards his face.

"Let me go," she threatened, holding herself very still. She was strong, she knew that, but the grip he had on her was one that would easily allow him to pull her from the saddle. This argument was already making her enough of a centre of attention, and she didn't need to have her dignity trounced as well.

"Then stop hitting me," he replied as he threw her hand away from him. Shaking his head, he put his heels to his horse and cantered back up to a spot beside Owen. Crushed by his desertion, Aislynn fell back to the end of the column, just before the wagons, and she rode on alone, Cheta at her side.

"I really have screwed this up, haven't I?" she asked the wolf. The *eesprid* just looked up at her, remaining silent as always. "At least you won't desert me, will you?"

The lonely ride continued long into the night, Eryk wanting to be home more desperately than he wanted sleep. Since they were following one of the main roads from the border, it was easy enough to ride in the dark, and it was after midnight when the king finally called a brief halt. The Bacovians were back in the saddle by the time the first sliver of the sun rose above the horizon, and the entire time, Aislynn rode alone.

It was early in the afternoon of the second day that the capital came into sight ahead. Aislynn could feel a surge of joy from Eryk at the prospect of finally being home, and she agreed with the sentiment. She put her heels to her gelding and rode up through the column, falling into place beside Eryk just as he reached the first gate into the capital. Aislynn had been riding close by as his bodyguard, but she felt it would be more appropriate to enter the city at his side, as his advisor.

"We need to talk," Eryk said, not glancing over towards her. "We have a few things to work out between us, given the past few days. Tomorrow morning, after your early morning practice session with Byron, meet me in my study." It wasn't a request, but Aislynn nodded her acceptance anyway. She wasn't sure what hurt her more; Eryk's flat voice, totally devoid of any emotion, or the maelstrom of emotions she could feel beneath his very careful control. The sadness, the longing, the love now destined to be unrequited.

They rode silently through the city, and approached the castle in short order. Reining in at the base of the stairs leading into the building, Eryk dismounted and tossed his reins to a waiting groom. The king waited for Aislynn to dismount and then offered her his arm, very formally. She placed her hand on it lightly and the two made their way into the castle.

"I'm very tired," Eryk admitted softly. "I know that it's only afternoon, but I'm pretty sure I can sleep through until tomorrow morning. I want you to send a message to the councilors, calling them to a meeting after breakfast tomorrow. We'll go over the whole thing with them and then get down to the business of planning this charade."

"I'll send Cheta with you now, and then get Marcus and Mateo to head up to your rooms as soon as they've changed," Aislynn commented. "I'll see you in the morning. And for what it's worth, I'm sorry."

Eryk nodded his head, acknowledging her apology, and then leaned down to brush the lightest of kisses across her cheek. "I'm sorry too," he admitted before turning away from her and walking slowly up the stairs towards his rooms. Cheta trailed along after him as she'd been asked, and Aislynn returned outside to the courtyard to pass along the assignment to the twins.

"Welcome back," purred a deep voice from behind her. As she whirled around to see who was at her back, she cursed her tiredness and her lack of care. Unfortunately, Warren was reaching out to wrap his arms around her waist as she turned, and Aislynn ended up facing him as he pulled her close against his body.

"You missed me too," he chuckled, leaning down with obvious intentions to kiss her.

"Let her go."

The command was quiet, pitched low to avoid a scene, but Byron followed up his words by putting his hand on Aislynn's shoulder and pulling her gently away from Warren. Warren's arms tightened reflexively, but he loosened his grip after only a few seconds, letting Byron pull her away.

"Are you staking a claim, little man?" Warren sneered. Being as tall as he was, he looked down on Byron with a good foot of height to his advantage.

"Yes," the captain replied very clearly, "I am."

Warren laughed. "You're a commoner, and she's a princess!"

"And you know nothing about her if you think that matters."

Warren stopped laughing and looked at Byron, a serious expression on his face. "Well then. May the best man win."

As the tall warrior strode away, Byron turned to look at Aislynn, meeting her startled look.

"What?" he asked. "I meant what I said to him. Just because I didn't do anything before now, it doesn't mean the feelings went away. Eryk, for better or worse, isn't part of the picture here."

"But…" Aislynn didn't know what to say, and her thoughts tumbled over themselves as she tried to make sense of everything. Wouldn't her being with Byron just hurt Eryk more? Could she honestly take the step towards her own happiness when she knew full well that he was so terribly unhappy? Confused and conflicted, Aislynn turned away from Byron and fled to the relative safety of her rooms, leaving Byron staring after her.

Chapter 9

The early autumn night was cool, with just the slightest hint of a breeze. The stars sparkled in the cloudless sky, but the brilliance of the full moon outshone them. A few dry leaves fluttered across the ground, a sure sign that autumn had arrived, and for now, the air smelled of freshly cut hay and late blooming flowers.

It was easy to see the guards walking the parapets of the castle, the moon throwing their silhouettes into sharp relief against the pale rock of the castle walls. With a full moon nearly bright enough to read by, the archers hiding below the walls had clearly defined targets. With a precision that was clearly planned and rehearsed, five arrows shot simultaneously up into the air, each finding its target. Just like that, five of the castle sentries were down, and grappling hooks quickly followed the paths of the arrows.

Once the hooks were set and the ropes tested, five men quickly scaled up the castle walls and pulled themselves over the edge of the parapet. Four of them quickly checked the guards, making sure that they would cause no more difficulties, and the last man descended to the courtyard to open the gate for his fellows waiting just outside. Soon, the main courtyard of the castle seemed filled with armed men, who quickly organized themselves into four unequal groups and then set off on their assigned tasks.

The first knot of ten men headed back up to take care of the rest of the guards walking the walls, and at the top of the stairs, they split into two groups, one heading to the right and the other heading to the left. The second large cluster of men left the courtyard and went over to the barracks to take care of the guards there, and the last two groups headed towards the castle proper. Once inside the main door, opened for them from the inside, the smaller group of four men split off and went through the small doors near the stairs and into the inner courtyard, while the other ten men made their way up the stairs to the second floor. Their instructions were to wipe out the council and kill the king, and the soldiers set about their tasks quickly and efficiently.

Byron came awake suddenly, as soon as the hand touched his arm. He lifted his head, reaching for his sword and met Jonathan's wide eyes. He realized that he'd fallen asleep at his desk while looking over some paperwork and his candle had burned out long ago.

"There's someone in the castle," his lieutenant whispered.

"And you're here waking me? Why aren't you ringing the bell?"

Byron got up quickly, and was just about to start berating his junior lieutenant when he heard some sounds in the hallway outside of his office door.

Sound was a common thing in the barracks. There were guards changing shifts at different times, some practicing here and there, and just the general noise of a large number of people housed in the same building. But the sounds that he heard now were different. Listening closely, Byron could make out the soft sound of footsteps, a few whispers, and the telltale sound of metal striking against metal.

His scabbard hung from the back of his chair, and he eased the weapon out, careful not to make a sound. Then Byron grabbed a dagger from his desk, crept slowly to the closed door and opened it just a tiny bit to peer out into the hallway. There were no windows in his office, so the moonlight pouring into the corridor from the open barracks door illuminated only the men standing there trying to get their bearings while keeping *him* hidden in the shadows. Within a few breaths, the intruders had broken off into two groups and were moving off through the building, weapons in hand. Byron knew that there was no way that he could take on all of the attackers alone, and he knew that if there were attackers in the barracks, they were also elsewhere in the castle.

"Sneak back outside and go ring the bell," Byron ordered Jonathan, before slipping out of his office and heading off in the other direction. He crept along the corridor, moving from shadow to shadow, heading towards the wing of the building he needed. Being familiar with the layout of the building, he was able to move quickly even while moving as silently as possible, and it wasn't long until he was approaching his destination. Unfortunately, one of the groups of invaders had headed in this direction also, and they were just ahead of him.

Byron knew the longer he stayed here trying to decide on a course of action, the more likely it was that Eryk would be in serious danger, to say nothing of the other people in the castle. So he just gripped his weapons more firmly and sprang ahead, bowling into the back of the group.

He led with his sword, driving it deep into the back of the man he encountered first, killing him instantly. Byron dipped his sword towards the ground, sliding the body to the floor, and sprang ahead again, his dagger slashing across the neck of the man who was turning towards him. Byron's goal was to get through this group of enemies as quickly as possible, ideally waking the sleeping guards in the process. He did not intend to be quiet, and he let out a bellow as he dashed forward to attack again.

Startled, the next few men in the group turned to investigate the sound made by the falling bodies. They were greeted by Byron's sword, which he slashed across in front of him at neck height, taking another two soldiers out of the fray in a spray of blood. Now everyone in the group was aware of his presence, and they were turning to face him. Byron desperately hoped that some of the nearest guards were awake now and would be coming to help him. He could not take on this whole group by himself, though he would certainly kill a number of them.

Byron plunged ahead, having nowhere else to go. With so many enemies, he had no time to think, just methodically slashing left and right, parrying blows that came at him, and driving himself ever forward.

He was no longer killing the men he attacked, but was merely wounding them and shoving them aside. He knew that he didn't have much farther to go to be free of the mass of men determined to be his demise.

Suddenly, he was through the press of bodies, and he turned to face his enemies once again. Slowly backing up, knowing that there was a doorway nearby, Byron defended himself from incoming attacks while searching for the elusive entrance to the sleeping chambers. Then he felt hands grab his shoulders, hauling him into the room and slamming the door behind him.

"Captain! Welcome to the slaughter," greeted the senior of his two lieutenants, Owen. Byron could hear combat at the other end of the room, and threw a questioning glance at the man beside him. Owen nodded to answer his unasked question. The enemy was attacking from both entrances to the room.

"This must have been an inside attack," Byron said. "It certainly looked like they knew exactly where to go when they split up at the entrance of the barracks. We have to get out of here and go defend the castle."

"What about the alarm bell?" Owen asked.

"I've sent Jon to ring it," Byron answered quickly. "We should be hearing it any time now, as long as he got there safely. We can't linger here though, so let's get this done."

The guards quickly regrouped and formed a plan of action, dividing themselves up into two roughly even groups of forty men. Then, after making sure that everyone was armed with whatever weapons were available, the men of the royal guard of Bacovia began to clear the enemy from their building.

The battle was intense from the moment it started. Both groups of guards started by suddenly throwing open the barricaded doors and letting their opponents inside. The goal was to keep the attackers blocked at the doors for as long as possible, limiting the number of them who could attack at a time. Unfortunately, the enemies rallied quickly and forced their way past the guards almost immediately, gaining access to the open area of the room. Instead of having a sense of control, the battle quickly degenerated into a desperate melee.

Byron was leading the attack at the door he had come through, while Owen was leading the attack at the other entrance when they heard the alarm bell start to ring. Spurred by the sound, Byron lost track of everyone as he lost himself in the fight, his vision narrowing to focus only on the opponent right in front of him. Byron slashed and parried, killing as many of his opponents as he could as efficiently as he could. He noted in a detached way that most of the people he faced were already sporting wounds from when he had forced his way through them on his way here, and he wondered if they were seeking him out on purpose. He dropped the man facing him with a sword thrust to the chest, and looked for the next one, only to see the last of the enemy fall to Owen's blade.

"Let's go and clear the rest of the castle, Captain," Owen suggested to Byron, who nodded and gathered his men with a sweep of his sword. Covered in the blood from their first battle, the remaining members of the royal guard left their barracks and dashed into the castle to take up the fight once more.

When he entered the castle courtyard, Byron looked around and saw Jonathan standing just a few feet away from him, facing off against two of the attackers, who moved apart as they tried to flank the young lieutenant. Byron started forward to help, but he knew that he wasn't going to get there fast enough as he saw both of the attackers stab forward at the same time. Jonathan tried to leap backwards, therefore avoiding the blows, but the sword coming at him from the left caught him anyway, plunging deep into his side. Jonathan slumped, the severity of the wound stopping him in his tracks, and the attacker striking in from the right swung his sword downwards, taking Jon's head off just as Byron plunged his sword into the killer's back.

Owen came up behind him, and clasped his captain's arm. "There's nothing more we can do for him."

"I know," Byron agreed, turning away from his young lieutenant's body reluctantly. With a deep steadying breath, he organized his men, including Marcus and Mateo who had been off duty and therefore in the barracks when the attack began, and sent everyone streaming into the castle.

Eryk woke to the sound of the clanging alarm bell and with the feeling that there was something not right in his bedroom. The moonlight flooding through the window lit the room, and it was by that light that he saw something move. It appeared as if a bit of shadow had detached itself from the wall near the window. Still feigning sleep, he rolled over slowly, and reached for the sword he kept in the bed.

Eryk had spent several weeks training with Marcus in secret, wishing to learn more about Aislynn's fighting style, and that training was going to be put to the test now. Initially, it had seemed odd to sleep with a weapon, but Marcus had insisted and Eryk had thought at the time that the man was even more paranoid than Byron was. He could hear Marcus in his head now, telling him to be prepared, to be ready to move. The advice was well timed, for just as Eryk settled his hand on the hilt of the sword, he heard the whistling sound that announced an attack coming his way.

With a sudden surge of adrenaline, he pushed off the mattress and rolled from the bed and into his attacker. The man stumbled away from the king, losing his grip on his own weapon, while Eryk remained in a defensive crouch and tried to assess the situation in the dark room.

Eryk could see that the man on the floor wore dark clothing, parts of his body blending so thoroughly into the shadows around the room that it looked almost like he'd had pieces cut off him. If his attacker had any friends in the room, Eryk feared that they would be dressed in a similar fashion, and therefore currently invisible. Things would be so much easier without the damned moonlight, he cursed silently to himself. At least then they'd all be invisible.

Parry and avoid. That was what Byron and the others had taught Eryk, the exercise drilled into him so meticulously over these past couple of months that he reacted on instinct, ducking out of the way of the next attack. He couldn't see it coming, but somehow he *knew*.

"Here comes another one."

He heard Marcus' voice in his head, and Eryk reacted immediately, bringing up his sword to parry the attack, this time coming at him from the left. The sound of metal on metal broke the silence in the room, almost startling in its loudness.

The attacks continued, and the sound of the swords clashing together filled the room. By this point, Eryk was certain that there was more than one attacker in the room with him, and he was starting to have serious doubts about whether he'd be able to hold his own until help came. Where were his guards? They must have heard all the noise by now, he thought, which must mean that they'd been killed, or they had deserted their posts.

Ducking another attack, Eryk spun away from his bed and towards the door. He stopped only when he nearly collided with another attacker, hidden in the shadows. Bringing his sword up to block that attack, Eryk took a hit to his back, gasping in pain as his enemy's weapon cut him.

The force of the attack made him spin, and Eryk found himself looking at the window, just in time to see yet another attacker enter his room. He swore under his breath and he knew that he couldn't last for much longer.

Mateo ghosted down the corridor, heading for one of the servant stairways at the head of a small knot of royal guardsmen. The stairs led up to the diplomatic suites, including Aislynn's room, from near the kitchens, and he could hear screams and commotion getting louder the closer he got to the area. It seemed very strange to Mateo to be rushing into battle without his brother to guard his back, but he followed his orders as he always did. Byron had sent him this way to reach Aislynn as quickly as possible while sending Marcus up the stairs near Eryk's suite.

He reached the hall just outside of the kitchens in time to see the retreating backs of some of the men who had invaded the castle. Unless he missed his guess, they were wearing Madelian uniforms, and Mateo wondered why they were leaving already.

He desperately wanted to follow them as they headed into the large room, to prevent them from getting into any more mischief, but he had his orders, so Mateo only glanced into the kitchen as he passed. The room was in chaos, full of weeping servants and a couple of people sporting what appeared to be minor injuries. It looked like the men had only passed through here on their way to their real destination. They weren't here for wholesale slaughter, apparently, but Mateo sent the rest of his group after them anyway and continued alone.

He rushed up the small servant stairs and pounded into the upstairs hall. The enemy had been here, as evidenced by the broken doors and scattered bodies. With a pang of worry, he dashed towards the princess's room, only to find the door open and the suite abandoned. With a curse, Mateo continued to run down the hall. He had to get to Eryk, and he had to know that Aislynn was safe. He hadn't been able to get to Aislynn fast enough last time she'd been attacked, and he didn't want a repeat of that scenario. As he ran, Mateo regretted having left the king's door when he'd been relieved earlier that night, and he prayed that he'd be in time.

Upon reaching the main foyer of the castle, Marcus and his group of six splintered from the others. Byron had been drilling the guards in emergency procedures since the war had started and the captain's hard work was paying off. The groups of men went immediately to the key areas of the castle, such as the council chamber and diplomatic suites, and then spread out systematically to search the grounds for the intruders.

The enemies seemed to be searching for someone or something in particular, and a group of them had been cornered the library, trapped there when the guards assigned to that area of the castle arrived. Marcus and his men paused there to help their fellows as the fighting commenced.

The Bacovians and Madelians came together with the clash of metal on metal, and one of the enemy fell immediately, a sword having cut open his belly, spilling his intestines onto the floor. Marcus found himself facing a large, heavily muscled man who carried a large sword that showed many nicks and faults in the metal along the edge. Either he was a man who saw a lot of battle, or he was someone who just had no idea about how to care for a weapon properly. Marcus suspected the former.

Part of their orders included capturing at least one of the intruders alive for questioning. Marcus was peripherally aware of the rest of the battle, but he focused his attention on the man in front of him, slowly swinging his sword from side to side as if the man was warming up. If Marcus were able to manage it, this man would be perfect to capture. The best way to do that would be a nice, quick blow to the temple. If he could get close enough, of course.

Marcus darted in to strike the man, who brought his sword up to block, easily defeating the attack. Marcus struck again, this time a lower cut aimed at the man's thigh, and the attacker parried easily once more. The solider he was facing had very good reflexes, and it was harder than he thought to try and *not* kill someone in battle.

The Madelian solider darted forward, once again showing his quick reflexes, and Marcus was forced back on his heels to avoid the attack. The man gave him no time to collect himself, pressing his attack and moving ever forward. Marcus scrambled back, desperately trying to escape, but not sure he'd be able to.

Chapter 10

"Eryk!"

Aislynn woke with a gasp, brought back to consciousness both by the alarm bell and by the feelings of fear and desperation throbbing down her link to her king. She was certain that he was in grave danger, and she paused only to grab her sword and dagger. Then Aislynn was out of bed and rushing to the door of her suite, Cheta right on her heels.

"Marja!" she yelled as she ran. "There's trouble in the castle, so stay here and keep safe." Aislynn didn't even stop to see if her friend had heard her, throwing open the door and starting to step out into the hall when a large familiar form blocked her.

"Warren! Get out of my way," she demanded, angry at the delay.

"Aislynn! There are several men in the castle and we're under attack. I came to make sure that you were okay." He looked genuinely concerned about her well-being, which would have been sweet if she wasn't in such a hurry.

"I'm fine," she stated. "Now get out of my way."

"I can't do that," he denied her. "If you leave your room, you'll be in danger."

"Not as much danger as *you're* currently in, trying to keep me here," she rebutted. "I told you to let me pass." She didn't have time for this and moved to push past him to gain entry to the hall beyond. Warren reacted instantly, reaching out to stop her passage.

"You're a lucky man, Warren. I don't have time to kill you right now," she growled, stepping back. Instead of trying again, she just whistled to Cheta, who had been waiting patiently behind her. Cheta gathered herself and sprang at Warren with a growl, knocking him prone before rushing down the hall.

Aislynn dashed out into the hall behind her wolf, and was off toward Eryk's suite far faster than Warren could regain his feet. Obviously still concerned for her safety, Warren came after her as soon as he could, catching up quickly with his longer stride.

"Where do you think you're going?" he demanded, panic starting to rise in his voice.

"Eryk's in trouble," she replied, picking up speed. "Stop staring at me Warren."

Warren shook his head, just now realizing that he *was* staring at her. She had obviously been asleep not long before. Her long brown hair was tousled, and she wore a light cotton nightdress, which was showing very enticing glimpses of her legs as she ran. It was then that he realized that she was carrying weapons.

"Where did you get that sword?" he asked, obviously flustered by the whole affair.

"It's mine," Aislynn replied with a wicked smile. "My father gave it to me for my tenth birthday."

Just then, they heard the sound of barking and growling coming from just up ahead, and as they turned the corner in the hall, they saw Cheta facing off against a group of armed men who obviously did not belong in the castle. They wore strange uniforms of dappled colors, gray, brown and green. Aislynn had seen clothing similar to this before.

"Madelians," she breathed, bringing her sword up. Ignoring Warren completely, she sprang into battle, sword slashing.

"Cheta!" Aislynn yelled as she attacked the closest invader. "Get to Eryk!" Cheta started to rush off down the hall, but then she came back, refusing to follow Aislynn's orders and leave her companion in danger.

Aislynn faced the man in front of her, directing a sword cut at his chest. As he sprang back to avoid her attack, she stabbed her dagger into his thigh, dropping him to the ground and taking him temporarily out of the fight. Two of his companions stepped over him to reach her, and Cheta slipped behind them to finish off the fallen foe.

"Cheta! Go now!" Aislynn demanded, and this time the wolf obeyed.

She slashed her sword across in front of her, from left to right and on an angle. She missed the first man entirely, and the second parried her attack with a downward sweep of his own sword. Aislynn stabbed out again with her dagger, attacking the man on her left, and he parried that attack too. She drew her sword back close to her body and then suddenly kicked out, taking the man on her right by surprise and connecting with his knee with enough force to send him tumbling.

Now faced with only one upright opponent, Aislynn jumped towards him, startling him enough that he jumped back in alarm. When he landed, he was a little off balance, and Aislynn used that to her advantage, rushing close to attack. A quick slash of her sword took him permanently out of the battle.

"Warren!" she shouted, knowing the large man was close. "Would you stop staring at me and help?" She could feel Eryk's anxiety building, and he was feeling pain too.

She stabbed quickly at the man she'd kicked, killing him, and then turned to see who was next. Warren shook his head and joined the fray, and between the two of them, they quickly dispatched the remaining Madelians before running off down the hall again.

"Aislynn?" Warren began. "What the hell was that?"

"Ask questions later," Aislynn told Warren, cutting him off as they reached the top of the stairs leading down to the main entrance of the castle. They could see that the door was wide open, and there were sounds of battle coming from the courtyard outside.

"You can either go help out there, or you can come with me, but decide quickly," she pressed, starting down the hall again and not waiting for his answer. The guards were not her problem, not with the panicked feelings coming from Eryk increasing in urgency.

Aislynn could hear Cheta's frantic whining coming from up ahead, and put on a last burst of speed to reach Eryk's closed door. His guards were nowhere in sight, and she wondered why there were no bodies on the floor. As Aislynn braced herself to open the door, she vowed that if his guards weren't dead around here somewhere, they would be by the time she was done with them. She threw herself against the locked door, slamming her shoulder into the wood, and the three of them barreled into the room.

Eryk had managed to escape the confines of his bedroom, and was currently fighting for his life in the reception chamber of his suite. Light from the hall flooded into the room, revealing four attackers and an obviously injured Eryk. With a growl of anger, Aislynn rushed to her king's aide.

Cheta was into the fight before anyone, leaping up and tearing the throat out of an unsuspecting Madelian. As she jumped away from the body, she turned her bloodied muzzle towards her next victim, who began to back away. Hackles raised, Cheta growled and started to advance.

Aislynn's first victim was the man closest to Eryk. The position of his sword worried her, so instead of attacking with her weapon, she focused on getting him away from his intended victim first. She flung herself at the man, rushing into him and intending to knock him off balance to give Eryk some breathing room. Her weight and the force of her blow pushed the soldier close to the window in the reception room, and Aislynn knocked her opponent back through window to fall to his death in a shower of multicolored glass.

Warren was still fighting with one of the two remaining attackers, and Eryk had collapsed against the wall, so Aislynn joined Cheta, who had backed her target into a corner, growling. The eyes of her opponent were on the obviously aggressive wolf, and he was paying little attention to Aislynn when a strong toss of her dagger took him in the eye. The man was dead before his body hit the floor, the blade finding his brain. Aislynn rushed over to Eryk without bothering to retrieve her weapon, trusting Warren to finish off his opponent.

Eryk's back was badly injured, and he was lying on the floor in a slowly growing pool of blood. Aislynn knelt beside him and placed his head on her lap. She caressed his cheek and brushed hair off his forehead gently, leaning down to whisper in his ear.

"Good job, your Majesty," she said quietly. "You did a magnificent job." He was fading, his breathing shallow and irregular, and she hoped that it was unconsciousness that she was losing him to, and not death.

She looked up and saw Warren looking at her, an odd expression on his face. She knew that he'd have more questions before the night was over, but that didn't concern her right now.

"Get the king a healer, Warren," she ordered, looking back to Eryk. She rolled him over carefully, found the worst of his wounds and did her best to slow the bleeding until Michael arrived.

"No!" Mateo screamed, seeing that Marcus was in danger.

The shout came from the door, and Marcus recognized his brother's voice. The man advancing on Marcus was not distracted at all, however, and continued to press his advantage. Their location in the room, separated from the others in Marcus' group by a series of tables, prevented any help from arriving in time to make a difference.

Mateo had finally found Aislynn, who was busy treating Eryk's grievous wounds. He paused only long enough to see that he wasn't needed before he continued on to secure the castle, following the sounds of battle down the stairs to the library. Now, he stared in horror at the scene before him. Bodies of both guards and attackers littered a floor that was slick with blood and other things, creating battlefield hazards. Marcus desperately tried to evade the rapid attacks coming towards him, and Mateo saw his brother slip on some entrails and fall as he staggered back from the large Madelian and his powerful attacks. Mateo sprang into the room, running towards the scene unfolding in front of him, but there was no way he'd ever make it in time, he knew.

The big soldier standing over Marcus raised his sword one last time, and stabbed downwards with his full strength behind the blow. The weapon sliced into Marcus' chest, reaching his heart and killing him instantly.

Mateo felt a very physical pain as he watched his brother die, but then his vision turned red and narrowed, so that all he could see was his brother's killer. He drove himself forward, leaping up on to a table that was in his way, and literally threw himself across the space that separated him from his target.

The full weight of his body barreled into the invader, bringing him crashing to the ground. The man's sword, still red with Marcus' blood, went flying free of his hand, and Mateo heard it skitter across the floor.

Mateo seized the man by his shoulders, and with a strength empowered by his rage, began to smash the man's head repeatedly into the floor. He didn't feel the man go limp after the third blow, and he couldn't stop himself from relentlessly continuing his attack until some of his fellow guards finally restrained him.

The men who had come rushing across the room in Mateo's wake had to use all of their strength to pry Mateo's hands from his victim. It took three of them to lift him off the man's prone body, with Mateo resisting the entire time.

"Mateo," said a voice, insistently. "You need to leave him alone. Eryk needs one alive, remember?"

Mateo did remember, but Eryk would have to find another one, because this man had killed his brother, and Mateo was determined that this one would die for that.

"Mateo," said that annoying voice again, distracting him from trying to reach the man he was determined to kill. "It's over. He's the only one left alive. You have to stop."

When he didn't halt, Owen slugged him hard across the face. The blow staggered him, and it was enough to make Mateo stop trying to attack the nearly dead man. Owen wasn't even sure the man would survive long enough for questioning, but he at least had to try to honor his king's wishes.

Mateo slumped in the arms of the men holding him, as the reality of his brother's death came crashing down. Owen directed a couple of the men to pick up the limp form of the Madelian soldier and had him carried out of the room before Mateo could resume his attack. The guards who were holding Mateo let him go, slowly and carefully, and Mateo slumped down onto the ground, gazing at his brother's corpse with an agonized look on his face. Owen ordered a couple of men to stay with him and left the room to report to the captain.

Byron entered Eryk's suite to see a scene of carnage. His eyes darted immediately to where Aislynn knelt, still cradling Eryk's head. Blood from his wounds had soaked into her nightdress, staining it a deep red. Byron blanched and started towards them.

"He lives," she commented, answering Byron's unasked question. "He held his own for longer than I would have thought possible. Warren's gone to get a healer."

Looking more closely around the room, Byron could easily identify which of the bodies was Aislynn's, given the dagger protruding from its face. He wondered what Warren thought of Aislynn now that he'd seen her fight, and he wondered if it would be a good thing or a bad thing, given the advances that he knew Warren had been making. There would be time enough to find out, he suspected.

When the healer arrived, Byron helped Warren carry Eryk back to his bed, being careful not to jar his injuries and restart the flow of blood. A quick examination and a few stitches, and the healer declared the king's injuries were not life threatening. He had lost a lot of blood, but the wound to his back hadn't caused any permanent damage.

When Eryk was sleeping as comfortably as possible, Byron escorted Aislynn out of the king's bedroom, leaving Warren behind as a guard. Aislynn left Cheta.

"The attack on the castle was carefully planned," Byron confided to Aislynn when they were out of earshot. "The Madelians attacked the barracks, the king and all of the council members, including those who reside in the city. It's a good thing that you left your door open when you left, or Marja likely would have been attacked too, since you were likely another target."

Aislynn looked shocked. "Do you think it was an inside job?" she asked.

"They *must* have had some inside help," Byron agreed. "They knew exactly where to go, and we lost a lot of people tonight."

"Did we manage to capture anyone alive?"

"Yes, but barely." Byron took a deep breath, knowing that Aislynn was close to her twin guards. "Marcus was killed, and Mateo is taking his death very badly. We all are."

"How did we fare, overall?" Aislynn wanted to know, pushing the news away with a shake of her head and a grimace.

"We're still counting the bodies," Byron answered. "We won't know for a little while yet. Mateo attacked the man who killed Marcus, and beat him badly, but he's alive for now."

"Hopefully we'll get some of the answers we need from him," Aislynn stated. "Could you please assign a pair of guards to this room? Mateo shouldn't be required to return to his duty quite yet."

They both knew that the coming weeks were going to be tough ones. Eryk was alive, but he'd be in no condition to run the kingdom for a while, and depending on how many council members survived… Only time would tell how this attack would affect Bacovia.

Chapter 11

Aislynn was exhausted by the time the sun broke above the horizon, but sleep was nowhere in sight. She had been busy during the early morning hours of the day, organizing and directing, trying to make some sense of who had survived the attack.

The guards had reported that three homes in the city had been set afire, but fortunately, the fires were extinguished before they could spread to any of the other houses in the area. The three homes had all belonged to members of Eryk's council: Father Jonas, Lord Aeron and Lord Harmon, and all three of the councilors were dead.

The death toll inside the castle was considerably higher. All ten of the guards who had been on duty on the walls had died, and seven men had died in the barracks. Byron's young lieutenant, Jonathan, had died in the courtyard after successfully raising the alarm, and Marcus had died in the library. In addition to the nineteen dead guards, nine more were missing. It was logical to conclude that these nine were the ones who had helped the Madelians and provided them with the information they had needed to execute such a nearly perfect attack. All of these losses cut Byron's force of royal guardsmen by almost a quarter.

The council members with rooms in the castle had fared better than those in the city had, since the guards had been able to fan out through the castle quickly. The attack on Mataline, in her room, resulted in some cuts and bruises, but her wounds hadn't prevented her from rushing around all night on whatever errands Aislynn set her. Lord Philip and

Michael, the Royal Physician, were unscathed, but the attackers killed Lord Geoffrey, Commander in Chief of the army, in the corridor outside of his room while trying to defend himself from his attackers. That meant half of the council was dead.

The guards Aislynn had put on body detail had been gathering the corpses of the attackers, piling them into a wagon. They would be carted away and burned once she finished with them. By the time the crew was finished, there were twenty-one bodies. Aislynn ordered them searched and stripped of their uniforms and equipment before being taken out of the castle to be disposed of. This search also produced a roll of parchment, stamped with the royal seal of Madelia, and the words written on the paper made Aislynn very happy.

Warren was hovering in the background, where he had been ever since Aislynn had ordered Owen to take over the duty of guarding Eryk. She knew, without a doubt, that she could trust him, but she wasn't so sure about many of Byron's men any longer. What a mess!

Shortly after dawn, Aislynn finally called it quits. Aislynn had assessed the damage, the corpses were gathered, and she was going to collapse from fatigue. The attack, on the heels of her previous sleeplessness during the marriage negotiations, was affecting her deeply. She ordered the four remaining council members to report for a meeting at noon, and then she walked back into the castle and up to her room. She was tempted to check up on Eryk first, but she knew that if she were needed for any reason, someone would come and find her. She needed sleep more than reassurance, and the feelings she got through the link told her that Eryk was still unconscious anyway. Knowing that he was receiving the best care was enough for her… for now.

"Aislynn?" The call came from behind her just as she reached the door to her suite.

Aislynn sighed and paused on the threshold. "What do you want Warren?" she asked tiredly, not even bothering to turn around. "Have you come so I can kill you? I do owe you that for touching me yet again…"

"Well…no, not exactly," he admitted.

"Then what, exactly, do you want? I'd really like to grab a few hours sleep before the meeting, if you don't mind." She turned her head to look at him.

Warren was staring at her again, but this time it wasn't entirely because of the way she was dressed. Granted, considering she was currently standing in her doorway wearing a tattered and blood soaked nightdress, it wouldn't be that odd for her current appearance to be shocking to some people.

No, Warren was staring because he was finally starting to put all of the pieces together in his head. He had the same look on his face that Eryk had when he found out about her… profession. She sighed.

"Why don't you come in, Warren? At least that way I can sit down." Aislynn opened the door and walked into her room, leaving the door open behind her. She knew that he would follow. Curiosity always got the better of them.

"Just wait here while I change quickly," she called, moving across the room and towards her bedroom. As she passed Marja's door, she could hear quiet voices coming from inside the room. Branden must still be here, she guessed. She knew that he'd come as soon as he was able after helping to fight the fires in the city, though he'd been unable to save the councilors. Branden had been at his family home in the city, getting things ready for Marja to move in after the wedding, and he'd fought bravely when the attacks had occurred. She'd excused him from any clean-up duties to be with his fiancée, knowing how worried he'd been about her. It only took one look at his face to see that, but he'd still fought with the guard to clear out the castle before he'd come here.

Slipping around the corner, she found Cheta fast asleep on the bed. Must be nice, she thought to herself while she started hunting through the wardrobe for some clothes. There wasn't much point in dressing for bed, since she could be awakened at any time, so she opted for comfort. Tradition be damned! Everyone had seen her running around in a nightdress with a sword in her hand, so coming to the meeting dressed in pants and a loose blouse likely wouldn't raise any comments at all at this point. She grinned to herself, finding that oddly funny.

Aislynn walked back into the reception room, belting the long cream blouse around her waist, and sat down on the couch. She pulled her feet up under her, curling herself into a little ball, and turned to look at Warren expectantly. He was staring again, and she wanted to reach out and slap the silly look off his face.

"You had something you wanted to say Warren?" she asked pointedly. This was going to take all day if she didn't get the conversation started.

"Um… yeah." He took a deep breath. "When you said that you'd kill me, you were being entirely serious, weren't you?"

Interesting question to start with, she thought as she smiled wickedly.

"I was deadly serious."

"So…um…" He was obviously nervous and toying with the idea of leaving right now. He fidgeted in his seat, trying to find an exit route that wouldn't take him past her. Aislynn found it really funny, and started to laugh quietly.

"Relax Warren. If I'd really wanted to kill you, you'd be dead already. Do you honestly think I'd want a dead body in my room? I'm rather tired of bodies today, having dealt with more than enough of them already."

Warren didn't relax, but she hadn't really expected him to.

"Besides," she added with a wry smile, "I need someone to take over Lord Geoffrey's spot on the council. I can't wait for Eryk to make a decision on that one. I need someone leading the army NOW."

Now Aislynn just sat on the couch and waited for Warren to process the information. She laid her head back and closed her eyes, hoping she didn't fall asleep before the conversation was over. It would be rude, and not at all the best way to start a working relationship with this man.

"So…" Warren trailed off again, obviously still having difficulty trying to phrase his questions in the least offensive way. He apparently didn't want to make her angry.

"Where did you learn how to *fight* like that?" It wasn't *the* question, but it was close enough. Aislynn answered it truthfully and in detail.

"I've trained to be an assassin, Warren, and I've been taught to fight like this ever since I was able to walk and hold a weapon. Somewhere around my fourth birthday, I think."

Now he really stared at her. He wasn't taking this as well as Eryk had, Aislynn thought to herself. Perhaps it was because he was a professional killer too, of sorts, and he was having a hard time reconciling the woman sitting in front of him with what he knew of killing.

"So are you really a princess then? Or is that just a cover?"

"I really am a princess of Evendell. I'm the youngest child of three, if you need to know."

"So then what's with the arrangement between you and Eryk? He's the king, you're a princess… I still don't get it."

Warren figured that he might as well find out if he actually had a chance, though he was really starting to doubt it. He'd seen the way she had reacted to Eryk in his room, despite their arguing and regardless of the fact that he was now Vivien's betrothed.

"I'm supposed to be his bodyguard," she replied, with a rueful shake of her head. Some job of it she'd done last night.

Warren blanched, the color leeching from his face as he put the tidbit of information into context with the events of the night. He gasped.

"I didn't know! Aislynn, I couldn't know. I'm so sorry. I would never do anything to hurt him. I just didn't… I swear I had no idea!" Warren was starting to babble, realizing that he could have contributed to Eryk's death. He'd tried to keep Aislynn here in her room for those precious extra moments…

Aislynn let him prattle on, knowing that she wouldn't be able to have a coherent conversation with the man until he calmed down. Eryk was hurt, but Michael said that he'd be fine. If he'd died though… Aislynn didn't want to think about that, or the fact that she would likely be hunting Warren down for his role in bringing that death about. She shook her head.

"So that's what Branden meant," Warren muttered as he gained control of himself again. Aislynn suspected that Warren was just as tired as she was, or he would never have been so open with his thoughts.

"What Branden meant about what?" she asked. So he'd been talking to Branden, had he?

Warren blushed. "Before I…uh…kissed you that first time, I had been talking to Branden. He said that I wouldn't be able to come between you and Eryk, so I had to try. Being told I would never be able to have you made it even more important that I try." His face was bright red and matched the color of his hair now, and Aislynn started to giggle. Boy, she really *was* tired, she realized.

"Yes, that's likely what he meant," she agreed, nodding. Aside from the fact that Aislynn's life was magically pledged to protect Eryk's, she also loved him. That was something that had really hit home at last when she'd seen him lying there on the floor…

"So I have no chance? No chance at all?" he asked, chagrined.

"No, Warren," she confirmed, thinking again of the letter her men had found on the dead Madelians. "You have no chance."

Seeing that the conversation was ending, Warren having received all of the information that he was looking for, she stood up. Warren jumped to his feet.

"I'll see you at the meeting at noon," she commanded, leading him to the door. "Go get some sleep."

Aislynn shut the door behind him and made her way back to her room. As she passed Marja's room, she heard that the quiet voices had stopped and everything was quiet. She opened the door with a touch and peeked inside.

Marja and Branden were asleep, the long night having caught up with them. Their blond heads shared a pillow, and he had his arm wrapped protectively around her. Aislynn shut the door with a small smile and made her way to her own bed, shoving Cheta out of the middle and over to one side. She sighed as she lay down, envying her friend for the freedom she had. Marja's relationship with Branden had progressed quickly, her friend knowing what she wanted, without any doubts.

Aislynn closed her eyes and drifted off to sleep, finally knowing with certainty what *she* wanted.

The Aislynn who strode into the council chambers was an Aislynn nobody but Byron had ever really seen before. She was dressed in tight, dark blue pants, and a long, loose cream blouse belted tightly at her waist. The sword and dagger at her side completed the outfit. She was done with pretending to be something she wasn't, and she'd decided that this war was as good a reason as any to be herself in public.

She walked to the head of the table, sat down in Eryk's seat and called the meeting to order. The gathered councilors just sat there staring for a moment at this unexpected development, but nobody said anything. Warren met her gaze and looked away first, and Byron chuckled at his reaction. When he'd commented yesterday afternoon that Warren didn't know anything about Aislynn, the fact that social status didn't matter to her was only part of what he'd meant.

"Lady and Gentlemen," she began, looking around at the much-reduced council of four, "we have suffered tragic losses from this attack. Half of this council died, his Majesty was seriously injured and we've lost nearly a quarter of the royal guard. The castle is compromised, and there is additional damage in the city from the fires at the councilors' homes. Furthermore, there has been damage in the barracks from the attackers there." Aislynn paused, reasonably certain that this was the longest speech she'd ever given in this room, and she wasn't finished yet.

"I have appointed Lord Warren as Commander in Chief of the army for the time being, and his Majesty can choose to make that position permanent. I will take any recommendations that you would like to put forward for the remaining positions so his Majesty can select the people he'd like to fill the empty roles on the council when he has recovered."

Aislynn took a deep breath. It was a little nerve-wracking to be here in front of everyone, taking the lead and making these important decisions, but she figured that it was better her than anybody else. Not that there really *was* anybody else.

"There was supposed to be a meeting this morning, as I'm sure you all remember, in order to review the terms of the agreement that the King and Queen Vivien came to. At this point in time, considering the attackers were dressed as Madelian soldiers and carried a very interesting missive, we need to decide how to respond to this attack."

"What did the missive say?" Mataline asked. "I also understand that there was a survivor. Will he be of any use determining a course of action?"

"The letter is a copy of Vivien's orders to the soldiers who attacked. Their orders were to kill the King and the council, and it was signed and sealed with her own hand," Aislynn commented. "As for the survivor, I've been informed that he is going to need a little time to recover from his injuries before we can try to… extract information from him."

"So what do we do?" asked Lord Philip.

"Well, we can be sure that the attack was deliberate," Aislynn explained. Taking a deep breath, she plunged ahead.

"Assuming that we do indeed have to end this war outside of the marriage contract, which is looking very likely, I have a few ideas about what can be done. I would like to know if any of you have any ideas, however, so the floor is open," Aislynn concluded, leaning back in her chair. She was still bone weary, having spent more time thinking about this than she had spent sleeping.

The room was quiet for a few moments, and then Philip asked for permission to speak again. Aislynn nodded in his direction, and he addressed his colleagues.

"Lord Harmon previously suggested striking at Queen Vivien directly, so I will put that idea back on the table. Though, with Harmon gone, I have to admit that I have no idea who to contact to make that work," Philip said, blushing. Little did he know, but half of the people in the room knew exactly who to contact. Aislynn smiled.

"Any other suggestions?" she asked.

When nobody put forth any thoughts, Aislynn sighed and began to outline her ideas. Mataline looked shocked, not having realized before that Aislynn was capable of thinking in this way, despite her role as Eryk's chief advisor. Warren nodded his agreement to Aislynn's statements and Byron stared at the ceiling, listening carefully and thinking things through.

Aislynn suddenly became aware of a stirring in the back of her head, a feeling the indicated that Eryk was starting to claw his way back into consciousness. She knew the summons would come soon, so it was time to wrap things up.

"Well," she stated, "if there are no further questions or comments, we'll wrap this up for now. I will confer with his Majesty before any final decisions are made, and you will all be informed of the final plan of action, of course."

Just then, a servant knocked at the door and came in.

"Your Highness," he said, addressing Aislynn with a bow. "The king is awake and he's asking for you."

"Thank you," Aislynn said with a smile, rising from her seat. "If there's nothing else?" she asked, addressing the council again. When nobody said anything, Aislynn left the room and headed for the stairs and Eryk's suite.

"Princess," Owen greeted her with a bow. Aislynn nodded to the lieutenant, and smiled as she walked past him and into the suite. She could feel that Eryk was in some pain, and she knew that he was feeling a little lonely and disconnected right now. Well, she could fix that.

"Hello, your Majesty," she said with a smile as she walked into the bedroom and sat down on the edge of the bed. "How are you doing? Is the pain okay?" She'd never told him about the link; it was her dirty little secret, and she intended to keep it that way.

"Aislynn," he greeted her, smiling back. "I'm okay, but really sore and stiff. Is that normal?"

Aislynn laughed, and Eryk blushed.

"Yes, that's normal. You're very lucky that Michael is as gifted as he is with his healing magic. I know firsthand how close to miracle workers your healers are, so be grateful. What isn't normal is for a man your age to never have had a serious injury." Eryk blushed, his cheeks darkening ever further.

Aislynn leaned a little closer and took Eryk's hand, turning serious. He noticed her mood, and tried to sit up a little straighter, but she pushed him back into his pillows.

"You need to rest, Eryk, and sitting up isn't going to make the news any better." She sighed, and then continued. "We lost half of the council: Geoffrey, Jonas, Aeron and Harmon. Mataline was hurt, but she'll be fine. We also lost about a quarter of the guard… and not all of them were deaths." She let that sink in for a moment, and felt the instant he realized what she meant.

"Will this court never to be free of traitors?" he demanded. She knew that it was a rhetorical question, but she answered him anyway.

"Probably not. Bacovia is a powerful nation, and that power comes with a price, unfortunately. That's part of the reason I'm here, remember?"

Eryk shook his head. "I'm aware of the price, and I'm glad that you're here," Eryk said, squeezing her hand. He looked up at her, and sighed. "There's more, isn't there? Tell me everything."

"I called a council meeting and we discussed some plans. We need to end this war, Eryk, and I'm not sure the marriage contract we just negotiated is the answer." He just nodded, waiting for her to go on.

"The soldiers who attacked the castle were Madelians, and they carried some very interesting information with them," Aislynn explained. "There was a signed and sealed copy of orders for the attack, so it appears that Vivien is making a serious bid for both kingdoms. We do still have a survivor to question, but assuming he confirms this, does that mean the wedding is off?"

Eryk picked up a small note of hopefulness in Aislynn's voice as she asked the question, and he looked at her. He tilted his head to the side and raised an eyebrow, silently asking his question.

Aislynn blushed and looked down. "Before you started yelling at me that night in the garden, I was going to tell you something very important," she admitted. "I love you, Eryk. I should never have let you agree to a marriage to Vivien. I… it was killing me to see you with her, knowing that she was going to get what I discovered I wanted for myself."

"Yes, assuming it can be proved that Vivien ordered this attack, the wedding is off. Given that there were people inside the guard who helped with the attack, it is more than likely that we'll have reason to terminate the contract, but we need to be careful." Eryk paused and took a deep breath. "I love you Aislynn, with all my heart. Aislynn, my beloved Aislynn, will you marry me? Will you become my wife and queen, and make me the happiest man in the kingdom?"

Aislynn leaned forward and kissed him, letting her feelings pour out into that brief contact. "Oh Eryk, I will! I love you too, and I'd like nothing more than to be your wife."

"I wish I could have gotten down on one knee and done this properly," Eryk admitted, blushing. "I had something made for you, waiting for this day. It's over on the dresser, if you wouldn't mind getting it."

Aislynn stood and walked quickly across the room, curious to see what Eryk had done. The rosewood box was sitting there waiting for her, and she picked it up and cradled it gently in her hands. There were butterflies in her stomach, her excitement and happiness bubbling over. She opened the box and gasped. "Oh Eryk, it's beautiful!"

Aislynn turned back towards her king, her eyes meeting his. Then she looked back down into the box, to the glittering diamond resting on the padded fabric inside. The large stone was set into gleaming metal, and she wrapped her hand around the grip and pulled the beautiful dagger from the box, testing its weight. The diamond, set into the end of the hilt, glittered in the light coming in from the window, and Aislynn ran her fingers lightly along the silver wire that twisted from the diamond to the base of the hilt. Sliding the dagger into her scabbard, leaving her old dagger behind, she returned to the bed and sat down once more.

"I have a plan," Aislynn said as she leaned forward to give Eryk a kiss, "and we just need your approval to implement it. It's a three-fold plan. First, we need to get the confirmation that the attack was a deliberate attempt to take the kingdom. Byron tells me that Owen, his lieutenant, is skilled at getting information, so we'll give him access to the prisoner when the healers say that we can."

"Okay, I can understand the reasoning there. What's the next part?" Eryk wanted to know.

"Well, then we need to plan the attack. We'd have to call some of the forces in from the border, choose our ground to give us the advantage, that sort of thing. This would be your job, with Warren to help. The question becomes how many men to recall, where the battlefield will be, that sort of thing."

"Okay. I'm still with you, though I have some ideas about that one. I'm thinking that marching the army across the border will send a *very* clear message. And the last part?" Eryk was impressed so far. He knew little about Aislynn's training outside of the weapons and fighting, but her grasp of tactics was good.

"We need to go after Vivien." Aislynn paused, waiting for his reaction.

"And it needs to be you," Eryk said in agreement. "You're here, and it would take at least eight days to get someone else from Evendell. That's eight more days of fighting, eight more days of people dying."

Aislynn nodded her head, agreeing with Eryk's words and his reasoning.

"Take Byron with you." Eryk sighed and slumped down a little more into his pillows. Aislynn had finally agreed to marry him, and he was going to send her away with one of the men who had been competing for her heart. "I know he'll keep you safe for me. Please be careful."

"I will," she promised. She stood up from the bed and leaned over to give Eryk another kiss, letting this one linger. Then she turned and left the room.

Eryk relaxed deeper into his pillows and closed his eyes. He desperately hoped that Owen got the confirmation he needed to burn the contract he'd signed and sealed just the day before. Moreover, he prayed that the woman he loved made it back to him in one piece, and with her feelings for him intact. Sending Aislynn into Madelia with Byron was a calculated risk, he knew. Eryk wasn't blind, and while he could say that he'd never seen or heard of anything inappropriate on the part of his captain, Byron wasn't completely able to bury his feelings for the princess either. On one hand, those feelings would drive Byron to keep Aislynn safe, but the two of them alone could lead to… more than Eryk wanted it to.

With a sigh, the king slipped back into sleep, hoping his plan didn't backfire horribly.

Chapter 12

As soon as she left Eryk's room, Aislynn headed off to find her traveling companion. She figured that she might as well give Byron as much warning as possible. Knowing that he'd still be cleaning up the mess in the barracks, she went straight there.

The sleeping chamber was as much of a disaster zone as she had expected it to be, given Byron's earlier report. There were servants and guardsmen busy clearing out the tattered bedding and clothing, and others were trying to scrub the bloodstains off the floor. Byron stood near one of the doorways, directing everyone and supervising the whole process.

"Captain!" she called, walking into the room. Byron immediately looked over at her, and started across the room when she gestured for him to come closer.

"We need to talk," Aislynn explained when Byron was close enough to hear her. "Is your office okay?" He just nodded, and led the way.

Aislynn noticed that he looked as tired as she felt, and she wondered if he'd gotten any sleep since last night. She suddenly felt guilty for the short nap that she had stolen earlier.

"What can I do for you, your Highness?" Byron asked as he settled himself heavily into his chair. Aislynn took a seat across from him and leaned her elbows on his desk.

"I was just talking with Eryk," she began. "I had been thinking about what Philip said, and Harmon before him, and I agree that something has to be done about Vivien. It'll be the fastest way to end all of this."

Byron nodded. "I thought that myself, when it was first mentioned, before the whole marriage fiasco."

"So I'm going after her, and you're coming with me." Aislynn knew that there was no point in beating around the bush. It was far easier just to say what needed to be said, and deal with it.

"Excuse me?" Byron asked, startled. "I can't believe Eryk would let you go, for one thing, or that you *would* go. Especially given last night… There's only one trusted guard to keep him safe if you leave, and who's going to run things while Eryk recovers? And why do you need me? I have things to do here, things that can't be left to just anyone." He had seen the way Aislynn had looked at Eryk last night, and Byron knew that regardless of his conversation with her yesterday, she would never be his. Aislynn's heart had been on her sleeve for everyone to see, so the thought of being alone with her… Well, it would be too hard.

"I don't want to leave him unprotected, don't make any mistake about that, but it will take too long to get somebody else from Evendell. It's easier if it's you and I. Eryk wants you to come with me. He said that you would keep me safe," she said with a smile.

"I know that there's a lot to be done here," Aislynn continued, "but can't you leave one of your lieutenants in charge? If I know you at all, then I know that they're well trained."

"It will have to be Owen," Byron said sadly, and Aislynn remembered that his other lieutenant had died last night. "When are we leaving?" he asked with a sigh.

"As soon as we get the confirmation we need from the prisoner, and we'll hopefully be able to question him later today. I'd also prefer Eryk to be up and out of bed, but time is of the essence here. We probably won't leave until the day after tomorrow, but it's possible that we'll be able to head out in the morning, so be prepared to leave at dawn just in case."

"I'll be ready," Byron agreed reluctantly. He'd be happy to have this war over and done with. After last night, Byron felt that he had a better understanding of what the men fighting at the border had been going through, and he'd be happy never to have to experience this sense of loss again. It had been a number of years since he'd fought as part of the army, and he hadn't been forced to watch his friends die back then.

With nothing left to say, Aislynn left Byron to return to his men and she headed to Eryk's study to find some maps that she knew she would need over the coming days. On her way back through the castle, she stopped a passing servant and asked for her evening meal to be brought to her in the study. Aislynn could feel that Eryk had drifted back to sleep, and she certainly didn't feel like company, so eating alone suited her fine.

"So Cheta, are you ready for a bit of a trip?" she asked the wolf as Cheta rejoined her at the door to the study.

The wolf, of course, said nothing, but as Cheta moved over to her rug in front of the empty fireplace, Aislynn thought that the wolf looked like she was grinning, the way her mouth was open, just a little. Aislynn laughed softly, knowing the Cheta was up for anything, as always. She knew what a blessing it was to have someone who understood her. Aislynn's also appreciated the wolf's willingness to take on any challenge.

It took a little while for Aislynn to find the maps she needed, mostly because there were so many maps to choose from. She finally decided on one that showed the most recent conflicts and razed villages. It would probably be easiest to cross the border in an area that had already been decimated since it was less likely to have active conflict happening.

Aislynn also searched high and low for a map of Madelia's capital city, but she was unable to find a single one. She knew where the city was located, but after that, she and Byron would be traveling blind. This was not going to be an easy job by any means, but it was a necessary job, and one that she was looking forward to, if she was going to be honest with herself. Aislynn hadn't liked Vivien at all, and she really didn't like the thought of her anywhere near Eryk. A dagger through the queen's heart stuck Aislynn as the perfect solution to all of her problems.

Sitting down behind Eryk's large desk, she found a blank piece of paper and began to sketch. Aislynn planned her route to the border, and then the route she hoped to take to the capital city. She made sure she detailed the full area to the best of her ability in case she and Byron had to deviate from their planned course.

She was just starting to plan possible ways to get into the city and castle when there was a knock at the door. Knowing that it was getting late, Aislynn figured that it would be a servant with her dinner.

"Your Highness," the servant said as he opened the door. "There's a gentleman here, and I'm not sure what to do. He wanted to see his Majesty, but he's… and then I thought about Lord Geoffrey, but he's gone, and…"

"You can show him in here," Aislynn interrupted with a smile. She knew that the servants were just as frazzled as everyone else was, considering everything that had happened in the past day.

A few minutes later, a guard showed a gentleman wearing an army uniform into the study. He was about average height and had brown hair. His eyes, however, were a startling shade of brown that seemed almost golden in the flickering light of the lamp on the desk.

"Your Highness," he greeted her, bowing at the waist.

"Commander," she replied, inclining her head. Either someone had told him who she was, or he kept up with the latest gossip. Assuming neither, she introduced herself.

"I am Princess Aislynn, his Majesty's chief advisor. The king is currently unavailable. Is there something that I can help you with?"

"My name is Petyr, and I came from the border to warn you about an attack," he said. "My men and I have been tracking a group of Madelians heading here to the capital."

"We know," Aislynn commented. "They attacked last night." She didn't go into any details, but the astute young man could tell that there had been a heavy toll.

"Too late again!" the young commander spat angrily. "We're always too late. Sometimes by a day, sometimes two, but we are never, ever on time to help the people who need us! Their army is always a step ahead of us."

"Commander!" Aislynn snapped, getting his attention. She could tell that he wasn't angry with her, but instead with whatever situation he and his men had found themselves in, apparently on more than one occasion. The man blushed again.

"I'm sorry, your Highness, but it's been very difficult, for me and for my men. We've seen a lot of dead villagers these past months, and now we're too late to help here as well. It's frustrating to always be cleaning up the messes you know that you could have helped to prevent, if only you'd gotten there sooner."

There came another knock at the door, and this time the servant entered with Aislynn's dinner. The thoughtful man had also brought a plate for her visitor, and Aislynn took both plates from him with a smile and a nod of thanks.

"Please, join me for dinner," she invited her guest. Aislynn took a seat on the couch and put the two plates on the table in front of her.

"Thank you," Petyr said, taking a seat in one of the chairs near the table and gratefully picking up the plate closest to him.

Aislynn thought about Petyr showing up here right on the heels of the attack on the castle. "How long did you say you and your men had been tracking that group from the border?"

"Two days," he replied looking up from the food in front of him. The smile on the princess's face startled him.

"And do your men feel the same way that you do?" Aislynn asked, taking a bite of her dinner. "Do they also feel that they should be helping to prevent further tragedy?" A plan was starting to form in her mind, or rather, her previous plan was starting to solidify.

"Of course they do!" Petyr replied, sounding offended. "We've seen some combat, after tracking down some of the raiders, and every time the men were eager to take revenge for the atrocities they've seen."

"That's good," she said with a smile. Yes, she definitely had a plan. "How many men do you have under your command, Petyr?"

"I have forty-four men with me, but only thirty-nine of them are ready for combat. The others are still nursing wounds."

"What would you say if I offered you a chance for further revenge? You and sixteen of your men."

Petyr looked intrigued, so Aislynn continued.

"We managed to kill seventeen of the Madelians who attacked last night, and I had the bodies stripped of weapons and uniforms before they were disposed of. We were thinking about sending men back across the border, scouting out their army and bringing that information back to us. His Majesty is planning to end this conflict, and he's going to need information when he marches the army across the border. If we had some of our men in Madelian uniforms, they'd be in less danger."

"But what about the men who escaped after the attack?" Petyr wanted to know. "The group that we were tracking was definitely larger than seventeen. If they get back across the border and spread news about the attack, we'll be in danger regardless of the uniforms."

Aislynn shrugged. "Unless you have a suggestion, that's a risk that we're asking you to take, you and your men. There is a lot of ground on the other side of the border. The chances of both groups crossing at the same point and meeting up with the same people are pretty slim, though it is a risk."

Petyr shook his head. "No, I can't think of a better idea. I'm not sure how much information we'll be able to find for you, but I'm sure I have sixteen volunteers for the job. Just the chance to strike back will draw most, if not all, of my men to the mission. I will agree to the assignment, on behalf of myself and my men."

"Thank you, Commander," Aislynn said sincerely. "This could make a huge difference towards ending this war. I will talk with the king, and he can pass along the specifics to you and your men."

The two finished their meal in companionable silence, each lost in their own thoughts, and Petyr left soon after to spend the night with the rest of his command. Aislynn made a note to Eryk with the details of her evening conversation, knowing that he still slept and not wanting to disturb him. She hoped to have time to talk with him in the morning, but wanted to have a backup plan in place in case she didn't.

Finally finished with the preparations she needed to make for her journey, Aislynn and Cheta retired to their rooms. Aislynn had some packing to do before bed, and she wanted to talk with Marja before they both went to sleep.

Marja was waiting for her when she entered the suite, and followed her when Aislynn didn't pause in the reception room and instead went straight to her bedroom. When Aislynn pulled out her saddlebags, Marja just sighed and sat down on the corner of the bed.

"Where are you going Aislynn?" she asked carefully. She knew from previous experiences back home in Evendell that she didn't always want the answer to that question.

"I have to go to Madelia for a little while," Aislynn replied. "We need to end this war."

Marja certainly couldn't disagree with that, but she was a little confused. Rumor was running rampant through the castle, and this was Marja's chance to find out the truth of last night's attack. Marja went to Aislynn's wardrobe and started gathering items to help her friend pack. She knew what Aislynn liked to work in, and she also knew what to pack for blending into a crowd. This wasn't the first time she'd done this, and Marja took the opportunity to ask some of the nagging questions she had.

"I thought the war was already ending," she commented carefully. "You and Eryk spent a couple of days in negotiations with Madelia, didn't you?"

"Yes, we did, and we brought back a signed contract," Aislynn admitted with a grimace.

"So why are you going to Madelia? Is there more that needs to be dealt with?"

"Most definitely," Aislynn agreed, a wicked grin on her face. She was going through her weapons and she tested the edge of her throwing daggers, envisioning them embedded in Vivien's body.

"The soldiers who attacked us last night left from the border over two days ago, which was before we finished negotiations with Vivien. It looks like we're going to need more violent means to end the war."

"When are you leaving?" Marja wanted to know as they finished up.

"I was hoping to leave first thing in the morning," Aislynn answered, "but that won't be happening now. It really depends on Eryk. I won't leave him until he's out of bed."

Marja nodded, agreeing with Aislynn's logic.

"You'll be careful, right?"

"Of course I will. I have too much to come back to. Besides, Eryk is sending Byron with me, to help keep me safe."

"Too much to come back to?" Marja echoed. "Does that mean what I think it does?"

Aislynn blushed and nodded. “Seeing him there on the floor… it made my heart stop, and it wasn’t just because I’m supposed to be keeping him safe. I love him, Marja, with all my heart.”

Marja smiled. “Finally! I wish you both the best,” she said sincerely, but then concern clouded her face. “Won’t it be strange to be traveling with Byron? There’s a little history there too.”

“I hope not,” Aislynn admitted. She remembered Byron’s words from the day before, his declaration of his interest, but he’d backed down for Eryk before and she suspected he’d do the same now. Aislynn cared for Byron, and considered him one of her dearest friends, but it was Eryk who had her heart and she had given it willingly and fully.

As Aislynn tied the straps closed on her saddlebags, Marja wished Aislynn good night and good luck. She went to bed, truly hoping that Aislynn would be here for her wedding in a few weeks, but knowing that it was possible that she had just spoken to her friend for the last time.

Chapter 13

Dawn found Aislynn awake and getting ready to leave for Madelia. She could feel Eryk's discomfort and frustration, which meant that he was awake and likely trying to get dressed. She also knew that he was intending to come and speak with her. This indicated that he was up and out of bed, so she was safe to leave on her assignment. That was fine with her, because the sooner this was over with, the happier she'd be. There was just one thing they had to do first.

The idea of leaving Eryk alone, without protection, made her very anxious, and she had toyed with the idea of leaving Cheta with him. But the idea of being without her *eesprid* on such a dangerous assignment made her even more ill at ease. Aislynn would just have to trust that Mateo could keep her king safe while she was gone, but the thought tugged at her as she made her way to Eryk's suite.

She had just arrived at his door when a servant brought word that the Madelian soldier they had captured was recovered enough to be questioned. According to the healers, Mateo had done a lot of damage during his attack on the man, but he was well enough to be moved, so the prisoner had been escorted to one of the few cells located beneath the palace. While Bacovia certainly wasn't entirely peaceful, the monarchy had a reputation for quick and final justice, so there were generally few occasions to use the cells.

The cell was cool and had a musty smell to it, but it was at least free of drafts. There was a hard bed and a stool for furnishings, and a torch on the wall outside of the cell cast an eerie flickering light over everything.

When Eryk arrived at the cell, accompanied by Warren and Aislynn, the prisoner was sitting on the stool with Owen standing right behind him. Mateo was lurking around in the corridor outside of the cell, occasionally throwing glares at the man who had killed his brother. He was still upset that he had been prevented from exacting his revenge, and he hadn't spoken a single word since the attack. One of the guards unlocked the cell, and they stepped in.

The healers had commented that the prisoner was lucky to be alive, and Eryk concurred, astounded by the man's appearance. His face was swollen and showed an incredible amount of bruising, with one eye swollen completely shut. The king, however, did not intend to keep him alive for all that long, so his state of health really wasn't that much of a concern. The fact that he could consider the death of this man so impartially bothered Eryk, but just a little bit.

"I thought you were dead," the Madelian spat, his words a little garbled from the swelling.

Eryk said nothing. He just stood there, looking down at the prisoner, and then he nodded to Owen. The big man stepped in front of the captive and Warren began the interrogation.

"How did you and your fellows get into the castle?" Warren asked.

The man spit at him, and Owen immediately slugged him across the face, rocking him on his stool. Byron's lieutenant had prepared for this ahead of time by chaining the man to the stool he was sitting on. Warren tried again.

"How did you get into the castle?"

"Through the gate."

Owen hit him again, and Eryk thought to himself that this was going to take a long time. He was in pain, and he wished that he'd had the foresight to bring himself a chair. Almost as if reading his mind, Aislynn slipped out of the cell and returned a few moments later with a stool identical to the one the prisoner was sitting on. Eryk sat down, and when Aislynn stood right behind him, he leaned back against her ever so slightly, willing to bear the pain in his back for a chance to be touching her.

"Look," Warren said, trying to sound reasonable. "This is going to go one of two ways. If you make us draw every little bit of information out of you, you will suffer more than you need to. I have it on very good authority that our friend here is very good at what he does, and if you're planning to make us hurt you in the hopes that you'll die before you give us what we need, then you are sorely mistaken."

Warren took a deep breath and crouched down beside the prisoner.

"Now, how did you and your buddies get into the castle?"

The Madelian clamped his jaw shut and shook his head, refusing to answer. Owen glanced back over his shoulder, meeting Eryk's eye. With a small sigh, knowing that it was inevitable, the king nodded. Owen turned back to the prisoner, and with a quick twist, he broke one of the fingers on the man's left hand.

"How did you get into the castle?" Warren asked again after the screaming had died down.

It took hours, and by the time they were finished, the man chained to the stool was pretty close to unrecognizable. The bones in both of his hands had been broken over the course of the interrogation, as was his nose and one of his ankles. His face was a mass of cuts and bruises, he was missing a number of teeth and both eyes were now swollen shut, but they finally ascertained the truth of the attack on the castle.

The attack had been planned well in advance. There had been a group of men in the royal guard who were bought by the Madelian crown, and it had been them who had arranged for the doors to the castle to be opened. All of those men had either been killed in the attack, or had fled the palace afterwards, so there was nobody they knew of left to punish for that act of treason.

Vivien had finally given the order to attack the city a few days ago, along with very specific instructions that had been outlined in the orders Aislynn had found. They were to find and kill Eryk, along with every member of his council. The queen wanted nobody with even a thought of taking power in Bacovia left alive.

"But how did you know exactly where to go, and who would be where?" This was a question that had been bothering Eryk, and he was glad that Warren asked it now.

The prisoner was definitely in rough shape, but once again the man gave his traditional response, spitting in Warren direction, though he succeeded mostly in drooling. Owen simply leaned his weight on to the man's broken left hand, and the prisoner screamed in agony.

"You do have a number of other bones for me to break, you know. Bigger bones that will hurt a lot more than the little ones did. It's in your best interest to just answer the question." Warren had to admit to himself that this man's defiance was quite something. They had had to literally drag each and every answer out of him, which unfortunately did carry with it the concern that the information wasn't valid. People being tortured had been known to lie in order to escape further pain and suffering.

The solider had apparently finally reached his limit, because he decided to answer this question without any further encouragement from Owen.

"Cora."

"Cora?" Warren asked. "What the hell is that supposed to mean?"

Eryk nearly gasped aloud when he heard the answer. He stood up, grabbed Warren by the arm, and drew him towards the corridor. Warren understood that they had the information they needed, even if he didn't understand it, and he called Owen off.

"Do you want me to get a healer for him?" Owen asked as he walked out into the hall.

"No," Eryk answered shortly. "He isn't going to need one."

Then he gestured to Mateo, who was still lurking nearby. A strange look came over Mateo's face, almost happy, and he walked into the cell sporting a truly disturbing smile and a wickedly spiked mace in hand.

As the group walked away, the prisoner in the cell started to scream. Eryk ignored the sound as best he could, but he shuddered as they reached the base of the stairs and the screams reached another, higher pitch. Aislynn rested her hand on his arm, offering support since she knew how difficult this was for him to do. Eryk wouldn't normally have condoned the torture of a prisoner, but they had needed the information too badly, and Mateo deserved his revenge. Eryk wondered if Aislynn's bloodthirsty personality was rubbing off on him a little, and he glanced over towards her.

Eryk went straight back to his room, leaning on Aislynn for support by the time they reached their destination, with Warren and Owen trailing along behind. Nobody said a word until the door was shut behind them.

"So what was that all about?" Warren asked. "The name obviously means something to you."

"Yes, it most certainly does. I'll admit that I never expected to hear that name again."

Eryk sat down on the couch, pulling Aislynn down beside him, and indicated that the other two men should sit down too.

"Owen, you should have at least a rough idea of the story, being Byron's lieutenant, but I'll go over all of it for Warren's sake. He's been a bit out of the loop, having been over in the east for so long." Eryk leaned back, trying to settle his weight more comfortably, and then launched into his recount of the recent events in the Bacovian capital.

"In the summer, a few weeks before midsummer actually, my father was assassinated. Aislynn was already here acting as my bodyguard, though I was unaware of it at the time, and after my father's death, things became very confusing very quickly.

"Branden started to act very strangely, and it appeared for a little while that he may have had something to do with the attacks, but in reality it was Durham. Durham was the uncle of Davin, my heir, and we believe that he was also the grandson of my grandfather's illegitimate brother. Durham felt that *his* grandfather should have inherited the throne, not my grandfather. That meant that moving down the generations, Durham should have been king, not me.

"Durham ended up being killed at the end of it all, but his sister escaped. His sister is Cora, and it looks like she's been providing the Madelians with inside information about the castle and council."

"Whoa," breathed Warren. "That's quite something. So what are we going to do about it?"

"I'm not sure there is anything we can do," Eryk sighed. "With luck, she'll be lurking around Madelia and Aislynn will run into her and deal with the problem for me." This he said with a smile for the woman sitting beside him. "Aislynn's task is to take care of Vivien though, not spending time hunting for Cora."

"Speaking of my task," the princess commented, rising, "I should be off. With luck, Byron and I can be out of here by midday. The sooner we leave, the sooner we get back and this will all be over with."

Aislynn leaned over and gave Eryk a kiss on the cheek, chaste considering the presence of the other men in the room. Then she left quickly, shutting the door behind her, to finish her final preparations.

"You really rely on her, don't you?" Warren asked, a thoughtful look on his face as he looked at the closed door.

"Aislynn? Yeah, I… I guess so. I've never really thought about it." Eryk blushed and looked embarrassed. With Aislynn it was all so easy and natural. Eager to change the subject, he turned to address Owen. "Thank you for your help, Owen," he said. Owen simply nodded. He was a man a few words, and Eryk couldn't even remember having had any form of conversation with him.

"What should I do with Mateo?" Owen asked.

"Well I'm hoping that the… quality time… he's had with our guest will be cathartic for him and that he'll regain some of his composure. I can only guess how hard it's been, but I need him back on duty."

"I'll keep him off duty for the rest of today and tonight, and assign him to you tomorrow morning. Who should I assign to be his partner?"

Eryk shook his head, at a loss. Mateo had always been partnered with his brother, and Eryk didn't know if the twins had even formed any close friendships during their time here.

"Is there anyone among the men who they were close to?" Eryk asked.

"I'm not sure. I know that they had some friends, but they kept to themselves a lot of the time. I'll ask around."

The late morning sun was streaming through the window and into the reception room of Eryk's suite, reminding him just how long they had spent below ground. He had missed his morning meal, and was suddenly very hungry; he expected that the others were too.

"I'll send someone down for some food, and then let the two of you get back to your men," Eryk said, moving towards the door.

"I appreciate the invitation your Majesty, but no thank you," Owen replied, standing. "I should get back to the men now and check in with the captain for any final orders before he leaves. We also need to work on some more drills for the defense of the castle; the men were not quite quick enough the other night."

Owen saw himself out, and soon afterwards, a meal arrived for Eryk and Warren. The two men settled back on the comfortable furniture to relax for what seemed the first time in days.

"Is it always so… crazy around here?" Warren asked.

Eryk laughed.

"It never used to be, but Aislynn seems to bring trouble with her," Eryk replied. "I'm sure that's not true, but life didn't become so interesting until she got here."

"Look, Eryk," Warren began as he looked away. "I'm really sorry for anything I said, or… um… did, in regards to your relationship with… her Highness."

Eryk looked up at the big man, wondering where that had come from. Warren was acting rather odd, totally unlike his usual confident and cocky self. Finally, Eryk remembered a fuzzy memory from the night of the attack and the look on Warren's face told him what he needed. He burst out laughing, and Warren raised his gaze off the floor, startled.

"You saw her fight, didn't you? You were there when she killed those men in my room." Eryk found this impossibly funny. Warren had been trying to get Aislynn to fall for him, to choose him over Eryk, and now he was backpedaling as fast as he could.

"When I spoke to Branden about her, he warned me that I shouldn't even bother. He said that you and she had a special bond. I should have listened to him, I guess." Warren looked honestly chagrined.

"Did she threaten you?" Eryk asked with a chuckle. It wouldn't be the first time…

Warren blushed. "After I kissed her, she told me not to touch her again. When I kissed her again the next day, she uh… knocked me to the ground and told me that she'd kill me if I ever laid a hand on her again. I didn't think she was serious…"

"Until the other night," he said, nodding. "Don't worry Warren, I understand. I had a similar reaction when I found out about her," Eryk confided. "Branden didn't tell you why he's no longer my chief advisor, did he?"

Warren shook his head. Now that he thought about it, Branden had actually avoided answering that question entirely.

Eryk chuckled. "Well I won't tell his story, but you should listen to Branden when it comes to Aislynn. He's gotten to know her very well, especially now that he's going to marry her friend."

The two men laughed, but then Warren turned serious again.

"You do need to consider what I said earlier," he said. "You rely on her for a lot."

"Yes, I do," Eryk agreed. "She's more than just my chief advisor, and she's important to me in so many ways." Eryk remembered the jealousy he'd felt not so long ago at the thought of Aislynn and Warren together. It was funny how his perception of things had changed in the last little while, knowing that he was finally going to be able to marry the woman he loved.

"So what happens if she doesn't come back?"

Eryk just looked at his friend, dumbfounded. He had known, logically, that there was a possibility that Aislynn wouldn't make it back from Madelia, but he had never really thought about it. Thinking of it now scared him. A lot.

"I don't know what happens," he admitted.

"Think about it. Think about it long and hard. Then, if it happens, you'll know what you need to do."

With that sobering thought, Warren left the room to return to his men. Eryk wandered around his room for a little while. He didn't want to think about what Warren had said, but now that it was at the forefront of his mind, he couldn't help himself.

What would he do without Aislynn? She was his chief advisor, and he relied on her for advice. She was his bodyguard, and he relied on her for protection. She was his friend, and he relied on her for companionship. And she was the woman he loved with all of his heart. How many holes would there be in his life if she didn't come back? What if neither of them came back?

With that uncomfortable thought, he gathered his strength and made his way down the hall to Aislynn's suite. Aislynn and Byron were going to be leaving very soon, and he suddenly had the need to kiss Aislynn just one more time.

It wasn't long after Aislynn was finished with her preparations that Eryk appeared at her door. He knocked quietly and let himself in just as she was swinging her saddlebags up and over her shoulder.

"I guess it won't be too long before you have this suite all to yourself," he commented as he entered. "Do you know if they're going to stay in the castle or get a place in the city after the wedding?"

"I'm not entirely sure. I know that Marja is leaning towards staying in the castle, at least for a little while, but Branden has been preparing his family's home in the city. It will be strange having to pick out my clothing myself every day," Aislynn commented with a smile. She relied on Marja to help her to choose the most appropriate dresses and accessories.

"You can have another attendant you know. We can even send for one from Evendell if you can't find a suitable one here. Are you ready to go?" Eryk asked, nodding towards the saddlebags. Aislynn nodded.

"There is just one thing more," she said. "It totally slipped my mind this morning, but it's important. I met with a young army commander by the name of Petyr yesterday evening. He and his men have seen a lot of murdered citizens and destroyed villages over the past few months, and they would like the opportunity to pay back the Madelians for some of the damages. He has volunteered some of his men for that one assignment I spoke to you about yesterday. They'll cross the border and gather information so that we know as much as we can about the Madelian army before the battle. Make sure that you meet with him sometime today."

"You've certainly been busy while I was being lazy in bed," Eryk commented. "You don't need me at all."

Aislynn shuddered inwardly at that statement, knowing with certainty that it wasn't true.

"I should get going," she said, choosing to ignore Eryk's comment. She settled her bags more comfortably and started towards the stairs. Eryk followed along a bit more slowly.

Outside, Aislynn found Byron and two horses, one of which was her familiar gray. She nodded her thanks to the captain, and slung her bags up behind the saddle. When she finished fastening the buckles and quickly checking over her tack, she turned to see Mateo standing nearby. He was still guarding Eryk and she intended to keep it that way, though he was supposed to have the rest of today off. She moved towards the man.

"Mateo," she greeted him. "I have matters to attend to, so I'll be gone for a while. I need you to take care of his Majesty for me."

Mateo acknowledged her with a bow.

"I have come to love and care for him very much, and if something happens to him while I'm gone, you had better be dead."

Mateo had seen Aislynn fight, here and back home, and he knew that she was perfectly capable of carrying out her threat. He nodded his acknowledgment of her statement.

"I intend to marry Eryk, so I need you to take good care of him. You wouldn't want me to end up with Warren, would you?" She asked this last question with a smile, and Mateo rolled his eyes, but he didn't smile as she'd been hoping. Impulsively, Aislynn wrapped her arms around the guard and hugged him before turning away and starting back towards her horse. While she walked, she glanced over and saw Eryk moving away from Byron. She wondered what they had been talking about.

Aislynn walked up behind the king, wrapped her arms around his waist and slid around in front of him. Then she ran her hands up his back, wrapped her hands in Eryk's long black hair and pulled his head down for a final parting kiss.

After she pulled away from her fiancé, Aislynn swung up into her saddle, shivering slightly in the cool air. Harvestide was only a couple of weeks away, and it was getting colder now. It wouldn't be long before they saw frost, or even snow.

Once Byron settled into his saddle, the two of them waved their farewells to the small group on the stairs and started through the gates of the castle at a trot. When they were past the gate, they nudged their horses into a canter and moved off through the city, Cheta keeping up easily.

"What was Eryk saying to you just now?" Aislynn wanted to know. She had been so busy talking with Mateo that she hadn't been paying attention to the link in the back of her mind.

Byron laughed. "He asked me to bring you back to him," he answered.

"And how did you answer that?"

"I told him that I would do my best, but that I was making no guarantees."

Aislynn laughed. "I wish you good luck with that," she commented.

"And Mateo?" Byron asked. "What were you saying to him?"

"I told him to keep Eryk safe because I intend to marry him if… when we get back."

Byron looked over at Aislynn and nodded. "It's about time," he said.

"You're okay with that? I mean, after the other day…"

"I have to be, don't I? Besides, we've already had this discussion. I won't get in Eryk's way if you're going to be with him, regardless of anything else."

After that, they both fell silent for a little while, their horses moving quickly over the last few cobblestones of the city road and off into the forest.

Chapter 14

Eryk watched Aislynn and Byron ride away and felt oddly empty. Ever since she had arrived a season ago, Aislynn had managed to insinuate herself into every nook and cranny of his life and Eryk knew that it would be very strange not to have her around. Even when they'd been fighting, she'd still always been nearby, a comforting presence, now that he thought about it.

As he walked back into the castle, Mateo fell into place behind him, making Eryk smile just a little. He had guessed that Aislynn would officially assign Mateo the task of keeping him safe, and he was likely the best trained for the job since the royal guard in Evendell completed part of their training at the Academy with the assassins.

Eryk reached his study and indicated that Mateo should follow him inside. He sat down behind his desk and the man took up a position on the other side, standing across from him.

"What did she say to you before she left?" Eryk had seen Aislynn deep in discussion with him and he was very curious. She got such intent looks on her face when she was revealing important information, and she'd had one of those looks.

Mateo stood there for a moment, trying to decide if he should say anything. He felt a little better now that he'd had his revenge, but it still seemed like the hole inside him where his twin used to be was going to devour him from the inside out. He felt that if he talked to anyone about Marcus, he'd start to scream and he'd never stop.

"She warned me that if I let something happen to you while she's away, I had better be dead before she finds me," Mateo said, deciding to try to answer the king.

Eryk laughed, but then took another look at the man in front of him. He stopped laughing and took a deep breath.

"Of course she meant every word of that, didn't she?"

"Yes," Mateo replied. "We once saw the assassin's guild punish a member who had betrayed his brothers. The assassins know exactly how to kill a person and exactly how not to kill a person. It took the punished man three days to die, and it was not a pretty sight."

Eryk swallowed audibly, his mind creating pictures of what they could have done to that man. He just couldn't wrap his mind around the idea of Aislynn being involved with something like that, but then he remembered earlier that morning. She'd had absolutely no problem with any of the torture inflicted on the prisoner.

"She just doesn't seem that dangerous to me," he commented. Mateo stared at him in shock, looking taken aback.

"Well most of the time," Eryk amended.

Eryk reached over to the pile of maps on his desk and started riffling through them.

"Would you please go and ask a servant to find Lord Warren for me?" he asked, clearly dismissing his bodyguard to be about the business of the day. Mateo passed word along to a passing servant and took up a position outside the study while waiting for Warren.

It took quite a long time for Warren to arrive in his study, which reminded Eryk that Warren had been going down to see his men on the plateau. Eryk shook his head, wondering at his lapse in memory, hoping it was just lack of sleep and recovering from his injury.

"Your Majesty!" Warren called as he finally walked into the room. He showed signs of having dressed hastily, and Eryk guessed that he'd changed to get rid of any blood that had been on his clothing. "You've been up and out of bed a lot today. How are you feeling?"

"I'm doing fine, thank you," Eryk replied, not entirely truthfully. "Please, have a seat."

Eryk looked back down at the map he had laid out in front of him.

"I understand that Aislynn appointed you as Commander of my army for the time being, and we need to formulate a plan."

Warren leaned forward to look at the map, happy to put his expertise to use.

The capital city of Bacovia was located on a large mountain plateau, backing onto the mountain range that acted as part of the border between Bacovia and Evendell. A wall surrounded the castle proper, but not the city itself. Instead, the populace relied on the remote location, the elevated ground and the maze-like roads for defense. The city wasn't the best place for a concentrated attack, and Eryk was inclined to take the army across the border, forcing the Madelians out of their guerilla tactics.

"We need to send scouts out to ascertain the location of Madelia's army before we can finalize anything, so this is just a hypothetical discussion," Eryk explained. "In order to keep the element of surprise for as long as possible, would your light cavalry be able to hide in a forested area until the main army is in position?" Eryk asked.

Warren thought about that for a few moments before answering.

"Possibly," he answered carefully. "I'd have to see how close the trees grow to each other, to make sure that there is easy egress for when the men are needed. And of course, that particular ploy will fail if the Madelians decide to approach your army through the forest."

"Do you have any other suggestions?"

"Well, if it's possible to choose an area with a lot of open ground, your heavy cavalry will have a much easier time charging, and the same is true for the lighter horses. It doesn't lend itself well to the whole surprise thing though, unless we intersperse the heavy horses with the light ones."

"But what if the Madelians decide to attack the cavalry? The heavy horses are armored, and your lighter horses are not."

"I guess we'll have to pick one idea or the other and take our chances," Warren said, with a touch of a smile. "We'll have to see what the land is like, I guess."

"So there's one part of the plan. Aislynn said that I should speak with a commander who arrived here yesterday evening. He will apparently be helping out with the rest of the plan."

"Really? How so?"

"You were part of the council meeting when Aislynn explained, I believe. This commander, Petyr, has volunteered some of his men to scout back into Madelia to learn about their army," Eryk explained.

"In that case, I suspect that the next discussion needs to involve him. I'll go and get him, if you'd like," Warren volunteered.

"That's a good idea. I'm going to head back up to my room before I'm in too much pain to make it that far," Eryk said, getting up. "I'll get the remnants of the council to assemble there as well, and we'll get this worked out."

Warren nodded as he stood, and after a quick bow to his king, turned and walked out the door. He was reasonably certain Petyr had camped beside his men down below the city. That would make him easy enough to find.

Eryk grabbed the maps off the desk and headed up to his suite as quickly as possible after sending a servant to find the council members. Eryk was determined to do what he could to support Aislynn's plan, and that meant getting the army assembled to march as soon as possible.

It didn't take long for the first knock to come, and Mateo opened the door to let Mataline and Philip into the room. They took seats at Eryk's bidding, and waited. Soon after, the door opened again to admit Owen and the royal physician, Michael. Finally, a little while after that, the door opened a final time for Warren and Petyr.

"Now that we're all together," Eryk began, "it's time to plan the end of this mess."

"Where are the others?" Philip wanted to know. He had a very concerned look on his face as he eyed Owen. Byron's second-in-command was a tall, imposing man, and his dark brown eyes glittered dangerously as he stared back at Philip.

"The captain and chief advisor are currently occupied," Eryk stated quietly but firmly, and his tone indicated that there would be no further discussion of the whereabouts of Aislynn and Byron. Philip swallowed audibly, and Eryk continued.

"Lord Warren and I have established a couple of possibilities for our army to make its stand, depending on what we find when we arrive in

Madelia. We want to hold the light cavalry in reserve until the Madelian forces are committed, and then use the horses to try to flank the enemy while the heavy cavalry attacks in the middle. After softening them up, the heavy cavalry can fall back, allowing the foot soldiers access to the enemy while the light cavalry can help to prevent any of the Madelian soldiers from escaping."

Eryk waited patiently while the councilors looked over the maps he had spread on the table between them. Petyr, who had a lot of experience with the lay of the land across the Madelian border, voiced his opinion about some likely areas for their army to be hiding. The council agreed that they would follow his recommendations, starting their search for information in those places.

"For those of you who have not had the pleasure, I'd like to introduce you to Petyr," Eryk said. "He's a commander in the army, and his men tracked the group of Madelians here from the border. He and his men have offered to help with the execution of our little plan."

Petyr cleared his throat and stood, preparing to address the group.

"My men and I want to express our deepest condolences, and our apologies for not being here to help during the attack. Ever since my command reached the border, we've been reaching village after village too late to do anything, and that remained the case here. We are all desperate for a chance to take a little bit of revenge against our enemies, and we're happy to volunteer."

Warren stood as Petyr sat down, and took up the thread of the plan.

"Seventeen of Petyr's men will take the uniforms her Highness scavenged from our attackers and head back to the border. Once they have crossed, they'll begin scouting the likely areas the commander has indicated, looking for information they can gather and send back to help us prepare."

"The rest of my men will act as couriers," Petyr continued. "They will head out on horseback to the various commands stationed along the border with orders for the soldiers to pull back to prepare for the attack. As they retreat, the Madelian force may follow, trying to take advantage of our weakness. This could allow us the chance to capture some of them, learning the location and specifics about their army that way."

"And we will prepare for the battle here, as best we can, until it is time for us to join the army at the border," Eryk finished. "Does anybody have any questions?"

The room remained silent. They had all heard the vague outline of the plan the day before, from Aislynn, so the filling in of the details didn't really raise any concerns.

"In that case, once this is all started, it will be up to the three of you to run things for a while," Eryk said with a wry smile for Mataline, Philip and Owen. "I'll be heading out with Warren when the time comes. I have to be involved with the final battle because the Madelians need to see that I'm alive and they can't just come across the border and claim Bacovia for their own."

As the councilors rose and prepared to leave, it struck Eryk how much had changed in just a few days. When he'd returned from the border, the war had been all but over, but now there was a battle looming on the horizon. A battle that would determine the future of this kingdom, and he didn't just mean the fight involving the army. Aislynn's mission was just as important, if not more so, and Eryk silently wished her luck one more time.

Chapter 15

Aislynn stretched slowly, and as her hands encountered the chill air outside of her blankets, she recoiled instinctively. This close to Harvestide, the nights were cool, and she knew that when she opened her eyes, she would see frost on the ground. Lovely, she thought sarcastically to herself.

Fortunately, she'd done her fair share of camping out over the years, and she had prepared for this the night before when the chill of the evening had heralded the coming frost. Her clothing for the day was under the blankets with her, warmed by her body heat, so at least it wouldn't be uncomfortable for her to dress. She nudged Cheta away from her side, and set about the task of getting ready for the day.

By the time she emerged from her tent, Byron had already started to strike the camp. His tent was packed and he was just burying their fire pit. She quickly packed her own tent and set about tacking up the horses.

She led Byron's horse over to him, and handed him the reins. In return, he handed her some warm breakfast that he had made before covering the fire. They both mounted up and continued on their way to the border, neither saying a word, enjoying the companionable silence.

Aislynn was still tired from the previous day. She and Byron had set off from the castle at about noon, and they had ridden the rest of the day, pushing the horses as hard as they could before the failing light of the evening forced them to make camp. They couldn't afford for a horse to break a leg stumbling around in the dark, but they both would have pressed on if it had been feasible.

Aislynn knew that being away from Eryk made her very uncomfortable, and she imagined that Byron felt the same way, though not likely for exactly the same reason. Her tie to Eryk may be stronger, but Byron had been protecting him longer than she had. They both wanted this over and done with, so they could be back where they belonged.

"We should reach the border sometime around midday," Byron said, breaking the silence. The sun was starting to rise, and the air was feeling warmer by the minute. The light frost from the night before was already melting, making everything sparkle in the sunlight as the sun's rays struck the water droplets.

"That's good," Aislynn said. "The faster we can get through the war zone, the better off we'll be."

Since Aislynn had been such an active part of updating the maps as the information came in from the front, she planned their route to pass through areas that had been devastated early in the fighting. They hadn't seen a soul since they'd left the city yesterday, which was just the way Aislynn wanted it.

"So do we continue to travel during the day once we cross the border, or would it be better to ditch the horses and travel at night?" Aislynn asked as they rode along.

"I'm not sure," Byron admitted. "We'll certainly be able to cover more ground on horseback, but there's something to be said for the security of moving at night. Their army shouldn't be active at night, and their campfires will make it a lot easier to avoid them."

"Unless we decide that we want to be captured," Aislynn amended. One of the strategies they had discussed the day before was being captured when they were close to the capital in hopes of being taken there as hostages. The difficulty of getting close enough to the queen was a popular topic of conversation right now, though getting through the active war zone was of highest priority for now.

"I'm not certain that's a good idea at all," Byron commented, shaking his head. "There's just too much that could go wrong."

"I know. I'd prefer to just enter the city like a normal person, scout things out and go from there."

"As long as we get to the city, there's nothing wrong with that. There is still the mercenary option for getting there," Byron said. It was common practice for mercenaries to find employment with an army when there was a war. He felt that this was the best option for the two of them, but Aislynn needed to get into the capital, not hang out near the border and the fighting. The mercenary option seemed better to her for escaping than for getting in.

"I think we'll just have to take things as they come," Aislynn said with a sigh. "We can't plan for every contingency, no matter how much we may want to. You and I both know that we can hold our own, so we'll just have to do the best that we can." She hated not having a plan. She was still alive, having survived the rigorous training as an assassin, because she knew how to plan.

It wasn't long before the path they followed led to the top of a rise. The pair paused there, looking down at the village below, or at least the remains of the village. According to what Aislynn remembered, this village had been among the first destroyed by marauding Madelians, nearly three months ago now. The fallen buildings remained untouched, but the weeds and flowers growing up among them softened their stark and blackened appearance.

Aislynn was the first to start moving again, kicking her horse into a trot and heading down through the ruins. Byron wasn't far behind her, and they moved past as quickly as they could, cantering by the time they reached the middle of town.

The emotions evoked by the razed village confused Aislynn. She had killed people before, with her weapons and with her bare hands, but this seemed so different. When someone took a contract out, there was always a reason, even if it wasn't a good one. While the assassin was impartial, or was supposed to be, there was always a motive behind the killing. The scene of the obliterated village before her seemed so impersonal. The death of dozens of innocent citizens made her feel uncomfortable and very, very sad. Byron noticed her reaction, but said nothing, riding in silence.

Once the village was out of sight behind them, Aislynn and Byron moved their horses off the path and rode along a parallel course through the woods. The border was coming up soon, and they didn't want to have to deal with any border guards. Aislynn sent Cheta back towards the road, with instructions to rejoin them once they were well past the markers and anybody stationed near them. It was unlikely that anybody would be at the crossing, but Aislynn and Byron both felt that it was better to be safe than sorry.

"The sad thing is that you get used to it," Byron said after a while, breaking the silence. Aislynn looked over at him quizzically.

"The destruction of that village back there; you get used to it after a time."

"You fought in the last war?" Aislynn asked, understanding that Byron spoke from experience.

"I started my career in the army," Byron replied, nodding. "All I had ever wanted was to be a soldier, so I joined up as soon as I was old enough. I was still very green when I went to war, barely knowing which end of the sword to hold."

"Well you obviously had natural talent, or you wouldn't have survived that, let alone gotten where you are today."

"I suppose that's true," Byron conceded, but he didn't sound convinced. "Part of me is pretty sure that most of my life has simply been luck, just being in the right place at the right time."

Aislynn wanted to ask questions, but the subject had obviously dredged up painful memories for Byron, and she didn't want to cause him any undue discomfort. Instead, they rode quietly through the forest, listening to the birds and the insects calling to each other.

By mid-afternoon, Byron and Aislynn came across a perfect place to camp. They were already well across the border, Cheta had rejoined them hours ago, and the nearby stream was too tempting to pass up. The air was pleasant, one of those rare truly hot autumn days, and the pair decided to camp early and take advantage of the water.

Aislynn went first while Byron started to set-up camp, taking her saddlebags with her. She decided to wash out her clothing and have a quick bath since she had no idea when she'd have another opportunity.

The water felt deliciously cool against her skin, and it felt wonderful to be clean. When she was done, she pulled a shift over her head and went back to camp, carrying her damp clothing over her arm.

"Don't you look lovely," Byron said with a smirk. "I didn't know that you'd packed a dress." He gestured towards the shift she wore and the slight bulge in her bag that showed the dress.

"Well, you never know when you may need to look like a proper lady," she countered. "Besides, a shift is by far the easiest thing to put on after bathing." She walked over to a convenient bush and spread out her clothing to dry in the sunlight.

"I'll go and get cleaned up myself," Byron said, "and then I'll head upstream a ways to catch some fish for our dinner. Something fresh would be a good supplement for our rations."

"I'll finish setting up here, and send Cheta out to hunt too. Maybe she'll bring us back something, just in case your fishing excursion doesn't go as planned."

Byron shot her a withering glare and started away towards the river. Aislynn laughed and gave Cheta an affectionate scratch around her ears before sending her off to hunt. Then she set about getting her tent set up and digging out the things she would need to get dinner ready when Byron and Cheta came back.

A short while later, sounds in the undergrowth nearby startled Aislynn into stillness. The noise was far too loud to be Byron, Cheta, or any of the local wildlife. Taking those options out of the equation, and that only left one likely answer - Madelians. Moving quickly and quietly in order to avoid detection, Aislynn grabbed her sword belt from where it lay nearby, slipped it across her chest, and scrambled up the nearest tree. Finding a spot against the trunk, she crouched down carefully and watched five armed men walk into the campsite below.

"This is interesting, isn't it boys?" one of the men asked the others with a laugh. He was poking through Aislynn's drying clothing. "Looks like someone's close by."

"Two someones," commented another man, gesturing towards the pair of horses grazing peacefully at the edge of the small clearing.

Aislynn hoped briefly that one of the intruders would approach her horse. He was a skittish creature, and prone to bite unfamiliar people.

Aislynn was fine up in the tree until the first man started to go through her bag, taking out clothing and displaying it to his fellows. Once the group realized that one of the people they were looking for was a woman, they started to look in earnest. The state of the camp proved that someone had been here not long ago, and the men started to fan out into the forest around the clearing.

"There are only five of them," Aislynn whispered to herself, slowly drawing her weapons from their scabbards. "I can take five, especially with surprise working for me." She carefully positioned her sword and dagger, knowing that it was easy to hurt yourself jumping with an exposed weapon, and waited for the right moment.

As soon as one of the men passed under the branch she crouched on, Aislynn leaped. She planted both of her feet into the man's back, bringing him to the ground, and then planted her sword between his shoulder blades. As she jumped away from the corpse and towards her next victim, she tugged her sword free and brought it across in front of her, slashing at the surprised man who was turning to investigate the commotion behind him. Aislynn's sword slashed across his chest and arm, nearly taking the limb off, and the second soldier dropped, his life's blood pumping itself out of the severed artery.

Hearing the screams from their companion, the other three men closed in on the camp. They hadn't really been expecting a whole lot of trouble, so they had just started to draw their weapons, a mistake that Aislynn was quick to take advantage of. As the first man reappeared from the trees, she dashed across the clearing, her weapons at the ready. The soldier managed to get his sword clear of his scabbard, but Aislynn batted it easily aside and plunged her dagger into the man's neck, sending up a spray of blood. She spun, looking for her last two opponents.

These final two soldiers had the opportunity to assess the situation when they jogged into the clearing, and for the first time, Aislynn met her victims on nearly even terms. Soldiers, trained to fight together, the two advanced towards her. Aislynn didn't want to be flanked by professionals, so she dashed ahead, taking the fight to them instead.

Crossing her weapons in front of her, Aislynn ran right into the first man, her momentum knocking him off balance and her weapons protecting her from his sword. As he stumbled backwards, she kicked out, connecting solidly with his knee and sending him sprawling, down but not hurt. She whirled in place, twisting her body to the side and catching the descending sword strike of her other opponent on her crossed blades. Aislynn pulled her hands apart, sending her sword and dagger crashing into the blade of her foe and making it vibrate uncomfortably. The solider was too much of a professional to drop his weapon, but the move did distract him long enough for Aislynn to disentangle herself and position her feet properly.

The two fighters met with the crash of sword on sword. The man was fast, meeting Aislynn's attacks with parry after parry, but he was unable to take the momentum of the attack from her. He was, however, able to keep her busy long enough for his partner to join the fray, and Aislynn found herself being attacked from both sides with only her dagger to protect her flank.

Parrying a sword with a dagger is never a good idea in the long run. The length of a sword's blade made it just a matter of time before it slipped past your guard and did a great deal of damage. Aislynn wanted away from the situation she found herself in as quickly as possible. Attacking with a dagger was just fine, but she was going to have to move fast.

She caught the next sword strike with her longer blade and then spun towards her attacker. With her sword still touching his, she forced his arm away from his body and used the momentum of her spin to drive her dagger deep into his exposed chest, deep enough that she felt the blade scrape bone.

Knowing there was no time to retrieve the smaller blade, and sensing an attack coming quickly from behind, Aislynn dropped her hand from the hilt of her dagger and spun under the arm of the man she had just stabbed, using his body briefly as a shield. She felt him jerk as his partner's sword struck home, and then she spun around his far side, bringing her sword around in a tremendous arc. She felt the impact of her sword striking her last opponent in the back, and the sharp blade traveled quite a ways through his body before the bones and muscles expended the energy of her attack. Aislynn let the body slide to the ground and bent to retrieve her dagger.

"Well, well, well," came a voice from behind her. "What's a pretty little thing like you doing out here all by yourself? And killing my men too…"

Aislynn whirled around, startled, and automatically dropped into a defensive crouch. In front of her was yet another man wearing the uniform of a Madelian solider, black pants and mottled green and brown shirt. He was of average height and build, with greasy black hair and cold blue eyes, and he wore a sword belted around his waist.

"You know that it's dangerous out here in the wilderness, don't you?" the man asked, taking a step towards her and seeming to ignore the fact that she was covered in blood and had two naked weapons in her hands. "So many horrible things can happen, especially to a lovely young lady such as you."

His smile was anything but reassuring, and Aislynn crept backwards away from him, still crouched defensively. The man was still talking, and Aislynn knew that he was trying to distract her. He wanted her to keep all of her attention focused on him so that the rest of his group could get into position around the small clearing. Aislynn tried to glance around her surreptitiously, but trying to see the camouflaged men was too difficult and the man was speaking loudly enough to cover any noise that they could be making. Cursing under her breath for her stupidity, she wondered how many more of them there were.

"A young lady needs protecting," the soldier said. "If you're a good little girl, maybe I'd be willing to be your protector." He grinned maliciously, and began to walk quickly towards her, hands fumbling with his belt.

Aislynn tensed, getting ready to spring towards her attacker, when she felt rough hands grab her from behind. She reacted immediately, instinctively, throwing her head back suddenly and smashing the nose of the man who had grabbed her. As he fell to the ground, trying to stop the flow of blood gushing down his face, she spun around, sword leading, but she missed.

"A feisty one!" the first man laughed. "I like the feisty ones. Grab her boys!"

Aislynn felt someone else grab at her arms and she kicked out behind her, trying to connect and do some damage to her assailant, but missed again. The man got a better grip on her and hauled her back towards him with an evil sounding chuckle, wrapping his thick arms around her and squeezing her lower arms so hard that she felt the bones grind together. With a gasp of pain, Aislynn felt her hands loosen from around her weapons.

"Now, now," someone said from the left. "You don't need those horrible things." The voice was getting closer as the man spoke, and Aislynn tensed, getting ready once again. She really wanted to know how many men she was facing, and she really wanted her weapons back. The man who had spoken picked up her weapons at the same time the man holding her squeezed the breath out of her, preventing her from kicking out at the man in front of her. Aislynn swore under her breath as she looked around the clearing, counting eight men including the one with the broken nose who was glaring daggers at her.

"You haven't been a good little girl, have you?" the leader asked rhetorically as he walked threateningly towards her once more. He was carrying his belt now, and he slapped it repeatedly into his open palm.

"I guess I won't be able to protect you after all. After I'm done with you, I will turn you over to my men, so they can have their revenge for taking their friends away from them." He was in front of her now, and ran his hand down her face and along her cheek in a mockery of a caress. "What a shame."

Aislynn brought her knee up in front of her before the man could move away, catching him in the groin and dropping him to the ground with a groan. A few of his men smirked while he recovered, but quickly made their faces impassive as he slowly got back to his feet. The man holding her tightened his grip.

The blow came quickly and brutally, the folded leather belt catching her in the face, cutting open her cheekbone and sending blood spilling down her face.

"That," the man hissed, "was for me."

He brought his hand back and swung again, this time hitting Aislynn in the temple and sending her staggering. Except for the hands holding her upright, she would have fallen to the ground.

"That was for the men you killed. And this is for not being a good little girl."

The belt whipped forward on more time, striking her across her face again, and cutting her lip open. She knew that there was no way she could take on all eight of them and survive, but Aislynn promised herself that she would kill that one man, the leader, even if it killed her.

"What a shame," the man reiterated.

"What are we going to do with her?" one of his followers asked. "There's somebody else with her, since there are two tents and two sets of bags."

"We'll take her with us."

With a gesture from their leader, the man holding Aislynn pushed her roughly to the ground. He crossed her arms behind her and pushed her shoulders into the ground, pinning her firmly. She couldn't get any leverage to get herself back up off the ground, so all she could do was kick out at anyone who tried to approach her.

As long as they couldn't reach her, she'd be safe, she figured, but part of her knew that she was lying to herself. She needed Byron or Cheta, and needed them now, but she suspected that they were both out of range of a scream. Aislynn screamed anyway, but that just got her face pushed into the grass while one of the men tied her hands roughly. Her captors hauled her roughly to her feet, and Aislynn took a deep breath and screamed again. The man holding her arms smacked her hard in the side of the head, sending her stumbling and cutting off the noise. The hit was hard enough to rattle her, and she stopped struggling for a moment.

"That's better," the leader commented as he walked towards her. "But I don't trust you." The full weight of his body pressed against her, and she could feel his hot breathe against her ear as he spoke.

"I'm going to enjoy this, and it's going to be as unpleasant as possible for you." He drew his sword, reversed his grip and slammed the pommel of the weapon into her temple. Aislynn crumpled immediately, the world going black.

Chapter 16

"You don't understand! This is something that I need to do."

Branden was angry, and getting angrier the longer he had to pace the floor of the suite. Marja sat on the couch, staring up at him with her big blue eyes rimmed with tears. Normally, he would have caved to her wishes, but this was simply too important to him.

"You have no idea what it's like, being trapped here with nothing to do, no reason to be here at all."

"Oh Branden!" Marja cried. "How could you say that?"

Branden sighed and settled down onto the couch next to his fiancée, the anger draining out of him at the depth of her distress. He reached up to brush her hair back from her face, and his action turned into a gentle caress.

"Look," he started, trying to explain. "I love being here with you, and I love you dearly, but I feel so…useless. I spent my entire life training for one specific purpose, and now that I don't have that, I feel unnecessary. I have to do something, and I'm a fair hand with a sword. Helping to fight off the invaders in the city the other night felt so right, and this is just the next logical step. Can't you understand that?"

When Branden had come to her this morning, a conversation about him leaving her a few short weeks before their wedding was not what she had anticipated. Marja knew that she was being a little selfish, wanting to keep him here with her, but she had already lost Aislynn and she felt very alone.

"Yes, I can understand the feeling of not being needed. I feel that way a lot." Marja sighed and laid her head on Branden's shoulder, snuggling closer. "But if this is something that means so much to you, then you have to do it," she said finally.

Branden leaned over and kissed her. "Thank you," was all that he said, and he stood up and left Marja alone in the suite once more. He'd have gone anyway, but it was easier to have her agreement, even if it was a little forced.

He set out from the castle on foot, having decided that if he walked all the way to his destination, then he would truly have the time to think things over. He wanted to be sure that he was making the right decision and that he was making it for the right reasons, and not just because he was feeling bored.

It was still quite early in the morning, and the air had a bit of a chill to it, especially in the shadows cast by the mountain range. As he walked, Branden looked around the city that was his home and was startled to notice that some of the trees were already starting to drop their leaves. It was shocking to think that fall would really be here soon, along with his wedding date. If he did this, if he left, would he be back in time for that? Would he come back at all?

Branden shook his head to clear away such negative thoughts, and told himself that the risk was worth it. To feel useful again… that would be worth almost anything.

Two very distinct camps currently occupied the plateau below the city. One, where Lord Warren had his men, was teeming with activity as the men exercised the horses, broke camp preparing to move to the border, and generally went about their daily routines. The other, where Petyr had stationed his men, was lifeless by comparison. Petyr had called his men to attention, and they had lined up as if for an inspection. Branden walked up to that camp in time to catch part of the conversation.

"Is it true that we're finally getting a real chance to strike back?" one of the men wanted to know.

Petyr paused and took a deep breath before answering the question. He hated that circumstances had forced his men to disobey commands in order to take what little action they had so far during this conflict.

"Yes, it's true," he told them. "The king was wounded in the attack on the city and castle, the attack that we were not here to help prevent, just like with all those villages. We can finally make amends for being too late, and that is why I've called you all here now.

"You have had a full day of rest, and you all look the better for it. Now it's time to get back into action, to take our revenge. Some of you will be accompanying me back across the border. Our mission is to scout the land, which we know best thanks to our illegitimate activities, and send information back to his Majesty and the rest of the army so that they can find the best possible place for the attack that's coming.

"Others will be acting as couriers, passing word of the order to fall back to the rally point at the border to the various commands currently deployed along the front. Finally, those of you who are still not fully recovered, you are temporarily assigned to the guard under the command of Lieutenant Owen, to assist in the preparation of the defenses of the city.

"I will take volunteers for the first group now."

It was a rousing speech, and Branden could see that Petyr's men were heartened by the idea that they could do something to help turn the tide of battle. He knew that these men were in no way to blame for the attack that had wounded Eryk, but if their commander felt that playing on their honor would encourage them to greater feats of valor, who was he to argue with that?

As if to prove this point, Petyr's call for volunteers resulted in far more men than he needed for the assignment. Every able-bodied man had stepped forward, and now Petyr would have to choose the sixteen best suited for the job from among them. It was just as he was about to start calling out names that Branded stepped forward.

"Commander," he called. "Could I possibly have a word with you?" He knew for certain that this was what he needed to do.

Petyr turned towards him, startled by the unexpected voice.

"Certainly, my Lord," he answered, stepping back from his men for a moment.

When the two of them had walked a short distance away from the gathered men, Branden spoke up.

"I'll get right to the point," he stated, "since I know that you're a very busy man, especially right now. I was hoping that you would accept me into your command. I'd like to come with you."

Petyr stopped and stared at Branden.

"My Lord, are you sure that's a good idea? I mean, you must have duties here that you would be leaving behind you." Petyr looked Branden up and down, and Branden had to admit to himself that he certainly didn't look like much of a solider right now. He was dressed in one of his finest silk shirts, decorated with subtle embroidery along the cuffs and collar, and the scabbard that held his sword was accented with gilded thread.

"I assure you Commander, I am more than capable of using this weapon, and I do not have any duties that I could not leave behind."

Petyr nodded his acceptance of that statement. He knew that Branden was currently at loose ends, having kept up with the court gossip as best he could. Petyr didn't know exactly why Branden was no longer Eryk's chief advisor, but he did know that Aislynn now filled that role.

"Well, my Lord, if you are that eager to try and get yourself killed, you are by all means welcome in my command. I have good men here, as you can see, and I think that you should be able to hold your own."

Branden actually felt a surge of joy at Petyr's acceptance of him, and wondered at it. Was he truly that desperate to belong? What was he trying to prove? He just hoped that he'd be able to find the answers that he was apparently looking for without getting himself killed in the process. Marja would never forgive him for that, and he certainly didn't want to break her heart.

"I will finish assigning my men their tasks," Petyr continued, "while you go back up to the castle and prepare your things. We are hoping to be underway within the hour. The afternoon promises to be hot, and that can make for difficult marching, so the sooner we are off on our way, the farther we will get."

Branden nodded, thanked the man, and headed back up the plateau to pack. He promised himself that he would stop in to see Marja briefly before he left, to say goodbye. Petyr turned back towards his men, who were all waiting patiently at attention for him. They were truly a good bunch of soldiers, and he was proud to be their commanding officer. He knew that they would acquit themselves well, regardless of which task he assigned them. He started with the injured men, since they were the easiest. He told them where to find Owen and then sent them to get their things and head up to the barracks in the castle.

Next, he assigned the men who were going to act as couriers. His command was a foot unit, used to marching for hours on end to get to where they needed to be. Petyr knew that some of his men had never ridden a horse, so for this assignment he picked those that he knew were at least comfortable with the beasts and had been in a saddle before. Warren, in his capacity as commander of the army, had provided him with maps showing the most recent deployment of forces, so his couriers would have some idea of where to find the various commands. The council had written a missive explaining the attack on the castle and the outcome of that attack, explaining that the orders were for the different commands to fall back in an orderly fashion to gather at the border before pushing across for a final attack. Petyr assigned his men, and ordered them to report to Warren for their horses and any specific last minute orders. Then he turned to the fifteen men remaining in front of him.

"You men have been selected to accompany myself and Lord Branden on what is likely going to be a very dangerous assignment. We will be crossing the border into enemy territory, wearing the uniforms of the men who carried out the attack on the castle. I have a copy of the missive the council has written, which we will say we took from a Bacovian courier that we captured and killed, in the event that the enemy finds us. The ideal outcome here is for us to cross the border around the area we know has recently seen enemy activity. We'll split up into smaller groups to scout the area, trying to find a good place for his Majesty to set up his camp, as well as any information we can get on the Madelian army."

Petyr paused, looking at the somber faces of his men. He could tell that they understood the gravity of their mission, and he was confident that they would accomplish their task.

"It is imperative that we do everything we can to find information for his Majesty. Go, get your things organized, and be back here and ready to march within the hour."

Branden rushed back up through the city, into the castle and up the stairs to his suite, taking the steps two at a time. He was anxious to leave this place now, eager to see battle. He hurried into his bedroom, threw open his wardrobe and started to rummage through his things. He already had his sword, and he switched the scabbard to a plainer, more practical one. He knew that they would be walking, so he didn't worry about taking anything that would be necessary for riding, concentrating instead on finding his most comfortable boots. Clothing flew through the air, landing on the bed, and was followed shortly afterwards by a pack. Branden packed only the most practical things, making sure to stuff some heavier clothing into the bottom of the pack since the weather was beginning to turn colder.

The last thing he did was change his clothing, dressing in a more appropriate outfit consisting of a light cotton shirt and heavier cotton pants. He pulled on his boots, belted his sword back around his waist, and grabbed his pack. It had taken him less then fifteen minutes to pack up his belongings.

As Branden left his suite for what could be the last time, he was surprised to find that he wasn't sad by the action. Regardless of the outcome of his current plan, he was not destined to remain here in the castle anyway. If things went as planned, after his wedding he'd be moving into his family's empty house in the city with his new bride, which was something that he was looking forward to.

He knew that it would be truly unkind to leave without saying goodbye to Marja, so his last stop was the suite that she still shared with Aislynn. He knocked on the door, torn between wanting her to answer it and hoping that she wouldn't.

As soon as she opened the door, it was obvious to Branden that Marja had been crying, and his heart contracted at the thought of causing her this much pain. Her blue eyes were red-rimmed and her blond curly hair slightly disheveled, but she was still so beautiful, he thought.

"I have to go," he said, not asking her to let him into the room. She stepped aside anyway, and taking his hand, drew him over the threshold.

"Are you sure? Are you positive that you need to do this? Why can't you just be happy here?" Marja demanded.

Branden didn't answer, having been over all of this already this morning. He started to regret having come to say his goodbyes after all. He took Marja's face in his hands and tilted it up so that he looked down at her.

"I will be back," he promised. "It is important that we end this war, and I'm going to do my part to make it happen. But I will be back, and so will Aislynn." Branden knew that at least some of this sorrow was for her friend and not for him.

"You had better not be late for the wedding," Marja threatened, drying her tears one last time. "You don't want to start your marriage by making your bride furious. It's not healthy for the relationship."

"I won't be late," Branden said with a smile. He knew that she would be okay, safe here in the castle, and that was all he really needed to know.

"Will you be saying goodbye to Eryk?" Marja wanted to know.

"No," he said, shaking his head. "He's still recovering from his injuries, so there's a good chance he's sleeping, and I'm not sure that he'd be as understanding as you are being." Branden wasn't sure if that last was true or not, but he still didn't want to face Eryk. If Eryk asked him to stay, his resolve may very well waiver. He loved Marja, but Eryk was his king and still his best friend.

"I have to go," Branden said again, and he leaned down quickly to give Marja a kiss. "I'll be back as soon as I can."

Marja watched him walk out of the door, and wondered how long it would be until he walked back across her threshold. She was going to miss him horribly, the way she missed Aislynn but for entirely different reasons. She laughed mirthlessly to herself and turned away, not wanting to think about the fact that it was possible that neither of them would make it back to her.

Branden hurried back down to where Petyr and his fifteen handpicked men were waiting. There was nothing left of their camp, with all of the soldiers having been redistributed along with their gear. He walked up to Petyr, gave a sharp salute that the commander acknowledged with a nod of his head, and Branden fell into place with the others.

"Okay men, here we go. Our goal is to make it to the border by the end of tomorrow, so we're going to have to push ourselves the entire way. We are going to try to avoid any conflict until we reach our goal, so our path will take us through some of the territory that we have already seen."

Branden decided that he liked Petyr, and knew that he would be able to follow the man's orders without any trouble. He spoke succinctly, took care of his men, and used his resources wisely. The commander was definitely someone Branden could trust with his life.

Petyr called Branden up to walk beside him as the group set out.

"Have you been privy to any of the most recent discussions at the castle?" he asked, wondering how well informed Branden had kept himself once he no longer held a position of power. Branden nodded, and just kept walking.

"How goes the rest of the plan?"

"I know that the two who were heading across the border left at noon yesterday, and have likely crossed already since they went by horseback. They should reach their destination sometime within the next two or three days, and will hopefully meet up with the army within the week.

"Lord Warren and his men are scheduled to be off the plateau by the end of the day, taking up their new position at the border within the next day or so, and your couriers will be gone by the late afternoon. It is expected that units will start to arrive at the rally point within two days, but everyone won't get there for at least five days."

"So we have two or three days before our army will be at the border to receive reports. That's good to know."

Petyr fell silent, and Branden suspected that he was running through plans and scenarios in his head, trying to determine the best way to accomplish their task in the time allotted.

This was definitely someone that he could trust.

Chapter 17

Byron was just reeling in his third fish when he heard a wolf howl. There were plenty of wolves here in the forest, but there was only one that he knew of that would be howling in the late afternoon. He jumped to his feet, grabbed his sword, and set off back along the river at a dead run.

When he burst back into the clearing where he and Aislynn had decided to camp, he wanted to be sick at the sight that greeted him. There was blood splashed across the tents, Aislynn's clothes were scattered across the ground, there were five dead bodies, and no sign of the princess. Cheta was prowling around the clearing, fury evident in every movement and sound she made, and the horses were going wild with the scent of blood so thick in the air.

Byron wasted no time, immediately starting around the edge of the campsite looking for tracks. He tried not to glance back into the camp, tried not to guess how much blood was Aislynn's, determined to keep his focus on the task at hand before dealing with the aftermath. And the task at hand was to find the princess and then kill each and every Madelian soldier in the vicinity.

Cheta starting sniffing around the clearing too, and when Byron noticed what she was doing, he paused. The wolf's nose was far better at tracking than he would ever be, so he just calmed the horses down while he waited. It didn't take long for her to find the trail that led away from the camp, but the way the wolf tracked her companion's scent confused Byron. Instead of sniffing along the ground, Cheta would pause every now and then and sniff at trees and bushes instead. Soon, the captain deduced that Aislynn had been carried away from the camp, and he didn't know if that was reassuring or not. She had likely still been alive when she'd been carried away, because there was no reason to haul a dead body, but why carry the prisoner instead of making her walk by herself? The implications made Byron's stomach clench in fear.

"Eryk is going to kill me," he muttered to himself as he slipped along the nearly invisible path the wolf was currently following.

The Madelians had the advantage here. They knew the terrain, they had a base camp to get back to, and who knew how many men waiting for them there. Byron had only Cheta, and while they were both motivated, common sense dictated that they move carefully and slowly, trying to avoid detection. Given their caution, it was well past twilight when the pair finally saw the glow of a campfire up ahead, and straining, Byron could make out the sound of voices.

Dropping into a crouch, Byron followed Cheta as she slinked silently through the undergrowth towards the camp. Again, he thought to himself how grateful he was to have the *eesprid* at his side. He'd never have found the camp without her, and Byron prayed that they weren't too late. It was obvious as they approached that the men were not expecting pursuit of any kind, and there was no sign of a sentry. Their mistake was going to be their downfall, Byron vowed.

As he approached the last bit of shielding foliage, he was finally able to view the camp. Five tents surrounded the central campfire, each big enough for three men. Quick calculations told Byron that there could be as many as ten soldiers in the camp, assuming Aislynn's five were the only casualties and that all the tents had started out full. Ten against one, two if he counted Cheta, were not odds that he liked.

Before he could stop her, Cheta started to edge around the clearing, belly low to the ground and still staying hidden from view. He followed her path with his eyes and drew in a shocked gasp when he saw what had caught the wolf's attention. Lying in a boneless heap near the forest was Aislynn. The flickering light from the fire showed that her shift was torn and stained, and what little he could see of her from where he crouched looked bruised. The princess looked like a doll that had been played with until it broke and then discarded because it wasn't fun anymore.

The soldiers didn't know what hit them. One moment they were sitting around the campfire sharing a meal, and the next thing they knew, there was some feral beast wrecking havoc among them. Then, to make matters worse, this man wielding a sword comes rushing out of the woods and starts slaughtering them where they sat.

Within minutes of Byron's arrival, he had two bodies on the ground, and Cheta had just finished tearing the throat from a third. The men scrambled to their feet, reaching for weapons and trying to appear like some sort of orderly military unit, but neither of their opponents gave them that chance. With a growl almost as ferocious as Cheta's, Byron advanced on the remaining men, sword held at the ready.

He feinted to the left and then slashed the sword up to the right on the diagonal, slicing his victim open from hip to sternum. Byron spun away from that man to the next just as Cheta lunged at the vermin. Cheta's weight knocked the man off balance, and as he staggered forward, Byron brought his sword up, impaling him and killing him quickly. With a twist of his wrist, Byron slid the body off his weapon and onto the ground, and then he looked around quickly for his next target.

Movement to his right showed the previously unseen sentry running into camp from wherever he had been, and Byron and Cheta were quick to attack the four men in front of them before the newcomer could join in. With a growl and a lot of snapping teeth, the *eesprid* drove one of the men backwards until he tripped over one of the guy ropes holding a tent in place. As he went down in a ball of flailing arms and legs, Cheta leaped on him, going for his throat.

Byron was too busy with the two opponents near him to worry much about what the wolf was doing. These soldiers had their weapons drawn and wouldn't be caught unprepared. Byron knew that there were two others around here somewhere, out of the line of his peripheral vision, and he plunged ahead while hoping he wasn't about to be stabbed from behind. His forward rush set the two men ahead of him back on their heels just a little, and instead of pressing his advantage, the captain reached down to grab another weapon from one of the bodies. While fighting two-handed wasn't his preferred method of combat, having two weapons where there were two foes just made sense.

As he stepped forward to attack, there came a whistle of air from slightly behind him. Byron threw himself sideways to the ground in order to avoid the incoming attack, and as he rolled over quickly, losing his extra sword in the process, he caught a glimpse of Cheta sailing over the spot where he'd just been standing. She crashed into the man who had tried to stab him in the back, sending him sprawling, but Byron's attention was back on his own attackers before he saw what Cheta did to the man.

Before he could regain his feet, the two men Byron had been about to attack were on him. He'd had some practice fighting while prone during his sparring sessions with Aislynn, but the tricky combat was not something he was very good at. He brought his sword up in front of him to block a descending cut and kicked out at the same time, hoping to drive one of his attackers back. Byron managed to parry the attack, but he missed with his kick, and the move had him slightly overextended and unable to attack again for a few moments. His opponents seemed to sense his greater disadvantage and advanced a little closer.

The campfire was crackling nearby, the light throwing odd shadows on his attackers, and the whole thing gave Byron an idea. He threw his sword up and out, a desperate attack that likely wasn't going to hit anything, but it did drive the two men back a little bit, giving Byron time to roll towards the sound of the fire. Two quick turns and he was close enough to grab a flaming stick, tossing it towards the men pursuing him.

One man jumped back from the fiery brand, and he landed off balance, something that Cheta took advantage of as she bowled him over. Byron used the momentary pause to get his feet back under him, and as his single attacker advanced, the captain lunged forward to meet him. With his sword extended, Byron flicked his wrist up and to the left, a quick slash of his blade. His opponent parried easily, sending Byron's sword down and to the right, and then he returned the attack with one of his own, cutting across in an attempt to take Byron across the throat.

It wasn't often that Byron was happy to be shorter than most other men were, but this was one of the few times that his height was an advantage. He ducked easily below the somewhat clumsy attack, not bothering to parry it at all, and then he drove the point of his sword straight ahead and into his enemy's knee. The man screamed in pain, and as he flailed around a little, Byron stood, slipped inside his guard, and ended the combat with a quick stab to the man's chest. Then he paused and looked around, trying to count the casualties. There should have been ten of them, and he could only account for nine; the sentry was missing.

Standing still and breathing heavily, Byron tried to still his breathing in order to make out any sounds that his missing foe might be making. Cheta had paused too, and as she looked round, the light of the fire showed her blood soaked muzzle clearly for an instant, making the *eesprid* appear more like a demon than a wolf. Then suddenly she was off like a flash, pursuing something she heard in the forest, and a man's screams soon confirmed that Cheta was dealing with the missing sentry.

Despite all of the bodies scattered around the campsite, Byron's gaze found only one, the one dressed in what used to be a white cotton shift. He walked quickly towards her, and crouched down to assess the damage. She was badly beaten but alive, though he had a feeling that she wouldn't want to be when she came to. There was a lot of blood – on her face, her chest and her legs. It was unfortunately obvious what the men had been doing before they grew tired of her, and it was evident that she'd fought back. Aislynn's hands were covered in defensive scratches and bruises.

Byron wrapped Aislynn tenderly in a blanket that was lying on the ground nearby, and searched the camp for water and a cloth of some sort. Better to get her cleaned up now, before she woke up, he decided. He'd take care of the rest of the mess after he took care of her and worry about their own camp and belongings tomorrow.

Aislynn came awake with a stifled groan. Part of her wanted to remain quiet, still pretending to be unconscious, until she knew exactly what the situation was. Anything could have happened after she'd been knocked unconscious the second time, and she didn't want to alert her captors, just in case. Unfortunately, the aches and pains she woke up to prevented her from remaining very silent.

Remembering the lessons taught to her in the Academy, Aislynn started a self-examination. She started at her feet and worked her way up to her head, flexing each muscle and testing each bone and joint with tiny little movements. She realized immediately that she was wrapped in a blanket and that she wasn't wearing anything. That couldn't be good.

Her check revealed what was likely a good number of bruises, but she wouldn't be sure until she looked. She was sore in places she didn't want to think about, so she pushed that thought out of her mind, and thought instead about the fact that nothing seemed to be broken. Her face was also very sore, especially her cheek, and she suspected that she wasn't a very pretty sight right now. She had only the barest recollections of what had happened, fuzzy memories that seemed more like dreams than reality.

Now Aislynn expanded her awareness out from herself, trying to get the feel for her immediate surroundings. She could hear the crackle of a fire nearby, and she felt warmth on her face. She also felt warmth at her back, and now that she was paying attention, she realized that it was Cheta behind her.

Aislynn immediately relaxed and tried to sit up, but the movement evoked such a bout of nausea that she gasped loudly. Byron was there immediately, helping her to sit up and being very careful to ensure that he wound the blanket tightly around her. Unable to help herself, Aislynn flinched away from his touch, gentle as it was.

"Take it easy there," Byron's voice said quietly. He tried not to be offended by the way she twitched away from him, but it was hard and it hurt him to see her do it. "You took a few hits to the head, and I'm pretty sure that you've got a concussion, so move slowly."

Once Aislynn was upright and settled, she tried to look around at the clearing and camp. It was at that point that she actually registered that one eye was swollen shut, and her resulting grimace pulled at her cut and swollen lip, making her gasp in pain once again.

"Oh Aislynn," Byron said sadly, settling beside her but being oh so careful not to touch her again. "I'm so, so sorry. I shouldn't have left you alone."

"Bull," Aislynn retorted. "You couldn't have known that they were there, and I should have remained hidden instead of attacking the five of them. If I hadn't been so cocky, they likely wouldn't have found me. It's definitely not your fault."

"But I should have known better," he maintained. "This is a war zone for crying out loud, and I know what soldiers are like. Rape, looting and destruction are the perks of the job, so I should have known, damn it!" Despite what Aislynn was saying, it was obvious that Byron blamed himself.

"You have no control over the way other people act, Byron, so stop being stupid."

"Eryk sent me to help protect you, and the first thing I do is get you…" He trailed off. "When he finds out, he'll never trust me again."

"Eryk is NOT going to find out about this, Byron. I don't want any word of this breathed to him, ever." Aislynn was adamant.

"Aislynn, he's got to know," Byron protested. "You're going to marry him, and a husband has the right to know. Especially if there's a chance of… long term complications."

Aislynn turned her head slowly to avoid making herself sick and looked him right in the eye.

"Byron, if you love me, if you have ever loved me, you will never, ever tell anyone what happened here. And I'll make sure I see Michael when we get back to ensure that there are no 'long term complications', as you put it." She shuddered a little at the thought. That would be intolerable.

Byron sighed and shook his head a little.

"You know that I love you," he said, actually saying the words aloud for only the second time since he had met her. "You know that I'll do pretty much anything for you, but I still don't agree."

"You don't have to agree. Now help me up," she ordered.

Byron rose and took her hand, helping Aislynn to stand and steadying her when she stumbled, trying to find her balance against the vertigo she was experiencing. She had let the blanket fall when she stood, and once she was steady on her feet, she looked down at herself with an odd sense of detachment.

Aislynn had bruises on her shoulders, arms and wrists from where she had been held down and hauled about. There were also bruises on her hips and thighs, and she knew that the whole left side of her face and neck was bruised and swollen too.

Not caring that Byron was there and looking at her, Aislynn searched for something to wear, realizing for the first time that they were not in their own camp. Seeing her searching glance, Byron passed her a clean shirt he's managed to find, and she dressed as quickly and carefully as possible. Then she turned to survey the rest of the clearing.

In the dark, the bodies looked like an indistinct mound just inside the trees, far enough away from the tents that the scavengers shouldn't bother the humans when they came to feed. Byron had picked up all of the gear that had been scattered during the fight and had tidied the rest of the camp while she had been unconscious.

"Did you kill them all?" Aislynn asked, a touch of malice in her voice.

"Not just me, no," Byron answered, "but between the three of us, we accounted for nineteen of them in total."

"Good."

Aislynn sat back down and shivered in the cool air. Byron lifted the fallen blanket up off the ground, and wrapped it around her once more.

"It wasn't your fault Byron, so you can stop being so solicitous of me," Aislynn stated. She wasn't used to people taking care of her and it made her feel a little uncomfortable.

"I'm still sorry that it happened," he replied.

"There's nothing to be sorry for. It never happened, remember?"

A little while later, Aislynn slept once more, Cheta wrapped protectively around her partner. Byron watched her for a little while, worried, but he knew that Aislynn would have to deal with the aftermath of the attack herself, so he would honor her wishes and not mention it again. Soon after, he lay down beside her and fell into a restless sleep.

Chapter 18

The sun slanting through the trees and landing across her face woke Aislynn from a sleep that had been full of nightmares. Still groggy, part of her wondered if it had all been a horrible dream, but an attempt to stretch ruled that out completely. She felt like she'd been trampled by a herd of horses.

Aislynn sat up slowly, unwrapping herself from her tangled blankets, and quickly realized that she would have to face her injuries and bruises again. Her clothing was soaked with sweat from her agitated sleep, and she needed to get changed before she caught a chill from the cool air.

Byron had apparently retrieved her clothing and her saddlebags sometime after she had fallen asleep, so at least she didn't have to contend with dew-soaked clothing, which would have gotten her nowhere. She sorted through her bags, selected a loose blouse and a pair of dark pants, and stripped off her damp clothing, letting it drop to the ground.

Her bruises were even more horrible now, between having had time to develop fully and the bright light that showed her every stark detail. She was a mottled black and blue from her neck to her knees, and some of the bruises looked distinctly like handprints. Lovely, she thought to herself as she bent down to gather up her clean clothing.

"As much as I would normally enjoy the view," came Byron's dry voice from behind her, "I'd rather prefer not to keep seeing it."

"Oh please," she answered. "It's not like you haven't seen it all before. Besides, I'm too tired to expend the energy on being modest right now."

"You didn't sleep well either, I take it?" he asked, though he knew the answer already from the blue-black bruises under her eyes.

Aislynn just snorted delicately in response to Byron's ridiculous question and finished dressing. Then she searched around for an instant, located the weapons that Byron had also kindly found for her, and belted her sword around her waist.

"I cooked some fish last night, so we can eat it for breakfast and be on our way if you want."

That sounded like an excellent plan to Aislynn, and she said so. She bent quickly to start packing up her few things, and then she went about saddling her horse. The familiar routine of the actions made it easy to keep her promise to herself to forget about the previous day.

True to his word, Byron said nothing to Aislynn about the attack or her bruises, and he pretended not to notice how much it hurt her to mount her horse and settle into the saddle. He knew that she didn't want Eryk to know, but that cut on her cheek was surely going to scar, so he wondered what explanations she was devising for the inevitable questions. It's none of your business, he reminded himself.

"How much farther do you think we have to go?" Aislynn asked, breaking the silence that stretched between them.

"Well, assuming that we don't run into any patrols or other trouble, I think we should be able to reach the city this evening some time."

"Trouble," Aislynn echoed. "We certainly don't need any more of that, now do we?" She laughed mirthlessly, and then sent Cheta on ahead to scout the way for them. It would be good if they were warned of any 'trouble' ahead.

With Cheta's help, Aislynn and Byron were able to push their horses hard that day, determined to reach the city before sundown when the gates would be locked. They were forced to travel in a zigzag pattern as Cheta identified groups of Madelian soldiers in the areas through which they traveled and they detoured around them.

It was late afternoon when the pair reached the edge of the forest.

This was where things would become more difficult, since they now had to move out into the open in order to close the distance to the city. There was a road nearby, just at the edge of their vision, but they were both unsure of whether or not they should take it.

"Why don't we head over towards the road and see what sort of traffic is using it?" Byron suggested. "Then we can try to come up with a plan. No offence Aislynn, but right now, your bruises really draw attention to you. We don't want anyone to remember us, if we can avoid it."

Aislynn grimaced, but she couldn't disagree. She was dressed like a boy, as Marja was fond of saying, and the left side of her face was still very swollen and bruised. It was obvious that she'd been beaten recently. Then, to top it all off, she was wearing a sword.

"In Bacovia, I know that my appearance would definitely draw attention, but Madelia is ruled by a queen, so perhaps the perception of women is different here," she commented hopefully. Byron just looked at her, and she was forced to admit that he was right. No matter where they were, her appearance would cause attention.

They reined their horses back into the cover of the trees, and headed off in the direction of the road, with Cheta scouting ahead, just in case. Aislynn was both eager and frightened to reach the city. She wanted to get this over with and get back home to Eryk so that everything could be normal again, but at the same time she was a little afraid to face him. The longer this assignment took, the longer she would have to figure out what she was going to do and say when she saw him again.

Soon, the trees showed distinct signs of thinning, indicating that the road was near, and they stopped a short distance away. Aislynn swung down out of her saddle, almost as gracefully as usual, and passed her reins to Byron. Then she slunk off through the shadows under the trees, Cheta by her side, to see what lay ahead.

The trees ended suddenly about a foot away from the edge of the road, and Aislynn crouched down out of sight. The road was currently empty, but she could hear voices coming closer.

"So what are we going to do when we get there?" a man's voice drifted towards her.

"I don't know," answered another man. "I guess we'll have to find the market first. We're really lucky that they even have stock this late in the year."

"I hope it's not just leftovers from the spring," the first man said. "All of the best ones get picked up before the nice weather. I'd really like to get a good one for around the house this winter, to help keep the cold away." The second man laughed.

Aislynn looked at Cheta, and together the two of them backed slowly away from the road. Once they were far enough, Aislynn stood and the two of them went back to where Byron waited with the horses.

"There's some sort of market going on," Aislynn said as she approached. "There are two men on the road right now, heading into the city. I don't really understand the references though. The one man said he was hoping to 'buy one to keep the winter cold away'?"

Byron looked at the confused expression on her face and sighed to himself. There were times when Aislynn seemed to be older than her chronological age and other times, like now, when she seemed to be very young and naïve.

"They're talking about a slave market," Byron explained. "The man wants to buy a slave to use to warm his bed throughout the winter."

The look on Aislynn's face was one of pure loathing and revulsion, followed quickly by anger. She turned back towards the road, hand on her sword, determined to kill the men before they could treat anyone like that. She had taken two steps back in the direction she had come before Byron stopped her, his hand on her shoulder.

"You may not approve, but slave-trade is legal here. And it's a perfect in."

"What are you talking about?" Aislynn demanded.

"You. We could pretend that I'm taking you into the city to be sold at the market. You've obviously been beaten, as would any slave who disobeyed her master."

The look of absolute horror that came next made Byron want to take her into his arms and comfort her. Instead, he drew her back towards the horses, keeping a firm grip on her arm.

"We're not actually going to go anywhere near that market, Aislynn, so don't worry. Nothing's going to happen to you. It's just the story we'll use to explain your appearance and get past the guards at the gate. It's logical and isn't likely something that anybody would remember, but we need to hurry."

Byron watched Aislynn mount back up, an unreadable expression clouding her face now, and she passed him her sword. He took it and he turned to mount his own horse. He gathered up Aislynn's reins and tied them around the pommel of his saddle, and then led her horse behind his over to the road. She kept her head down, just staring at her hands, until the change in the light indicated that they were free of the trees.

"Stop a minute," she commanded quietly.

Once Byron had complied, Aislynn slipped down out of the saddle and knelt beside Cheta. Something wordless passed between them while Aislynn ran her hands through the wolf's thick fur, but soon Cheta was bounding away into the forest and Aislynn was back in her saddle.

"What was that all about?" Byron asked.

"She can't exactly come with us into the city, now can she?"

Byron hadn't thought about that aspect of this mission.

"It's up to you to keep me safe now," she added.

"And I've done such a wonderful job of *that* so far, haven't I?" he replied bitterly. Aislynn didn't reply, not feeling up to the argument right now.

They continued along the road for only a short time before they caught up with the men that Aislynn had seen from the trees. The two men on foot moved over to the side of the road to let the horses pass and one of the men noticed that Aislynn's horse was being led.

"Excuse me, good sir," the first man called. "Where are you headed?"

"To the market, of course," Byron replied, contemptuously.

"You selling her?"

"Well obviously, or I wouldn't be going, now would I?" Byron turned his head away, and nudged his horse to increase his speed a little. They quickly pulled ahead of the two men. Aislynn shuddered when she heard the muttered comment that came from behind her.

"Well she looks like a good one for your winter fun."

It took every bit of self control Aislynn had not to jump out of the saddle and strangle the men where they stood. But she had a role to play, and she kept her head bowed and her eyes on the road. It would all be over soon enough.

The guards at the gate asked Byron a few cursory questions and passed the two of them through and into the city without any difficulty. The sun was beginning to set, and Byron headed off in the direction of the market, following the directions the guards had provided, but he turned into a side street as soon as they were out of sight of the gates. Byron threw Aislynn's reins back to her, and the two of them continued up the road until it crossed another main thoroughfare.

"We'll just find ourselves an inn and get a room," Byron said. "Then we can figure out what to do next."

Aislynn just nodded and began to scan the businesses along the road until she found one that suited her. The building she indicated had a sign over the door that sported what looked like a crescent moon attached to a handle – the Crescent Dagger. They rode through the archway and handed their reins to the groom on duty before grabbing their bags and entering the building.

The main room of the inn was nearly empty as Byron slid into a chair opposite Aislynn. He signaled for breakfast to be brought over to them and when it arrived, he dug into it with a vengeance.

"Hungry?" Aislynn asked with a smile on her lips.

"Definitely. Aren't you?" Byron raised his head and watched Aislynn push her food around with her fork. Her face was looking better today, he noticed. The bruises were already fading into that lovely yellow color. She'd always been a fast healer, he knew.

"What's wrong?" he asked.

"Nothing. I'm fine."

"Liar."

Byron knew that there wasn't any point trying to get her to talk about what she was feeling, so he changed the subject.

"Why are we up before the crack of dawn?" he pondered aloud.

"So that we can take a look around and figure out what we're going to do with ourselves," Aislynn replied. "First thing in the morning is the best time to look around. The streets aren't crowded, and we can move from place to place quickly and efficiently."

"Well let's get started then," Byron said, pushing aside his empty plate and rising from the small table. Aislynn rose quickly to join him, and the two of them left the inn.

Aislynn led the way through the maze of streets towards the centre of the city. There, the pair could see the pale hulk of a building rising above them. The palace that was home to the Madelian queen was constructed of a pale marble, and it shone slightly in the light of the setting moon. From this distance, the walls surrounding the castle looked smooth and featureless, but Aislynn knew that up close they would be pitted and rough enough to climb. Or at least she certainly hoped so.

The front of the building wouldn't provide them with any answers, so Aislynn led the way around to the back. There was a small gate set into the wall here, and a bunch of men were standing around. They were obviously waiting for something.

Byron found a good place for them to watch while hidden, and he pulled Aislynn into the shadows of an alley. There were a number of barrels and boxes near the entrance to the street, and the pair hid behind them. Soon, a wagon full of baskets appeared, rumbling down the quiet, empty street.

"Morning deliveries," Byron commented, nodding towards the wagon.

"Exactly," Aislynn said.

She watched carefully as the waiting men lined up, accepted a basket from the back of the wagon, and turned towards the small castle gate. The gate was opened to let the line of men inside, and then was shut behind them. Less then ten minutes later, based on her slow count, the men reappeared at the gate and they repeated the process.

It took about a half hour, and three trips, for the wagon to be fully unloaded. When the workers returned the final time, this time to the empty wagon, they received their wage and wandered off. Aislynn smiled in satisfaction, pulling Byron out of the alley and back in the direction of the inn.

"You look very proud of yourself," Byron said, looking at the odd smile on Aislynn's face. "I take it that something just went according to plan?"

"Definitely. We just found you a way into the castle."

"You want me to deliver produce?"

Aislynn nodded, still smiling.

"It's perfect. You show up tomorrow morning and wait around with the others. Then, when you carry your load in, you just don't come out again."

Byron shook his head in disbelief.

"Do you honestly think that it would be that simple? I'm sure that there are guards at the gate counting the workers as they come and go, to say nothing of the fact that I will certainly be noticed. Those men have never seen me before."

"I didn't notice anybody talking to each other, so I doubt that they're friends. And I'm sure you're right about the guards. You're just going to have to make sure you're very well hidden so that they don't find you when they search."

"Oh is that all?" Byron asked, rolling his eyes.

By this time, they had reached the inn once more and Aislynn led the way inside and upstairs. They entered their room, and Aislynn immediately started to rummage through her bag. She pulled out a bundle of dark fabric and shook it out, revealing a plain skirt. She slid the skirt on over her pants and then slipped her pants off from underneath, effectively changing her clothing.

"What did you do that for?"

"All of the women here seem to wear skirts, and I don't need to draw any undue attention to myself," she explained. "We still need to find a way to get *me* into the castle."

"Can't you just go over the wall or something?" Byron questioned.

"I could, yes, but then I'd be going in blind. It would be much better if I could find a way into the castle today, so that I can scout around and know the layout of the place before we both go in tomorrow."

"And we'll finish our business tomorrow and be away from this place," Byron stated. Aislynn nodded, just about as eager as he was to head home. There was just that one little thing that she needed to do first.

By the time the pair headed back out into the streets, the crowds were beginning to build as the citizens of the city started their day. Having nowhere in particular to go, Aislynn and Byron followed the crowd, allowing the flow of people to pull them along. It wasn't long before they came to the marketplace.

As was common in a number of cities and larger villages, there was a permanent market where farmers and artisans could sell their wares. Now, at the height of the harvest season, the stalls were full to overflowing with food and goods, and the market was bustling.

Aislynn wandered around, Byron close behind, and they just listened. Any crowd of people was a good place to pick up on local gossip, and conversations were as plentiful as bargains right now. For each merchant making a deal, there was a least one person chatting with a friend about the current news in the city.

"Well I heard that he was dead," Aislynn overheard one woman say to another. "Apparently, the soldiers cut his head off and burned down the city!"

"Well that's not true," her friend replied. "If the city was burned, why would the army be getting ready to go and attack it?"

Aislynn smiled slightly to herself as she moved on to the next conversation.

"Well I don't know about you," one man was saying to another, "but I think she's crazy. Who in their right mind steps up a war in the fall? Winter's just around the corner and she's sending them out? It's crazy."

The man's companion nodded his head in agreement as they walked past her. Aislynn turned to look over her shoulder at Byron, wondering if he had heard the comment. He gave a slight nod of his head before turning to look at the array of belts and buckles on display in the stall beside him.

They continued to wander and eavesdrop on various conversations for most of the morning, not really learning a lot that could help them. They knew that most of the populace wasn't pleased with the idea of advancing the line of the army this close to the first snow, and that bode well for the end result of their plan. If Aislynn could manage to kill the queen, then chances were very good that the war would come to a grinding halt. There wasn't anybody willing to pursue it through the winter.

Unfortunately, they learned absolutely nothing that would help them with their task tomorrow. There was no reason for anyone to discuss the layout of the castle or the normal day-to-day business of the place. There was no mention of an upcoming audience or court session, or anything else that would allow the general citizens access to the palace.

Aislynn was starting to get frustrated and concerned that she would indeed have to go into her mission blind when she and Byron reached the far end of the market. Here, there was a big open area set up and there were a large number of people both in the area and arrayed in front of it. They had found the slave market.

At this particular instant, there was a man walking up and down the line of men, women and children on display. He was wearing what was obviously a uniform, and when he turned around, Aislynn noticed that he bore the winged serpent crest of the Madelian throne on his breast. Suddenly, Aislynn had an idea.

"You have to sell me," she whispered urgently to Byron, who looked at her like she'd suddenly grown an extra head.

"What?" he asked, obviously confused.

"Look! That man there works in the palace, and he's buying slaves. It's a way to get me in. You have to sell me, and you need to be quick about it."

"How can you ask me to do that? I can't do that," he replied, shaking his head. "First, how would I get you out again? And second, they treat slaves like animals, not people. Who knows what they'll do to you?"

"It can't be much worse than what's already happened," she said quietly. "And slaves are invisible too. I could learn a lot, just being inside the castle and invisible to everyone around me. I'm not as worried about getting back out again. That we can deal with when we need to."

Byron continued to stare at her, dumbfounded. Did she honestly have any idea what she was asking him to do?

"Hurry up! He's going to be leaving in a minute, and then we'll have missed our chance. Just give me a few days, let's say three, and then make sure that you get into the castle and stay hidden. We'll find some way to take out the target and get out. Don't worry."

Aislynn sounded so sure of herself that Byron found that he couldn't turn her down, regardless of how crazy the plan seemed to be. With a sigh, he grabbed her by the back of her shirt and started to propel her through the crowd and towards the open area. The man, who had collected four slaves from those who had been presented to him, was just getting ready to leave when Byron came up.

"Excuse me sir!" Byron called. "I have one more for you to consider." He pushed Aislynn, who stumbled and fell to her knees in front of the man. "I see that you're looking for good slaves, and this one is good. She works hard and she's healthy. I'll sell her to you for a good price."

The man in the livery looked at Byron doubtfully.

"If she's as good as you say she is, then why are you selling her?"

Byron grabbed a fistful of Aislynn's hair and yanked her head up. He pushed her hair off of her face, displaying her healing bruises.

"This one needs a firm hand," Byron explained. "I'm a working man myself, and there isn't anyone around to keep as close an eye on her as is needed, that's all. I'm hoping to buy a more docile slave with the money I make off of this one." He let go of her hair, and Aislynn let her head fall back down, staring at the ground in front of her.

The man still looked doubtful, but he decided to take a look at Aislynn anyway. He looked at her calloused hands, her teeth, her eyes and her limbs. The more he checked her over, the more he seemed to relax. Aislynn knew that the deal was as good as done.

"She seems to be as healthy as you claimed, but if she's a troublemaker… Well, I can only pay so much for a slave that will cost me in overseer pay."

"Oh, a good beating here and there, and she'll come around, I'm sure. She's quite strong, and I think that helps to balance out her behavior."

Byron and the man haggled a little over price, and the next thing Aislynn knew, she was being herded into line with the other new palace slaves. As Aislynn was marched off in the direction of the castle, secretly beaming inside, she couldn't help but notice Byron's worried expression. I'll be fine, she thought to herself as she walked by, not looking in his direction again.

The walk was an easy one, and as they passed through the main gate of the castle, Aislynn began to look around surreptitiously. After all, the idea behind this was to gain as much information as possible about the castle layout so that she could plan for the upcoming attack.

The slaves were all herded across the courtyard and down a small alleyway between the castle and a large outbuilding. At the end of the alley was another courtyard, this one considerably smaller than the first. There were buckets of soapy water waiting there, and the five of them, all female, were ordered to strip and clean themselves thoroughly.

Aislynn followed the order without complaint or hesitation. The man who had purchased them wandered back and forth while they cleaned themselves, and he stopped once behind Aislynn.

"Looks like you were used for more than just the cleaning," he muttered quietly to her, noticing her odd bruises, and Aislynn couldn't help but shudder. The man grinned an evil little grin and continued his pacing.

When they were all clean and dry, they were each handed a rough cotton dress to wear. The dress was plain and had no sleeves, and it was tied at the waist with a length of black cotton. It seemed that one size was meant to fit all, so Aislynn's dress was quite short on her, coming up nearly to the knee. That didn't bother her at all though, because it gave her a much wider range of motion and freedom of movement.

Finally, the five new slaves were herded together again, and led farther into the castle grounds. When they reached an area just behind the kitchens, they were ordered to stop again and line up against the wall. As Aislynn did as she was told, she noticed a fire pit in the middle of the area, with what looked like a piece of metal lying in the smoldering embers. A sick feeling began to form in her stomach.

The man picked up the metal rod, drawing it out of the pit, and he advanced towards the first woman in line. Two nearby guards stepped forward and took hold of the woman, holding her still. She wasn't able to move, but she was certainly able to scream, and the scream she uttered when the brand touched the skin of her arm was enough to make glass shatter.

Aislynn swallowed hard, suddenly having second thoughts about her plan, but it was far too late now. As the next slave in line was branded, a small voice in her head gave a mocking laugh. It looks like you're starting a collection, the voice said. First a birthmark in the shape of the Bacovian royal seal, and now a brand in the shape of the Madelian one! Eryk was going to owe her for this…

Aislynn braced herself as the guards held her, determined not to scream. She'd done enough screaming in these past couple of days, she decided. Besides, she thought, it can't be worse than the pain she'd felt when the pact had chosen her to leave her home to become Eryk's bodyguard, sending a burning pain down her arm as her birthmark had flared into visibility again. She was wrong, on both counts, and she screamed as loudly as any of the others.

She had little time to recover herself, as the slaves were immediately led into the castle through the kitchen door. The kitchen was busy and full of people going about their various tasks, but one particularly nasty looking man stepped out of the crowd to greet the man in uniform. He had short black hair and beady dark brown eyes, and he looked the slaves over with obvious interest.

"Here's your new batch," the uniformed man said. "Be careful with the tall one. Her former owner said that she could be a bit of a handful, but that she's a good worker." The nasty looking man nodded, and turned to face the five of them.

"Now listen up," their overseer said, "and listen well. Your job is a simple one. Do what I tell you, when I tell you, and we'll get along just fine. If you do not do what you are told, you will be beaten. If you disobey again, you will not be fed. If you disobey a third time, you will be killed."

Aislynn stood very still and looked at the floor like a good little slave. As long as this man didn't lay a hand on her, she and he would get along just fine, but she wouldn't guarantee that her temper would let him beat her.

They were assigned their first tasks, and Aislynn was sent off with three other slaves to scrub floors. She went about her job without any complaint or issue, working silently and quickly, making sure there was no need for anyone to complain about her work. She had to fit in to become invisible, and until she had proven that she could be trusted to do her work, she would be watched too closely to accomplish her goals.

By the end of the day, when all of the slaves were herded into their little locked rooms, Aislynn had seen most of the castle. She knew where the stairs leading up to the suites were, and she knew where all of the important rooms in the castle were located. She had also heard that Vivien used the anteroom of her suite as a council chamber and small court, so Aislynn knew the most likely place to find her target when the time came in three days.

Now she just needed for Byron to show up on time, find somewhere to hide inside the castle and escape detection. Then she needed to get free of whoever was with her at the time, find Byron, locate Vivien and kill her. Finally, the two of them needed to escape the castle alive.

No problem.

Chapter 19

Branden was sweating under the glaring noonday sun, desperately trying to maintain his place in the formation. He'd thought that he was in good shape, but the marching these past two days had proven how wrong he was. And this morning, he had done no better.

The men who walked in the formation with him pretended not to notice his difficulties, helping him to maintain his pride, at least a little. But despite the problems, Branden was still sure that this was where he was meant to be, and he vowed silently to himself that he would endure. It was a promise he made about every two hours.

Finally, in the shade of a large stand of trees, Petyr called a halt so that the men could eat their noon meal. Branden practically crumpled to the ground, his knees weak with exhaustion, and it took him a few moments to even get up the energy he needed to eat. Someone passed him a canteen of water, and he drank deeply before passing it on to the man next to him.

"Well men, this is it," Petyr stated, gathering the gazes of his soldiers. "We are well across the border now, and should be able to split up and start scouting after the meal. You've all got the story straight, right?"

There were nods all around the group. Petyr and Branden had drilled them all with the details of the story of the attack on the castle and their supposed purpose here across the border, and any of the men could have recited the story in their sleep. That was a very good thing. And since it was entirely possible that members of this group could be captured and questioned individually, they had even prepared individually tailored stories to go along with the various thrusts of the attack. If all else failed, they wanted to appear as Madelian soldiers on their way back to rejoin the army.

Petyr's small command had been following the trail of a Madelian raiding party for the past day and a half. It had initially seemed strange to Branden that Petyr had known exactly where to go to find a trail, but one of the men in the group had noticed his confusion and explained everything to him.

"We've been seeing these trails ever since we were assigned to this area," the solider, Petyr's lieutenant Anders, commented.

"At the beginning, the Madelians were sneaky with what they did. They would slip across the border at night, wreak some destruction, and slip back. We had some good trackers and could have pursued them, but our orders explicitly stated that we were not to follow the enemy across the border.

"Once they realized that they weren't going to be punished for their actions, the buggers became bolder. They would still attack mostly at night, when the villagers were easier to subdue, but they started taking livestock and other useful things with them when they fled. The trails they left were plainer than day, and still we weren't allowed to pursue them, though we did, on occasion.

"Over and over again, we arrived too late to help the villagers and we could do nothing but bury the bodies. It was almost as if they knew where we were going to be and would attack somewhere else. The Commander would get so frustrated, and we were some pissed off too."

Branden couldn't understand the logic behind the decision not to pursue the Madelian raiders, but he hoped the reasoning was sound. He could only imagine what these men had been through, and they were all so eager to be finally able to take some revenge.

The break was over far too soon, and Branden found himself back in his spot in the formation, walking along the road towards who knew what. Or perhaps plodding along was a better description. They could see a rise in the road ahead, and Petyr wanted them to stop there to break up into their smaller scouting groups. It was less then half an hour later that the group topped the rise and all thoughts of being tired fled from Branden's mind.

There, laid out below them in a large mountain valley, was the assembled force of Madelia in all its splendor. One of the men in the group let out a low whistle, impressed by the view.

"Well," Petyr said, "this changes things a little, doesn't it?"

The force arrayed in the valley was at least half again larger than the Bacovians had suspected. There was a group of command tents in the middle of the mass of men below, and it looked like seven companies, each broken into nine commands, were organized around those tents. Everything was neatly organized, and despite the initial appearance of chaos, it soon became obvious that things were actually totally under control.

"Well we know where they are now, don't we?" somebody asked.

Branden just shook his head in disbelief. Just like that, their mission was over and they'd found what they were looking for. Now they just needed to get the information back to their own army.

"We shouldn't have anybody on this side of the border yet," Petyr commented, "but the army should be massing just on the other side by now. The question becomes whether or not we all head back or if we just send a couple of runners."

The commander signaled for them to fall back. They wanted to be farther up the road and out of sight of anybody keeping watch from the camp before they settled down for a discussion about the tactics appropriate for this situation. Soon, the seventeen men were huddled in a copse of trees, hidden from sight and trying to be quiet while the pros and cons of both plans were tossed back and forth.

"We might as well all head back to the border," one of the soldiers argued. "What's the point of having anyone stay here? It just increases the likelihood that they'll catch one of us. I know that this is a dangerous mission, we all know that, but why tempt fate?"

"Moving as a group is more likely to get us all caught and killed," commented another man. "It's harder to hide a group, and it's just luck that nobody has found us yet. Who would have thought that the whole army was so close to the border?"

The discussion continued for a little while longer while Petyr weighed his options. He agreed that it was dangerous for the men to stay where they were, and he agreed that smaller groups were easier to move secretly. Finally, he called his men to order and laid out the revised plan.

"We're all going to head back to the border," the commander stated, "but we're going to go in small groups of two and three. That way, we can split up and have a better chance of getting the information to his Majesty, and we'll all be safer."

Nods greeted his orders, and Petyr started to divide the men. "The first group will head out now, followed by the next in five or ten minutes. We'll all leave from here staggered like that. I want you all to spread out across the countryside to head back, looking for ideal locations for our army to set up their camp. The Madelians are firmly established in the valley over there, and attacking from the higher ground has advantages and disadvantages, given the cavalry. We would like to give his Majesty as many choices as possible."

Once it was time for him to set off again, Branden certainly wasn't feeling tired any longer. He felt his palms grow moist with nervous sweat as he pulled himself to his feet and took a quick look around the area outside of the copse of trees. He was accompanied by Petyr and Anders, and they were about to walk away from the enemy encampment and try to sneak back to the border to pass along their findings. He truly hoped that this went according to plan, because if it didn't, they were all dead.

No sooner had the thought crossed his mind then Branden knew that he was in trouble. The sound of a sword whispering out of its scabbard was the only warning, but Branden had spent a lot of the past two months attacking Eyrk at random times, and he knew the sound intimately. Hand on the hilt of his own sword, Branden was drawing his weapon as he spun around to confront the threat. Anders didn't give Branden the chance to bring his sword to bear, stabbing forward violently with his own weapon and stabbing Branden in the back, just above his kidney.

"You can go ahead and drop your weapon, commander," Anders ordered, turning his head to look at Petyr as Branden slid to the ground, blood flowing rapidly from his wound. Anders made sure that Branden was no longer a threat, and then he brought his sword around and leveled it at Petyr's chest.

Petyr was not about to go down without a fight, and he charged straight for the man he thought was his friend, hoping to catch Anders unprepared while he finished with Branden. Anders was an expert swordsman, however, and he spun around as soon as Branden's weight was free of his blade. Anders was moving the weapon into position to parry Petyr's attack before he'd even set his feet.

Their swords met with a clash, and as his sword rebounded away from the other blade, the commander stepped towards his lieutenant and brought his sword crashing back towards the man. Anders lifted his blade over his head, catching Petyr's weapon and bending his knees to help absorb the force of the blow and then he straightened suddenly, heaving Petyr up and away from him. As Petyr stumbled back a little, Anders was quick to pursue, stabbing forward with his sword and catching the other man along the outside of his arm. Petyr acknowledged the cut with a swift intake of breath, but didn't let the wound slow him, bringing his sword slashing down towards Anders' shoulder.

Anders twisted aside to avoid the strike, guiding his sword towards his enemy as he did so. The blade sliced in towards Petyr, who had his own weapon already engaged in the attack on his traitorous lieutenant, leaving the commander with very few options. Petyr abandoned his attack and dropped down towards the ground to try to get below the slashing sword, but Anders simply corrected his angle to compensate, bringing the blade to a stop just a fraction of an inch away from Petyr's throat.

"Drop the blade," he commanded again.

"Why are you doing this?" Petyr asked, dropping his sword to the ground. "You've been with us for almost a year. Why now?"

"Because we're close enough to home that I can get away with it," Anders replied. He retrieved Petyr's weapon from the ground, and started to march the man back towards the Madelian army.

As the two men entered the encampment, they drew attention from all sides. They were dressed in dusty and torn uniforms, so they had obviously seen either combat or some very rough living, but one man had the other under guard, which was certainly unusual. Was this a disciplinary issue?

Despite the attention, nobody stopped them and they were able to walk right up the middle of the camp to take a position in front of the command tents. When they stopped, Anders called for help in order to secure his prisoner, and then they just waited. It didn't take long for someone to exit the command tent to see what was going on. The man, apparently an aide of some sort, looked Anders up and down with disdain.

"What do you want?" he demanded.

"I have come to report a successful attack and to present a very important prisoner," Anders said with a courteous bow of his head.

"So? Why do you have to report here?"

"The attack was on the castle and King of Bacovia," Anders answered, refusing to be offended by the aide's tone of voice, "and this is one of his army commanders."

The man said nothing, but Petyr noticed his eyes widening at Anders' statement, and he slipped back inside the tent. Moments later, the aide was back and gesturing for them to follow him inside. With a shove, Anders directed Petyr roughly into the tent.

The inside of the command tent was well organized and furnished. It was obvious that the army had been camped here for some time, and the commander of this huge army liked his luxuries. There were rugs covering the ground, solid wooden furniture laid out neatly, and a curtain that separated the front part of the tent from the rear, where the sleeping area would be.

The man seated behind the field desk was surprisingly young, sporting light brown hair and startling green eyes. Petyr decided that the man was only a few years older than he was, and he wondered if it was hard to have this level of responsibility. The man straightened as they entered, pushed aside some papers that he had been reading, and gave the Bacovians his undivided attention.

"So, soldier. My aide informs me that you have some important news."

Anders nodded and stepped forward slightly so that he was just beside his prisoner. He bowed at the waist, but didn't take his eyes off the man seated behind the desk.

"Five days ago, a squad of Madelian soldiers successfully penetrated the defenses of the Bacovian capital. They attacked the castle, with strikes on the barracks, the king and the council members who lived on the premises. They also attacked the council members who lived in the city."

"Oh did they now? And how do you know that?" The man was obviously skeptical.

"We arrived after that battle, and as this man's lieutenant, I have been privy to information about the attack. According to the reports, someone from Madelia managed to make earlier contact with some of the royal guard who were dissatisfied with their current lot in life. It didn't take very much to convince them to help us, and we were able to obtain a map of the castle and the locations of the whereabouts of everyone important."

"And?"

"All three of the council members who were housed in the city were killed and their homes were burned. They also killed a number of the guards, leaving the guard quite weakened, if you also take into account the desertions. Finally, they attacked and wounded the king, who has subsequently started to gather his army for a push across the border, and his target is here."

"Well," said the army commander. "This certainly makes things interesting. So the army is gathering at the border?"

Anders nodded, but saw no reason to comment.

"Well sir, you are to be commended for a job well done. You can join the Fifth Company. They have seen recent losses and could use a good man. Stop by the commissary to commission new uniforms and take your prisoner to the pit."

"Yes sir. Thank you sir."

Anders bowed at the waist, gathered Petyr and then turned and left the tent. He led the commander to an area not far from the command tents, which the soldiers referred to as the pit. There were three tall poles hammered into the ground, and the area around the poles was covered with sand. Anders tied Petyr to one of the poles before taking himself off to wherever the commissary was located.

"That seemed to go well," Petyr said sarcastically to himself, rolling his eyes. "What happens now? Why am I even still alive?"

As the sun was beginning to set, Petyr noticed a commotion just to the east of their location. It looked like a courier was heading out at full speed towards the capital city, and he hoped that whatever the message was, it put a quick end to the misery he was currently experiencing.

By the time the sun rose once more, it was obvious that fall had arrived. Each leaf and blade of grass was turned into a glittering jewel with the frost that had arrived with the dawn, and it was very chilly before the sun was up far enough to warm the air.

Petyr had only slept due to sheer and utter exhaustion, and that had only been a couple of hours in the middle of the night. He was tired, very cold and very sore. The sun was actually a blessing, even though it blinded him as it rose. Petyr had stopped shivering hours ago, his body shutting down, and the sun was likely the only thing that was going to keep him alive through the day.

The main camp was starting to stir all around him, and he knew that he needed to be ready for whatever was coming, but it was difficult to focus. Almost as soon as the sun was fully above the horizon, men started to trickle down from the tents to the large open area to the east of the camp, just beyond the last row of tents.

"Looks like I get to watch some drills," Petyr commented quietly, talking to himself to try to stay alert. "I should be able to gather some pretty valuable intelligence about how the Madelians fight. Not that it's going to do anybody any good," he added bitterly.

As the commander passed the time leaning against his pole and watching the Madelians drill, he actually found the whole process rather fascinating, comparing their techniques to the ones he'd drilled into his own men. The Madelians worked as a team with sword and shield, bows and spears, and it was obvious that these men knew how to fight as a group. That would make them formidable opponents, he knew.

Their company commander kept them busy all morning, and they received only a short midday break to eat and rest. Nobody seemed to have time to even think, let alone talk to each other, so Petyr learned nothing interesting. Their afternoon duties were soon upon them, and the companies that had drilled in the morning left the practice grounds to attend to their camp chores while other companies came down to drill. The practice ground was busy until sunset, and not once did anyone come to speak to the prisoner.

It was quiet for a time as the sun began its decent, the Madelians all eating their evening meal, and Petyr reviewed what little he had learned.

"They are very well prepared. They have discipline and know how to fight effectively. I get the feeling that their hit-and-run tactics have been only to draw us out, meaning to deceive us into thinking that they are less formidable than we are. And we fell for it, didn't we?" he asked himself.

Petyr realized that this army was a much better match for their own army at home than they had ever thought possible. Bacovia had long rested on the laurels of their well-disciplined and effective army, and nobody had ever conceived of one of their enemies being able to accomplish what Bacovia had accomplished. But Madelia *had* accomplished that very feat, and there was no way to warn the people at home.

Chapter 20

"According to the reports I have here, the closest commands started to arrive two days ago, just like they should have." Warren glanced up from the papers in his hands and looked over towards where Eyrk stood at the door of his tent. "Everything seemed to be going smoothly. My men had arrived the day before, so camp was already in the process of getting set up, and the heavy cavalry got here yesterday, with us."

Eryk had to admit to himself that it was somewhat comforting to have an army between him and the enemy army he knew couldn't be far away. It was hard to imagine that if everything went as planned, he would be crossing the border very soon, and then Madelia would be playing host to the dead and dying. War was a horrible thing.

"You haven't summoned the whole army here, have you?" Warren asked, walking up behind the king and startling Eryk out of his reflections.

"Of course not," Eryk answered, throwing Warren a look of disbelief. "The commands I summoned are only those who were closest to this area of the border. By now, about half of our expected units should be here, collapsing in entirely from around this section of the border, and any of the army that isn't from around here has orders to remain where it is. We'll end up with about one third of the whole army, once everyone is assembled."

"Are you sure that this plan is a good idea?"

"No," Eryk admitted, "but what else can we do? We've been totally unable to engage with the Madelian army in any way that matters. Every now and then, we'll chance upon a unit, but for the most part they just fade away like smoke whenever we get near them. This is the only way to draw them into a real battle."

Eryk turned away from the door suddenly, forcing Warren back a step.

"What do you want from me?" Eryk demanded, suddenly angry. "You've done nothing but ask uncomfortable questions for the past five days. Are you my conscious or something? That little voice in my head that you seem to think I've been ignoring?"

"What do you mean?" Warren asked in reply, backing away even farther from the irate king. "I wouldn't even begin to question your judgment."

"Oh no? Then why the questions about what I'm doing and why I'm doing it? Why are you so very interested in everything I'm thinking?" Eryk took another step, advancing towards Warren with a dangerous look in his eye.

"I have had my fair share of traitors in this court since I took the throne. I have been attacked four times in three months, not including the attacks my guards spring on me from time to time to make sure I'm paying attention to what's going on around me. I have had a man tortured to get information, and I've hanged others for not giving me the information I wanted. I have sent the woman I love into a foreign and hostile country to assassinate their ruler to end this war, and I'm about to lead my army across the border to make sure that the blow is decisive. Do you honestly think that I need someone playing my conscious? Do you think, for even one second, that I haven't thought about each and every action that I have taken until I can't sleep properly anymore?"

Warren had his hands up now, as if to ward off an attack, and he was still backing away. He had never seen Eryk like this before, and he wondered if the stress of ruling was starting to get to him.

"No, of course I don't think that. I'm sure that you've weighed every decision carefully before you've made it. That's not what I was saying at all!"

Eryk calmed down just as suddenly as he had gotten worked up. He straightened and took a step away from Warren.

"Look," Eryk said, turning away from his commander in chief. "I didn't mean to attack you like that. I guess I'm just tired. I really don't sleep very well anymore."

"Well I can understand that. You've had a lot on your plate for the past few months." Warren forced himself to smile.

"All I meant when I asked about the plan was that your army is going to fill this area, especially once you take into account the extra bodies that make up the cavalry. This place is full to bursting as it is, and there are still a number of commands to report in. Where is the fighting actually going to happen? Have we heard anything from the scouts we sent across the border yet? Knowing where the Madelian army is would be a big help right now."

Eryk turned back to the door and looked out once again at the army gathering outside. Warren was right, he realized. They needed more up to date information so that the plan could be adjusted. What had happened to Petyr and his men?

"It looks like time to call a command meeting and get things underway. Without the reports from Petyr's group, we're going to need to send out more scouts, and the sooner the better. Would you please send someone to gather the commanders who are already here?"

Warren nodded and left the tent quickly. He was glad that Eryk seemed to be keeping his head together, at least most of the time. He knew that if he were in Eryk's position, he would have snapped under the pressure by now. The sooner this was all over with, the better it would be for everyone.

Warren returned much faster than Eryk had expected, pulling a man in a dusty uniform along behind him as he strode into the tent without pausing. The king sensed his bodyguard tense at his back, and was a little surprised that Mateo didn't draw a weapon. The man had been very tense and on edge ever since Eryk had arrived here in the war zone.

"This is one of Petyr's men," Warren explained happily. "It turns out that they found the Madelians two days ago, and Petyr sent them back here in pairs and small groups, improving the chance that we got the message."

"And what sort of information do you bring?" Eryk asked the man, who looked very tired but who snapped a smart salute and bowed at his waist all the same.

"The army is big, your Majesty," he said. "Much bigger than we were expecting. There looked to be seven full companies of men, which would be about three thousand men."

"We're going to be outnumbered," Warren commented quietly, "by about two to three."

"What about the cavalry?" Eryk asked. "Surely they'll help to even the odds."

"They should, yes," Warren agreed. "We have one hundred of each of the light and heavy cavalry, but how they are used is what will really determine how they'll even things up."

"And the rest of the foot soldiers? When should they arrive?"

Warren glanced at his notes once more. "They should all be here the day after tomorrow, and we'll likely be able to attack four days from now, assuming we march out right away."

Eryk took a deep breath and prepared to speak again, but then the first of the commanders arrived. By the time they had all gathered, there were twenty commanders for the foot soldiers and another four for the cavalry, each of them responsible for fifty men.

"Well gentlemen," Eryk began, "we have some bad news. Our scouts have reported that the Madelian army is camped about two days from here, and they are larger than we expected them to be. We will be outnumbered."

"Madelia is not a large kingdom."

"It looks like there are about three thousand men," Warren answered honestly, and his comment was greeted with shocked gasps. Bacovia was used to being the largest group on the field of battle.

"Should we call in more men?" another commander wanted to know.

"There are still about half of the commands left to report in, so our numbers should double over the next couple of days. Beyond that, we can't leave our border totally undefended," Warren said.

"Besides," Eryk continued, "depending on the location of their camp, we may be able to use our cavalry very effectively." The king looked expectantly over towards the scout, and the man cleared his throat self-consciously.

"They are camped in a mountain valley," he said. "The road leads down into the valley and out the other side, so they are literally sitting across it. They fill the valley, except for a large empty area to the front of their encampment. That's likely where they drill."

"Were there any cavalry at all?" one of Warren's men asked, and the scout shook his head.

"If they are filling so much of their valley with their tents and equipment, it may be best to try and attack them right there in the camp. They won't have a lot of room to maneuver." The suggestion came from the back of the group, one of the younger commanders speaking up for the first time.

"But we won't have a lot of room to maneuver either," came the reply from someone else.

"I think that the cavalry will be able to help with that, at least somewhat," Warren put in. "With the hills around the valley, assuming they are clear enough, the cavalry will be able to build up a lot of momentum. The heavy cavalry especially should be able to ride through their encampment, especially if we can take them by surprise.

"The light cavalry up the middle, along the road, should be able to get through the camp fast enough to prevent escape out the other side, and likely pick a few of them off along the way. The foot soldiers can follow the heavy horse in and use the open area as their staging point."

Nods came from all around the tent as the commanders envisioned the plan that Warren laid out for them. A few of them asked questions, but it quickly became obvious that they couldn't decide anything until someone had scouted the area in detail.

"So do we send out scouts from here or do we move the army and take it as it comes?" someone asked.

"We definitely send out scouts," was Eryk's quick reply. "The only way this will work is if the area is laid out ideally, and I'm not willing to risk the army on the hopes that the geography of the area is the way we need it to be. We won't be ready to march out of here for another couple of days anyway, so send out scouts on fast horses and we'll see what happens."

Warren spoke to the light cavalry commanders quickly, selecting men to act as scouts while the rest of the group broke off and went back to their men. They had drills to do and an attack to plan, even if they only had a few vague descriptions to go on. It would be better to have some idea of what to do than no idea at all.

"We've actually done it, haven't we?" Eryk asked, shaking his head. "We've gathered our army and we're about to go and get who knows how many of these men killed.

Warren paused at the entrance of the tent. "No, your Majesty, *we* haven't. The Madelians push our borders and our people over and over again. Either we fight or we surrender the kingdom."

After Warren left, Eryk decided to head out into the camp and survey his army. He knew that he wouldn't actually be doing any of the fighting in the days to come, and he felt it was important that the soldiers could see that he was still here with them even if he would be relatively safe while they were the ones in mortal danger. He started out from the tent, Mateo right at his heels.

Mateo went everywhere with him now. He would stand at Eryk's shoulder while he ate or met with anyone, and he had even taken to sleeping on a cot in Eryk's tent at night. Mateo hadn't accepted anyone that Owen had offered to be his partner, and he'd never said a word to anyone after that one brief conversation with Eryk days ago. Mateo was a ghost of his former self, and Eryk found it more than a little disturbing. Unfortunately, there wasn't anything he could do to help the man. He hoped that Aislynn would be able to get through to him when she came home. Eryk was looking forward to that day too.

As Eryk walked along, he thought about his final meeting before leaving the castle to come out here to the border. He'd met with his much reduced council, and explained his wishes. Owen remained in charge of the guard while Mataline and Philip shared ruling privileges until Eryk returned. Michael had accompanied Eryk to the border, feeling that his medical expertise and healing magic would be of benefit to the soldiers who would inevitably be injured during the upcoming battles. Nobody was particularly happy that Eryk was leaving the city, but nobody could force him to stay there either.

Marja had been waiting in Eryk's room when he arrived to pack, and she'd risen gracefully to her feet as he entered. The king gestured for her to sit back down on the couch, and he'd taken a seat beside her, and reached out to take her hand.

"It's hard, not knowing how he is," she'd said quietly. "How do you do it?"

"I try not to think about her, in all honesty, but sometimes, I can't help myself. All I can do is hope, and that's all you can do too."

"I'm so afraid that he's not coming home," Marja had confided, her voice breaking. As she'd started to cry, Eryk had gathered her into his arms and just held her.

Eryk thought about the moment now, and realized that he wished he was able to break down, just a little. After Marja had dried her tears, she had seemed somewhat more relaxed and at ease, and Eryk wished for that release. He was wound so tightly right now, he sometimes felt that he was about to snap.

Eryk pulled himself together and finished his walk around the camp. When he returned to his tent, he moved over to the small desk that he had in his reception room. There were a number of papers there that he needed to deal with, and it was a good way to pass the time.

Chapter 21

Byron was waiting outside of the small gate in the morning just like he was supposed to be, and just like he had the past two days. There were other men there, but nobody looked at him or questioned his right to be there, which made his job for today a lot easier. Maybe Aislynn had been right about this being an easy ticket into the castle, he thought. Today was the third morning since she'd disappeared into Vivien's castle, and today he was going to get her back.

He was tired and he hadn't slept well at all the night before. Ever since he'd sold Aislynn into slavery, regardless of whether it was a good cover or not, Byron hadn't been able to stop thinking about her and wondering about what they were making her do. He hoped she was okay and that things were going as smoothly for her as they appeared to be going for him, but he wasn't sure that that hope was reasonable.

Damn that woman, Byron thought for at least the tenth time. How do I let her talk me into these crazy schemes of hers?

It was still dark as the heavily laden wagon rumbled up the road, and the men gathered in anticipation of its arrival. Byron held himself towards the back of the group, as he had the past several days, and got himself ready to help unload the supplies.

When the wagon came to a halt, the driver jumped down and climbed up onto the back to begin passing baskets of fresh fruits and vegetables down to the men waiting below. After taking a basket, Byron joined the queue of men waiting to pass through the now open gate, and then he found himself once again inside the castle wall, easy as that.

Byron kept his gaze fixed straight ahead, not wanting to be caught looking around and drawing attention to himself. He was following a path of crushed gravel that led from the gate straight towards the castle, passing underneath an archway in a second wall. Before him was an open door, and he could hear the bustle of a busy kitchen beyond.

As he passed through the open door and into the busy room beyond, Byron was happy to see the sheer number of people walking around and working there. There were cooks busy preparing the morning meal and getting ready for the rest of the day, servants carrying and fetching… and slaves busy cleaning. Byron quickly scanned the area and he almost didn't see Aislynn, who was kneeling in front of a large, empty fireplace. This was the first time he'd seen her on his forays into the castle, and he was reassured to see that she appeared fine.

She was busy scrubbing the brick clean, and didn't look up or apparently pay attention to anything that was going on around her. He was able to see that there were some fresh bruises on her arms, and with a sigh, wondered what trouble she'd managed to get into. It certainly seemed like she was being punished, having by far the dirtiest job in the kitchen.

Byron followed the cleared pathway through the kitchen to a door located farther down the wall on the left side. After crossing the threshold, he found himself walking down a ramp leading into a cold room that was mostly underground. Byron deposited his basket where the others had left theirs, and then turned around to head back to the wagon for a second trip.

As he walked back across the grounds, Byron carefully worked one of his daggers loose from the scabbard at his waist. Very carefully, he slid the weapon up under his right sleeve, blade pointing down towards his hand, effectively hiding it from view.

Upon reaching the wagon, Byron took the basket that was passed to him, hefted it up onto his left shoulder, and turned back towards the castle. As he turned, he took careful note of how many baskets remained to be carried in to the kitchen. He needed to make sure that he timed his exit properly - not too soon and not too late.

This time when Byron entered the kitchen, he took a careful look around to see who was paying attention to whom. Upon ascertaining that nobody was looking at either him or Aislynn, he dropped his right hand down beside his leg, letting the dagger carefully slip into his hand. With a quick flick of his wrist, he tossed the dagger into the fireplace that Aislynn was cleaning, where the clatter of its impact was lost within the general noise of the room. By the time he was heading back out of the door, the dagger was gone, and so was she.

Byron made sure that he lagged behind a little on his trip back to the wagon, and he managed to be last in line for his final trip. The wagon was empty and this time, after he placed his basket with the others in the cold room, he didn't turn to go back up the ramp. Instead, he found himself a shadowed corner behind some boxes and hid there until he heard the door shut and the lock slide home with a loud click.

He sat there in the pitch darkness, grimacing at the thought of being locked in this tiny underground room, and tried to formulate a plan. Byron was on the castle grounds, certainly, but he was no closer to accomplishing the mission that Aislynn had laid out for him than he had been outside the walls.

After a time, Byron realized that it wasn't totally black inside the little room after all. He could see light seeping in around the door at the top of the ramp, and there was a little bit of light coming from somewhere else too. As his eyes adjusted to the darkness even more, he was able to make out two faint rectangles of light up near the ceiling. Windows. There were two of them, each emitting a rectangle of dim brown light.

Byron knew that he certainly couldn't stay where he was, at least not without getting caught, so he carefully arranged some boxes and crates to give him better access to the ceiling. Climbing carefully, testing his weight with each step, he made the painstaking ascent to investigate his only possible exit.

The windows were very dirty, crusted with dust on the inside and dirt on the outside. They were also made of glass, which gave Byron an idea. He remembered seeing burlap sacks below, used to store wheat, corn and other seeds, and it was possible that they could help him escape.

He carefully climbed down his makeshift stairs and felt around in the near darkness for the sacks that he remembered. Finding them, he felt around until he located one that was near empty, and then he used his other dagger to cut the excess fabric free of the top of the bag. Finally, Byron slit the seam and brought his cloth with him as he climbed the boxes one last time.

Byron carefully wrapped the burlap cloth around his hand and arm, positioned the top box to catch the broken glass, and then punched the window with all the strength he could muster in his awkward position. The glass shattered into dozens of pieces, scattering in all directions, and Byron carefully cleaned the sharp bits away from the window sill. Concerned that he cover all of his tracks, he picked up as much of the glass as he could reach, storing it in the box he had used to catch the falling glass.

Slowly poking his head out, Byron looked around as best he could. It looked like the windows were at ground level in a garden, with a number of carefully manicured plants and hedges scattered around within view. Listening carefully, he heard nothing but the trickling water of a nearby fountain. Nobody had heard him, apparently.

Being very cautious so as not to cut himself, Byron eased his way out of the window and into the early morning light. The garden was still in shadow next to the building, so he relied on the darkness to keep him hidden and took a few moments to unwind the cloth from around his hand and arm and then position it over the now open window. Hopefully, when someone eventually looked into the storage room, the burlap would filter the light sufficiently so that they wouldn't notice the broken window right away. The more of a head start he got on any pursuit, the better.

Satisfied that he had done all he could to escape detection for the time being, Byron slipped along the side of the building looking for a good place to hide. He eventually came upon a part of the garden that looked perfect. There were a number of thick bushes growing close to the wall of the castle, and the soil looked freshly turned, which meant that the gardeners shouldn't be back to this particular area today.

Byron slipped in among the bushes, finding the hollow he had been hoping for. He reached out of his hiding place and brushed away the prints he had left in the rich soil, and then he settled in for a wait. It was times like these that he wasn't unhappy being as short as he was. It certainly made hiding easier!

Looking up at the brightening sky, Byron noticed a balcony overhead, and then the set of stairs leading down from it. Excellent, he thought to himself. Later, when it's time to continue with this little endeavor, I'll have easy access to the castle.

Aislynn had heard the men come into the kitchen with their baskets, but she was too occupied with her own thoughts to bother looking at them as they passed by her. Granted, part of her was afraid to look because she didn't know what she would do if Byron wasn't there like he was supposed to be, but the greater part of her was too busy scrubbing at the fireplace while trying to keep a hold of her temper.

While the slaves were usually up at dawn to begin their duties, Aislynn had heard the key in the lock of her door before the sun came up this morning. She knew that it was early because her usual waking time was just before dawn, so she should have already been awake when the jangling keys put in an appearance. The oddity of it put her on her guard, and Aislynn was up and out of her cot as quickly as she could be.

The overseer walked into her room wearing a nasty little grin.

"I've heard some interesting stories about you," he said as he walked closer. "I understand that your prior master taught you some… special skills. I was thinking about seeing how well you were taught."

Aislynn was literally sick to her stomach at the man's words. She knew, right then, that she was going to have to kill the overseer, something that would destroy her chances of completing her mission, but nobody was EVER going to abuse her again. She was unarmed, but he was only one man, and Aislynn knew that she could kill him easily. As he approached, she dropped into a defensive crouch, ready to do whatever it took.

The overseer's grab at her was clumsy, and it was easy for Aislynn to move out of the way. When his second attempt to reach her was equally clumsy, she decided that maybe she could take care of this man without jeopardizing her mission after all. The third time, she let him succeed, and as he pulled her towards him, she bit his arm as hard as she could.

Her assailant screamed and reflexively pulled away from her, exactly as Aislynn wanted him too. Unfortunately, as soon as there was a bit of space between them, the overseer unexpectedly swung his fist into the left side of her face. The cut along her cheekbone reopened, and she felt her lip cut on her teeth. The blow was hard enough to stun Aislynn briefly, and the overseer used her momentary weakness to grab both of her arms, hard enough to raise new bruises, and throw her back down on to her cot.

Aislynn had a lot of training that dealt exclusively with fighting while lying on her back, and she put that training to good use now. As soon as he approached the bed, Aislynn kicked out twice in rapid succession, once to his face and once to his groin. The man doubled over in pain, and finally decided that pursuing her just wasn't worth it today. She breathed a sigh of relief when he left, but he got his revenge soon after when he assigned her the dirtiest job he could get away with. Aislynn considered it a small price to pay considering he could have taken his revenge with a group of his buddies. Fortunately, it seemed like he didn't want it known that he'd been beaten back by one of his slaves, and a female one at that.

Considering how distracted she was, Aislynn was surprised, and relieved, when the dagger came whistling by her to land in the fireplace. She was also very happy that she'd been making Byron practice throwing daggers from time to time over the past months, as the blade had come very close to her arm. She didn't really need any more scars on this trip.

As quickly as she could, Aislynn reached over and grabbed the dagger, slipping it under her skirts before anyone could notice. She was nearly finished with this particular fireplace, and she would have to move soon. Now that she had it, she certainly didn't want to leave the weapon behind. It would give her an edge that she didn't think she would have.

Soon, she finished up where she was and stood to move on to the next room, being careful not to drop the dagger. The overseer had informed her this morning that all of the fireplaces needed to be swept and cleaned in preparation for the coming winter, and Aislynn was happy enough for the excuse to move around the castle. It was, however, an incredibly dirty job. She was already covered in soot and ash, and this was just her first fireplace.

Aislynn moved into the dining hall, where there were a few early risers eating their morning meal. She walked quickly and quietly to the fireplace and got to work, listening carefully to the conversations going on around her while making sure that she did nothing to draw attention to herself.

"So what do you make of that meeting last night?" one man asked the gentleman sitting beside him. "They were up half the night, I heard."

"Apparently," replied the gentleman, "a courier came in from the border early yesterday morning, and they were trying to figure out what to do about the information he brought."

"And?"

"It sounds like we're going to attack. The Bacovians have been gathering at the border, and our spies say they are getting ready to attack our army. The courier was supposed to head back out first thing this morning with the attack orders."

"So this war might be over soon?"

"That's the hope."

Aislynn was very happy to hear that Vivien had already issued the orders to attack Eryk and the army. They needed to have the army massing in order to do the damage they wanted to do, and if Aislynn killed Vivien before the order came, their plan could totally fall apart. As it was, there was no guarantee that everything would work out the way they all hoped, but the more pieces that fell into place, the more likely it was for a favorable outcome.

The rest of the time in the dining hall passed uneventfully. Aislynn cleaned the fireplace to the best of her ability and then prepared to move on once more. Before she left the room though, she was able to snatch a cloth napkin from a nearby table. She used it to wrap the blade of

Byron's dagger carefully like a makeshift scabbard, and then used a piece of cotton she tore from the hem of her dress to secure the dagger around her thigh. That kept the weapon hidden and her hands free. It was a very good thing that nobody paid much attention to the slaves.

The stairs leading to the second floor of the castle were not far from the dining hall, and Aislynn decided to try and press her luck. Her orders were to clean the fireplaces, but she hadn't been told explicitly which ones to clean. The upper rooms had to have fireplaces too, after all.

She made it up the stairs without difficulty, servants and castle guards alike ignoring her as they passed. Slaves were, after all, invisible, which was something she was totally counting on.

The first room she came to was a bedroom suite, and apparently unoccupied. The suite had that sterile clean but unused look, and Aislynn got right to work cleaning out the fireplace. There was something innocuous about cleaning an empty room, and if someone came to check on her, she'd have a perfect excuse to be where she was.

Slowly but surely, Aislynn made her way ever closer to the royal suite as the day progressed. She made sure she stopped in every room and cleaned every fireplace, leaving an obvious trail of her whereabouts. She never saw anybody checking up on her, but there wasn't anybody looking for her either, which suited her just fine.

She was wandering down the hall towards her next room when strong hands suddenly grabbed her from behind.

"What do you think you're doing up here?" sneered a low voice close by her ear. The voice was female, and definitely angry. "This hall isn't for vermin like you."

"I…I was just… I was just cleaning the fireplaces," Aislynn stuttered, lifting up her buckets and brushes, but not looking around at whoever had hold of her.

"Well you don't belong here," said the voice again, and Aislynn fought down the urge to slam her bucket into the side of the woman's head.

"But I have to clean all of the fireplaces," Aislynn tried to explain in a quiet voice, but it was pointless. The woman had no patience for a slave.

Aislynn felt the grip on her shoulders tighten briefly, and then she was falling forward, pushed from behind. The buckets went flying from her hands, spilling ashes and dirty water all over the plush red carpet. Another guard came around the corner ahead.

"What's going on here?" the new woman demanded. "What's this slave doing here?"

"She claims that she's cleaning fireplaces," the first guard answered.

Aislynn was down on her hands and knees trying desperately to clean up the mess she'd made. She knew, logically, that it wasn't her fault, but she also knew that whose fault it was wouldn't matter. If she didn't get this cleaned up, she'd get a beating. Then she'd have to kill the person who did it, and that would likely ruin her chances of completing her mission here.

Suddenly, a door opened behind Aislynn. She couldn't see who was behind her, being crouched on the ground in front of the mess, but she saw the sudden change in body posture of the two guards in front of her. They stiffened to attention, and she could hear their breath starting to speed up. Whomever they had disturbed, it was somebody important.

"What is all of this commotion out here?" asked a cool, controlled voice. Vivien's voice.

"We're very sorry, your Majesty," one of the guards replied. "We caught this slave sneaking around out here and were just taking care of the situation."

"Oh were you now? Then why is there such a mess? Bring her in here," the queen ordered.

The guards grabbed Aislynn by the upper arms, causing her to hiss in pain as they put pressure on the fresh brand on her arm and her new bruises from the overseer. The two women picked her up and then they practically dragged her through the open door. Inside, Aislynn found herself on her knees once again, this time on a luxuriously thick dark green carpet. She kept her body hunched and kept her eyes on the floor, not daring to look at her target. How lovely of the guards to bring her into striking distance, Aislynn thought to herself.

"Now, explain to me why you've disturbed my afternoon conference?" Vivien demanded.

"As I said, your Majesty—" one of the guards began, but Vivien cut her off.

"I want this *creature* to explain," the queen sneered.

Aislynn felt one of the guards nudge her, obviously wanting her to begin speaking. She took a deep breath.

"I was told to clean all of the fireplaces in the castle, to get them ready for the winter. Nobody told me that there were fireplaces that I shouldn't clean, so I was up here doing what I was told, and then I… tripped and spilled the buckets on the carpet. I was trying to clean the mess when the guards came and…" The entire time she was speaking, Aislynn kept her body posture carefully submissive and her voice slightly breathless. She was trying to convey fear and she spoke quickly. She was also hoping to disguise her voice somewhat, not something she had a lot of practice with.

"I know that voice," said a woman over to Aislynn's right. "Where do I know that voice from?"

Aislynn stiffened involuntarily, and shook her head slightly, trying to deny what she had just heard.

"Let me get a look at her," said the voice again.

One of the guards grabbed a handful of Aislynn's hair and yanked her head up so that the speaker could get a good look. The woman recoiled in horror, hands coming up in front of her defensively.

"You!" Cora gasped. "Guards! Kill her immediately!"

The guards weren't entirely sure how to react. Their queen hadn't issued an order, but the other woman was obviously afraid of this slave. They grabbed Aislynn once again, and hauled her to her feet, but didn't draw their weapons. Not yet.

Aislynn glared at the woman recoiling away from her, all illusion of submissiveness gone.

"You look different," Aislynn said. "You're not the timid little thing you were when last we met. I guess not having your big brother around has done wonders for your self-esteem."

"How dare you talk about my brother, you murdering bitch," Cora replied. She straightened, hands reflexively smoothing her long brown hair. Cora looked at the queen once again.

"Your Majesty, may I introduce you to her Royal Highness, Princess Aislynn of Evendell."

Vivien started to laugh, a low throaty sound. She swept around in front of Aislynn, and the guards tightened their grips on her arms.

"Well isn't this a pleasant surprise," Vivien commented. She wore a dress of dark blue silk, slashed with red, and her long black hair was unbound, tumbling around her shoulders. "We haven't had the opportunity to chat in days now! And since I returned from our negotiations, Cora's told me *all* about you."

"Oh has she?" asked Aislynn. "Then you're either a fool or she hasn't told you everything."

"And why is that?" Vivien wanted to know.

"Because you haven't ordered your guards to kill me yet."

The guards were holding Aislynn's arms, but not her hands. Aislynn stomped her foot down hard on one of the guards' feet, and the woman let go of her and stumbled backwards. Aislynn reached over to her left, drawing that guard's sword. With a quick twist of her hand, Aislynn brought the sword swinging straight back and thrust into the guard's stomach. The angle was perfect for a good hit, and the sword was very sharp, so it left the guard bleeding from the deep belly wound, taking her out of Aislynn's way. Cora screamed and backed into a corner.

Aislynn quickly whipped her sword back towards the other guard, forcing her to let go, and she took two steps backwards, still facing Vivien. She tuned Cora's screams out, forcing her into the background, and kept her eyes on the guard. The one she had wounded lay still, clutching her stomach, and Aislynn went after her first, finishing her off with a stab through the heart.

Byron was dozing in the gardens when he heard the screams coming from above him. Reacting instinctively, he sat up quickly, forgetting that he was lying in the middle of a clump of bushes, and tangling himself briefly in their branches. He drew his dagger and dashed out of hiding, heading for the stairs leading up to the balcony and the open door he could see above him.

He slowed as he reached the stairs, not wanting to draw attention to himself as he climbed them, and not wanting to attract the notice of whoever was causing the screams. All he knew was that there was a lady in trouble, and every fiber of his being needed to help her. He guessed that it had something to do with having four sisters, and all of them younger than he was.

As Byron slipped past the curtains and into the room, the scene that greeted him was not the one that he had pictured when he'd heard the sounds of fighting from below. The screaming woman had backed into a corner to his left, and a quick scan of the room showed that she was in no immediate danger. Directly in front of him was a guard wearing a Madelian uniform protecting a tall, regal woman. And directly in front of *them*, Aislynn stood over a body, holding a bloody long sword in her hand. Her eyes met his briefly and then flicked back to the guard she was advancing towards, but other than that quick look, she gave no hint that there was anyone else in the room.

Byron got over his shock very quickly, and advanced silently towards the woman in front of him. There was only one reason that Aislynn would be attacking these people, and that meant that the woman with her back toward him must be Queen Vivien. Byron settled his dagger in his hand, eyes skimming down the woman's spine, counting the vertebrae he could just see beneath her dress, looking for the perfect spot to strike.

Aislynn had moved on to the next guard now, but this one wasn't as easy a target as the first had been. She met Aislynn with the sound of metal on metal, their swords meeting so violently that they struck sparks. Aislynn was taller than the woman she faced, and she sought to use that height to her advantage, bringing her sword up over her head for a downward chop. The guard darted forward, quick as a snake, and slashed her sword across Aislynn's unprotected stomach.

Aislynn saw the attack coming, and bent forward at the waist to try to minimize the damage. She accepted the blow, bringing her sword down with every bit of her strength, cleaving into the woman's collarbone. The guard's arm and hand went limp, and her sword dropped to the ground. Blood from the wound ran freely down the guard's arm, and she looked at it in shock. She was still looking at the blood on her arm when Aislynn's sword took her head off.

Byron knew that it was time to strike, and he gathered himself in preparation for his pounce. He drew his arm back, took a step forward, and instead of plunging his dagger into the queen's unprotected back, he grabbed her around the waist instead, bringing his dagger to rest lightly against her neck. He just couldn't bring himself to stab a woman in the back.

Aislynn caught Byron's eye and shook her head in disgust. He could have ended it, right here and now, and instead, now they had a prisoner. She turned away from the queen, and took a few quick steps, bringing her right up in front of Cora. She grabbed the woman around the throat, and Cora's screams ended in a strangled gurgle.

"Just what are you doing here?" Aislynn asked menacingly.

"This is my home," Cora replied quietly once Aislynn eased up on her throat a little, allowing her to speak. "I came here when my brother didn't come for me."

"She has been very helpful over these past months," said Vivien, speaking for the first time since the fight had begun. Her voice was steady and she sounded unconcerned, despite the knife at her throat that was drawing a thin bead of blood. Cora threw her a look of horror before turning her gaze back to meet Aislynn's.

"I haven't done anything, I swear. Please don't kill me!" she pleaded.

"And why shouldn't I? You wanted me dead, after all. For all I know, you were in on the attack your brother led, and you were certainly involved in the recent attack."

"I wasn't, I promise. Please, let me go."

"So you can summon more guards? I don't think so." Aislynn squeezed again, and Cora began to choke, but instead of simply strangling her to death, Aislynn brought her sword hand up. Turning the weapon, she brought the pommel down hard against Cora's temple, and the woman collapsed to the ground. She could deal with her later, Aislynn knew, and the queen was the target here. Cora would be unconscious for more than long enough for her and Byron to do what they had to. Aislynn turned back to look at Byron and Vivien.

Vivien wasn't going to go down without a fight. She twisted her right hand in an odd little motion, dropping a knife from a hidden sheath on her arm into her hand. She reversed her grip on the handle and drove her arm backwards, stabbing the knife up to the hilt into Byron's stomach. Byron gasped in pain, releasing his captive and dropping his dagger.

Aislynn was across the room in just a few seconds, but it was still long enough for Vivien to bend down and retrieve Byron's dropped weapon. Vivien then stepped behind Byron quickly, bringing his own weapon up to his throat. Byron's eyes widened as he looked at Aislynn.

"Drop the sword, or he dies," Vivien commanded, glaring coldly at Aislynn from her protected position behind Byron.

Aislynn was truly torn. Part of her wanted to just end this, to attack Vivien and Byron be damned. But a larger part of her knew that she couldn't do that. Despite her intention to marry Eryk, and despite her love for the king, she loved Byron too. She dropped the sword, and the sound of it falling to the ground seemed unnaturally loud.

"Good," Vivien purred. "Now, back to a proper kneeling position with you, slave."

Aislynn folded her knees and dropped straight to the ground. The skirt of her dress puffed out away from her as she fell, and she buried her hands in its folds, settling into a submissive position once more. She tried to appear non-threatening as she inched her hand slowly closer to the dagger she still had hidden under her skirts.

Vivien started to chuckle again.

"You are far too concerned for your partner to be a proper assassin," she said. "You're weak."

Aislynn didn't reply. She knew that she should have just attacked, but if she lived through this, she didn't want to have to explain to Eryk that she'd killed Byron simply to accomplish her mission. Not as long as there was any other way. She stretched her hand under her skirts just a little bit farther, and her fingers brushed against the dagger.

Everything after that happened very quickly. Vivien pressed the dagger deeper into Byron's neck, drawing blood, and started to pull the knife across his throat at the same time as Aislynn pulled the dagger out from under her skirt and threw it in one smooth motion. The dagger flew wide, scraping along the side of Vivien's face and opening a huge cut along her cheek and ear. It wasn't fatal, but it was enough to make the queen drop the dagger she was holding against Byron's throat as she grabbed at her face in surprise. Aislynn was up in an instant, rushing at the queen and pushing Byron out of the way.

Vivien tried to fend Aislynn off, but Aislynn was stronger and far better trained, and Aislynn didn't need a weapon to be deadly. A quick sweep of her leg swept Vivien's feet out from under her, and the queen fell backwards, cracking her head on the wall behind her.

Aislynn was back on her in an instant, hands reaching for her neck. Her thumbs found the small hollow of Vivien's throat, and she leaned forward, effectively crushing Vivien's windpipe. It was over quickly.

Aislynn stood and turned back to her fallen companion. Byron was laying face down on the floor, and Aislynn carefully rolled him over. He was bleeding heavily from both of his wounds, and she was suddenly concerned that he was going to bleed to death before she could do anything. Vivien's body was closest, and Aislynn ripped fistfuls of silk off her dress to press against Byron's neck and stomach to try to staunch the bleeding.

Byron was still conscious, but groggy, and he certainly wasn't going to be any help during their escape from the palace. It was only a matter of time before someone came to look in on the queen, and they had to get away now if they wanted to make it out of the castle alive.

"What the hell happened to you?" Byron asked with a small smile, taking in her new bruises and cuts.

"The overseer and I had a… disagreement," Aislynn replied.

"Did you kill him?" he asked, and she shook her head.

"Maybe I'll take care of him next time we vacation here," she suggested.

"You should leave me," Byron rasped quietly, moving on to a more important topic of conversation.

"Like I should have just let Vivien kill you? Or killed you to get to

Vivien? Or when *you* should have stabbed her in the back when you had the chance? Why start doing the easy thing now?"

"I got my just desserts for that screw up, didn't I?" Byron asked with just a hint of a hoarse chuckle.

Aislynn used more cloth to bind Byron's wounds as best she could and then she turned to the bodies of the guards. Working quickly, she stripped one of the bodies and slipped into the uniform. She would be considerably less conspicuous dressed as a guard, and this way she could still carry a sword.

Ready to leave the suite, Aislynn helped Byron to his feet.

"Is there any way out of this place if we go down the ladder?" she asked.

"I don't know," Byron said, swaying gently on his feet. "I never had the chance to investigate. It looked like a walled garden, similar to your garden at home."

"Well we have a better chance getting out of there than we do walking through the halls. Let's go."

Slowly and carefully, Aislynn and Byron made their way down the stairs and set off across the garden. Aislynn could see a wall in the distance, and she hoped they'd be able to find a way off the palace grounds. But when it came right down to it, Aislynn knew that it didn't really matter if they made it out. The queen was dead, her mission accomplished, and making it home was just a bonus.

Chapter 22

The farther Aislynn and Byron walked into the garden, the more alert Byron seemed to be. Aislynn knew that only adrenaline kept him going right now, and she dreaded the inevitability of him running out of it. Despite the fact that his wounds didn't seem to be bleeding through the makeshift bandages, he had still lost a lot of blood, and that was going to have consequences.

Byron, for the most part, walked with his head down, carefully choosing his footing. He could feel how light-headed he was, and he didn't want to fall. Considering Aislynn was currently bearing a lot of his weight, any fall he took would bring her crashing down too. They needed speed to get out of here, not accidents slowing them down even more.

"Hey," Byron said in alarm as he caught something out of the corner of his eye. "You're bleeding."

Aislynn just nodded, even though Byron couldn't see it. She knew that she was injured, but that wasn't an issue right now. She needed to reach the wall, and get over or through it, before Byron lost consciousness.

"Aren't you going to do anything about it?" Byron asked, sounding concerned.

"Not right now, no," she replied since he obviously needed her to acknowledge his questions. "We don't have time, and it's not that bad."

Byron fell silent again, and Aislynn felt him sway against her. It wouldn't be long now until she'd have to carry him. Please let us make it over the wall first, she prayed silently.

When they reached the back of the garden, after what seemed like an eternity stumbling forward, Aislynn was disappointed to find that there wasn't a doorway in sight, in either direction. Why should it be easy now? she wondered to herself.

Picking a direction at random, she turned them to the right, and they followed the wall until they reached the back corner. Here, the wall would be easiest to climb because they'd be able to use the two walls to brace themselves. Byron was going to need all the help he could get.

It was cool and shadowed under the trees, isolated, and Aislynn was just starting to relax a tiny bit when she heard a noise behind them. The noise was too big to come from an animal, which meant that it was likely either a guard or a gardener.

She pushed Byron up against the wall and pressed herself close against him, using her body to hide the gash across his stomach. Then she reached up, wrapped her arms around his neck, and just as whomever it was pushed through the bushes behind them, she leaned in. Aislynn used her height to her advantage as she leaned over Byron slightly, pressing her cheek against his, and pretending to kiss him. She murmured reassuring nonsense while they waited to see if their ruse worked.

The gardener who had stumbled across them thought that he was interrupting a couple in the midst of something… private, and he stumbled loudly back into the bushes. He noticed the uniform the young woman was wearing and didn't want to get involved. The queen's guards had notoriously short tempers and the gardener valued his life.

Aislynn pulled away and met Byron's eyes with a smile as the sounds faded. Byron had a shocked look on his face, his eyes wide.

"What?" Aislynn asked. "You expected to kiss me again?"

"Yes. I mean no! That would horribly inappropriate, considering…"

Aislynn laughed softly at his discomfort. "Relax, Byron. I just don't think you should mention it to Eryk. You remember how you were afraid that he'd behead you for helping me stretch way back when? Imagine what he'd do to you if he found out that you kissed me all those months ago. Or that you want to do it again," she added with a wink. Aislynn gave him a quick peck on the cheek, and with a little evil laugh, headed up the wall.

Aislynn braced herself carefully and peeked over the top. At the back, the wall came right up to the edge of a hill, and it was a long way down to the buildings of the city below. To the right, there was a courtyard and then more of the castle building. There was certainly no easy exit there. She knew that the far end of the garden from where she was now was the kitchen courtyard, where it was possible that someone would recognize her.

She slipped back down the wall after a quick scan for guards. Byron had slumped to the ground, fading fast, and Aislynn had to shake him a little to get him to wake up.

"I'm sorry Byron, but this isn't going to be comfortable. Our best bet is to go over this back wall, and then down the hill and into the city. It's a long way down though, and I'll have to drop you off the top of the wall."

Byron nodded his head weakly, not really understanding. Aislynn sighed and helped him to stand. She couldn't see any guards from her current vantage point, but time was running out so she decided to risk it. She boosted Byron up towards the top of the wall, and he was able to cling there briefly while she ascended herself. Then she grabbed him by the arms, lowered him over the side as far as she could, and let him drop before jumping down herself.

Byron fell like a stone, knees buckling as he hit the ground, and then he fell forward. The momentum of his fall caused his body to start rolling down the hill, and Aislynn hoped that he didn't hit anything too hard on the way down. She jumped down from the wall, landing precariously but on her feet, and then she started down the hill after him.

Byron was lying in an unconscious heap, covered in dirt and bits of vegetation by the time Aislynn reached him. The wound on his neck was beginning to bleed again, and she retied the bandage before picking him up and hoisting him over her shoulder. She was certainly strong, but he was dead weight, and they were on the wrong side of the castle from their inn.

Sighing, Aislynn started the long walk back, hoping that anyone who questioned her would be willing to believe that Byron was merely drunk. It was getting close to the dinner hour, so it wasn't entirely impossible that he's been drinking heavily for most of the day and had done this to himself. As long as nobody saw the wounds, they should be okay. All of this was assuming that the guards didn't mobilize from the castle before she got to the inn. At least the fact that they'd search the castle first would buy them a bit of time.

It was well past dusk by the time Aislynn stumbled into the lit doorway of the Crescent Dagger. She'd answered questions a couple of times on her way here, but the citizens believed her story about Byron's drunkenness. The common room was packed, so she was able to walk through the room and over to the stairs without anybody noticing them, or at least not commenting. She let Byron slip off her sore shoulder and leaned him against the stair rail for support while she maneuvered his body up to their room. Opening the door, she literally pushed Byron over onto the closest bed and collapsed in exhaustion.

Soon, however, Aislynn forced herself to her feet and retrieved her saddlebags from under her bed. After lighting the lanterns in the room, she fished through her bags for some of her own clothes and gratefully rid herself of the soiled and torn uniform she had purloined from the guard she'd killed.

As she changed, she made note of the injury she had sustained, which looked like a bright red slash across her flat stomach. It wasn't anything to worry about and it was scabbed over already. Just one more addition to her long list of scars.

Next, she pulled her emergency kit from her bag and walked wearily over to where Byron lay sprawled across the mattress. His breathing was shallow, but even, she was happy to note, though his color was horrible. She set about cutting his shirt free and examining his wounds.

The stab wound in Byron's belly was a deep one, but the tiny knife Vivien had used had still been too short to hit any major organ or blood vessel. Aislynn threaded her needle with a special silk thread she kept for this purpose and set about methodically stitching the gaping hole closed. She wasn't much of a seamstress, but it would do.

Next, Aislynn bent to take a closer look at the damage Vivien had done to Byron's neck and throat. The cloth she had bound there was sopping with blood, and the wound still oozed a little bit. It looked bad, but she forced herself to stay calm. She knew that if Vivian had cut a major vein or artery then he would have been dead already.

Again, she set about methodically stitching the wound closed. It went from just below his jawbone across his throat about half way, nicking his voice box. Aislynn used the smallest stitches she was capable of making, trying to minimize what would undoubtedly be a horrible scar. When she was finished, she washed both wounds with the hottest water she could handle, spread them with salve from the healers and then bound them tightly.

Finally finished, she arranged Byron more comfortably on the bed and went back down the stairs for some food. It was important that she act as normally as possible so that nobody would remember her and Byron when the guards inevitably questioned people in the city.

It was quite late now, but the common room of the inn was still packed to capacity. Everyone was talking, and it took Aislynn some time to sort out enough of the conversation to understand why everyone was so worked up. It seemed that news of the queen's death was spreading rapidly, and there was a lot of speculation about what would happen next.

Vivien had been the only child of the previous king, and she had no children of her own, so now there was the issue of succession. There were a number of cousins waiting in the wings to take the throne, but most of them were all equally blood related to the late queen, so the issue was likely going to take some time to decide.

As Aislynn took a seat at a table in the back corner of the room, she smiled a little to herself. They had been hoping that Vivien's death would throw the court into disarray, which was why they risked sending Aislynn here in the first place. The slight ring of panic in the voices of the crowd was everything Aislynn and Eryk could have wished for.

Soon after finishing her meal, Aislynn retired to her room. She checked on Byron, who was doing as well as she could expect. Then she lay down on the empty bed and fell into a deep and dreamless sleep.

Aislynn woke up to the sound of someone pounding on the door to the room. Feeling groggy and very stiff, she rolled out of bed and onto her feet before stumbling in the direction of the sound. She was just about to unlock the door when the pounding came again.

"Open up in there! Open this door in the name of her Royal Majesty!"

Aislynn sprang back from the door, her head suddenly clearing. She cursed, remembering exactly where she was and exactly what had happened the day before. Apparently, she'd slept far longer than she intended to, and now the man or men in the hall had her trapped in her room. Sparing a quick glance for Byron, who was still asleep in his bed, she dashed for her weapons, which Byron had kept safe for her.

The pounding on the door sounded a third time, and this time the hinges gave way, the door falling to the ground with a resounding crash. Aislynn rushed the door, sword leading, determined to keep the men from crossing the threshold. The doorframe was only so wide, and if she could keep them in the hall, they'd only be able to attack her one at a time.

The first guard was entirely unprepared for Aislynn's attack, and didn't even have a weapon up to block her strike. Her sword slipped past his non-existent guard and plunged into his chest, finding his heart. He dropped to the ground, and as his companion went to step over him, Aislynn glanced briefly over her shoulder. Byron slept on, and Aislynn thought that if the noise hadn't woken him yet, nothing was going to. She shook her head in dismay and prepared herself for the next attack.

The man who tried to force his way across the threshold was more prepared than his fellow had been. He had a sword in his hand, held defensively in front of his body. Aislynn wondered what these men knew about her and whether or not they believed it. She also berated herself for leaving Cora alive, Byron having distracted her with his injuries. The woman had obviously recovered enough to tell tales, and the guards all across the city likely knew what she and Byron looked like by now.

The need for escape became more pressing with each passing

second, and Aislynn darted forward to attack once more. Her sword flashed in from the left, and the guard parried the attack before bringing his sword back to centre, ready to defend again. The same thing happened the next time Aislynn attacked, and the time after that. The man never advanced and never made an attack of his own.

Growing suspicious, Aislynn moved to her right, forcing the man in the doorway to twist to keep even with her. Looking past his shoulder towards the stairs, Aislynn could see that he was alone in the hall, and his actions began to make sense. He was stalling, waiting for more guards to arrive to help capture or kill her.

Aislynn darted forward again, sword flashing in a flurry of blows. The man was able to parry them easily, but it wasn't the sword that concerned her. Just as the last of her attacks struck his blade, she kicked out. Her foot connected with the man's knee, and she heard a loud pop. The man went down, howling in pain, and Aislynn plunged her sword into his back.

The hall was clear for a moment, and Aislynn rushed back towards the beds. She had no time to be nice to Byron, so she grabbed the basin of water left over from the previous night and tossed it in his face. As he sat up, shocked and sputtering, Aislynn had already turned away and was busy throwing things into saddlebags.

"What's going on?" Byron asked, confused. His voice sounded a bit hoarse and deeper than she remembered.

Aislynn nodded her head in the direction of the door and kept packing. Byron glanced over at the broken door, took note of the bodies, and rolled unsteadily to his feet.

"Be careful, and make sure you lean on something," Aislynn directed him over her shoulder. "I'll pack up. You just concentrate on finding your balance. I can't carry you again."

"Carry me?"

"Yeah. I had to carry you half way across the city yesterday. You, sir, are very heavy."

Aislynn finished stuffing the last of their belongings into bags – they'd sort out whose was whose later – and handed Byron his sword. He strapped it around his waist and went to take a set of saddlebags from her. Aislynn shook her head and headed for the door.

"The second one was stalling, so we may have company outside," she explained. "You are still recovering from some nasty injuries, so I'll carry the bags, if it's all the same to you."

She helped Byron over the bodies, and together they moved down the stairs as quickly as they could. Aislynn rushed outside into the courtyard, dropping the saddlebags by the door, and ran into the stables to grab their horses. She tacked up Byron's horse first, just throwing the saddle over the beast's back and yanking the cinch tight. Then she just threw her own tack over her horse's back, fully prepared to ride out of the city bareback. She led both animals out into the courtyard and left Byron to mount while she pulled herself onto her gray.

Just as Aislynn leapt up, four more guards appeared in the courtyard. When their fellows hadn't emerged from the building on time, they had gathered to come and see what was keeping the two men, and now they found the people they were looking for.

There was only one way out of the courtyard, and that was past the four guards who had their weapons ready. Aislynn drew her dagger and threw it at the closest guard, catching him in the throat and dropping him to the ground. While the other three were momentarily stunned by the suddenness of their comrade's death, Aislynn spurred her horse into a canter, and slashed at the next closest guard as her mount rushed by. She knew that Byron's animal would follow, and she hoped that he was able to get past the remaining two guards without difficulty. It was times like these that horses were particularly useful. As long as Byron didn't stop, the naturally competitive nature of his beast ensured that it would follow hers, keeping pace and hoping to overtake the lead.

"We're going to have to rush the gate," Aislynn called back to Byron once they were both free of the inn's courtyard and were dashing along the road. "The guards will have our descriptions and I really don't feel like stopping to fight them. Do you feel up for it?"

"I don't have a lot of choice in the matter, now do I?" Byron answered. He was grateful for the pommel of his saddle, and he held onto it as tightly as he could, happy that Aislynn had chosen a canter and not a gallop. The gallop would be faster, but the canter's smoother pace made it easier for him to hold his balance. He couldn't believe how dizzy he felt, and he knew that he certainly was not up for a fight of any sort.

The two horses pounded down the nearly empty road, skidding around the corner and onto the thoroughfare that led to the gate they needed. Aislynn kept them to the side streets for as long as she could in order to give the guards the least amount of time possible to prepare to intercept them. Seeing the gate ahead, Aislynn kicked her mount into a gallop, Byron's horse following suit.

Byron grimaced in pain as the jarring gate of his horse pulled at his unhealed stomach and the new stitches, and he felt the world spin. He grabbed onto the sides of his horse with all the strength he had in his legs, and gripped the pommel of his saddle even more tightly. He noticed, in a strange detached way, that his knuckles were white. He'd thought that was just an expression.

The guards noticed them coming and were obviously planning to stop them from leaving the city. The four of them had spread out across the road and were starting to brace spears, something that could be disastrous if they had time to get fully into position Fortunately, both Aislynn's mount and Byron's were war trained, and wouldn't hesitate to run the guards down, unlike a normal horse which would shy away, regardless of the weapons. Aislynn spurred her gray on, and he charged the guards, bull rushing one aside as he passed, slicing his shoulder open on a spear's blade as he did so. The gray let out a loud whinny of pain, but Byron's horse was right behind and kept pace despite whatever warning Aislynn's mount had been trying to communicate. Then, just like that, they were free of the city.

Aislynn didn't let the horses slow down until they reached the edge of the forest, long out of sight of the city walls. She looked back over her shoulder to check on Byron, who was still with her but looking horrible. His face was white and pasty, his eyes partially closed, and it was obvious to her that Byron was still only in his saddle by sheer force of will.

"It won't be long now," Aislynn called to him, and then she turned back around and started to scan the forest. She had to be here somewhere!

Soon, there was a sound in the underbrush, and Cheta came bounding into view. Aislynn slid off her horse's back and knelt down on the road, opening her arms to the wolf. Cheta came close and licked Aislynn's cheek, and Aislynn buried her face into Cheta's thick fur for a few seconds.

Pulling away, Aislynn sat back on her heels and looked Cheta directly in the eye.

"We need a safe campsite," she said, "and then we need meat. Byron's hurt, and we need to rest, but they are following us." She knew Cheta understood, even if she didn't know how. Cheta stood, licked Aislynn's hand and bounded off into the forest.

Aislynn turned to Byron and helped him down from his horse. He slid down into her arms, barely able to hold his own weight. There was sweat all along his forehead, and Aislynn could see blood staining his shirt over his stomach wound. She gathered the reins of both the horses, and led Byron slowly off the road and into the forest.

"Cheta will be back soon with a safe place to rest until tomorrow. That'll make the world of difference for you. We'll just rest here and wait for her to come back."

Byron nodded his head and slumped down to the ground. He rested his head on a tree and closed his eyes. Aislynn watched his breathing settle and the time between breaths lengthen, and she knew he was asleep.

When Cheta returned, Aislynn woke Byron and helped him to his feet before following the wolf to the site she had selected. A natural rock formation protected the area on two sides, and it was hidden from view by thick bushes and trees with low overhanging branches. Aislynn got the camp set up while Cheta hunted for the three of them, and after everyone ate, they all settled in for the day to rest and recover before the final push for home.

Chapter 23

Eryk stood just outside the entrance of his tent, waiting to call the meeting to order. It was just past dawn and cold, the feeble sunlight trying to break through the early morning fog and failing miserably. He'd called in all of the commanders of the various units of the Bacovian army, and they were just waiting for the last of them to gather. Michael was there already, and a short while later, Warren came riding up. They were finally all present and accounted for, and Eryk called the meeting to order.

"The enemy has been located, the area has been scouted, and it is time to discuss the last minute details of our course of action," the king said. "You have all been drilling your men, and the soldiers are ready for this."

"The attack will be tomorrow," Warren continued, picking up the thread of the presentation. "We expect that the Madelians will launch an attack soon, and we want to attack them before they can break camp. If we can attack on schedule, we'll also have the advantage of having the sun behind us, so part of these plans is to make use of that."

"Why are you so sure that they will attack?" one of the commanders wanted to know. "Couldn't we just sit here and wait them out? Winter isn't far away, and once the snow flies, they'll have to retreat from the border, won't they?"

"From the letter that was found on the castle's attackers, we know that Vivien sanctioned that attack in an effort to kill his Majesty and the council," explained Warren. "We imagine that her plan was to clear the capital of anybody who had a chance of governing the kingdom until Davin could arrive from Evendell, which would make it pretty easy to take. So while they could sit here and stare at us, Vivien has wanted our land for a long time, so she's more likely to make that final push now. We're actually in a better position than they are for a wait, being that little bit farther south, so it is in their best interest to attack and finish this war sooner rather than later."

"So this is it then," another commander commented.

"Yes it is," Eryk agreed, "and I want to thank you all for the dedication you've put into training your men. Tomorrow is going to be a big day, and it's going to determine everything."

Warren walked forward to the open area in front of the commanders, and bent down to sketch a rough map of the area in the dust.

"Our army is gathered here, and the Madelians are here," Warren said, pointing to the respective areas on his map. "I have the heavy cavalry in waiting here and here, and they will lead the attack, heading directly through the Madelian camp. The light cavalry will join them, heading up the middle of the encampment before wheeling to attack again from the rear. The foot soldiers will follow the pathway that the horses cleave for them."

Warren continued to outline the specific details of the plan of battle, such as where the men would wait until the attack began and where the soldiers would fall back to in the event that they needed to retreat and regroup. Warren was sketching on the map while he spoke, and the commanders listened and watched attentively.

Once everyone was fully acquainted with the particulars, Eryk dismissed the commanders back to their men to get what rest they could. They were going to start leaving from this main camp just after the noon meal, reporting to their holding areas for the night. Everyone had to be in place for the dawn attack, so they needed to move closer to the Madelian camp during the day today and into the early evening.

Eryk watched the commanders as they walked away, and then turned his gaze out over the area below where his tent was pitched. The campfires of his army were hundreds of dots in the faint light, and they started to wink out like the eyes of hundreds of monsters settling down to rest while waiting for the right moment to attack. The men were putting the fires out and starting to tidy their camps in preparation for their departures. The tents would stay where they were, and only minimal gear would accompany the soldiers to the battlefield, so the army would have somewhere to come back to after the battle.

Tomorrow was going to be a very long day.

Everyone in the camp stopped what they were doing to watch the courier's horse pound into view. The man leapt from the back of the animal before it came to a full stop, and he dashed into the command tent. Once the flaps of the tent had settled into place once more, whispered conversations began everywhere throughout the camp.

"I assume that he's carrying a message from the queen. What else could be so important?" Petyr commented wearily to himself from where he hung from his pole. "Maybe I'll find out and maybe I won't," he added, his tone of voice showing that he really didn't care either way.

Less then an hour later, Petyr noted that the company commanders were starting to arrive, filing into the main command tent accompanied by a lot of whispered conversations that were too far away for him to make out. In spite of his isolation, Petyr still found out what all of the fuss was about a short while later when Anders appeared before him.

"Well *sir*," his former lieutenant sneered, "this is it. The order just came from the capital, and it's finally time for us to attack. We sent word to her Majesty that Eryk has been gathering his army for an attack, and the queen wants us to take the fight to them and show your king that Madelia isn't going to be pushed around any longer. This is our chance to end this conflict once and for all. Our scouts will be heading out any time to find out what's going on with Eryk and his army so that we can plan properly."

"When did it become 'we'?" Petyr wanted to know. "Are you Madelian and just posing as a loyal Bacovian solider? Are you Bacovian and a traitor?"

"Not that it really matters," Anders replied, "but I'm Madelian, born and bred. There are more of us than you think in the Bacovian army. This takeover has been planned for a very long time, and the pay is excellent."

As Anders finished speaking, Petyr's attention drifted briefly to the scouts leaving the area and heading towards Bacovia. Turning back to the traitor, he shook his head. "So this is just about money? No patriotic reasons? Not taking revenge for past wrongs?"

"Nope, just the money," Anders agreed. "That's why you're here and Branden isn't. I was paid to kill him if I got the chance, to weaken Eryk by taking away his best friend. You, on the other hand, being a high ranking military officer, are potentially useful to us, and nobody paid me to kill you."

"Paid by whom?" Petyr wanted to know, but Anders just laughed at him.

"Oh no you don't," he said. "It wouldn't do at all to betray my employer. How would he ever trust me again?"

Anders seemed to gather his thoughts, and then he stepped closer to his former commander. "The commander wants to ask you some questions. Simple things, like size of your army, where they are camped, all sorts of interesting facts."

The Madelian soldier untied Petyr from the pole where he'd been hanging for the better part of four days without food and only minimal water. Petyr was very tired and very weak, and he stumbled and fell when the support of the pole was no longer there for him. Anders didn't even bother to draw a weapon, knowing that the commander was too weak to be a threat. Instead, he just hauled Petyr roughly to his feet by the rope used to secure him to his pole, and dragged him up to the main tent.

"What am I going to do now?" Petyr asked himself under his breath as he stumbled along behind Anders towards the command tent. "Is Eryk's army even ready yet? Did any of my men make it back?" He didn't find the questions particularly reassuring, but there was one thing that he did know. Petyr knew that he needed to stall for as long as he could. The longer it took him to give up any information, the longer the

Madelians would delay their attack, giving Eryk more time to prepare. On the plus side, he really didn't know all that much about his king's plans.

The Madelian commander seated behind the desk didn't even glance up as Anders led Petyr in. Anders dragged Petyr to a halt a few feet away from the seated man, and then pushed him down to his knees, a very easy task given Petyr's current weakened state. Only then did the enemy commander speak.

"Where is the Bacovian army?" the Madelian asked.

"I don't know," Petyr replied truthfully. The expected blow came and snapped his head to the side, Anders doing the honors.

"This can go one of two ways. You can answer my questions truthfully, or your friend can beat the truth from you."

"I did answer truthfully," Petyr stated as firmly as he could. "When I left the capital, the army was still stationed along the border, so I have no idea where they are now."

"How big is your army?" was the next question. This one Petyr did know the answer to. There were approximately six thousand foot soldiers in the army at any given time, and he said so. That made the Bacovian army twice as big as the Madelian one, without taking into account the cavalry. Petyr's understanding was that there were likely around two thousand horses and soldiers in the army, but he didn't mention the cavalry at all.

"What is the plan of attack?"

"I don't know," Petyr replied, earning himself another cuff from Anders. This time, the power behind the blow as enough to knock him sprawling to the ground, and Anders had to drag him back up into a kneeling position.

"What is the plan of attack?" the Madelian commander asked again, his voice still even and calm. It was obvious that the truth wasn't going to do the trick, so Petyr lied. A little misdirection wouldn't be a bad thing anyway, in Petyr's opinion.

"The king will start with arrows, filling the sky with fiery death," Petyr started. "Then he'll send in the soldiers, from three sides if he can flank you, and he'll cut your men to pieces."

"When are the Bacovians going to attack?" was the next question, and Petyr wasn't sure what a good lie was for this one. On one hand, he could try to scare them and say tomorrow, but he could also try to lull them into a false sense of security and pick a later date.

"I don't know," was the reply he picked, which earned him another trip to the floor of the tent.

"It is painfully obvious that you are going to be of no real use to us here," the commander commented. "As enthusiastic as our young friend is, he isn't really getting us anywhere, is he? I think that it would be best to send you to the capital for some real… questioning."

Anders hauled Petyr unceremoniously to his feet and dragged him back out of the command tent. He expected to go back to his familiar pole, but Anders led him instead behind the tent and deeper into the camp, heading towards where the couriers were stationed with their beasts.

Apparently, he was going to be leaving for the capital sooner rather than later.

When they set out from their shelter the next morning, Aislynn was pleased to note that Byron looked a lot better. Granted, he was still very unsteady on his feet and he had black shadows under his eyes, but his slightly fevered complexion gave him some color. He looked like hell, but it was an improvement, and he seemed more alert.

"We're just going to push straight for the border," Aislynn said. "I think that the sooner we get out of this damned kingdom, the better."

"That makes sense. We may not be safe from pursuit once we cross back into Bacovia, but we should have a better chance of getting away on familiar ground."

They mounted up and Cheta led the horses back to the road before the wolf dashed ahead to scout. There would be no riding along beaten tracks this time, and they pushed the horses into a canter as soon as the way was clear. Aislynn and Byron traveled at a canter for as long as the horses were able to sustain the pace, and for as long as Byron was able to hold his balance, and then dropped down to a walk to allow everyone to rest before pushing the horses back to a canter again.

Cheta raced back towards them at a run, signaling to Aislynn that it was time to hide at the side of the road again. Neither she nor Byron wanted to deal with any other travelers, so they would rein in and let the horses graze for a little while under cover whenever the wolf let them know someone was coming.

"We must be getting close," Aislynn murmured quietly to Byron, who nodded in agreement. "There are a lot more people on the road now."

As the sound of hoof beats came closer, Aislynn held her breath and wrapped her arm around her horse's muzzle to keep him quiet. Their cover here was very thin, and it would take next to nothing for someone to discover them. Everything was going according to plan as the pair of horses drew abreast of their position, then Cheta started to growl deep in her chest.

"What are you doing?" Aislynn hissed at the *eesprid.* "You're going to get us caught."

Cheta just growled a little louder and then dashed out of cover, rushing towards the closest horse. Aislynn cursed under her breath and drew her sword before breaking cover herself.

The first horse was shying away from Cheta as Aislynn dashed forward and surveyed the scene. The Madelian solider astride the first beast was panicking at the sight of the wolf and he was passing his anxiety on to his mount, who was dancing nervously. Glancing over, she saw that the second horse had a man slumped over and tied to his saddle, his horse tethered to the first with a lead. He looked vaguely familiar.

The Madelian solider was too busy with his horse and Cheta to worry about her, so Aislynn's first move was to cut the rope that tied the two horses together. As soon as the second animal realized that it was free, it backed away from its agitated companion, moving over to the side of the road to graze. Like most animals, it was unconcerned by the *eesprid*, something that Cheta was making sure the other man didn't notice by growling and snapping at his legs.

Once Aislynn was sure that the unconscious man was out of the way, she called Cheta off and advanced. If the *eesprid* was going to this much trouble to go after the Madelian, then Aislynn was going to follow her wolf's advice and take care of him. She pulled her dagger from the scabbard at her waist, drew her arm back, and launched the weapon at the man.

The soldier twisted in his saddle to follow Cheta as she retreated, changing his position and knocking Aislynn's dagger askew. Instead of hitting him in the back, right at his heart, it embedded itself into his arm, knocking him sideways in his saddle from the force of the blow. She was right behind her dagger, leaping at the man and knocking him to the ground. She wrapped her hand around the hilt of her knife, ripped it from the man's arm, and held it to his throat.

"Where were you going?" she asked.

"To the capital," the wide-eyed man replied. He certainly saw no reason to lie to the armed and obviously dangerous woman.

"And that man?" Aislynn questioned, gesturing towards the second horse with her free hand.

"I'm just taking him to the capital. He's some sort of prisoner."

Aislynn pressed her dagger more firmly into the man's throat, and then turned to look at the unconscious man again. He had bruises on his face and a black eye, but now that she was taking a closer look at him, the princess recognized Petyr. She turned back to the man on the ground in front of her and smiled.

"I don't think you'll be taking him anywhere," she stated firmly, and then she quickly drew her dagger across his throat, stood, and went to collect the Bacovian commander.

"It seems we have company," she informed Byron as she approached. "It would appear that our mission has also become a rescue and recovery, so our friend Petyr will be accompanying us home."

Byron glanced over at Petyr and winced in sympathy. "He's going to be pretty sore when he wakes up." Aislynn tossed Byron the reins for Petyr's horse, and then the three of them set off up the road, retracing Petyr's steps. Aislynn pushed her horse into a canter, and the other horses followed.

The trio alternated between a canter and a walk for the rest of the day, and it was late when the tired horses topped a rise and Aislynn and Byron found themselves looking down on a valley full of armed men. They had found the Madelian army.

"Oh my gods," breathed Aislynn. "Would you look at that?"

"There must be two or three thousand men there," Byron stated, a look of wonder on his face. Neither of them had ever seen such a huge concentration of people.

"We have to do something."

"Like what?" Byron demanded. "What could the three of us do against all of them? Even if we were all fine, which we are not, we couldn't do anything to turn the tide of this battle."

They pulled back down the road and made camp a little way behind the enemy army. Aislynn and Byron untied Petyr from his saddle and lowered him carefully to the ground. The commander groaned and regained consciousness only long enough to drink a little water before closing his eyes and slipping away again.

As darkness fell, Aislynn changed into her assassin's garb. The mottled black outfit blended completely into the darkness, and a little soot from the fire took care of her face. She honed her daggers, darkened the blades with a special cream so they wouldn't give her away, and turned to face Byron.

"Are you sure?" he asked. Aislynn nodded her head, nearly invisible in the firelight.

"I have to do something to help, even if it's just a little something. Eryk shouldn't be far from here, and we need to do what we can to help."

"Be careful. Eryk will kill me if you die tonight, so close to him."

Aislynn smiled, her teeth looking even whiter than usual against her darkened skin. Then she turned towards the enemy camp and faded into the darkness, leaving Cheta behind to guard Byron and Petyr.

Chapter 24

As Aislynn slipped through the darkness, quiet as a shadow, she mentally reviewed the list of what she wanted to accomplish. There should be sentries about, and she needed to deal with them first. Byron and Petyr were in no condition to defend themselves, and even Cheta could only do so much. She just needed to find them.

With a camp as large as the one spread out in the valley below, any guards posted would have a specific area to monitor, not the entire perimeter. That made it less likely that someone would report the missing men since there wasn't the constant check and balance of guards passing each other on rotation. And since she'd left this little foray of hers until last watch, there wouldn't be a shift change to worry about once she made her hole in the Madelian defenses.

The sound of footsteps coming from her left alerted Aislynn to the presence of the sentry she was looking for. Sentries, she corrected herself, hearing a voice mutter something softly in the darkness and a second voice reply. She had her sword belted around her waist, just in case, but Aislynn drew her daggers slowly and silently as she crept towards the voices she'd heard. The smaller weapons were better for the close quarter fighting she planned.

The assassin was just about to take another step when the pair of Madelian soldiers came through the thin bushes right in front of her. She knew that she was mostly invisible in the darkness, but Aislynn didn't want to risk losing the element of surprise, so she lunged forward quickly, slicing the first man across the throat with the dagger in her left hand. His companion paused, startled and shocked, and Aislynn took care of him with the dagger in her right hand, bringing the blade up beneath his ribs and stabbing into his heart. He was dead instantly, and the body dropped to the ground like a stone, freeing Aislynn to finish the first soldier. Slicing a throat was a great way to make sure someone didn't sound an alarm, but death could take a little while. Aislynn kneeled down beside the man, placed the tip of a dagger where she wanted it, and leaned down until the knife slid home, ending the man's thrashing. Finally, she wiped the daggers clean of blood using the uniforms of the fallen, sheathed the weapons and continued on her way.

Now that one group of sentries was disposed of, she wanted to find the pairs to the left and right of this group, which would give her a larger area of unprotected camp to escape from. Aislynn wasn't sure what the layout of the enemy camp was, and she didn't know how long her errand would take, so it was best to have as many exits from the area as possible. She ghosted through the night to find her next targets.

It took less then an hour to find the other two pairs of soldiers and kill them, so it was still a few hours until dawn when Aislynn finally made her way to the very edge of the enemy camp. She knew that Vivien had sent the order to attack, and it was only a matter of time before the camp packed up and moved, so Aislynn was going to delay the move as best she could. An army without commanders wasn't about to go anywhere.

The army was organized into companies, something that she'd seen when looking down on the camp earlier. Each squadron of soldiers within that company would have a commander, and the company itself would have a commander too. Then, somewhere around here, there would be someone in charge of everything, similar to how Warren was in charge of Eryk's army. Aislynn's self-imposed mission was to assassinate as many of the commanders as possible, and she knew that the highest ranking of them would be in the centre of the camp, where she and Byron had noticed many tents and a lot of activity. The problem was getting there unnoticed.

Since it was the last watch, those dark and lonely hours before dawn, the fires outside of the tents had burned low, and many were out entirely. Those few remaining embers cast long, dark shadows that Aislynn made good use of as she crept along, moving as quickly as she dared in order to make the best use of the time remaining to her. She bypassed the tents of the common soldiers, picking them out easily because of their size. The two-man tents were only large enough for the bodies that slept inside of them, while each squadron's command tent was larger and easy to pick out. She'd visit those on her way back out, if she had time.

The area of camp that Aislynn was aiming for was easy to pick out. The ten tents clustered together were the only ones that showed any life or movement. Not all of the tents had lights, of course, but from where she stood currently, she could see bodies silhouetted against the sides of six of them. The fact that these commanders would still be awake, or would be awake so early, lent credence to the idea that the army was about to move. Aislynn figured that she might as well start with the easiest of the targets, and slipped up to the darkened tent that was closest to her.

The Madelians had been in this valley for a while, and that was something that Aislynn planned to use to her advantage. When pitching a tent, you tie the guy ropes that help to support the structure around pegs that you hammer into the ground. With time and weather, those pegs will loosen, and the ropes tied to them will be less taut than they once were. This gives the walls of the tent a bit of slack, and that let Aislynn slide under the back wall of the first tent she approached.

Like most of the larger tents, the back area was for sleeping and the front was used for meetings and planning. Since this tent was dark, Aislynn expected to find the commander asleep, and she wasn't disappointed. Drawing one of her daggers, she slipped through the darkness until she stood beside the cot of the sleeping man. Once again, she positioned the tip of the weapon carefully, and then a quick shove pushed the blade home. She withdrew her dagger, wiped it clean with two quick swipes across the commander's blanket, then she was slipping back out the way she'd come.

She entered the four darkened tents and killed the commanders in exactly the same way, making Aislynn grateful for mass produced command tents that were all constructed and erected the same way. She was also pleased that the guards were as lax in their duties as she hoped they would be. There was a pair at the front entrance of each of the tents, she saw as she slipped silently among them, but they were all tired and nobody was making any rounds. Anything that made her job easier was fine with her.

The next six commanders would be more difficult, she knew. Because of the lanterns within the tents, her silhouette could be thrown against the canvas in the same way as the commanders themselves were right now. Aislynn knew that she'd most likely be able to sneak up on the commanders, but a guard who happened to glance over at just the wrong time was going to see an extra body moving around, and that could be disastrous.

It would be easiest to work from the outside of the tent, keeping the body of her target between her and whatever guards were on duty, so before she slipped into her next tent, Aislynn surveyed the guards to note their positions carefully. Then she picked a tent and crept towards it, crouched low. Once again, there was some slack in the tent wall, but this time there wasn't enough for her to slip under. Cursing silently, she put her dagger against one of the seams in the tent wall and drew it down along the stitches very carefully. Aislynn didn't want to disturb the canvas and thereby alert her target, who was sitting at the small camp table.

Once she'd created enough give to slip under, Aislynn reversed her grip on her dagger, laying the blade down along her arm. Then she rolled ever so carefully under the tent wall and rolled up into a crouch as soon as she was clear, bringing her right arm up before her body, dagger at the ready. Fortunately for her, this commander was actually asleep at his table, which made her job much easier.

Aislynn stole forward, still in a crouch, and she stayed low when she reached the table. Mindful of the fact that this man's guards weren't far away, she reached her arm up, positioned her dagger against the commander's throat, and then drew her blade back towards her savagely, cutting deep. The man came awake with a start, hands reaching for his throat, but Aislynn laid her weight across the man's lap and held him as steady as she could until the weakness from the loss of blood overtook him. She eased away, careful not to make any noise, and slipped out of the tent, leaving a smear of the commander's blood on the tent wall as she passed under it. The man had bled out all over her, but it was a small price to pay to keep him quiet while he died. The tent wall and the grass had wiped some of the blood away, but Aislynn disregarded the rest of the warm, sticky fluid as she moved on. She didn't have time to worry about that sort of thing.

The next few tents were more of the same, with commanders asleep in the working areas of the tents, and apparently not quite as dedicated as they had initially seemed to be. Unfortunately, Aislynn could see movement in the last tent she approached. Dealing with a man who was awake and moving was going to be difficult if she didn't want to draw any attention to herself, so she paused to try to formulate a plan. Looking once again at the placement of the guards, and knowing the layout of the tents, Aislynn decided to sneak in through the back, and then attack from the partition between the two halves of the tent.

She approached the tent and slid smoothly underneath the back wall, coming to her feet before moving to the flap of cloth that blocked her view from the commander. Dagger in hand, Aislynn carefully pulled the canvas aside just a little, peeking through the opening she created to assess the situation. The commander was pacing back and forth across the carpeted width of the tent, his gaze fixed on the sheaf of papers in his hand and absently running his free hand through his light brown hair. From the luxury of the furniture and accessories in this particular tent, Aislynn surmised that she'd found the commander in chief, and she was determined to make sure that this man died, even if she couldn't manage to take out any of the squadron commanders. If this man died, the army would grind to a halt, especially since all of the company commanders were currently enjoying their final rest.

Aislynn knew that she was certainly good enough with a thrown dagger to wound the man from where she stood, but a killing blow from the side with a thrown weapon was next to impossible. Also, if she did manage to drop him from here, his guards would certainly notice the sound of his body hitting the floor, even if it was carpeted. Attacking him certainly wasn't an option, considering *that* would definitely bring the guards running.

With a silent sigh, Aislynn drew a tiny vial from her clothing and popped the cap open. She disliked using poison when she killed. It seemed like cheating somehow, and she'd much rather rely on her own body and skills than some toxic substance to get the job done. But sometimes circumstances warranted its use, like now.

Aislynn regretted the impending loss of one of her paired daggers, which was silly because it was easily replaceable, but assassins relied on their familiar weapons. Besides, it was a small sacrifice to make in order to behead this army. Then she remembered the beautiful weapon Eryk had commissioned for her, and remembered its heft and balance. That blade would be a more than satisfactory replacement for the one she was about to throw, even if that did mean that her daggers would no longer be a matched pair. Feeling considerably better, Aislynn carefully coated both sides of the blade with the poison from the vial and then carefully tucked the tiny container away.

Her weapon ready, Aislynn eased the flap separating the two parts of the tent aside once more, taking stock of the commander. She watched him pace, measuring his stride and making sure that he was indeed walking in a predictable pattern. There was only one shot with this, since a miss would bring the guards in and lead to a battle that could wake many of the surrounding soldiers. Still, she felt that the chance to kill this man was worth the risk.

Aislynn took careful aim, holding her dagger by the hilt instead of by the blade as she usually would, and then threw, leading her target and catching him in the side of the neck. The blow was far from fatal, and the commander's hands reached instinctively for the embedded blade, but the poison started to act before he could touch it. The poison Aislynn used, on the few occasions that she used it at all, was a very powerful one, and lethal in small doses. She'd used far more than she needed to, in order to ensure this man's death, and she'd hit him in the neck because the brain had a dedicated blood supply. The vessels in the neck carried blood between the brain and heart exclusively, so dumping poison into that area of the body ensure the most rapid spread possible.

The commander slumped to his knees as the weakness spread, and then fell forward. He was still conscious enough to try to stop his fall with his arms, but they wouldn't move and the slight blue tinge starting to spread across his face showed Aislynn that the poison had already stopped his lungs and heart. He was a dead man, and she slipped back out of the tent confident that even if the guards found him right away, there would be nothing they could do to save him.

With the most important part of her mission accomplished, Aislynn slipped quietly from shadow to shadow, avoiding the guards as she made her way back into the rest of the camp. Judging from the dark sky and the sliver of the moon above the horizon, she still had an hour or so until dawn. That would certainly be enough time to take out a few of the squadron commanders while she made her way back to the edge of the camp.

Aislynn traveled from command tent to command tent in a zigzag pattern through the camp, being careful not to draw a straight line from the central cluster of tents to the point where she finally left the rest of the Madelians to their slumber. By the time she slipped back into her own camp, still covered in dirt and dried blood, the tiniest sliver of the rising sun had just breached the horizon.

"Successful night?" Byron asked wryly as she slumped to the ground.

"Very," Aislynn commented with a wicked grin. "Now I need a little bit of sleep."

"I think you should likely clean yourself up first," he disagreed, grimacing at the sight of her. "Is any of that yours?"

"Not a drop."

Instead of taking Byron's advice to wash up, Aislynn simply lay down and pulled a blanket over her. She'd had a few long days in the past little while, and being up all night exhausted her. She fell into a deep sleep, certain of the fact that Cheta could keep them safe, and knowing that Byron would wake her if he needed to.

Chapter 25

The attack was supposed to begin at dawn.

The sun, rising this morning looking like a giant red ball, cast a lurid glow over the Madelian army below. The Bacovian cavalries were ready and waiting on the edge of the valley, only needing enough light so that the horses could see well enough to attack with reasonable safety.

In the enemy camp, around the cluster of command tents, everything was in disorder. As dawn had approached, the camp aides had gone to wake their commanders only to find them dead in their tents. Some died while asleep, others seemed to have died while sitting or standing, reading or going over last minute plans. Nobody had any idea who had done it, and nobody had apparently seen or heard anything either. What everybody did know was that they were in trouble.

The squadron leaders were fighting amongst themselves while trying to establish a new pecking order, and as the news of the dead commanders spread, there were rumors circulating about the whole attack being population control, designed to reduce the number of mouths to feed on the slim resources Madelia had. Scouts who left the day before hadn't returned and there was speculation that maybe those men had known something the rest of them didn't. Then there was a rumor that the queen had only ordered the attack out of desperation, being caught by surprise by the advancing Bacovian forces. While the less senior officers scrambled to get the army up and prepared to march, the giant red sun that appeared did nothing to improve the confidence of the Madelians, especially when the growing light revealed what was waiting for them.

All along the top of the ridge that bordered the valley, the soldiers could see the massed horses of the Bacovian cavalry. The reddish glow of the sun glinted off the armor of the men and horses, making them appear to be an army of dead, washed in blood.

In the Bacovian camp, there were worries as well.

"What's taking so long?" Eryk wondered aloud, pacing back and forth along the prominence where he and his command team were prepared to oversee the upcoming battle. Mateo followed closely behind him, but he didn't answer the king's question.

His enemy filled valley below, his own army lined up rank upon rank above them, just waiting for the command to attack. Eryk could just barely see his archers as they spread out along the top of the valley and prepared to support the cavalry. It shouldn't be too much longer, or so the anxious king hoped.

Finally, the order to attack came from Warren, and the first strike belonged to the cavalry, as planned. The light cavalry was also lined up along the top of the valley while the heavy horse were in flanking positions to the left and right of the camp, and for the king and his entourage waiting above, it was like the attack began out of nowhere and with no warning. The horses were just suddenly moving, the frost on the ground helping to prevent a rising cloud of dust. The men were silent, so the only sound was the growing roar of the thunder of hooves.

Safe upon his prominence, the differences between the two types of cavalry doing what they did best struck Eryk profoundly. The heavy cavalry, men and horses alike in armor that glinted in the early sun, were much larger than their light counterparts were. The horses were akin to the large draft horses that farmers used to plough their fields, with hooves as large as a man's spread hand and muscles that propelled them forward to crush their enemies. The light cavalry, by contrast, were instead similar to the smaller horses used by couriers. Riders and horses alike had only the lightest of armor, meant for speed and maneuverability more than sheer power.

The light horse quickly outdistanced their heavier cousins, tearing down the road that led from the ridge and through the Madelian camp. The enemy soldiers hadn't been expecting an attack, so the road still stood clear, but that would change quickly once the camp mobilized. For now, the skirmishers readied their bows, and soon arrows were flying out into the camp, taking soldiers down as they exited tents, grabbed for weapons and readied themselves for battle.

Eryk was very glad that he'd been able to convince Mateo and the rest of his advisors of his need for a viewing platform of sorts. It was obvious even to him that they would never allow him onto the field of battle, but he had threatened to do exactly that if he didn't have some way to oversee the fight. He'd learned many things from Aislynn in her time with him, including how to bully and threaten to get what he wanted. And it worked! The king was now able to pace along the prominence his commanders had found for him, looking down over the action below. He had the visibility he wanted and the safety his guards insisted on.

Warren sat astride his horse at the edge of the valley, looking out over the area where the battle was beginning. Some small bushes obstructed his view slightly, but he could see well enough to keep track of the general flow of the battle. It looked to him like most of the Bacovian light cavalry was now through the camp, so he expected that they should be wheeling around to attack from the back of the camp any time now. He nudged his horse into movement, skirting along the edge of the valley, getting ready to join the battle himself as part of the heavy cavalry unit. As far as he could tell, things were going well for his side. Now it was time to finish this war, decisively.

The horses were as much a danger to the foot soldiers as their riders, plunging fearlessly into the fray and trampling people as they charged in from the sides, effectively attacking the enemy camp on three fronts. Warren had come out of hiding far down the enemy line, and he gathered the wheeling cavalry with a wave of his arm. A few moments to pause and collect themselves, and then they were off again, plowing back into the camp. Warren slashed his sword from side to side, attacking the soldiers that his horse couldn't reach and heading the wedge that bisected a group of soldiers who were trying to form a cohesive defense.

It took some time for the Madelians to organize any form of effective defense against the cavalry attack, and until they did, the horses literally just ran them down. Warren could see his lieutenant ahead of him, leading his group of men parallel to Warren's, and the swath of destruction the two groups had left in their wake was impressive. There were bent and broken tent poles, strewn belongings and dead bodies everywhere, most of the last wearing Madelian colors.

Warren had his sword held high, ready to slash down upon his enemies once more, reveling in the feeling of power he had when he fought astride his horse. He loved this feeling, and it was why he had joined the cavalry in the first place, back when he'd started his fighting career. The formation of the light unit, which was even now circling the camp again, still firing their arrows carefully into the massing Madelians, was a logical extension.

As Warren reached the edge of the broken line, he attacked a man standing on his right, cleaving open his shoulder and forcing him to drop his weapon. Warren withdrew his blade and looked up, searching for his next victim, when he suddenly felt his horse shudder underneath him. Confused, he looked down, and saw a pair of soldiers holding a long spear, which his mount had just impaled himself on.

The horse shuddered again, and began to pitch forward, dead as the spear pierced his heart. Warren didn't have time to free himself from the stirrups, and went down with the animal. The horse crashed down on top of him, pinning him underneath. There was nothing Warren could do to defend himself as the enemy soldiers approached.

It was mid-morning when the order for the foot soldiers to attack came down from Eryk. The king could see that Madelians were finally organizing themselves, and the tide of battle had now changed. The advantage Eryk's men had earlier, picking off individual disorganized groups of soldiers and causing chaos, was now gone. He could also see that the cavalry was starting to lose more and more horses, forcing the riders to fight on the ground, and he knew that it was time to engage the

Madelian army with his own. The cavalry had done their job, and Eryk passed the order to fall back to his runners. Their job now was to keep the enemy from escaping.

The archers who were advancing on foot prepared to fire into the grouped Madelians as the order for the foot soldiers to charge rang out. The warriors on the front lines dashed towards their enemies, running down the incline, as a volley of arrows flew overhead, knocking holes in the line of men that was starting to form the defense of the Madelian camp. Then the foot soldiers reached their destination, and the battle broke out in full. The din was immediately deafening as men fought and screamed and fell. Swords met shields, spears found openings in defenses, and everything was chaos.

Eryk watched what looked like a wave ripple through his army. As the front line of men advanced to close ranks with the enemy, the second line moved forward, then the third and so on, all the way back to where Eryk waited with his guards. He imagined that a similar wave was moving across the Madelian army too, if in a more disorganized way, and wondered how long it would take before both armies fully engaged.

Petyr was barely able to lift his head on his neck when he heard the pounding thunder of hooves seemingly coming towards him. He was beaten and delirious, feeling fevered and sick, and he wasn't certain if it was actually the arrival of the cavalry or a dream of his impending rescue. Hoping that it was reality he was experiencing, Petyr silently bid his comrades good luck, and then he passed back into unconsciousness.

Shaking her head, Aislynn glanced worriedly over at Byron. "He doesn't seem to be getting any better," she commented. "He's been barely conscious since we camped. I don't know what to do with him."

"Well, considering the sounds coming from over the ridge, we'll hopefully be able to get him to a healer sometime in the next little while. Just keep on with the water and we'll bide our time." Byron wasn't in great shape himself, his color off and his eyes dull with pain.

"Get both of you to a healer, you mean," Aislynn corrected, straightening. "I'm going to go take a look. I'll be back soon."

She slid silently out of the bushes she'd used to conceal their small camp before Byron could object, Cheta slipping through beside her. Aislynn could hear the battle not too far away, and it called to her. She was a warrior, and while she hadn't fought in a large-scale battle before, the thought of sitting by while her soon-to-be countrymen were fighting and dying just didn't sit right with her.

Aislynn lay down on her stomach and inched up to the edge of the valley, looking down on the chaos below. The Bacovian cavalry looked to be finished, starting to gather in groups away from the main concentrations of fighting in order to preserve their mounts. From the number of dead horses scattered throughout the valley, they had taken some heavy casualties, and the fighting was too intense for Aislynn to be able to decide if the results were worth it. She hoped so.

Though she really wanted to help the Bacovians below, it was immediately apparent that it wouldn't be a good idea. The battlefield was chaotic, and she had no armor to protect herself if she waded in. Aislynn knew that she was good with a sword, but she wasn't sure how to join the conflict without getting herself immediately killed. With a sigh, she was about to pull back to her camp to wait when a fireball slammed into one of the groups of retreating Bacovian cavalry.

Aislynn jumped to her feet with a curse, moving down the ridge towards the battle before she had even made the conscious decision to do so. Cheta's whine brought her to a halt, and the wolf pushed up beside her as Aislynn scanned the battlefield quickly. In her months in the Bacovian court, she had become accustomed to the lack of mages and magic, but now she remembered that this lack was not the norm for the surrounding kingdoms. Her own home kingdom of Evendell had a Mage School as part of the palace complex, along with the Academy where she had trained, and the use of mages in battle was common practice. Especially fire mages.

Fortunately, being born with magical gifts was a rare talent, so it was likely that the Madelian army had only one mage with them, or two at most, and they should be easy enough to find. On one hand, fire mages tended to be flashy and draw attention to themselves, and on the other hand, like attracted like. Cheta, being a magical creature herself, would be able to track the mage or mages easily, once they made it down to the valley.

Another fireball arced up and over the battling foot soldiers to smash into another group of horses and riders. Getting a general idea of where the fireball had come from, and reasonably certain that there was only one mage to contend with given the time between attacks, Aislynn and Cheta resumed their decent into the valley. Taking care of the mage was one thing that Aislynn *could* do.

As she jogged through the back of the camp, mostly alone because the fighting was towards the front where Eryk's foot soldiers had joined battle with the Madelians, Aislynn was surprised by how quiet this part of camp was. The cavalry had already been through here, so there were scattered belongings and destroyed tents here and there, along with a few dead bodies, but the air seemed almost still. It was similar to the feeling you got just before a thunderstorm began, the atmosphere almost alive with energy that was about to be harnessed into something devastating.

Cheta seemed to feel it too, and the *eesprid* whined softly as she lifted her nose to the nonexistent breeze and tried to catch a scent of the mage that they were tracking. Always ones to be mindful of their personal safety, the mage should be back behind the line of battle somewhere, but high enough so that they'd be able to choose their target area.

Another fireball shot overhead, heading towards the front of the camp and the battle waging there, and Aislynn realized that their target had positioned himself a little way up the ridge, back the way they'd come. Cursing, she and Cheta turned back, and Aislynn scouted around for some cover. Mages could be very difficult to kill if they knew that you were coming, so it would be easiest to strike from concealment.

The lightly wooded ridges had small trees and bushes that made their way down into the valley as well. The road, along with a few feet to either side of it, was clear of obstructions, but the mage was nowhere in the open area. Aislynn knew that the mage would need line of sight in order to keep throwing those fireballs, so he had to be around here somewhere. She knelt and gave Cheta directions, and then sent the wolf off to track down their prey while she remained hidden in a small clump of nearly leafless shrubs. Aislynn was glad that she was still wearing her dark clothing to help her blend in with the few shadows that were available for her to hide in.

Cheta's bark and the sudden appearance of a wall of fire alerted Aislynn to the mage's location. Her *eesprid* must have attacked for there to be a fire shield, and she noted that it was facing only one direction. Shaking her head at the obviously inexperienced mage, Aislynn slipped farther up the ridge to approach from above. The fire shield would have stopped her too, if it had been wrapped entirely around her target, but this was a mistake that she was prepared to take advantage of, and quickly.

As she approached from behind, Aislynn heard the growls and barks that Cheta was making as she half-heartedly tried to get around the shield to attack the mage. The wolf would dart close and then dance away from the flames, and then she would try to get around the wall of fire and attack the mage's flank, forcing him to move his shield. Aislynn was grateful to note that her wolf never attacked too far back, leaving that direction unprotected for the assassin.

Aislynn readied her remaining dagger and then threw it towards the back of the mage's neck, following her toss immediately as she drew her sword. The dagger hit home but didn't bite as deeply as it should have, and the mage whirled around in surprise, letting his shield drop as his concentration broke. Cheta was on him instantly, throwing herself at the man's back just as Aislynn reached them.

The wolf's weight caused the mage to stumble forward slightly, and Aislynn brought her sword up on an angle, hoping to impale the man and end this quickly. She wasn't that lucky, and the man threw himself sideways as soon as he saw her. Seeing that he was off balance, Cheta sprang at the mage once more, knocking him farther to the side and making him lose his balance. As he reached down towards the ground to catch himself and stop his fall, Aislynn darted in with her sword, sweeping the blade down and across from right to left. The sword caught the mage at the junction of his shoulder and arm, cleaving the limb off before it continued to travel downwards on the diagonal, slashing into his chest until it finally reached his heart.

Aislynn put her foot on the dead mage's chest and heaved on her sword, pulling the blade free with difficulty. Then she searched around the ground in the area until she found her dagger and sheathed both blades. Turning to look back down at the battlefield, Aislynn realized that the battle was starting to end, so she headed back up to the top of the ridge and returned to camp once more.

All across the battlefield, men screamed, and bled, and died, Some screamed in pain, and others simply found themselves caught up in the moment and needed some way to verbalize what they felt. Some men were covered in their own blood, and others were covered in the blood of their friends or their enemies. Most were covered in a combination of all three.

Eryk, who had never left his post atop the prominence, knew that the battle was almost over when the carrion crows started to feast. The writhing masses of men arrayed in the valley below him had been gradually slowing in their movements as more and more soldiers were wounded and found themselves unable to continue the fight.

The king had ached to join his men, to help them turn the Madelians away, but he knew that was not his role here. Even if he'd honestly thought that he was capable of holding his own in battle, which he did not, Eryk knew that there was no way that Mateo, or anyone else, would have allowed it.

The cavalry attack had decimated the enemy camp early in the day, and the Bacovians had been able to attack the remaining soldiers with considerably better odds than they'd had in the beginning. The fireballs that had suddenly appeared had in turn devastated the Bacovian ranks, but those had fortunately been short lived.

As the sun passed its midpoint and started to descend into afternoon, Eryk sent out another order, calling the cavalry away from the far side of the camp. The Madelians, now having a route of escape, opted to chance an attack from behind in order to have a chance of living. Eryk could see some of the enemy streaming away from the battle now, pursued by groups of the cavalry.

Aislynn and Byron, being camped behind the enemy army, were the first to know for certain when they started to break and run. Between the deaths of their commanders, the devastating cavalry attack, the loss of their mage, and the organized assault by the foot soldiers, the Madelians were finished.

Small groups and individual soldiers broke away from the fighting first, and they started to run down the road back towards the capital. Once the retreat started, the end of the fight was inevitable as more and more soldiers saw their fellows turning tail and running and then decided to join them.

By the time the sun set, it was all over.

Chapter 26

The battle had literally lasted the entire day, so crews had to go out carrying torches in order to start the clean up. Most of what needed doing would happen after the following dawn, but Eryk knew that it was important that the injured be treated as soon as possible, and the dying be put out of their misery. He didn't envy anyone who had that duty.

Michael had set up a hospital of sorts early in the day, just above the valley where the Madelians had been camped, and the stream of the injured during the battle had been constant. Now, that stream was a river, with more injured soldiers flooding in every minute.

"We need to get these men organized," Michael stated. He grabbed a couple of soldiers who had the misfortune of being nearby, and drafted them into his service. He set up areas outside for those soldiers whose injuries were not life threatening, and then he had the most seriously injured men brought into the tent. He knew that infection was a serious concern, so Michael felt that he could treat them better with this arrangement.

Eryk wandered around the camp, doing what he could to consol the wounded and dying, but he knew that all he was doing was trying to make himself feel better. He didn't like to feel helpless, and he had certainly felt helpless for the majority of the day. It was a strange thing to be in charge of life and death decisions when you are only observing the battlefield.

"Your Majesty," a call rang out. Eryk turned, not quite recognizing the voice, and couldn't believe what he saw. Riding up the path towards him was Byron, leading a pair of horses, one of which he recognized as Aislynn's gray. The other was carrying an unconscious man who seemed tied to his saddle.

"Byron!" Eryk rushed towards his captain of the guard, happy to see him back safely even if the empty saddle gave him feelings of foreboding.

Byron reined in his horse, letting the reins fall to the ground, and he nearly fell out of the saddle as he tried to dismount. Eryk caught him by the arm and helped to steady him, getting a good look at Byron's injuries for the first time. He gasped.

"What happened to you?" Eryk asked, astonished by the bandages Byron sported around his neck and horrified by his pale color.

"Vivien's blade was even sharper than her tongue," Byron joked weakly. "It's a long story, and one that will have to wait until tomorrow, I'm afraid. Aislynn asked me to send her deepest sympathies for the cancellation of your wedding, and to tell you that she'll be up soon."

A grin of relief flashed across Eryk's face.

"I was afraid to ask… I saw that you were leading her horse."

"She stayed below to help the crews giving mercy. The princess figured that she might as well continue to put her skills to good use. She can help to end their suffering quickly, and she's not going to be nearly as traumatized as some with the duty."

Byron knew that Aislynn was actually trying to delay the moment she'd have to face Eryk as long as possible. The fact that she could do so legitimately was just a bonus.

"Help me get Petyr down?" Byron asked, his rasp even more noticeable as he leaned weakly against his horse. "He needs to see a healer."

"And it sounds like you do too," the king commented, his face turning serious. Byron tried to resist, stating that there were soldiers injured far worse than he was, but Eryk overruled him. Rank had to have some privileges, after all, and Michael was soon at Byron's side while one of his assistants attended to Petyr.

"How did this happen?" Michael asked as he peeled away the bandages from Byron's neck and side. Eryk was curious to know the answer to that too, but Byron just shook his head. This was neither the time nor the place to reveal the details of his trip.

"Aislynn stitched me up, if that's what you mean," he answered instead.

"Well, she did a reasonable job, I suppose," the physician commented. He smeared some salve over the healing wounds and ordered Byron up to a tent to rest. "It would do more harm than good to take the stitches out just to try and minimize the scarring. You'll be able to resume your duties by the time we get home, but you'll have to rest during the trip," Michael stated, fixing the captain with a stern stare. The royal physician hadn't had a lot of opportunity to treat Byron before, but he knew the personality type, and knew that Byron would have a hard time with the resting part. Petyr would likely be just as bad, Michael added to himself, glancing over to where the commander was getting his bruises treated.

Just as Byron was preparing to leave, helped along by a pair of Michael's assistants, Cheta loped into the tent, followed closely by Aislynn. She looked around, and spotting Eryk, came right over. It would be horribly rude to do anything else, after all, and she *had* missed him terribly.

"They told me that you were here," she said as she approached, eyes only on Eryk.

Eryk said nothing. He just took Aislynn into his arms and kissed her, not stopping until Byron made a discreet noise, reminding him where he was. Eryk loosened his grip on Aislynn, just a little, and looked down at her. It was then that he noticed her blood spattered clothing, the healing bruises and the new scar across her cheek. He reached out a finger to trace the red crescent-shaped mark.

"What happened?" he demanded, a look of concern on his face. He felt Aislynn stiffen in his grasp.

"Nothing," she replied. "I'm fine. It was no big deal."

Eryk could tell that she was hiding something, it didn't take a genius to figure *that* out, and he took a breath preparing to ask her again. Then he happened to catch Byron's gaze, and he let the breath out. Byron had a look of concern on his face, but he was shaking his head, warning Eryk to drop the subject.

"Well, we could all use some rest, I'm sure," Eryk said as he stroked Aislynn hair. He decided to follow Byron's advice for now and changed the subject. "Let's head back to my tent for a quick meal and then you can get some sleep. There's nothing more we can do over here tonight anyway."

Eryk kept his arm around Aislynn's shoulders as they walked slowly away from the battlefield and towards the camp that had been set up for the Bacovians. Mateo followed a step behind, and helped Byron along. Aislynn glanced back over her shoulder and took a good look at the guard.

"How is he doing?" she asked Eryk, knowing that Mateo was still taking Marcus' death very hard. Eryk followed her gaze, saw Mateo, and sighed.

"Mateo really hasn't been the same since the attack on the castle, and he hasn't said a word to anybody since just after you and Byron left."

Aislynn pondered that while they walked, but didn't say anything else.

Just outside of Eryk's tent, everyone said their goodbyes and Byron headed over to the tent that Eryk indicated would be his for the night. Eryk then led Aislynn inside and over to the table, where some food was waiting.

While they ate, they spoke only of inconsequential things. Eryk didn't ask about what had happened to Aislynn while she was gone, and Aislynn didn't ask about Branden, Warren, or the battle. There would be time enough in the morning to sort it all out. Now that she was safe, Aislynn felt dreadfully tired, and there was nothing she wanted more in the world than a good night's sleep.

"We did it," Aislynn said quietly just before Eryk left her to sleep. "She's dead, with all of the succession issues that go with it."

Eryk kissed his fiancée softly on the lips and saw her eyes drift closed. When she slept, he left the tent quietly.

Dawn found Aislynn and Eryk walking back out through the Bacovian camp. Cheta ran ahead of them, and Mateo followed closely behind. All three of the humans wore swords at their waists, and everyone was a little tense and nervous. There was always a chance that the Madelian retreat hadn't been a retreat at all, but instead just a chance to regroup before they attacked again.

As they walked down and into Michael's camp, the sheer number of injured men struck them immediately. On one hand, it was good that these men were injured instead of dead, but Aislynn had to wonder how many of them would succumb to their wounds later today, tomorrow or even a few days from now. And for those who didn't die of their wounds, how many would die from subsequent infection? She knew that the plan was to pull back to the larger camp today and then proceed back to the capital tomorrow, and Aislynn wondered how many of their men wouldn't make it all the way back.

The bodies of the dead were being laid out downwind from the camps, and there were dozens of people wandering back and forth among the corpses, trying to identify them. When a body was identified, a clerk would make note of the man's name and any other known information, and then the body was loaded up into a cart for burial at a site that had been selected not too far away. Soldiers were burning the enemy bodies down in the valley since none of the Madelians remained to claim them.

According to the scouts Eryk had sent out, there was no sign of an army gathering beyond the valley, so the pair continued farther down into the war torn fields, followed closely by their guard. There were still a large number of corpses scattered around, the body detail not having reached them yet, and the sheer number of dead on both sides threatened to make Eryk sick. Aislynn held his hand and picked up the pace. Their destination wasn't too far away, in an area where the dead were already fully cleared away. Eryk would be able to breathe more easily there, she suspected.

The prisoner camp was composed of two parts: an area for healing and an area for waiting. The guards, soldiers from Eryk's army, kept watch on the Madelians as they sat or slept. Most of the prisoners sported bandages, and they all looked very tired.

"What are you going to do with them?" Aislynn asked as they approached, gesturing towards the prisoners.

"I'm not really sure," Eryk admitted. "Winter is right around the corner, and we don't have the stores to feed them, so we can't take them back with us. I'm honestly leaning towards hanging them all."

Aislynn looked over at him, surprised. Eryk grimaced, and explained.

"If they had only been here for the battle, that would be one thing," he began. "Instead, they have been burning our villages and slaughtering innocent civilians, and that is unforgivable. If it were a different time of year, I would hold them for a proper trial, but that isn't going to be possible. The only thing stopping me right now is the possibility of starting my relationship with the new Madelian ruler on good terms. Sending the living home may be a good start towards a treaty, but if not, at least I don't have to worry about feeding and housing them."

Aislynn thought about that for a moment, and then nodded her head. Her training told her not to leave an enemy standing, but what Eryk was saying made sense. It would be nice to try to work towards peace with Madelia. She had killed many of the enemy soldiers in the past day and a half, but now that the fighting was over, she really didn't see the need to slaughter the ones who were sitting there on the ground looking up at them.

"I think sending them home is a good idea, but how are you going to do it? Chances are very good that there aren't many commanding officers in that group there." She said that with a touch of a smile, and Eryk looked at her questioningly.

"Later," she promised.

"We'll tie them together and send them down the road," Eryk explained as they reached the camp. "I'm planning to fortify along the border anyway, so the men I send there as the first group on duty will be able to keep an eye out in case any of them head back our way."

Aislynn scanned the men all seated on the ground, singly or in small groups. They all looked young, and scared. Walking slowly among them, leaning on a stick for support since he was still a little unsteady, was Petyr. Seeing Aislynn's confused look, Eryk smiled.

"That man refused to stay in bed," he explained, "so I gave him this supervisory position until I order him back to the main camp in a little while. I think that he just needs to feel useful, given that he wasn't capable of participating in the battle, and Michael said that other than exhaustion, he's fine."

Seeing the two of them approach, the man spoke a few quick words to the nearest red and black uniformed guard, and then he headed slowly towards them. He bowed low as he reached them, or at least he tried, and Aislynn reached out to steady him when he stumbled.

"Your Majesty," he greeted Eryk. Turning to Aislynn, he bowed again. "Your Highness."

"Petyr," Eryk said, grasping the man's hand firmly. "It's great to see that you're doing well here. Did you find out how your men fared?"

Petyr smiled slightly. "Not too badly, all things considered. We are currently nine, with another three confirmed dead. I'm afraid that leaves four of my men still unaccounted for. What about Lord Branden? Did you find him?"

Eryk nodded his head sadly. "We found him just before dawn, thanks to the information that you gave us last night, but it's not good. He's alive for now, but his injuries are very severe and there's infection in the wound. Michael will summon me if he wakes up before we pack up and leave."

The king took a deep breath to clear his thoughts and then continued. "There will be a council meeting at the castle as soon as we return," he said. "I'd like you to be there."

Petyr bowed his head in acquiescence and then excused himself to go back to his duties keeping an eye on the prisoners. Even after a night of sleep and a couple of good meals, he was still weak, and the fact that he was tiring was pretty obvious by how much of his weight he was putting on his stick.

"You have plans for him, don't you?" Aislynn asked, recognizing a certain light in Eryk's eye. He nodded.

"I got word late last night, after you were asleep, that Warren is dead. They pulled him out from under his horse somewhere out in the middle of the battlefield. I'm going to promote Petyr, and give him Warren's job."

"Well he certainly seems like a good man, given what little I know of him. The fact that over half of his men survived what was a very dangerous mission bodes well for his command ability, and he's certainly dedicated. I think he'll do a good job."

After leaving Petyr with the prisoners, the couple went back up to the hospital to check in with Michael and his healers, hoping that Branden might finally be awake. Cheta, noticing their anxiety, whined softly and raced ahead, beating them to the tent that was in place to help protect the most seriously injured while they were treated.

Branden still lay pale and unmoving on a cot surrounded by healers. After removing his torn uniform, Michael treated the ghastly wounds down the left side of his body. The stains on his bandages gave testimony to the amount of blood that he had lost. Aislynn, shocked, was sure that he looked even worse than Byron had, especially given the obvious infection spreading out from under one of the bandages.

"Where did you find him?" she asked nobody in particular.

"In the copse of trees a little way up the road," replied one of the soldiers standing nearby. "Petyr told us what happened when he was captured once he regained consciousness briefly last night, and we went immediately."

"You mean he was out there, seriously wounded, for days?" The soldier just nodded his head, agreeing to the statement.

Aislynn knew that it was nobody's fault that Branden wasn't found before this, but she still felt angry. If anything happened to Branden, Marja would be crushed, and Aislynn felt that everyone had lost enough over the course of this conflict, especially in the recent weeks. The upcoming wedding was something to look forward to, a ray of sunlight after the storm of the war. She sighed.

Aislynn and Eryk left the healers to do their work and headed back up to Eryk's tent, still trailed by their ever-present and ever-silent guard.

Nobody interrupted them, and Aislynn turned to face her king.

"Is that everyone then?" she asked. "Are we all present and accounted for, in one way or another?"

"Yes," Eryk said. "We'll be heading back to the main camp soon, and we should be back to the castle within three days. Once we arrive, we'll gather for the council meeting and decide what we do from here."

Everyone pulled out of the smaller makeshift camp over the course of the day, and Eryk sent the Madelians on their way as he'd promised Aislynn. Branden and Byron, along with some of the other badly wounded soldiers, were loaded into wagons for the trip back to the capital within another day, and within a week of the battle, there was nothing left in the valley and surrounding area except debris.

There was an excited feeling to the conversations happening around the council chamber that first afternoon after Eryk and his entourage returned from Madelia. Everyone knew part of the story, since rumor was running rampant through the castle, but this would be the first time they found out about everything that had happened over the past couple of weeks. Aislynn looked around her as she entered the room, noticing that everyone looked different, older. The war had changed them all.

Eryk called the meeting to order, and everyone took their assigned seats. Eryk smiled slightly, happy to be meeting in the chambers again instead of out in a tent near a battlefield. He looked around the table, taking note of the still empty seats in the room. He'd have to appoint new councilors as soon as possible.

"Okay everyone," he started. "As far as the cavalry could tell, the Madelians were heading away from the border at top speed, and they don't seem likely to return anytime soon, so the war is over for now. I've called you all here so that we could review the details of what has happened and make a plan to move forward.

"As many of you know, the attack that we planned had multiple parts, and there were members of this council who were involved in different ways. Her Highness and the captain took on one role, Petyr and his men another, while the foot and cavalry units took on a third. I regret to inform you all that Lord Warren died during the battle, but the effectiveness of his unit was everything that he promised it would be. The light cavalry definitely helped to end the battle quickly, complementing our heavy cavalry very nicely.

"I will turn the floor over to her Highness to explain what happened in Madelia."

Aislynn took a deep breath. She had thought long and hard about what she was going to say at this meeting. The only ones at this table who truly knew her were Byron and Eryk, and she saw no need to change that. Her role, and the role of her predecessors, had been kept secret for decades, and she wasn't about to break the silence. There were some of the guards who knew that she was an assassin, but her bond to Eryk remained undisclosed to them too. Only Byron knew the true depth of that bond.

"The captain and I went across the border to arrange for the death of Madelia's queen," she said honestly. "It took some doing, but I can assure you that she is dead and that the court is going to be dealing with the problems of succession for some time to come. Vivien had no declared heir, and I understand that the closest relatives are cousins – and that there are a number of them."

As Aislynn finished, Eryk gestured to Petyr, who cleared his throat and prepared to take up the flow of the story.

"My men and I, disguised as enemy soldiers, made our way across the border and found the army camp there. I divided my men and sent pairs and small groups back across the border to report our findings. My traitorous lieutenant betrayed and captured me, and Lord Branden was seriously injured. The Madelians sent word to their capital about the impending attack, but his Majesty attacked their camp before they were able to mobilize and come to strike at us."

Eryk took a deep breath and continued.

"For now, we will be increasing our patrols along the border, and in the spring, we will be building permanent command posts in strategic locations. Are there any questions?"

The councilors, all of them intelligent people, realized that there were details missing from the various accounts of the battle, but nobody was willing to question Eryk right now. Seeing that there was nobody brave enough to ask questions, the king continued.

"There are a number of seats on this council that still need to be filled," he said. "It is my great pleasure to announce the promotion of the commander here." Eryk gestured towards Petyr, who blushed, surprised.

"I officially confer upon Petyr the title of Lord, and grant him the position of commander in chief of the army, replacing our fallen comrades, Lord Geoffrey and Lord Warren. The rest of the positions will be filled within the next few days, so there will be a full council for Lord Branden's wedding." Eryk made no comment about the condition of the groom-to-be, preferring to think positively. "You are all dismissed."

As the council filed out of the room, Eryk gestured to Byron to wait a few moments, and he sat back down. When the room was empty, Eryk walked up to the captain and sat down in a seat beside him. Aislynn hung back a little.

"So are you two going to tell me what happened yet?" he asked, turning to look at them both as he spoke. Byron looked at Aislynn, and she took a deep breath.

"We needed a way to get into the castle, and there was a slave market happening at the time. There was a representative from the castle there, and I made Byron sell me to him," Aislynn said. She ignored the look of horror on Eryk's face and the rush of disgust that traveled to her through the link, and kept talking.

"I was able to move almost freely around the castle after a couple of days, and Byron was able to sneak in with the morning deliveries. We met up in Vivien's suite, where we also ran into Cora. I killed the guards, and Byron captured Vivien, but she stabbed him before we could finish the job. Vivien then attacked Byron, injuring him further before I managed to kill her."

"And that's it?" Eryk asked, sensing that there was still something she wasn't saying.

"That's it," she said firmly. "We made our way back here, and I spent a few hours the night before the battle ridding the Madelian army of most of its commanding officers, as well as the mage that was throwing fireballs around during the battle."

"Do you want to add anything?" Eryk asked, addressing Byron. Byron just shook his head, not trusting himself to speak. He couldn't lie to his king, but he wouldn't betray Aislynn's confidence either, so he just remained silent.

"Fine," said Eryk, accepting their stories since he had no other choice. If there were more, he'd find out eventually. He had just gotten Aislynn back, and he wasn't about to make her angry by pushing her.

Byron left the council chamber to return to his room to rest, following the orders of the healers in a most uncharacteristic way. Aislynn and Eryk retired to the study to go over some paperwork and other administrative stuff. Life would be able to get back to normal now, they hoped.

Chapter 27

The next few days passed in a whirlwind of activity. Marja, generally an optimistic person, had held off on the last minute wedding preparations in case Branden hadn't made it back from his mission with Petyr. Almost as soon as she heard of his survival from Aislynn, Marja had been busy getting things ready for her big day.

Aislynn was incredibly happy to help Marja with whatever she needed. She was content to be swept up in Marja's bliss – it kept her thoughts from drifting towards darker places. Marja kept her busy from dawn until well after dusk, only grudgingly allowing her time to eat and attend to her duties at court. It was going to be a fabulous wedding, and helping her friend was a pleasant distraction.

It was just two days before the wedding when Branden was finally feeling strong enough to leave his bed, and Eryk was only happy to keep him company.

"So what's going on with the ladies?" Branden asked as he settled himself into a comfortable chair in Eryk's study.

"I don't know the specifics," Eryk replied, "but I do know that all Aislynn's spoken about since she returned has been your wedding. Apparently, since I'm a *man* I wouldn't understand the intricacies of wedding planning."

Branden rolled his eyes. "From what I've seen, Aislynn doesn't exactly have an eye for the finer things either," he commented with a chuckle and Eryk laughed with him. The men just didn't understand the need the women felt to plan and execute the perfect day. You show up, the priest marries you, and you're done.

"So when will it be your turn?" Branden asked, turning a smiling face towards his best friend.

"I honestly don't know," Eryk answered, his face falling. "I missed her so much while she was gone, but she doesn't seem to feel the same way. She's been distant, almost cold, since she and Byron got back. I had been hoping for a spring wedding, but I really need to talk to her about everything first."

"Have you asked Byron about it?"

"I've tried, but he won't answer my questions. He keeps trying to change the subject too. I could order him to tell me what they're hiding, but I don't think that would be the right thing to do. And I'm honestly not sure that he'd tell me the truth."

"That's odd," Branden commented, and Eryk nodded his head in agreement.

Eryk had wracked his brain trying to figure out what was going on, but he couldn't come up with anything. He had briefly considered the idea that Aislynn and Byron had become romantically involved while they were away, but Aislynn acted the same as she always had with Byron. Only her feelings for Eryk had apparently changed.

Shaking their heads at the unknowable minds of the women, the gentlemen settled in for what they hoped would be a relaxing afternoon.

Aislynn stretched out on the couch in her room while Marja posed for her and Anna. She looked absolutely stunning in her wedding gown, which she was modeling for them as part of her final fitting.

Marja had opted for a plain gown, made from the finest white linen with an overdress of white lace. It was tight in the bodice, showing off her tiny waist, and the skirt flared out from her body as she turned. There was no train.

"It's perfect!" Marja exclaimed, twirling around again and watching the fabric move around her. She gathered the skirts in her hand and pretended to dance, giggling as the dress swished and swayed with her movements.

"I will stitch the crystals and beads onto the lace today," Anna promised, smiling. Marja's joy was contagious, and it was impossible not to smile with her.

"What are you going to do with your hair?" Aislynn asked.

"I'm going to leave it down, and weave some ribbons and beads through it," Marja said. "That way, it won't get all messed up with the veil."

After Anna left, taking the dress with her for the final alterations and finishing touches, Marja collapsed onto the couch next to Aislynn. The stress of these last minute preparations was starting to get to her, though she seemed determined not to show it.

Aislynn laid her hand on her friend's leg.

"Don't worry," she said. "Just a couple more days and this part will all be over."

Marja smiled tiredly at her friend. "And then the fun begins, right?"

"Has it been hard, having Branden still recovering and not here to help?" Aislynn wanted to know.

"Honestly, it's been rather nice," Marja said, blushing. "He wouldn't have been that much help anyway, and his injuries have kept him out of my way."

Aislynn laughed, and then got to her feet.

"So what's next? We've done the dress thing, and you know how you're going to wear your hair. We did flowers yesterday and met with Father Nicholas at the church. Are we done?"

Marja sat up, surprised. "You know what? I think we actually *are* done!"

"So we honestly get to relax tomorrow? Wow, that'll be different."

"You're kidding, right? How could I possibly relax on the day before my wedding?"

"Well, *I'll* get to relax then," Aislynn said with a wink and a laugh. Marja threw a pillow at her.

The morning of the wedding, Aislynn found herself in the barrack's courtyard for the first time since returning from Madelia. It was cold this morning, and the cobblestones were slick with frost. It wouldn't be long until she would be out here in the snow, she knew.

Aislynn walked slowly around the courtyard, testing her footing before starting her warm-up. The last thing she needed was a sprained ankle or some other injury, so this would be a slow and controlled set of exercises, she decided. Cheta settled into her usual corner, and curled up with her tail covering her nose.

The princess drew her sword and began a slow sword dance that her Master had taught her long ago. She started with her sword pointing upwards to the sky, feet shoulder width apart, and then she moved. Shifting her weight back and forth as she danced, she brought her sword down and across her body slowly, cutting graceful arcs though the air. Closing her eyes, she lost herself in the dance.

Aislynn knew that Eryk was there. She sensed him as he approached, and she could feel his admiration now as he watched her exercise. But she could also sense his worry and concern. She finished her dance in the same position as she had started in, and turned to face her king.

"Good morning," she said with a smile. "Why aren't *you* here exercising?"

"I was planning to wait until Byron could be back here," Eryk said, blushing.

Aislynn laughed at his discomfort and moved closer to him. He reached out to embrace her, but she dodged aside with a smile, then darted in and planted a kiss on his cheek before moving away again. Warming up to the game, Eryk eagerly pursued her around the courtyard, and it wasn't long before Cheta was playing too, running interference for Aislynn.

A little while later, Eryk had managed to back Aislynn into a corner, with help of her traitorous wolf who had switched sides at the last minute. Eryk embraced her, and gave her a kiss on the nose, trying to ignore the way she stiffened in his arms.

"I admit that I'm really surprised to find you here this morning," he said. "I thought that you'd be totally occupied helping Marja get ready.

Goodness knows you've spent every waking moment with her for the past week." Aislynn could feel a touch of jealousy surging down her link to him.

"I needed some time to focus, and I really needed some exercise," she explained, ducking under his arm to escape the way he confined her. "And now, I really need to go." She blew him a kiss as she dashed away, and Eryk sighed before following more slowly.

He intended to return to the castle to see if Branden needed any help getting ready, but changed his mind as he walked through the barracks building. Eryk had finally reached his limit with Aislynn's evasions and secrets, and he was determined to get answers. She would tease and throw him the occasional kiss, but as soon as he tried to get close, tried to embrace her and give her a really good kiss, she would stiffen and shy away. Eryk turned towards Byron's room and soon after, he was knocking on the door.

"Your Majesty, come in. What can I do for you?" Byron asked, startled to find Eryk in his quarters. Judging from the look on Eryk's face, the king was not happy. He slid up in his bed, trying to be as presentable as possible while still obeying the healer's orders to rest as much as possible. The journey back to the castle had been harder on him than anticipated, and Michael had extended Byron's convalescence for another few days.

Eryk walked in and shut the door behind him, leaving Mateo in the hall. He intended this to be a private discussion.

"I've had enough," the king began. "You need to tell me what's going on, right now."

"I can't do that, your Majesty," Byron said, shaking his head and knowing exactly what Eryk was talking about. "You need to have this discussion with her Highness, not me. I've already told you that."

"I've tried!" Eryk complained, throwing himself into the only chair in the room. "She avoids the question, avoids me, and evades."

"I'm sorry I can't help you," Byron commented honestly.

"What if I ordered you to tell me?" Eryk asked.

"I would still have to refuse, regardless of the consequences," Byron replied without hesitation. He'd already had this discussion with himself, knowing that Eryk would eventually demand answers. Eryk sighed, trying very hard not to get angry.

"How long has this been going on between the two of you?" the king asked quietly.

Byron thought briefly about pretending not to know what Eryk was talking about, but he already felt bad enough about evading the previous question, especially since he didn't agree with Aislynn keeping the attack a secret.

"About as long as she's been here," the captain replied. He couldn't miss the flash of anger in Eryk's eyes.

"She's *mine*, Byron," Eryk growled, and Byron nodded his agreement.

"I know that," he agreed quickly. "I've always known that. I don't have, nor have I ever had, any intention of pursuing a relationship with her Highness. Not while you're interested in her; my loyalty to you is deep and true." He figured that keeping it formal might help him convince Eryk of his sincerity.

"We're only friends, Sire," Byron continued. "Closer than most, admittedly, but only friends none the less. I am loyal to you, your Majesty, as always, but I am loyal to her as well. *When* she is queen, it will be the same, and you will always know that you can trust me."

"Do you love her?"

Again, Byron considered not answering the question, but come what may, he needed to be as honest as he could be with his liege.

"I do."

"And does she love you?"

"You'd have to ask her that, your Majesty. I wouldn't presume to dictate her Highness's feelings, but I am confident in saying that if she loves me, she loves you more."

Eryk sat back in his chair and closed his eyes, trying to think.

"What am I supposed to do Byron?" he asked quietly, sounding a little defeated. "I thought that she just needed time to unwind from the mission and the battle. She's been so tied up in wedding preparations with Marja, but hasn't mentioned anything about our wedding. Now you tell me that you love her, and she probably loves you too. Do I just give up?"

"I can't tell you what to do in this case, Eryk," Byron answered him just as quietly. "I said before that I couldn't dictate her emotions, but I do know that she loves you. Before you make any decisions, you need to talk with Aislynn. It could just be that she's avoiding the conversations out of respect for her friend. You know that she'd never overshadow Marja's big day with her own announcement."

Eryk stood and made his way to the door. His hand on the latch, Eryk looked back over his shoulder at Byron, who met his gaze steadily.

"You promise that nothing has happened with her?" he asked one last time.

"I promise that nothing has happened between her and me," Byron carefully worded his reply.

Still not satisfied, Eryk left the barracks, shaking his head at Byron's parting remark. He had a lot of information to mull over, but not the answers he had originally been looking for.

Back in the castle, Aislynn made her way up to her rooms. She knocked lightly on the door to announce her arrival, and then slipped in, quickly closing the door behind her being careful not to catch Cheta's tail. It wouldn't do for anyone to see the bride before she was ready, after all.

Marja was just finishing her bath, and the air in the suite smelled of roses and lavender from the dried petals someone had added to the water. Aislynn took a deep breath and sighed. The lavender was a nice touch, nice and relaxing.

"What's wrong?" Marja asked, walking into the room. She was dressed in a white linen shift, and was drying her long blond hair with a towel.

"Nothing," Aislynn replied. "I'm just going to miss you, that's all. This suite is going to be very empty without you."

"I'm not going very far," Marja said. "Branden's taken possession of his family's old house in the city, so I'll be able to be come back here whenever you need me to be. Ever since Alexius was banished, nobody's been using it, so he figured that it might as well be ours."

"I know you'll be close, but it still won't be the same." Aislynn walked over to her friend and gave her a big hug. "I'm so very happy for you. Truly happy. It'll be a wondrous wedding and a magnificent marriage for you both."

Aislynn helped Marja finish drying her hair, and got herself dressed while Marja twisted her perfect curls with ribbons and crystals. The effect was stunning, with Marja scattering rainbows around the room every time she moved her head.

Soon after, a knock at the door announced Anna's arrival with Marja's gown. Aislynn helped her friend to get dressed, carefully holding the various layers of fabric so that they wouldn't ruin Marja's hair, and when it was all done, she stepped back to admire the bride.

The white dress skimmed along Marja's body, accentuating her figure while at the same time seeming demure and modest. The beadwork Anna had added to the neck, sleeves and hem were the same as the beads in the Marja's hair, and they drew the whole look together. Aislynn helped Marja to position her lacy veil, collected her bouquet from the vase on the table, and they were ready to go.

The wedding was to take place at noon at the Cathedral in the city, with Father Nicholas presiding. This would be his first ceremony since he was appointed to the council and Aislynn hoped for the sake of everybody that it went smoothly. Afterwards, the reception would take place in the ballroom of the castle, and the girls knew that everything was already set up there.

"You're sure your father won't mind that I'm using the carriage?" Marja asked as she prepared to leave the room for the last time.

"I'm positive. You are nobility, *Lady* Marja, so you can certainly make use of it. You may not have the royal crest for your own, but it won't hurt to show that you come from Evendell."

"It's too bad nobody could make it from home," Marja sighed. "I know that the passes are closed early because of the snow, but it would still have been nice."

"Then you should have planned a summer wedding," Aislynn said with a wink. "At least they sent a really nice gift with the courier."

The ladies descended the stairs and walked out the great wooden doors and into the courtyard. Their carriage was waiting for them, drawn by a white horse that a groom had thoughtfully decorated with flowers woven through his mane and tail. They took their seats inside, and they were on their way.

Outside the Cathedral, Eryk was waiting with Mateo. The guests were already inside the church, and Eryk knew that Branden was nervously pacing in front of the altar. The groom had recovered well from his injuries, though he would bear some very nasty scars until his dying day. Today, without his recovery to occupy his thoughts, he was feeling nervous while he waited for his bride.

When the carriage rolled up to the base of the stairs, Eryk started down the steps to greet the ladies as they emerged. He offered Marja his arm, leaned over to give Aislynn a quick kiss, and Aislynn and Cheta led the way back up the stairs.

They all parted ways at the entrance to the cathedral, with Aislynn walking down the aisle alone to take a seat in the front pew. She threw Branden a reassuring smile as she sat, and he smiled back before turning to look up the aisle towards the doorway. Then the music began to play, the guests stood, and Marja was escorted up the aisle on the arm of the king.

Tall vases of flowers decorated the church on either side of the altar, and each pew had a decoration of flowers and ribbons. All of the flowers were white and pale pink, which were very hard to come by this late in the season. Aislynn had spent an entire day combing the city and surrounding countryside for enough flowers to decorate to Marja's wishes.

After Eryk placed Marja's hand in Branden's, he sat beside Aislynn and the two of them enjoyed the service. During the ceremony, both Marja and Branden spoke their vows clearly and without faltering. Father Nicholas proved to be an animated speaker, and Aislynn was actually looking forward to having him on the council. He was certainly more interesting to listen to than Father Jonas had been, which automatically made Aislynn prefer him to his predecessor.

The bride and groom never took their eyes off each other during the whole ceremony, which proved to be a bit of a problem when Branden missed Marja's finger with the ring, dropping it on the ground instead. Blushing, he bent down to pick it up to the laughter of everyone in the church, and then he placed the golden band around her finger.

Just as the ceremony concluded, and Branden leaned over to kiss his wife for the first time, Eryk leaned close to Aislynn to whisper in her ear.

"Look how happy they are," he commented with a sigh. "When will it be our turn?" His tone was wistful and light. Aislynn knew that he expected an answer, but she didn't provide him with one. She could feel that he was worried, but she wasn't sure exactly what he was worried about. She'd been too busy to think about their wedding, knowing that they had time to figure that out. Assuming he still wanted her, once he found out about what had happened in Madelia.

At the reception, everyone ate and danced long into the night until it was time for Branden to take his bride to their new home. True to tradition, Branden swept his bride off her feet and literally threw her over his shoulder before carrying her off to the waiting carriage. Eryk glanced at Aislynn, and caught her looking speculatively at the newlyweds.

"Is everything all right?" he asked her.

"Yeah," she replied quietly, her eyes starting to well with tears. "Everything's fine." Then she turned away and walked quickly back into the castle.

Eryk stood there for a few moments, and then just shook his head. She had been acting so strangely, and he really wished he knew what was going on. With a sigh, he followed Aislynn back inside.

Chapter 28

The meeting between Aislynn and Byron the next morning was certainly not typical for the pair.

"You want me to do what?" Byron stared at Aislynn, a look of incredulity on his face. "Why aren't you being your own thief?"

"I told you," Aislynn replied, forcing herself to be calm. "I'm going to be busy setting everything up in the garden."

The morning had dawned bright and clear, the sunrise turning the few clouds in the sky a pale pink as it rose. The sky was lightening to a deep shade a blue, the kind that would accent the colored leaves perfectly. It was going to be a gorgeous day, and Aislynn planned to take advantage of it.

"Setting what up in the garden?" Byron pressed, wanting to know. "If I'm going to do this, I need to know why, and it had better be a damned good reason too."

Aislynn turned away from him, but not before he caught the telltale sign of a blush. Byron stepped closer and put his hands on her shoulders, intending to turn her around to face him. Just as he was about to touch her, Aislynn whirled to face him, a mischievous look on her face.

"Can't you just consider it a favor?" she asked. "Surely you could do this one tiny thing for me?"

"Haven't you used up a lifetime of favors?" he asked in return.

Byron stood there and just looked at Aislynn, waiting for her to continue. Instead, she just stared right back at him, an expectant look on her face.

"Fine!" Byron exclaimed, exasperated. "I'll do you this favor. If you really think that you need them, then I guess I'll go and get them for you. I would just feel so much better if I wasn't stealing from a church."

"You're not stealing them. They don't belong to the church, and they're just going to be thrown out anyway. I figured that I might as well us them before they all wither and die. Just get me the flowers and bring them to the garden, okay?"

Byron nodded his assent.

"Eryk and I need to talk," Aislynn explained, "and I want everything to be as perfect as possible. He's still pushing for answers."

Byron took a few steps forward and wrapped his arms around Aislynn tightly. "It will be okay," he assured her before letting her go. "I know that you've made the right decision, and I know that you will both be happy after you're married."

"Thank you," Aislynn responded, honestly touched. "Now go and get the flowers and don't be late."

As Aislynn walked out of the barracks, back straight and anxiety apparent in every line of her body, Byron sighed to himself and then followed along more slowly. He watched her disappear into the castle proper just as the first rays of sunlight touched the courtyard, and then he turned for the gate and headed out into the city towards the cathedral.

Aislynn didn't look back once as she made her way towards her destination. She knew that Byron would do what she'd asked of him, and she knew that the rein on her anxiety was precarious at best. She could hardly wait for this discussion to be over.

With a sigh, Aislynn turned into the library and made her way towards the back wall. Then, with a slight smile on her face, she slipped through the doors and into the garden beyond. She had a lot to do to get ready.

Eryk rolled over with a groan. He could see light behind his eyelids and knew that it was day, but he had no idea what time it was. He did know that his head was aching – likely because he had overindulged the night before at the wedding.

As he lay in bed, trying to get back to sleep, Eryk heard noises suddenly coming from outside his bedroom door. Thinking that odd, he rolled out of bed and started to make his way over to the door.

The partially open bedroom door flew open just as Eryk reached it, admitting a very agitated Cheta. The wolf ran full speed into the room, jumped up onto Eryk's bed, and then flung herself back off and sped off back into the reception room. Confused, Eryk followed behind her, eyes following her chaotic movements around the room.

"What's up with her?" Eryk asked, nodding towards Cheta.

Mateo shrugged his shoulders, his face mirroring Eryk's own confused expression as he watched Cheta bound around the room. Then the wolf dashed back out of the suite and into the hall, leaving as precipitously as she had arrived.

Shaking his head, Eryk turned and made his way back towards his bedroom and his waiting bed. His sudden exit from his warm blankets had done nothing to ease his headache, and he figured that a bit more sleep wouldn't hurt. But no sooner had he sat down then Cheta was back, rushing into the room and jumping back onto the bed.

This time, the wolf didn't leave the bed. Instead, she lay down across the middle of it, and growled at Eryk when he tried to move her. It was obvious that Cheta had no intention of letting him go back to sleep.

Giving up, Eryk moved over to his wardrobe to find some clothing and get dressed. This, apparently, was exactly what Cheta wanted, and she leaped off the bed again and dashed over to Eryk, where she began to pace impatiently. When he finished dressing, she ran over to the door, doubling back to Eryk before running for the door of the suite.

"Geesh! Think she wants me to follow her?" Eryk asked Mateo, a silly grin on his face. Mateo said nothing, his face devoid of expression. He fell into place behind the king, and the odd trio made their way out of the suite and down the hall.

It quickly became obvious that Cheta was leading Eryk to his study, and he picked up the pace, causing the wolf to dash on ahead. Sure enough, he found her waiting outside the closed door to the room, and when Eryk let her inside, she made her way directly to the doors leading out into the garden. Once again, Eryk opened the door to let her out and then stepped through himself.

As soon as he was outside, Cheta laid down across the entrance preventing Mateo from coming out into the garden while also stopping Eryk from going back inside. Knowing that he had arrived at his destination, Eryk turned away from the wolf and started walking deeper into the garden.

While he walked, Eryk thought about the times that he had played in this garden as a child. He remembered the way the frost would edge each leaf and petal before the cold sent everything into hibernation until the spring. He recalled playing outside here in the snow, building forts and lobbing snowballs at unwary servants. Eryk also remembered the disarray that it had fallen into after his mother's death, and he was happy to see how much better it looked now that Aislynn had used most of a season to work on it. He knew that she liked the peace here, and liked to have somewhere to go away from everyone. After a few months at court, Eryk knew that Aislynn was still considerably more comfortable on the battlefield than caught up in the social situations at court.

It wasn't long before he found a new addition to the garden. Tucked away in the back corner was a lovely gazebo. Each of the four corner posts was made of wrought iron shaped like vines and flowers, and these posts supported a white linen canopy that protected the small breakfast set below from the sun. The small table was set with a light breakfast – juice, bread and cheese – which was appropriate for someone nursing a hangover. There were also large vases of flowers at each corner, and Eryk thought that they looked strangely familiar. Aislynn was nowhere to be seen.

No sooner had he commented to himself about her absence, Eryk heard the crunch of gravel on the path behind him. He smiled as he turned around, knowing that she had made the noise on purpose to announce her arrival. Aislynn's footfalls only announced her presence if she wanted them to.

She stood there on the path, the warm fall sunlight catching hints of red in her brown hair as the slight breeze blew it softly around her shoulders. She was wearing a plain white dress that skimmed along her body and came to just below her knee, almost like a young girl's dress, and the breeze played with the hem of the skirt too. The short sleeves and pale color of the dress set off the tan of her skin perfectly, and Eryk couldn't remember if she had ever looked more beautiful.

Aislynn, feeling the play of Eryk's emotions along their link, smiled at him as she walked forward. She stepped up close to him and leaned forward slightly to whisper in his ear.

"Do you like it?" she asked. Eryk just nodded dumbly, not knowing what to say.

"Come and eat breakfast with me," she said, picking up his hand and guiding him towards the small table. "I have something I want to talk to you about."

It wasn't until they settled under the canopy of the gazebo, breakfast spread out in front of them, that Eryk noticed the brand on Aislynn's arm. She had been careful not to wear anything with sleeves short enough to reveal it until now, and now she felt that the time for secrets was over.

"What's that?" he asked, curious. Eryk reached out to brush his fingers softly across Aislynn's marked arm. "It looks almost familiar."

"It should," she replied with an ironic smile. "It's the royal crest of Madelia. They brand their slaves."

Eryk looked up, meeting Aislynn's calm look with his own look of horror.

"I'm fine," she said reassuringly. "It hasn't bothered me in a long time. Besides, I figured that I was starting a nice little collection."

She smiled and lifted her left hand, revealing to him again the mark of Bacovia's royal family. "All I need is a tattoo of my own country's crest and I'm all set!"

"Aislynn, that's really not funny," Eryk commented with a scowl.

"Then it's a good thing that this isn't what I wanted to talk to you about," Aislynn said, gesturing to her arm.

"No? Well, what did you want to talk about?"

Aislynn took a deep, steadying breath, and then looked Eryk straight in the eye.

"I wanted to tell you again… to reassure you that I would be your bride," she said. "If you'll still have me, that is."

When Eryk heard Aislynn say that she wanted to be his bride, it was almost as if he stopped listening. Aislynn could feel his happiness and his excitement, and she sat at the table waiting for the rest of what she had said to register.

"That's such wonderful news!" Eryk exclaimed, jumping up from the table and walking around to her. He knelt down beside her and wrapped his arms around her waist.

"I hoped that if I was patient, if I just gave you the space you needed, that you would talk to me. I hoped that you just needed time to unwind after all the fighting. This is going to be so great – we really are perfect for each other. When do you what to have the ceremony?"

"Eryk, did you hear me?" Aislynn asked instead of answering his question.

"Of course I heard you," he replied. "You said that you'd marry me."

"I said I would marry you if you would still have me," she clarified.

Eryk let her go and rocked back on his heels as the importance of her words sank in.

"What do you mean, if I'll still have you?" he asked.

He remembered the way she had been acting ever since she and Byron had returned from Madelia, cold and distant. "Aislynn? Tell me what happened while you were gone."

She wanted to tell him, she really did, but she just couldn't force herself to say the words. Aislynn knew that Byron was right, and Eyrk deserved to know the truth.

"I can't tell you that Eryk," she answered, tears in her eyes. "I'm sorry, but I can't talk about it, not yet. I just can't seem to force myself to say the words."

His initial reaction was to be angry, and that reaction caused him to stand up and step back from where Aislynn still sat. He was about to demand that she tell him what was going on, that he had a right to know why she thought he wouldn't want her anymore. He was sure that Byron must have lied and that their relationship was the reason she thought he wouldn't want her.

He was actually about to walk away from her, to get some distance, but something just didn't seem right here. Instead, he walked back over to her and drew her to her feet, taking her in his arms again. Feeling the tenderness of his embrace, and feeling the anger of his emotions die away, the walls that Aislynn had built over these past weeks dissolved and she let herself cry on the shoulder of her fiancé. She trembled in his embrace as all of her bottled-up emotions poured out and she melted into his arms, knowing that she was safe here, with him.

Eryk suddenly realized that he didn't need her to tell him what had happened. He just knew, and the reason he knew was because Aislynn was crying. He had watched this woman kill people to protect him, and he had seen her viciously wounded, but he had never seen her cry. He was sure that the list of things that could do this to her was very, very short, and he was able to compare her recent behavior with that list and figure it out. Feeling Aislynn comforted by his embrace felt so right to him. The revelation horrified Eryk, and he longed to do more for her than just hold her tightly and let her cry. He was also sure that he didn't want to know the specifics of her mission in Madelia.

"You have nothing to worry about," he whispered to her as she started to pull herself together after a little while. "Of course I still want you, regardless of what happened to you while you were gone. You are the only one I have ever wanted, and nothing will ever change that."

Aislynn looked up at him and smiled, possibly the biggest smile she had ever shown him. And this time, the smile reached her eyes and her tears were tears of joy.

Epilogue

Alexius stalked across the room before whipping around to glare at the messenger. How dare he come in here with his announcements! It was bad enough that her brother had found a bride, but this! This was inexcusable.

Ever since Eryk banished her to this estate, Alexius' life had gone downhill, and very quickly. Only a few months ago she had been at the top of the court circles, envied and admired. Now she was a pariah, and nobody spoke to her or about her. And that bitch was to blame for all of it.

Alexius was certain that those women from Evendell must be sorceresses of some kind. How else could you explain that they could show up out of nowhere and have husbands faster then you can blink? It had to be magic.

Even if it wasn't magic, that princess was unnatural. Branden had known that, and he had told Alexius as much. Now he was married to the princess's best friend, so somehow that bitch had blinded Branden to her oddness.

Slowly getting her temper under control, Alexius managed to thank the man for his information. She passed him a coin as a token of her appreciation and the man left. The fact that she had to pay for court gossip was truly a testimony to how far she had fallen. Fortunately, she had plenty of money, and she knew exactly how she was going to spend it.

Alexius walked to the window and sat down on the seat there. The sunlight that streamed through the glass brought out the various shades of golden highlights in her hair and made her blue eyes sparkle. The beauty of this woman would have captivated anyone walking into the room at that moment, but anybody who knew her knew that the sparkle in her eye was far from saintly.

Aislynn had stolen her king, shipped her off into exile, and had made her life a living hell, and Alexius was determined that she would do anything in her power to return the favor. They may currently be planning a wedding for the spring, but if Alexius had her way, the bride-to-be wouldn't live to see her wedding day.

LaVergne, TN USA
23 November 2010
206014LV00006B/20/P